SHARE THE BREATHTAKING ADVENTURES OF THESE DARING PIONEERS OF THE EARLY WEST AS THEY FORGE A MAGNIFICENT LEGACY IN A TEMPESTUOUS AND RUGGED LAND. TRAVEL WITH THE BOLD FOREBEARS OF LEGENDARY WAGONMASTER WHIP HOLT WHO SEEK THEIR DESTINY IN YOUNG AMERICA . . . FOLLOWING THE WIDE MISSOURI, CROSSING THE VAST ROCKIES, AND BLAZING A PATH OF PASSION, CONQUEST, AND GLORY ACROSS A BRAVE NEW NATION.

OUTPOST!

THEY ARE THE MEN AND WOMEN OF THE YOUNG WEST . . . ADVENTURE SEEKERS AND VISIONARIES DRIVEN BY DREAMS OF POWER AND PASSION, CONQUEST AND GLORY . . . STRUGGLING TO CARVE OUT THEIR DESTINIES IN A HARSH, UNFORGIVING LAND CALLED AMERICA

CLAY HOLT—Born into a violent, lawless land, the hot-tempered, hardworking eldest Holt has known his share of bloodshed . . . and heartbreak. Now he heads north to Canada, where a deadly enemy lies in wait, bent on destroying the only man who can foil his twisted dreams of conquest.

JEFFERSON HOLT—A rugged frontiersman and trapper, he only wants to live in peace with his wife and young son. But a chilling act of treachery will soon divide him from his family and turn him into a hunted fugitive framed for a crime he didn't commit.

MELISSA MERRIVALE HOLT—Beautiful and spirited, she has always been controlled by her domineering father . . . until her life is shattered by tragedy and she must risk everything to save her beloved husband.

CHARLES MERRIVALE—For years, this ruthless North Carolina businessman has schemed against the son-in-law he despised. But now his careful plotting backfires when he becomes a victim of greed and ambition—at the hands of the one man he trusted above all.

SHINING MOON—Clay Holt's loving Oglala Sioux wife, she suffered a terrible ordeal at the hands of her vicious Blackfoot captors. Reunited at last with her husband, her faith is shaken when another woman's shocking claim threatens their peaceful union.

PROUD MOON—Shining Moon's brother, he will fulfill his Sioux destiny and prove his valor on the field of battle when he risks his life to save another's. But his mettle will be tested when he meets his match in a warrior who is fearless, strong—and female.

FLETCHER McKENDRICK—Driven by greed and bloodlust, he has turned the American territory into a land of violence by setting brother against brother. But his work won't be finished until he destroys his old enemy Clay Holt once and for all.

FATHER THOMAS—Sent west to establish a mission in Sioux territory, he was determined to bring peace to a wild, untamed land. A man who has never known the love of a woman, he will find himself irresistibly drawn to another man's wife—the enigmatic and beautiful Shining Moon.

TERENCE O'SHAY—The big, brawling Irishman is quick with his fists and just as quick to come to the aid of a friend. A sailor and a smuggler, he will come up with a clever plan that could help Jeff Holt clear his name—or get them both killed.

WAGONS WEST
FRONTIER TRILOGY
VOLUME 3

OUTPOST!

Dana Fuller Ross

 Producers of **The Holts, The Patriots,
The First Americans, and The White Indian.**

Book Creations Inc., Canaan, NY • Lyle Kenyon Engel, Founder

BANTAM BOOKS
NEW YORK • TORONTO • LONDON • SYDNEY • AUCKLAND

OUTPOST!

A Bantam Book / published by arrangement with Book Creations Inc.

Bantam edition / July 1993

Produced by Book Creations Inc.
Lyle Kenyon Engel, Founder

ISBN 0-553-29400-8

Published simultaneously in the United States and Canada

Bantam Books are published by Bantam Books, a division of Bantam Doubleday Dell Publishing Group, Inc. Its trademark, consisting of the words "Bantam Books" and the portrayal of a rooster, is Registered in U.S. Patent and Trademark Office and in other countries. Marca Registrada. Bantam Books, 1540 Broadway, New York, New York 10036.

PRINTED IN THE UNITED STATES OF AMERICA

OPM   0 9 8 7 6 5 4 3 2 1

OUTPOST!

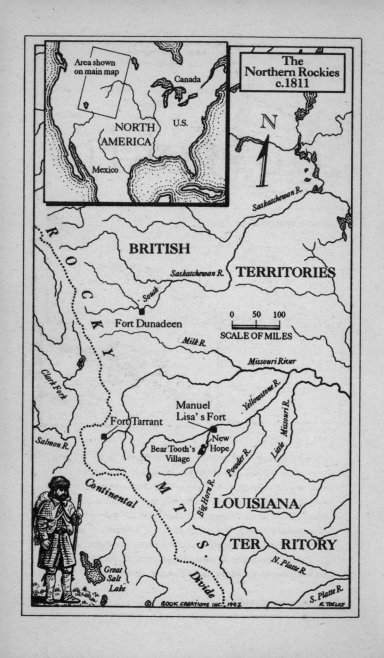

Area shown on main map

Canada

NORTH AMERICA

U.S.

Mexico

The Northern Rockies c.1811

N

Saskatchewan R.

BRITISH

Saskatchewan R.

TERRITORIES

South

Fort Dunadeen

Milk R.

Missouri River

0   50   100
SCALE OF MILES

Clark Fork

Manuel Lisa's Fort

Yellowstone R.

Little Missouri R.

Salmon R.

Fort Tarrant

Bear Tooth's Village

New Hope

Powder R.

Big Horn R.

LOUISIANA

Continental

M
T
S.

TER   RITORY

Great Salt Lake

Divide

N. Platte R.

S. Platte R.

© BOOK CREATIONS INC. 1992

R. TOELKE

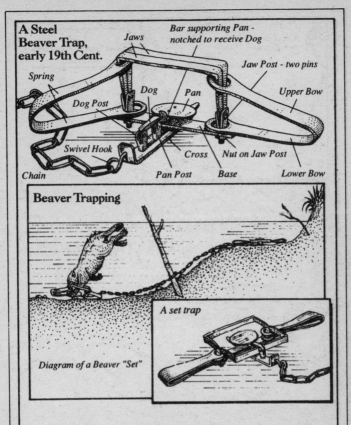

A Steel Beaver Trap, early 19th Cent.

Jaws

Bar supporting Pan - notched to receive Dog

Spring

Dog Post

Dog

Pan

Jaw Post - two pins

Upper Bow

Swivel Hook

Cross

Nut on Jaw Post

Chain

Pan Post

Base

Lower Bow

Beaver Trapping

Diagram of a Beaver "Set"

A set trap

After preparing a bed for a beaver trap in shallow water, a trapper placed a foot on each jaw of the trap, forcing open the spring and setting the trap. He carried the chain into deeper water, where he linked it to a stake, which he anchored in the streambed. Then he daubed castoreum, or "beaver medicine," onto the end of a branch and suspended it over the trap. Beavers could detect the scent of castoreum from a mile away and would come to investigate, springing the trap. Once snared, an animal would swim for deep water and, weighed down by the heavy trap, ultimately drown.

R. TOELKE '92

PART I

The territory west of the Mississippi belonging to the United States, and extending from that river to the Rocky Mountains, has evidently two characters, so distinct, as regards the external appearance, that they cannot justly be included in one general description. The part which lies immediately on the Mississippi, and extends from one hundred to two hundred and fifty miles westward from that river, has a thin covering of timber, consisting of clumps and of scattered trees. From the western limits of this region to the Rocky Mountains, the whole is one vast prairie or meadow, and, excepting on the alluvion of the rivers, and, in a few instances, on the sides of the small hills, is entirely divested of trees or shrubs. The extent of this region is not accurately known, on account of the real situation of the Rocky Mountains not yet being truly ascertained; but it appears from the account of hunters and travellers, that in some of our best maps and globes they are laid down considerably too far to the eastward.

—JOHN BRADBURY
"Travels in the Interior
of America 1809–1811"

PROLOGUE

The big man in buckskins strode down the St. Louis street, surveying his surroundings with eyes accustomed to seeing dangers that others might miss. Clay Holt had not been there since the spring of 1807, and in the two and a half years since then, the bustling young settlement had rapidly grown. St. Louis was a city now, a sprawling conglomeration of buildings spread along the west bank of the wide, deceptively placid Mississippi River.

Clay was a frontiersman. He did not like cities at all, but he knew that sometimes a man had no choice but to venture into them, at which times it paid to stay alert. Being in a place with more than one or two buildings meant never knowing where trouble could be hiding—that was Clay's philosophy.

The young man walking beside him looked over and grinned. "Don't look so worried, Clay. I don't think there are any Blackfoot or Ree lurking around here, waiting to jump out and take your hair."

"Might be some things even worse," Clay growled.

Aaron Garwood chuckled. "Man'd have to be a damn fool to tangle with a couple of old grizzlies like us."

In truth, both men were fairly young, Clay in his late twenties, Aaron in his early twenties. Both of them wore buckskin trousers and buckskin jackets over homespun shirts, and high-topped moccasins on their feet. A coonskin cap was settled on Clay's rumpled thatch of black hair, while Aaron sported a gray felt hat with a rounded crown and a wide brim that all but hid his brown hair. Clay had shaved recently, but his beard grew in so thick and dark that his face always looked as if he had several days' worth of stubble on it. Aaron's features were smoother, gentler, lacking the craggy strength that Clay's possessed. He was also several inches shorter and considerably more slender than Clay, and his left arm was thinner and weaker than his right, the result of being broken three years earlier—in a vicious fight with Clay Holt.

Their enmity had passed. After months spent together in the mountains, after numerous hardships and dangers endured together, Clay and Aaron were now staunch friends, and even though Aaron might not look as much like a seasoned frontiersman as his companion, Clay knew he was as tough as they came. There was no one Clay would rather have beside him in a fight than Aaron Garwood—except for his own brother Jefferson, who was somewhere back East.

Both men were well armed. The .54 caliber flintlock rifles canted over their shoulders were made at Harper's Ferry in 1803. Each of them wore a brace of North and Cheney flintlock pistols tucked under his broad leather belt. Clay also carried a heavy-bladed hunting knife in a fringed leather sheath, as well as a wicked-looking tomahawk under his belt. The 'hawk drew some looks of surprise from passersby, but not too many. The citizens of St. Louis were accustomed to seeing men like Clay and Aaron in their midst since the city was the jumping-off point for the growing fur trade in the lands to the west.

From all over the country men came to St. Louis, outfitted themselves, then headed up the Missouri and down the Yellowstone and the other tributaries to the rugged heights known as the Rockies—or, as the natives who had lived there first called them, the Shining Mountains. Others headed cross-country instead of following the rivers, to unknown destinations.

Clay, however, was a man of the rivers and the mountains and knew the vital relationship between them. They were his home.

And he was ready to go home again.

He had been ready to turn around and head back to the mountains as soon as he and Aaron had arrived and safely delivered Miss Lucy Franklin to her hotel. Lucy, the only surviving member of an ill-fated scientific expedition led by her late father, Professor Donald Elwood Franklin, was on her way home to Boston and Harvard, taking with her the copious notes and the plant and rock specimens that were her father's legacy. Clay, along with his Hunkpapa Sioux wife, Shining Moon, her brother, Proud Wolf, and Aaron Garwood, had encountered the expedition in the mountains and shared a series of harrowing, ultimately tragic adventures with the professor and his companions, which had culminated in the professor's horrible death by torture.

Because of everything Lucy had gone through, Clay and Aaron decided not to leave the unfortunate young woman on her own in St. Louis and had spent the past three days there, waiting for her transportation to arrive. Finally earlier that day the young woman had boarded the keelboat that would take her down the Mississippi, then up the Ohio River to Pittsburgh, where she could buy a ticket on a coach that would convey her east. With Lucy's departure an ending of sorts had been written.

But it was also a beginning for Clay Holt, because there was a little matter of revenge to be taken care of. . . .

"Let's stop in here and have a drink," Aaron said, breaking into Clay's brooding mood as they passed a tavern. "Then we can go see about picking up the rest of our provisions."

"Can't be soon enough to suit me," Clay said. "I'm ready to get those canoes back in the water and head upstream again." He looked up and down the narrow dirt street, which had at least a dozen buildings on each side, and added, "Too damned crowded around here."

Aaron's suggestion was a good one, though, Clay thought. The proprietor of the store where they had purchased the supplies for their trip had told them that the goods would not be ready until late afternoon —still enough time to pack them in their canoes and paddle a mile or two upriver before making camp. Clay was glad they would not have to spend another night in town, but in the meantime, they might as well have a drink.

Aaron led the way into the tavern, and the two men stopped just inside the doorway. It had real planks on the floor instead of split-log puncheons, a real bar on one side of the room rather than boards laid across the tops of whiskey barrels, and red-checked cloths on the tables.

Clay looked around and scowled. "What the hell kind of a place is this?"

"I'm not sure," Aaron replied. "Sign over the door said it was a tavern, but it doesn't look like any I've ever been in."

Several men were lined up at the bar, drinking, while others sat at the tables with women wearing low-cut dresses. Aaron looked at the women with obvious eagerness, while Clay paid them much less attention; no doss-house girl could ever be as beautiful as Shining Moon.

"Well, let's sit down and see what they've got to drink in this place," Aaron said, gesturing at an empty table in a rear corner of the room. He and Clay pulled out honest-to-God chairs, not the rough-hewn stools they were used to, and sank down on them, then stowed their rifles on the floor at their feet.

A serving girl came over to take their order. Her lustrous raven hair reminded Clay of Shining Moon's, but her skin was olive instead of burnished copper. She smiled at them and said with a trace of an accent that Clay identified as Spanish, "What can I get you gentlemen to drink?"

"Whiskey," Aaron said.

But Clay shook his head. "Better make it ale." Something about the place made him nervous, and he did not think it was just that the surroundings were fancier than what he was accustomed to.

"We have aguardiente," the girl said. "The only tavern in St. Louis that serves it."

"What is this agar—agard—aguardiente?" Aaron finally managed.

"Spanish brandy," the girl replied. "The very finest."

"Bring us a bottle of the stuff," Aaron declared.

This time Clay thought better about disagreeing with him. Aaron had gone through a lot in the mountains, and Clay supposed that if Aaron wanted to cut loose a bit, he should be allowed to. Besides, Clay was interested in the aguardiente, too. He had never had any Spanish brandy.

The serving girl favored them with a big smile and went to the bar, then returned with a tall, heavy bottle of smoked glass and a couple of crystal goblets. Clay noticed there was a crystal chandelier hanging from the ceiling, too, and he knew it must have cost a fortune to be brought out from the East. He would have hated to have been the riverboatman with the responsibility of delivering the chandelier unbroken to its owner.

After the girl had filled the goblets with brandy, she deftly scooped up the coins Aaron slid across the table to her. Clay had been unsure how much a bottle of foreign liquor would cost, but evidently Aaron had guessed close enough to the price, because the girl smiled yet again and said, "Enjoy your drinks, señores. And if you would like, when my time to work is over, I will come back and sit with you."

Aaron's face lit up with anticipation, but before he could answer, Clay said, "We won't be here that long. We've got to pick up supplies in a bit."

The girl shrugged and pouted. "That is to regret," she said, then moved away from the table.

Aaron leaned toward Clay. "Why'd you tell her that?" he hissed. "We don't even know how long a time she was talking about."

"Doesn't matter. Before you knew what hit you, that gal would have you buying another bottle of this stuff. That's the only reason she offered to sit with us, and you know it."

"I don't know any such thing," Aaron complained. "Could be she was just charmed by my youth and good looks."

Clay's voice was wry as he said, "Yep, could be." He lifted his goblet. "Why don't we try this expensive liquor you just bought?"

Aaron picked up his brandy. He took a small sip, smacked his lips, and then downed half the glass. His eyes widened.

Clay was sampling his drink with more moderation. "Mighty smooth," he commented, "but it warms up as it goes down."

"Yeah," Aaron said, his voice halfway between a croak and a whisper, "it does, doesn't it?"

Clay had to admit the aguardiente was good, and after a few glasses of it the olive-skinned serving girl with the white, off-the-shoulder blouse looked better to him. He had not seen very many Spaniards in his life and certainly not many Spanish females. She had a sultry beauty that could set a man's mind to spinning, if he was not careful. Clay reminded himself firmly that he was a *married* man.

No such constraints applied to Aaron, however, and when the girl finally came back and sat down at the table without being invited, he moved his chair closer to hers. He began a low-voiced conversation with her as Clay tipped the last of the liquor into his glass and savored it. They had already stayed at the tavern longer than he had intended, but there was no real hurry, he supposed. The store where they had to pick up their supplies would be open late; the proprietor had told them so.

Gradually Clay realized that he was a little drunk. Aaron, on the other hand, was a *lot* drunk, and Clay decided it was high time they left. Trouble generally followed too much liquor like a hound after a rabbit.

The decision was too late. Four men came swaggering up to the table, a couple of them typical riverboat toughs in homespun shirts and corduroy pants. The other two, though, had the same olive complexion as the girl and wore town clothes—expensive ones at that. They wore beaver hats on their sleek, dark hair and short jackets that cinched tight at the waist. Clay was certain they were both Spaniards.

The Spaniards glared down at Clay and Aaron, and one said without any preamble, "You are brave men, señores, to sit so with a man's sister and dishonor him."

"She sat down here on her own accord," Clay countered. "We didn't invite her."

The other Spaniard said angrily, "You dare to call my fiancée a loose woman?"

Clay looked up at the men, and a smile broke out on his rugged face. He was not so drunk that he did not understand what was going on. The girl was probably neither sister nor fiancée to either of the men; mistress to both, maybe. Or maybe just another player in a scheme that had undoubtedly worked many times before. She had gotten Clay and Aaron to buy the expensive aguardiente and had probably overheard them talking about the supplies they were supposed to pick up later. That meant they would be carrying a goodly sum of cash—cash that could be lifted from their senseless bodies once the four men got them outside the tavern on the excuse of avenging a "lady's" insulted honor, then beat the hell out of them.

Aaron blinked bleary eyes and leaned forward. "Clay?" he said nervously. "Clay, what's going on here?"

"Seems that we insulted these gents by sitting with this gal." He turned to the Spaniards and said calmly, "We didn't mean any offense. You can ask the lady. We were gentlemen."

"Gentlemen," repeated one of the men in a sour voice. "Backwoodsmen such as yourselves do not know the meaning of the word. What did they say to you, Juanita?"

The girl made her lower lip tremble, and two tears rolled down her cheeks. "They were very rude to me. They spoke to me as if I was a—a woman of the streets."

The one who was supposed to be her brother caught his breath—an excellent portrayal of righteous indignation, Clay thought—and demanded, "You will come with us outside, and we will settle this. Now!"

They probably thought he was a lot drunker than he really was, Clay mused. After polishing off a bottle of that smooth but potent brandy, most men would probably be a long way in their cups. However, he had not been feeling the liquor very much to start with, and danger always had a sobering effect on him. He warned himself not to underestimate the men, even though they looked like dandies. No doubt they had pulled this trick successfully in the past, and they had a couple of brawny riverboatmen backing them up. With odds of two to one, he and Aaron would have to be careful.

"What if we don't go?" Clay asked, adopting a drunken but belligerent attitude as he hunched forward.

One of the Spaniards slipped a hand inside his jacket and took out a small pistol. With a smooth motion, he pulled back the hammer. "Come with us quietly, or I will kill you right now, backwoodsman," he ordered, his voice pitched low enough so that it would not be easily overheard at nearby tables. No one else in the room seemed to be paying any attention to the drama unfolding in the corner.

"Watch it, Clay!" Aaron exclaimed, finally alarmed. "He's got a gun!"

"Not enough of one," Clay said. He pulled the trigger of the North and Cheney he had slipped out from under his belt and was holding under the table.

Suddenly Clay's flintlock pistol boomed. The Spaniard with the gun screamed when the ball from Clay's weapon tore through the muscles of his thigh and shattered the bone, knocking him off his feet. Then Clay crashed the table into the other Spaniard and drove him back against his two brawny cohorts. For a moment all four of them had their feet tangled.

The quarters were too close for Clay to bring the long-barreled flintlock rifle into play. Instead, he shoved the empty gun under his belt and immediately brought out the second pistol. When its cock snapped down, however, there was only a faint sputter as the powder in the pan misfired. Given an unexpected chance, the second Spaniard pulled a gun from underneath his jacket, while Clay reached for his tomahawk and brought it around in a sweeping, backhanded blow. Just as the Spaniard leveled his pistol, the 'hawk's blade caught his wrist, the keen edge sinking deep. Blood spurted, and the gun fell. The

Spaniard staggered back, shrieking and trying to stem the crimson tide coming from his wrist.

That left the two riverboatmen, who cursed as they jumped Clay. They were fast and strong, and as one of them grabbed the hand holding the 'hawk, the other barreled into Clay and pinned his back to the floor.

Aaron kicked at the man who had landed atop Clay, but before his foot reached its target, the serving girl jumped on his back and clawed at his eyes with her fingernails. Aaron yelped in pain and staggered forward, tripping over one of the legs of the overturned table and falling on the floor near Clay. He grabbed at the girl's wrists and tried to pull her off.

Clay managed to hold on to the tomahawk, and he slammed the flat of the blade against the skull of the man punching him in the face. The man reacted defensively, which allowed Clay to throw a punch of his own squarely into his opponent's jaw and knock him off to the side. Suddenly a heavy boot was coming at Clay's face, and he rolled desperately the other way. The second riverboatman's attempt to stomp Clay into the floor missed, and that miss threw him off balance. Clay drove an elbow into the back of the man's knees, knocking him down.

He could have probably killed both of them with the tomahawk, but he chose not to. They were nothing but hired strongmen and did not deserve to die for their poor judgment. But he could sure make them wish they had decided otherwise. He kicked the second man in the side, then caught the first one with a well-timed punch as the man struggled to stand. A couple of swings of the 'hawk, using the flat of the blade again each time, made both men go down and stay down.

Clay looked around. Aaron had finally subdued the serving girl, but he had his hands full trying to keep her from attacking him again, and she spat continuous curses at him in Spanish—at least the words sounded like curses to Clay.

The tavern had cleared out in a hurry when the trouble started. Nobody was left but the bartender and a couple of patrons too drunk to flee. The two Spaniards were both lying on the floor, alive but in poor shape from their wounds. Clay gestured at them with the tomahawk and said to the bartender, "Better get help for those two before they bleed to death— that is, if you want to go to that much trouble. It doesn't matter to me."

He slid the tomahawk under his belt again, picked up the pistol he had dropped, and retrieved his fallen cap. "Come on," he said curtly to Aaron. "We've got things to do."

"Dammit!" Aaron exclaimed as he tried to hang on to the serving girl's wrists. "If I let her go, she's liable to come after me again."

Clay laughed. "That's a problem, all right. Here, hold my rifle."

He handed the flintlock to the startled Aaron, who let go of the girl to take it. Before she could attack again, Clay stepped to her in a half crouch and grabbed her. She screamed as he straightened and tossed her over his shoulder, but in that position, with his arms clamped like iron bands around her legs, all she could do was beat futilely on Clay's back as he strode out of the tavern.

On the far side of the street was a horse trough. Clay sauntered over to it and dumped the girl into the murky water with a huge splash. As her head emerged from the water and she clung sputtering to the sides of the trough, Clay said to her, "That little trick you and your friends tried might've done the job —if I hadn't known to be suspicious of *anybody* who lives in a city. From now on maybe you'd best steer clear of us poor old backwoodsmen. We're not all as dumb as you seem to think we look."

With that he turned to Aaron, who had followed

him out of the tavern. The sun was nearly down; it was past time to be picking up their supplies and putting St. Louis, and its so-called civilization, behind them.

"Come on," Clay said to Aaron. "Let's go home."

CHAPTER ONE

Do not grieve—misfortunes will happen to the wisest and best men. Death will come, and always comes out of season: it is the command of the Great Spirit, and all nations and people must obey.

—from Sioux burial oration, as quoted in JOHN BRADBURY's "Travels in the Interior of America 1809–1811"

"Think we'll be able to find the village?" Aaron Garwood called as his paddle bit into the water of the Yellowstone River and sent the vessel upstream against the current.

Clay Holt was paddling the other canoe just slightly ahead and to one side of Aaron's canoe. "We'll find it," he replied confidently over his shoulder. "This is big country, but Bear Tooth's band will range only so far. And they'll be settling down for their winter camp pretty soon, too, if they haven't already done so."

"Big country" was an understatement, Clay thought, looking around. This was about the biggest country a man could ever find.

St. Louis was five weeks behind them. They had traveled up the Missouri River along the great curve of that stream that took them far to the north through flat, treeless plains—an area that Clay had first visited with Lewis and Clark's Corps of Discovery—then southwest again on the Yellowstone, which angled gracefully toward the mountains. They had already passed the junction of the Yellowstone and the Big Horn, where a Spanish fur trader named Manuel Lisa —who had helped outfit the Corps of Discovery for Lewis and Clark—had established a fort that had become the center of the trapping industry for the Rockies. Clay and his brother Jeff had been members of Lisa's party and helped build the fort, but in the time since then, the Holt brothers had gone their own ways, Clay becoming a free trapper and Jeff heading back to Ohio to be reunited with the wife he had left behind. Clay had expected to see Jeff and perhaps even Jeff's wife Melissa before now; since that had not happened, he thought perhaps his brother had decided to stay in Marietta, where the Holt family farm was located. Clay missed Jeff, but he himself had no desire to travel any farther east than St. Louis.

The Yellowstone ran west through a pass in the Absaroka Range before turning south to cut through the region sometimes called Colter's Hell, after Clay's old friend from the days with Lewis and Clark, John Colter. Clay had heard Colter's description of the area with its bubbling, brimstone-stinking mudholes and geysers that shot columns of steam high into the air. The back door to hell, Colter had called it, and while some folks had scoffed at his tales, Clay suspected he was telling the truth. John Colter was not a man given to flights of fancy.

Clay and Aaron would likely arrive at their destination before they reached Colter's Hell, however. The band of Hunkpapa Sioux led by Bear Tooth ranged up and down the eastern slopes of the Absarokas for the most part, sometimes venturing over toward the Tetons or the Wind River Range. During the spring, summer, and fall, Bear Tooth's people would frequently move their village, following the buffalo that wandered along the plains at the foot of the mountains. As winter drew nearer, though, they would begin looking for a permanent home until the following spring. As far as Clay could tell, it was an age-old routine, and it would probably remain so for as long as the mountains reached their snowcapped peaks toward the sky. He hoped so, anyway.

Wherever Bear Tooth's village was, there would be Shining Moon and her brother, Proud Wolf. Clay was looking forward to seeing his brother-in-law again, but there was an ache inside him when he thought about Shining Moon. His wife had endured torture and rape while a captive of the Blackfoot collaborators of Fletcher McKendrick's group of English trappers, who had come down from Canada, and it seemed as if the effects of the horrible ordeal might never go away completely. Shining Moon had changed, and Clay had hated to leave her behind while he and Aaron escorted Lucy Franklin back to St. Louis. But he had given his word to Professor Franklin, and since the professor had sacrificed his own life to save the rest of them, including Shining Moon, Clay had felt bound to honor his promise.

Maybe a few months with her own people had helped Shining Moon, Clay thought as he paddled toward the Absarokas. He certainly hoped so.

The mountains shouldered up out of the plains, their steep sides covered with trees. Among the evergreens were splashes of color where the leaves of de-

ciduous trees had turned orange, brown, and russet
with the advent of fall. The wildflowers, so common
earlier in the year, were gone now.

As they paddled closer to the mountains, Clay
saw moose, antelope, and deer grazing several hundred yards away from the riverbanks. Prairie dogs
and ground squirrels would stick their heads up, peer
inquisitively toward the intruders in their canoes,
then disappear into the tall grass again.

With each stroke of the paddle, Clay's joy at being home grew. In another few days at the most, he
and Aaron would spot Bear Tooth's village, and they
would be welcomed back with feasting and dancing.
Then Clay would join Shining Moon in her tipi, and
their reunion would be complete. . . .

"Smoke over yonder," Aaron called, breaking
into Clay's thoughts.

Instantly Clay's instinct for survival took over.
He lifted his paddle from the river and let the gentle
current bring his canoe alongside Aaron's. The
younger man was pointing to the south, toward a valley that curved between two peaks.

Clay spotted the thin column of grayish black
smoke. He should have noticed it before now, he
chided himself. He had let his happiness at being
back in the wilderness and his anticipation of seeing
Shining Moon cloud his mind and his eyes.

"That's too much smoke for a campfire," Clay
said, his voice grim. "There's trouble over there."

"You think it could be coming from Bear Tooth's
camp?"

"I plan to find out."

Clay again stroked hard with the paddle, sending
the canoe ahead through the water.

About a quarter of a mile farther on, a small creek
ran into the Yellowstone from the south. Clay piloted
his canoe into the smaller stream, Aaron following
closely behind. The narrow stream led straight toward

the valley where the smoke continued to rise into the clear sky.

Until they got there, there was no way of knowing if the smoke was coming from a Hunkpapa village, let alone if the village was the one of Bear Tooth's people. But it was highly likely, Clay thought. He had been all over that part of the country, trapping beaver in small, winding mountain streams just like the one they were floating on, and he knew this was the kind of territory favored by Bear Tooth's band. He felt his heart beating faster.

He and Shining Moon had come through so much. It would not be fair if anything came between them now, when they were about to be together again.

Without giving any thought as to whether Aaron could keep up with his canoe, Clay's paddle rose and fell with amazing speed and strength. But when he finally grounded his craft against the bank of the creek, Aaron was still right behind him.

"We can get there quicker going overland now." Clay stepped out of the canoe and pulled it up on the shore. "I remember this creek. It winds around too much as it gets closer to the mountains."

He picked up an extra powder horn and shot pouch from inside the canoe and slung them over his shoulder. Aaron followed suit. They were venturing into the unknown, and it always paid to have plenty of ammunition along. After checking his rifle to make sure it was loaded and primed, Clay set off in a ground-eating trot toward the origin of the smoke, which was thicker now.

The Hunkpapa could run all day over these plains and rolling hills, and Clay's stamina approached the same level. Aaron struggled to stay with him, however. Clay knew he could not afford to slow down. The only thing that could cause that much smoke from an Indian village was for tipis to be on fire—and that meant a raid by a war party from a rival tribe, in this case, most likely Blackfoot or Crow or Arikara, sometimes called Ree by mountain men. All of them were dangerous, and there was plenty of bad blood between them and the Sioux. The main body of the Sioux Nation stayed farther east on the plains, but the bands of Bear Tooth and several other Sioux chiefs had expanded into the mountains—Teton Sioux, they were now called—causing hard feelings among the other tribes. Of course, a Blackfoot warrior did not need much of an excuse to raid a band from another tribe. The Blackfoot were the most hostile bunch Clay had ever encountered.

When he and Aaron topped a small rise in front of the mouth of the valley, Clay's worst fears were realized. Below him lay the half-circle of tipis, open to the east, with their entrances facing east as well so that the Hunkpapa could greet the sun each morning as it rose. The camp should have been a tranquil scene; the sun overhead was warm, and the sides of several of the tipis were rolled up so that the crisp autumn breeze could pass through and ventilate them. But a half dozen of the tipis were blazing furiously, set afire by the raiders who had transformed a peaceful camp into a place of chaos, havoc, and death.

Clay's keen eyes could distinguish the markings on a few of the tipis not yet burning, and he recognized them. "It's Bear Tooth's band, all right," he called to Aaron, his voice choked with anger and fear for the safety of his wife and friends.

"Are—are those Blackfoot?" Aaron was panting from exertion.

Clay's face was grim. "Yeah. Piegans, I'd say. And they're getting more of a fight than they bargained for, I reckon."

Even from that distance, Clay could tell that the Hunkpapa were battling back with the desperation of a people defending their home from ruthless invaders. Muskets boomed, arrows flashed through the sun, blood sprayed from the heads of tomahawks swung through the air.

Clay nudged Aaron and pointed at one of the Blackfoot, a tall, brawny warrior wearing an elaborate headdress of eagle feathers and ermine fur. The warrior did not seem to be joining in the fighting, but he was waving his arms around and exhorting his comrades on to greater atrocities.

"That one's a leader in the Blackfoot Horn Society," Clay said. "He's got powerful medicine—supposed to be able to just point at a man and strike him dead." He lifted his rifle to his shoulder and cocked it. "Let's see how he likes being pointed at."

"But, Clay," Aaron started to protest, "it's at least three hundred yards down there—"

Clay's rifle boomed, and a second later, the Blackfoot warrior was thrown backward, arms flung out to the sides, as the heavy lead ball struck him. The warriors around him set up a howl of surprise and outrage.

"Seems that Horn Society medicine's not as strong as powder and shot and a Harper's Ferry rifle," Clay said with a wry smile. "Come on!"

He reloaded on the run as he charged down the hill toward the Hunkpapa camp, then stopped to fire again. Aaron had wisely waited until he was closer before trying his first shot, and both men hit their targets. Clay pounded forward again in leaping strides. In a matter of moments he would be in the thick of the hand-to-hand fighting. He knew he had to keep his mind on what he was doing; otherwise, he would probably not survive the next few minutes.

But at the same time in the back of his mind a frantic voice was crying out for Shining Moon, and the part of Clay Holt that still prayed sent a plea heavenward that his wife was not already a victim of the Blackfoot raid. . . .

* * *

Just before the Blackfoot raid began, Proud Wolf was sitting outside with the two other young men who shared his tipi, Walks-Down-the-Wind and Cloud-That-Falls, carving shafts for arrows. Although the band had an arrow maker who specialized in that task, one man could not keep up with the band's need for arrows, so all the men carved their own shafts for hunting, allowing the arrow maker to devote his attention to fashioning arrows for war.

And war came that day with no warning, announcing its deadly presence in the boom of muskets and the screams of the women.

Proud Wolf leapt to his feet, dropping the shaft he had been carving, and reached for the rifle that lay near his feet. A gift from Clay Holt, the Virginia flintlock was the finest gun Proud Wolf had ever seen. He polished it frequently so that the wood of the stock and the brass patchbox gleamed brightly. A gun that beautiful had stronger medicine and shot truer, Proud Wolf believed. He now proved it to himself by bringing the rifle to his shoulder and setting the sights on a Blackfoot warrior about to smash the skull of a Sioux brave with a tomahawk. Before the 'hawk could fall, Proud Wolf pressed the trigger. Powder flashed in the pan, and the weapon kicked against his shoulder with a loud explosion. The Blackfoot tumbled backward, his collarbone shattered by the ball.

There was no time to reload. Blackfoot were everywhere, swarming through the village, killing wantonly. Proud Wolf wondered how they had been able to get so close to the campsite without being discovered by Bear Tooth's sentries, but he had no chance to ponder the question. One of the raiders leapt toward him, and he swung the rifle one-handed to block a sweeping knife thrust. With his other hand, he plucked his own knife from its sheath and plunged it into the belly of the Blackfoot.

Proud Wolf was shorter, and his build was more slender than most young men his age, which was seventeen summers. As a young boy he had never been good at the games the others played, and the rigorous training to become a warrior had seemed beyond his abilities. Many had scoffed when he had gone into the sweat lodge to seek his vision and emerged with a tale of a gigantic wolf bestriding the mountains, full of arrogance and power and pride. He had taken the name Proud Wolf from that vision, and while none had denied him that right, few believed he would ever deserve the name.

Then Clay Holt had come to the Shining Mountains, and everything changed, not only for Shining Moon but for her brother, Proud Wolf, as well. He was a warrior now and had counted plenty coup. He had fought not only Blackfoot, but also white men from the north, from the cold lands. Clay Holt had taught him something that Proud Wolf would never have believed a white man could teach: A man fights on, no matter what the odds.

He would fight well this day, Proud Wolf vowed, and whether he lived or died was in the hands of the Great Spirit, Wakan Tanka.

He had no idea where Shining Moon was, but he began fighting his way toward the center of the camp where Bear Tooth's tipi was located. The Hunkpapa defenders would rally there, he knew, and that was where the back of the Blackfoot attack would be broken. Proud Wolf wanted to be part of that.

A high, keening chant that was audible even over the chaos of the battle caught his attention, and he looked over to see a Blackfoot in an ermine and eagle headdress. Proud Wolf felt a chill go through him as he recognized the trappings of the Horn Society. Its leaders had the most powerful medicine of any warrior group, and for a moment Proud Wolf's spirit faltered. If the Hunkpapa Sioux were opposed by the Horn Society, surely there was no way they could defeat the invaders—

Then the Blackfoot in the headdress was driven

backward by something; blood appeared on his beaded buckskin shirt as he flopped to the ground and died. The warriors with him shouted in rage and gestured toward the hill that overlooked the village. Proud Wolf followed their pointing fingers.

Two men were up there, two men in buckskins who carried long rifles.

Proud Wolf's heart leapt. Although the men were too far away for him to see their faces clearly, he knew in his heart that they were Clay Holt and Aaron Garwood.

And as white men Proud Wolf had known might have phrased it, those damned Blackfoot did not know how much trouble they were in now.

Proud Wolf lunged into the center of the battle. Feeling invincible, he used knife and tomahawk on the raiders, suffering a few scratches himself but killing or badly wounding several of the Piegan Blackfoot. Suddenly, as he passed one of the tipis that had been set afire, he saw a young Hunkpapa woman sprawled on the ground, her back to him, trying to crawl away from the Blackfoot warrior who loomed over her, his tomahawk raised for a killing strike. With a harsh cry, Proud Wolf flung himself at the larger, older man, grabbing his arm and diverting the blow as the 'hawk fell.

The impact as Proud Wolf crashed into the Blackfoot threw both of them off balance. Proud Wolf felt himself falling and tried to catch himself, but he was too late. He hit the ground with enough force to knock the breath from his lungs. Gasping, he rolled over and tried to locate his opponent, and at that instant the Blackfoot's tomahawk smashed into the ground where Proud Wolf's head had been a second earlier.

Proud Wolf looked up into the face of his enemy. Diagonal stripes of red paint ran along the Piegan's cheeks. The Piegan lashed out again with the 'hawk, aiming the blow at Proud Wolf's head. The young

Hunkpapa brought his arm up just in time to block the blow, but the wooden handle of the tomahawk cracked against his forearm with numbing impact. The knife he held slipped out of his fingers.

Desperately, Proud Wolf swung his own 'hawk at the Blackfoot. The raider ducked, giving Proud Wolf the chance to roll to the side and put a few feet between them. He sprang to his feet as the Blackfoot lunged at him again.

Using his smaller size and quickness to avoid the next couple of blows, Proud Wolf somersaulted and came up next to the unprepared Blackfoot. A fast sideways swipe with the 'hawk opened up the enemy's belly, but the man made no sound as he grabbed at himself to keep his entrails from spilling out. Even as the raider was dying, he swung again at Proud Wolf, although the blow was slower and less powerful than the others.

Dodging the Piegan's final strike, Proud Wolf swung his own tomahawk in a looping blow. The blade sank deep into the side of the man's neck. With a gasp, the Blackfoot raider died on his feet, then tumbled to the ground in a heap as Proud Wolf wrenched his weapon free.

"Proud Wolf!" a voice cried. He turned to see that the young woman whose life he had just saved was scrambling to her feet. He now recognized her. Butterfly was a year younger than he, but despite her being younger—and female—she surpassed him in height, and her shoulders were as broad as his. Her body was lithe and strong in a buckskin dress, and her lustrous black hair fell around her shoulders. Proud Wolf had thought many times that she would have been quite attractive, if it weren't for the fact that she was the most annoying female on the face of the earth.

Now she threw herself at him, swung her arms around him, and pounded him heavily on the back as she embraced him. "You have saved me! My vision was right! Oh, Proud Wolf—"

The last thing he wanted to hear during a battle with Blackfoot raiders was Butterfly chattering about one of her visions. In fact, over the last two years he had heard more than he ever wanted to about Butterfly's visions, most of which had to do with the ridiculous notion that someday the two of them would be joined in union.

Proud Wolf pushed her away and turned to prod the fallen Blackfoot with his foot, just to make sure the invader was really dead. Proud Wolf's chest filled with pride as he saw the way the man's head lolled loosely on his shoulders.

Suddenly something slammed into his back, and the impact propelled him over the Blackfoot's body. As he fell facedown on the ground, he heard an arrow whip through the air over his head. Someone let out a hoarse cry of anger. Only when he rolled over did he realize that the noise had come from Butterfly. She snatched up the tomahawk that had been dropped by the dead Blackfoot and lobbed it through the air and straight into the forehead of the Blackfoot who had just loosed the arrow at Proud Wolf. The 'hawk split the raider's skull. The man dropped to his knees, then fell forward in death.

Proud Wolf swallowed hard as Butterfly looked at him pensively. Like it or not, she had just returned the favor and saved his life. He knew the arrow would have hit him had she not knocked him out of its path. And judging from the expression on Butterfly's face, she was just as aware of that as he was.

"It is meant to be," she said solemnly. "Fate cannot tear us apart."

Proud Wolf scowled, climbed quickly to his feet, and barked, "Find a safe place with the other women." Then he picked up his knife and turned to rejoin the battle. There were still attackers to be driven off.

But he had seen the injured expression in Butterfly's eyes, and he felt guilt gnawing at him. Although the girl sometimes buzzed around him like a fly after something sweet, he had truly not meant to hurt her. But perhaps it was for the best. Butterfly's visions could never come true.

And in the meantime, there was still a battle to be won.

Shining Moon huddled against the buffalo hide wall of her tipi, hoping that none of the Blackfoot would come in and discover her. She listened to the yipping cries of the raiders as they wreaked destruction on the camp and smelled the acrid smoke from the burning tipis. She was more frightened than she had ever been in her twenty-one years.

Her eyes went to the long rifle lying on the ground nearby with its powder horn and shot pouch. She could load and prime it and have it ready to fire in less than a minute; her husband had taught her that. Clay Holt had taught her many things, in fact— to smile, to kiss, to revel in the feelings he had aroused in her during their courtship and the early months of their marriage. She had given herself fully to those things, and she knew she had been a good wife to him.

But then everything had changed, and she knew her life would never again be as it had been.

Before, she had been quick to fight when challenged. She had battled at her husband's side, had taken charge when he was injured. She had killed evil men to save herself and her friends. Now she could only sit and shiver and pray to the Great Spirit to protect her, because in her mind she heard not only the cries of these Blackfoot warriors, but also the cruel laughter of the others, the ones who had worked for the Englishman, the ones who had violated her and tortured her until she almost prayed for death. The laughter, the harsh grunting as they took her, her own screams as knife blades bit into her flesh . . . the sounds echoed endlessly in her mind. Her once-proud spirit had been driven out by those hellish noises.

Shining Moon wept in terror.

Suddenly the flap over the entrance of the tipi was thrust aside, and a leering face painted in white and vermilion stripes looked in at her. Shining Moon cried out as the Piegan stormed into the tipi and reached for her. There was a knife at her belt, but she did not snatch it from its sheath and slash at the raider, as she once would have done. Instead, she cowered from him, making futile pawing motions with her hands as she pushed her feet against the ground and tried to scuttle out of his reach. He caught her arm and closed his hand so tightly around it that she cried out again, this time in pain. The Blackfoot dragged her toward the entrance.

A part of her brain screamed that she had to fight back. But fear and pain had paralyzed her, and in her mind she was back once more at Fort Tarrant, far to the north and west, where she had undergone the ordeal that would forever scar her soul.

The Piegan dragged her through the opening and into the autumn sunlight. Shining Moon, her eyes wide with terror, saw the bodies scattered around the camp, bodies of Hunkpapa and Blackfoot alike. She stumbled over the limp, outstretched arm of a young Hunkpapa girl, no more than twelve, whose throat had been slit, and would have fallen if not for the grip her captor had on her arm. He pulled her along, and suddenly the most frightening realization of all burst through Shining Moon's mind.

He did not intend to kill her. He was taking her prisoner.

She knew what that meant. When they reached a place of safety, the Blackfoot warriors would rape her repeatedly until they tired of her. Then, depending on their whim, they would either kill her or take her with them back to their village, where she would be a slave, tormented daily by Blackfoot women.

Shining Moon stiffened. She could not endure that. Better to die here and now.

Uttering a sharp cry, she threw herself at the warrior, trying to get her hands on the tomahawk he held. She kicked him, clawed at his face, tried desperately to twist out of his grip. Growling a curse in his own tongue, he let go of her arm and backhanded her viciously, knocking her off her feet. As he stood over her, his face was easy to read: She was too much trouble and might as well be killed now. He raised his 'hawk.

Suddenly his back arched as a gun blasted from nearby. The Blackfoot swayed momentarily, his mouth opening soundlessly. Blood trickled from it, and then he fell, collapsing beside Shining Moon.

She looked around in amazement. Her husband was standing ten feet away, a flintlock pistol in each hand.

"Shining Moon," Clay said, his voice filled with emotion. He tucked away the guns and raced to her side, kneeling to take her into his arms.

A Hunkpapa woman did not cry, she reminded herself, ashamed of the tears already on her cheeks. Several great shudders went through her as Clay held her and finally lifted her to her feet. His arms tightened around her, as strong as iron and at the same time as gentle as the touch of a breeze on the petals of a flower.

She had been anticipating and dreading Clay's return, knowing that she was no longer the woman he had married, and now he was here. All he seemed to be feeling was joy at being reunited with her; he stroked her hair and murmured soft words in her ear. Soon he would see the change in her, she thought, and then he would be repulsed by her, would no longer want to call her his wife.

But that was in the future. For now all she wanted to do was stand here and be held by him.

Gradually Clay became aware that the sounds of battle had died away. He took a deep breath and surveyed the scene, keeping his arm tight around Shining Moon's quivering shoulders. She was shaking like a deer, he thought, but then a Blackfoot attack was enough to make anybody a little jumpy.

The raiders had been driven out of the village, but at great cost. The fire had spread until half the tipis were destroyed. Bodies were sprawled everywhere, and while many of them were Blackfoot, too many were Hunkpapa. Young and old, men and women and children alike, all had fallen victim to the bloodthirsty Piegans. Clay felt a certain satisfaction when he looked at the body of the Horn Society leader he had shot from atop the hill, but as satisfaction went, it meant little. At least Shining Moon had survived the raid, and so had Proud Wolf. Clay saw him not far away, trying to ignore a tall and seemingly persistent young woman and look dignified at the same time. He was not succeeding very well at either one of those things, Clay thought, smiling briefly.

Aaron Garwood walked up, his face grimy with powder smoke, the sleeve of his jacket ripped and bloodstained where a Blackfoot tomahawk had left a shallow cut. He said to Clay, "Well, we're home, I guess."

Clay nodded. They were home, all right, and some things never changed.

CHAPTER TWO

*E*verything *changes*, Jefferson Holt thought as he
picked up his son. *You turn around a couple of
times, and everything is different. Nothing stays the
same.*

Well, a few things did, Jeff amended, looking
over at his wife, Melissa, whose lustrous dark brown
hair and sparkling brown eyes were as beautiful today as the day he'd met her. More importantly, their
love was as strong as ever.

Jeff, Melissa, and their son, Michael, were walking down a waterfront street in Wilmington, North
Carolina. The blond-haired toddler, nearly two years
old, twisted around in his father's arms and pointed
to the ships lying at anchor in the harbor. "Boats!" he
cried happily.

"That's right," Jeff told him. "You like boats,
don't you, Michael?"

The youngster nodded his head enthusiastically. In truth, Michael liked anything having to do with travel. He loved wagons and could watch for hours as they rolled past. Anytime anyone was going anywhere, Michael wanted to go along.

The boy had his uncle Clay's restless nature, Jeff had thought more than once. Clay had never been content to stay in one place for very long, and Michael was going to be the same way.

But maybe he was leaping to conclusions, Jeff reminded himself. After all, he had only known his son for a brief period. In fact, only a couple of months earlier he had not even known that he *had* a son.

At that time he had returned to Wilmington from a hazardous wagon train trip to Tennessee and confronted his father-in-law, Charles Merrivale. Once a prosperous businessman in North Carolina before moving inland with his wife and daughter to Ohio, to a farm near the Holt place, Merrivale had reestablished himself in the coastal city by purchasing a successful mercantile store and several warehouses near the docks, which were conveniently located for the storage of trade goods that he, in partnership with a man named Dermot Hawley, purchased from incoming ships and then freighted elsewhere.

Jeff thought bitterly about Dermot Hawley, who had tried to have him killed during the journey to Tennessee. He hated to think how close he had come to dying without ever being reunited with his wife or knowing that he had a child. While Jeff was off trapping in the Rocky Mountains with Clay, Merrivale had packed up and left Ohio to return East, taking his wife, Henrietta, and his then-pregnant daughter with him. And he had covered his tracks well. Jeff was now sure that Merrivale had bribed the postmaster in Marietta not to turn over a letter Melissa had left for Jeff that told him she had gone to North Carolina with her parents.

Charles Merrivale had always opposed Jeff's

marriage to his daughter, and Jeff knew the move to Wilmington had been partly motivated by Merrivale's desire to destroy their union. He had come close to succeeding, too. Jeff had searched for Melissa for many months and had been on the verge of giving up his quest when fate brought him to Wilmington.

Even then, unaware of how close he was to Melissa and the son he did not know existed, he had left town to work for the very man who, for reasons of his own—among them, wanting to marry Melissa himself —had tried to arrange Jeff's death. But Dermot Hawley's effort had failed, and Jeff returned to Wilmington, armed with the knowledge that his wife was there. He had gone to Merrivale's office to confront his father-in-law.

There he had seen Melissa and, for the first time, his son. Now, at Melissa's insistence, he was on his way to Merrivale's office again. An uneasy truce existed between Jeff and his father-in-law, and for Melissa's sake Jeff was willing to give Merrivale the benefit of the doubt. Merrivale had insisted that he knew nothing about Hawley hiring someone to kill Jeff—and disavowed the notion that Hawley was behind the attack—saying he had not even known that Jeff was one of the men guarding the wagon train bound for the settlements in Tennessee. Grudgingly, Jeff had accepted Merrivale's word.

As for Dermot Hawley, he seemed to have vanished from Wilmington, and that was all right with Jeff. If he had seen the man, he might have been tempted to put a pistol ball through him. For despite Merrivale's firm belief in his partner, Jeff had a dying man's word that Hawley wanted Jeff dead.

Michael's happy jabbering as his father carried him along the street pulled Jeff away from dark thoughts of Dermot Hawley. The boy had been shy with him at first, and it had taken him a while to get used to the fact that Jeff was his father, but now he seemed delighted. As was Jeff. He found himself pick-

ing up Michael whenever he had the chance, as if to
reassure himself that the child was real. He basked in
the knowledge that he had a son.

It was a lovely day with a warm salt breeze blowing in from the Atlantic, although to Jeff the tangy
smell it carried was unpleasant. As Michael waved
his pudgy hand at the boats, Jeff looked at them and
wondered where his cousin, Ned Holt, and Ned's
friend India St. Clair were. Somewhere at sea, he wagered. For a landlocked Holt, Ned had taken quickly
to sailing when he had accompanied Jeff down the
Atlantic coast from New York on a ship owned by
another relative, Lemuel March. Of course, the chance
to be around India had a lot to do with Ned's attitude.
Jeff suspected that Ned was more than a little attracted to the enigmatic young Englishwoman who
disguised herself as a young man, thus enabling her
to work as a sailor on merchant vessels plying coastal
waters. Jeff, on the other hand, had done more than
enough sailing to suit him; his stomach had never
grown accustomed to the motion.

"I'm glad you agreed to come to Father's office,"
Melissa Holt said, breaking into her husband's reverie. "It's a nice gesture on your part."

Jeff shrugged. It seemed to him that he could
have talked to Merrivale just as easily at the man's
house, since he was staying there. For the past couple
of years the house had been home to Melissa and then
Michael after his birth, and Jeff did not want to uproot
them until they had decided what to do next. He in-
tensely disliked accepting Merrivale's hospitality,
which had been offered with ill grace, but he could
put up with almost anything for Melissa's sake. Besides, Hermione Merrivale was a charming woman,
and Jeff got along well with her. He could not imagine how his mother-in-law had put up with such a
pompous, arrogant blowhard for so many years.

He pulled at his cravat and the collar of his shirt,
trying to ease the discomfort of having something so

tight around his neck. He was used to open-throated homespun shirts and buckskin breeches, not the town clothes Melissa had him wearing. And the beaver hat perched on his thick, sandy hair would have gotten him hooted right out of the stockade at Manuel Lisa's fort. The fur trappers might depend on such fashions to provide a market for their pelts, or plews as they called them, but they would have a good laugh out of seeing Jeff in such a getup.

Jeff felt his nervousness growing as he and his wife and son neared Charles Merrivale's office. Melissa had suggested the meeting—an opportunity to eliminate hostility, tension, and suspicion, she had said—and she had insisted that she and Michael come along. But Jeff wished he was far away in the high country, breathing in the cool, crisp mountain air rather than the humid ocean breeze laden with the pungent dockside miasma of human sweat, dead fish, and spoiled food.

Melissa gently touched her husband's cheek. "It'll be all right. You'll see. My father is a reasonable man."

Jeff made no reply. One thing Charles Merrivale was not, he thought, was reasonable.

Gulls circled overhead and squawked, and Michael waved at them and yelled, "Birds! Birds!"

Jeff smiled tightly. For his wife and his son, he would make the attempt to get along with Merrivale. But he did not have to like it.

Charles Merrivale's office was in a single-story building beside one of his warehouses. Six steps led up to the covered porch on the front of the office building, and that porch continued on to become a loading dock for the warehouse next door. Several wagons were backed up there, and bales of cotton and tobacco that Merrivale had acquired from inland plantation owners were being unloaded from the wagons and carried through the huge warehouse doors by the landholders' burly slaves, who were stripped to the waist in the hot sun. The empty wagons were refilled with crates of trade goods being carted out of the warehouse by Merrivale's employees. Although his house servants were slaves, his warehouse workers were white men who earned wages for their efforts—though Jeff suspected Merrivale paid them as little as he could.

The cotton and tobacco would soon be shipped both north and across the Atlantic to England. It was a lucrative business, and Merrivale was a wealthy man who made no pretense of being anything else. Jeff could understand why Merrivale had returned from Ohio; he was the type who could make a fortune in commerce, but as a gentleman farmer he had been much less successful. And Merrivale was not the kind of man to tolerate the slightest degree of failure.

When they reached the bottom of the steps, Jeff paused and asked Melissa, "Your father *does* know we're coming, doesn't he?"

Melissa hesitated before answering, and Jeff felt a sense of foreboding.

"I'm—I'm certain he'll be glad to see us. Father never minds when Michael and I visit him. In fact, he always seems happy that we're here. He shows Michael all through the warehouse, doesn't he, Michael?"

The toddler pointed at the building and said, "Paw-Paw!"

"Yes, well, when you came down here to visit Paw-Paw before, I wasn't with you," Jeff dryly pointed out. "He doesn't know anything about this meeting, does he, Melissa?"

She looked exasperated. "The two of you can't keep ignoring each other. All this polite hostility is driving me mad! He's my father, Jeff, and he's Michael's grandfather. I don't want you hating each other."

"I thought we were ignoring each other, not hating each other," Jeff said, then winced inwardly as

anger flared in Melissa's eyes. Pointing out her incon-
sistencies was not a move designed to win favor, he
realized belatedly. To placate her, he added, "I'll talk
to him. I don't mind doing that much. But I can't
promise anything, Melissa. He's going to have to
make an effort, too."

"Paw-Paw's silly," Michael said.

That was not a word Jeff would have ever used to
describe Charles Merrivale, but perhaps there was
good in the man that he just had not seen, Jeff told
himself. After all, Merrivale had fathered Melissa,
who was the most wonderful woman he had ever
known.

"Let's go in," he said quietly.

"You'll give him a chance?"

"I'll listen to anything he has to say, and I won't
lose my temper." Jeff hoped he could keep his promise.

They went up the steps, across the wide porch,
and into the building. The door led into a small recep-
tion area, which was separated by a wooden railing
from several desks used by Merrivale's clerks. On the
far side of the room was a door that led to Merrivale's
private office, and on the right was a corridor that
opened into the warehouse.

The desks behind the railing were occupied by
pale-faced men with stooped shoulders and haunted
expressions. Jeff repressed a shudder at the thought of
being cooped up all day, every day, sitting at a desk
and scratching out numbers with a quill pen. He was
sure he would go insane in less than a week if he had
to make his living in such a manner.

One man looked up and blinked in surprise at
the sight of the three visitors. "Miss Melissa!" he exclaimed.

"Hello, Harvey." Melissa smiled at him. "We've
come to see my father."

Harvey glanced at the door of Merrivale's office,
and Jeff wondered why he seemed so nervous.

"Mr. Merrivale is having a meeting right now. He gave orders I wasn't to let anyone disturb him, but seeing as it's you . . ."

Harvey's quandary was apparent: He wanted to obey Merrivale's orders, yet at the same time he did not want to risk offending his employer by refusing admittance to his daughter.

Sensitive to the situation, Melissa said quickly, "We'll just wait out here, Harvey. No need to bother my father. We're in no hurry, are we, Jeff?"

"Nope," Jeff said hollowly. "No hurry at all."

In truth, he badly wanted to get out of there. The pots of ink on the desks stank, and the smell made his stomach queasy. He had not wanted to talk to Merrivale in the first place. Maybe the delay would get him out of the unpleasant task.

"Actually," Jeff added, turning to Melissa, "if your father is too busy, we ought to come back another time—"

The door of the inner office swung open, ruining the hastily laid plan Jeff was devising. Charles Merrivale stepped out, still in earnest conversation with his visitor, a handsome, well-dressed man in his thirties, with curly brown hair, a mustache, and an expensive beaver hat held casually in one hand.

Melissa took one look at the man and gasped, "Dermot!"

Jeff stiffened, although his pulse began racing at the sight of the man who had arranged to have him murdered. Carefully placing Michael on the floor, he took a step toward Hawley. Hawley, seeing Jeff Holt, clenched his hands into fists and stood his ground, an easy smile on his face but a flicker of alarm in his eyes.

"Melissa!" Charles Merrivale exclaimed. "What are you—the three of you—doing here?"

"We came to talk to you, Father," Melissa said coldly. "But we didn't expect you to have company of this sort."

"Hello, Melissa. It's good to see you again," Dermot Hawley said. He looked at Jeff and went on, "And this must be that husband of yours I've heard so much about."

Jeff's pulse pounded in his skull, keeping time with the anger vibrating through his body. He wished he had a gun, a knife, a tomahawk—any sort of weapon with which he could teach Dermot Hawley a lesson he would never forget.

"You know damn well I'm Jeff Holt," he snapped. "We have some unfinished business, mister."

"I'm afraid I don't know what you're talking about, Mr. Holt. I've heard of you, of course, since in my business dealings with Charles I've visited his home several times, but I assure you—"

"Forget the lies. Don't you remember? Amos Tharp brought me to your office, and you personally hired me to go with that wagon train of yours to Tennessee. But what you really wanted to do was get me off in the middle of nowhere so Tharp could kill me!"

"Jeff . . ." Melissa touched his arm and looked down meaningfully at Michael, who was taking in the exchange with wide-eyed interest. "Not here, Jeff. Not now."

"What better place?" Jeff shot back at her. "Right here in front of your father, the man who started it all!"

"See here!" Charles Merrivale protested. With his face ruddy with righteous indignation and his shock of white hair, he looked every bit the Old Testament prophet. "Whatever the bad blood between you and Dermot, Jefferson, I had nothing to do with it."

"No, nothing," Jeff snarled. "You're probably the one who put him up to having me killed, that's all."

Hawley's smile evaporated. "Charles told me about the vicious lies you've been spreading about me, Holt, and I warn you, they've got to stop. Otherwise, I'll have no alternative but to take legal action against you. You can't just go around slandering a man—"

That was all Jeff could take. He lashed out and cracked his fist against Dermot Hawley's jaw.

Hawley lurched back from the blow, and Melissa let out a scream.

"Stop it! Stop it, I say!" Merrivale shouted.

Jeff stepped closer to Hawley and hooked a solid left into his midsection.

Merrivale yelled to his clerks, "Grab him! Stop him!"

The clerks hesitated—Jeff Holt *was* a strapping man—but fear for their jobs overwhelmed their temerity. The three of them swarmed out from behind the railing, grabbed at Jeff, and tried to hold him back.

Vaguely, Jeff heard Melissa pleading with him to stop, and he heard Michael crying as well. When he realized that the fight had to be scaring the child, he let the clerks pull him back.

Now that Jeff and Dermot were apart, Charles Merrivale stepped forward, planted his hands on Jeff's chest, and shoved him back even farther. "Stop this insanity!" he demanded. "You can't come in here flinging accusations around and then attack my business partner. Why, Dermot would be well within his rights to have you arrested."

"There won't be any charges pressed," Hawley cut in sharply. He had regained his balance and straightened up after doubling over momentarily from the blow to the stomach. He dabbed at a small trickle of blood running from the corner of his mouth, then looked at the smear of crimson on his fingertip and smiled coldly. "You're upset, Holt, and I'll make allowances for that. But don't ever touch me again, or you'll regret it, sir. I can promise you that."

Jeff's chest was heaving with rage, but Melissa's hand on his arm held him back. She yanked his sleeve, and he allowed her to lead him to a corner of

the room. He heard Merrivale apologizing profusely
to Hawley.

Jeff felt a tug on his trouser leg, and he looked
down to see Michael staring up at him. He scooped
up the child and drew strength and calmness from the
presence of his son.

"Why you hit that man?" Michael asked, looking
anxious.

Jeff cast a glance at Hawley and then replied in a
low voice, "Because he's a bad man who tried to hurt
your ma and pa."

"Paw-Paw make him go away!"

Melissa patted her son's shoulder and then
turned to face her father. "Yes, Father," she said angrily, "make him go away."

Merrivale stared at her in surprise. "What?" he
finally managed to say.

Melissa leveled a finger at Dermot Hawley, who
had watched the exchange with cool detachment. "I
want you to make him leave. And I don't think you
should do business with a man like that. He lied, and
he tried to hurt Jeff."

"I'm the one bleeding, my dear," Hawley
pointed out.

"Don't talk to me, you—you scoundrel!" Melissa
turned back to her father. "If you want us to stay in
Wilmington, Father, you'll dissolve any sort of partnership you have with Mr. Hawley and never have
any dealings with him again."

Charles Merrivale's eyes narrowed angrily. "I
won't be dictated to by a woman. Not even my
daughter."

"Very well. In that case, we'll move out immediately, and you may never see your grandson again."

Michael was apparently following enough of the
conversation to know something of what was going
on, for he cried out, "Paw-Paw!"

The look in Merrivale's eyes softened, and he
sighed heavily. "Very well—although you were

raised not to talk to your elders like that, young lady!"

"I was raised to believe in right and wrong," Melissa retorted sharply.

Merrivale started to say something else to her, but he turned to Hawley instead. "I'm sorry about all this, Dermot. It looks as though that deal we were discussing will have to be set aside."

"I'm sorry, too, Charles." Hawley took a silk handkerchief from his breast pocket and wiped away the last of the blood on his chin. "But I don't want to cause any more trouble, even inadvertently." He bent down and picked up his fallen beaver hat. With a nod to Merrivale and a cold glance at Jeff and Melissa, he left the office.

The clerks looked relieved that the trouble was over, and they scurried to their desks.

Charles Merrivale folded his arms across his chest and glowered at Jeff. "Your behavior was abominable! I'll thank you—both of you!—to stay out of my business dealings in the future."

"You won't have to worry about that," Jeff promised. He jerked his jacket around until it hung straight again. It had bound a bit when he swung at Hawley, and Jeff knew that if he had been wearing his buckskins, the punch would have been harder.

"I'm sorry, Father," Melissa said. "We didn't mean to cause trouble by coming here today. I just don't see how you can stand to have that man in your office, knowing the things he's done."

"For which we have no proof but your husband's word." Merrivale nodded curtly, adding, "If there's nothing else, I'll bid you good day. I have work to do."

Michael ran over to him. "Paw-Paw! Pick up!"

Again the expression on Merrivale's face softened as he bent to lift his grandson into his arms. He patted Michael on the back, rumpled his sandy, blond hair, and kissed his cheek. "You go with your mother now," Merrivale said as he handed Michael to Melissa. "I'll see you at home tonight."

With that he turned and stalked into his office and shut the door behind him.

"I'm sorry," Melissa said to Jeff. "That didn't go as it was supposed to, did it?"

"I guess not." Jeff took a deep breath, then exhaled loudly. He wished he could regard Charles Merrivale with the same cold hatred he felt for Dermot Hawley. That would make things simpler. Then he could just pack up his wife and son and head for the frontier. But he saw the effect Michael had on his grandfather. The boy touched something in Merrivale that no one else was able to, not even Hermione. Somewhere, deep down, there was decency in Charles Merrivale's soul, despite the things he had done. And that left Jeff with the worst dilemma of his life.

"Come on," he said, slipping an arm around his wife's shoulders. "Let's get out of here."

As was his habit, Charles Merrivale worked later than his employees. He was still seated behind the large desk in his office when night fell, his ledgers open on the desk and spread out in front of him. As he went over the figures his clerks had entered in the ledgers, he frowned. He did not tolerate sloppy work, and a single careless mistake was often enough to make him fire one of them.

He sighed. It was difficult to concentrate on what he was doing when he was still so angry with his daughter. Melissa had been standing up to him more and more often in recent weeks, and he found it increasingly annoying. Never before, though, had she dared to meddle in his business affairs. That was intolerable, and he knew his daughter would never have done such a thing had it not been for the bad influence of that ruffian of a son-in-law.

Not for one minute did Merrivale believe the

wild stories Jeff had told about Dermot Hawley. Hawley was an upstanding businessman, a prominent member of the community, a young man with a fine future ahead of him. Merrivale laid his pen aside and shook his head. If only Jefferson Holt had died out there in the Rocky Mountains. If Holt had never come back, it would have been a relatively simple matter to have him declared dead or to arrange a divorce for Melissa. In either case, by now Melissa might have been Mrs. Dermot Hawley, and everything would have been fine.

The creak of a floorboard in the outer office made Merrivale look up sharply. He heard the noise again, and his pulse began to race. He had not heard the outer door open, but he had been so lost in thought, it was not surprising. Could it be a thief trying to sneak in and rob him? he wondered. If so, the man was going to be in for quite a surprise. Merrivale noiselessly opened a desk drawer and took out a small flintlock pistol. His eyes were fastened on the partially open door to the outer office as he lifted the gun.

"You won't need that, Charles," came a familar voice, a touch of mocking amusement in the words.

Merrivale sagged against his chair. "What are you doing out there, Dermot?" he asked as he replaced the pistol in the drawer. "The way you were skulking around, I thought you were a thief!"

Hawley pushed open the door and swaggered in. "I just wanted to make sure that son-in-law of yours wasn't here," he said. "I didn't want to be attacked again."

"Not likely." Merrivale snorted in disgust. "It would be just fine with me if Jefferson Holt never set foot in this office again. It's bad enough that I have to have a near-savage like that living under my roof. If you knew the family he came from, you wouldn't be surprised by his behavior. A worthless lot, those Holts." Merrivale gave a discreet cough. "The oldest son took advantage of one of the local girls out in

Ohio, then ran off to the West rather than marry her. It was quite a scandal."

"I can imagine." Dermot Hawley smiled and perched on the corner of the desk. "And I can understand why you were hoping that my quest to win Melissa's affection, not to mention her hand, would be successful. You deserve better, Charles, and so does she."

"Indeed," Merrivale agreed. He leaned back in his chair. "But there seems to be nothing we can do about that now. What brings you here tonight, Dermot?"

"I just wanted to be sure that the arrangement we came to this afternoon is going to proceed."

Merrivale held up his hands. "I'm sorry, Dermot, I truly am. But you heard the promise Melissa forced me to make—"

Hawley waved away the plea. "I heard you mollify your daughter so that that barbarian husband of hers would settle down. That doesn't have an effect on our dealings, Charles, and you know it."

His brow furrowed in thought, Merrivale asked, "You propose that we continue with our plans?"

"Melissa doesn't have to know anything about them," Hawley pointed out. "Everything is arranged. You have the goods, Charles, and I have the wagons to deliver them. Both of us stand to make a profit."

"Well, that's true. . . ."

"And you and I can continue to meet at night like this so that Melissa's sensibilities are protected. After all, Charles, business is business."

Merrivale slapped the desktop. "You're right, Dermot. Business *is* business. And I'll be damned if I'll let my own daughter decide how I should run mine." He thrust his hand out to Hawley. "You've got a deal."

Hawley shook hands, then slipped a couple of cigars from his coat pocket. Handing one of them to

Merrivale, he said with a grin, "I knew you'd be sensible, Charles."

"Of course. No reason not to be." Merrivale cast a shrewd gaze at his visitor, then asked, "Dermot, there's no truth to the things Holt has been saying, is there?"

"That I attempted to have him killed?" Hawley laughed. "Really, Charles, I'm surprised you even have to ask such a thing."

"Sorry, sorry," Merrivale muttered quickly. "Of course it's not true. I should have known better."

"However," Hawley said slowly, "Jeff Holt strikes me as quite a hot-tempered young man. He's going to find himself in a great deal of trouble one of these days, mark my words. And when that day comes—"

"Then you and I can be partners openly once again," Merrivale finished for him. "And perhaps Melissa will finally come to her senses and realize that the best man for her has been right here all along."

"We can only pray that you're right, Charles," Hawley said smoothly.

Jeff stalked back and forth in the elegantly furnished parlor of the Merrivale house. His steps were muffled by the thick rug on the floor, but every so often he drove his fist into the palm of his other hand, and a resounding crack filled the room. His nerves were jumping around like grasshoppers, and he could not be still.

Melissa and her mother watched him from the long divan with its brocaded cushions and ornately carved mahogany arms. "If you keep that up, Jeff," Melissa said with annoyance, "you're going to wear a hole in the rug."

"Sorry," Jeff muttered as he came to a stop. He clasped his hands together behind his back, took a deep breath, and ordered himself to calm down.

Ten seconds later he was pacing again.

Melissa sighed in exasperation and looked at her mother, who wore a tolerant smile.

"Your husband has a great deal on his mind, my dear," Hermione said quietly, smoothing back her graying reddish hair, "and some men are just not meant to sit."

Jeff overheard his mother-in-law's comment and smiled. If only Charles Merrivale had been more like Hermione, they could have worked out their troubles. Hermione was a sweet-tempered woman, and she had a long-standing habit of trying to make the best of things, no matter how unpleasant they might be. Having been married to Charles Merrivale for many years, Jeff imagined she had had a lot of practice at it.

"Guess I'm just a troublemaker," Jeff said as he came to a stop again. "But I never meant to cause you any grief, Hermione."

"I know that, Jeff," she assured him. "Besides, you've made Melissa happy. A mother couldn't ask for anything more for her daughter."

Jeff took another deep breath. He had reached a decision but had decided to postpone talking about it until Merrivale got home from the office. He wanted to wait until after they had all eaten before broaching a subject that he knew was going to cause more trouble. But there was no sign of Merrivale, and Jeff was debating whether to go ahead and announce his decision before his father-in-law got home.

Just then he heard heavy footsteps on the veranda. A few seconds later the door swung open, and Merrivale strode into the foyer. One of the housemaids was there to meet him and take his hat and coat, and then he walked into the parlor. He frowned at the three people he found waiting for him.

"Where's Michael?" Merrivale asked without preamble.

"He's already been put to bed, dear," Hermione replied. "You know his bedtime is seven o'clock. If you want to see him in the evenings, you should try to get home before then."

"A business doesn't run itself, you know," Merrivale chided her. He swung around to face Jeff. "And what do *you* have to say for yourself after that disgraceful display this afternoon?"

"Really, Father," Melissa said before Jeff could answer. "The moment you walk though the door you make trouble—before we even have dinner."

"Make trouble? I ask a simple question, but do I receive the courtesy of a reply? How is that making trouble?"

"That's all right, Melissa," Jeff cut in when she started to answer. "You don't have to defend me to your father. I can speak for myself."

With a haughty glare, Merrivale said, "Then by all means do so, young man."

No point in waiting, Jeff decided. His father-in-law was clearly in no mood to put up a pleasant facade through dinner, and neither was he.

"I'm sorry I haven't lived up to your expectations as the husband of your daughter and father of your grandchild, sir." Jeff found himself enjoying the look of surprise that crossed Merrivale's face. "And I honestly don't believe you had anything to do with Dermot Hawley trying to have me killed." He held up a hand to forestall the protest that Merrivale started to make. "Don't bother defending him. If that matter is ever settled, it will have to be between him and me. What we have to address now is the fact that you don't want me here."

"Nonsense, Jeff!" Hermione said quickly. "You're Melissa's husband, and you're welcome in this house for as long as you want to stay. Isn't he, Charles?"

"Let's just hear what else the boy has to say, Hermione," Merrivale said heavily. "Go ahead, Jeff."

"All right." Jeff glanced at Melissa and saw the apprehension in her eyes. She suspected what he was about to say, he thought, even though he had not discussed it with her. "I don't think the feelings of resentment and dislike in this house are good for Michael. I think it would be better for Melissa and Michael—for all of us—if the three of us leave."

"No!" Hermione exclaimed. "There's no need for that." She looked up at her husband. "Say something, Charles!"

Her husband did not seem overly surprised by Jeff's announcement. He folded his arms across his chest and asked, "Just where exactly do you propose to take my daughter and my grandson? To those Indian-infested mountains where you and your brother lived?"

"No, sir. There are no real settlements out there yet. For the time being, I thought Melissa and Michael could live in St. Louis. It's a real city, a growing city, and they'd be fine there while I trapped. I'd be able to see them pretty often. A couple of times a year, anyway."

Melissa's voice was taut as she said, "Jeff, I wish you had talked to me about this before you made up your mind. I might not want to live in St. Louis."

"A wife's place is with her husband," Jeff said stubbornly. "Isn't there something in the Scriptures about how a woman's supposed to leave her parents when she gets married?"

"Don't you dare quote the Scriptures, boy," Merrivale growled. " 'Honor thy father and thy mother'—there's one for you, Melissa. You've certainly done us no honor by marrying this—this—" Merrivale's face grew mottled with anger, and words failed him for one of the few times in his life.

Into the heavy silence that fell over the parlor, Hermione said tentatively, "Shouldn't we perhaps have dinner now?"

"I'm not hungry," Merrivale barked.

"Neither am I," Jeff said. They continued to glare at each other.

Melissa stood up. "We can't settle this tonight. We have to talk about this, Jeff."

"Talk all you want," he said to her without taking his eyes off her father. "It won't change anything. It won't change his mind about me."

"Nothing could do that." Merrivale snorted. He pointed a blunt finger at his son-in-law. "I'll tell you one thing, Jeff: The only way you'll take Melissa and Michael away from here is over my dead body!" He stalked out of the room.

Clenching his teeth, Jeff left the parlor, too. But he turned the other way and wrenched open the front door to walk off his rage in the cool night air. Behind him he heard sobbing, but he could not tell if it was coming from Melissa or Hermione. Either way, it was a lonely sound.

CHAPTER THREE

The deviation from the true curvature of the earth is much greater on the approach to the Rocky Mountains. This gives an increased velocity to the currents of water, and produces a more powerful attrition on their beds. The consequence is, the valleys in that part are deeper, and the surface more rugged and broken.

—JOHN BRADBURY "Travels in the Interior of America 1809–1811"

Always wary of an ambush by any one of their many enemies, the Sioux tended to locate their camps in open areas, near water but away from any thick timber. This was the case with the Hunkpapa Sioux camp that had been attacked by Piegan Blackfoot raiders. However, the creek running near the Hunkpapa camp formed a fairly deep gully between high banks, and the Piegan Blackfoot had used this convenient trench as a cover to launch their onslaught. The sentries that Bear Tooth had placed near the creek had been silently killed by Piegan arrows, allowing the raiding party to mount a surprise attack on the camp.

The Blackfoot had not reckoned on the fighting ability of the Hunkpapa, though, and had probably underestimated the number of warriors in the camp as well. Also, they had not counted on Clay Holt and Aaron Garwood taking a hand in the fight and downing several of the war party, including the leader from the Horn Society. That, as much as anything else, had turned the tide of battle.

The Hunkpapa were still cleaning up the devastation of the raid when several of the young men, led by the warrior called Walks-Down-the-Wind, approached Bear Tooth. Clay was standing nearby and noticed Proud Wolf among the group. An angry Walks-Down-the-Wind asked permission to speak to Bear Tooth.

The stolid, middle-aged chief of the band said, "You may speak. This is your right."

"I ask a meeting of the council." Walks-Down-the-Wind crossed his arms and glared at Bear Tooth.

"For what purpose?"

"So that we may plan our pursuit and punishment of the Piegan dogs who have done this to our people!"

Bear Tooth nodded. It was evident that Walks-Down-the-Wind's request did not come as a surprise to him. Work stopped now as Walks-Down-the-Wind's loud voice drew the attention of the other villagers. They drifted toward Bear Tooth, anxious to hear what his reply would be.

For a moment Bear Tooth did not speak, and Clay could see the impatience growing in the young men. Finally the chief said, "Soon the cold wind will blow and the snow will fall. The children will be hungry and will cry, but their mothers will not have food for them because the warriors are gone, chasing Blackfoot. The old ones will be cold from lack of firewood because the warriors are gone, chasing Blackfoot. The women will be restless in their sleeping robes because the warriors are gone, chasing Blackfoot. Is this what you and these others want, Walks-Down-the-Wind?"

The young warriors grew angrier as Bear Tooth lashed at them. A few, however, Proud Wolf among them, seemed to understand what Bear Tooth meant. They cast down their eyes as Walks-Down-the-Wind said hotly, "So you mean to let the Blackfoot escape and go back to their tipis to boast of how they killed so many of the Hunkpapa and none pursued them? You mean for this violation they have committed to be unavenged?"

"I mean we will take our vengeance at the proper time!" Bear Tooth thundered, his tolerance at an end. "The Blackfoot are as cunning as the fox. They planned this raid knowing there would not be time to pursue them before winter came. They burned our tipis and destroyed our stores for the difficult days ahead. We must spend our time hunting now so that there will be food for the children when the cold lies on the land. We must gather firewood so that the old ones will have warmth. If we desert our people to chase Blackfoot, we will be doing more harm than this raid has done. And if that happens, Walks-Down-the-Wind, the Blackfoot will have won."

The nods and murmurs among the people indicated that nearly everyone was convinced of the correctness of the chief's decision. Stubbornly, however, Walks-Down-the-Wind said, "It is not right to let such a thing go unpunished."

Bear Tooth smiled coldly. "Remember: The winter will go, and the warmth of summer will return. And when it does"—the chief's hand closed tightly on the lance he held, and he raised it into the air to shake it over his head—"then the people will have their vengeance on the Blackfoot!"

Cries and shouts went up from the survivors.

Through the long, cold months ahead, the Hunkpapa Sioux would nurse their hatred, and then, when the time was right, the Piegan Blackfoot would rue the day they had raided Bear Tooth's village.

Clay looked over at Shining Moon as the cries of righteous anger swept through the village. He would have expected her to join in, but instead she was sitting quietly beside the entrance to her tipi. She was staring off into the distance, and she seemed not even to be aware of the tumult around her. It was almost as if she were in a different world, one with its own peculiar sights and sounds that no one else could distinguish.

Glumly, Clay went about helping the Hunkpapa clean up the destruction around the camp. Shining Moon and Proud Wolf were safe; he was thankful for that. But his homecoming had certainly not been what he expected.

It was late afternoon, and Shining Moon was in the tipi she would once again share with Clay when he stepped inside, holding an oilcloth-wrapped package in his hand.

"Aaron retrieved the canoes we left below the camp, and he and Proud Wolf carried up the supplies we bought in St. Louis. This is for you," he said, his words slightly gruff with awkwardness.

Shining Moon recognized the tone quite well. Clay had never been one to give voice easily to his feelings.

He went on, "I know you didn't say you fancied anything, but I wanted to get something for you."

Shining Moon smiled stiffly. So far, things between them had gone just as she had expected: badly. Not that she was unhappy to see Clay again. She had thanked the Great Spirit for his safe return and would continue to do so in her prayers every day. But she could tell he knew something was wrong with her. The long months of nightmares and hellish memories had taken their toll. Whatever had given life to her soul was now gone; what remained was only a husk of what she had been.

He thrust the package out at her, and she had no choice but to take it. Her fingers moved as if without conscious thought as she unwrapped the oilcloth. Bright colors radiated off soft cloth, cornflower blue and yellow like the sun. She lifted the cloth and shook it out so that it hung from her hands. It was a dress— a white woman's dress.

"It—it is very beautiful," Shining Moon heard herself saying as if from a great distance.

"Try it on," Clay urged.

She hesitated. Was this the way he wanted her to look now? Like one of the white women he had seen back in St. Louis? Like the women he had left behind in the Ohio Valley?

She sighed and stood up. If this was the way Clay wanted her, she could at least try to please him. She began unlacing the buckskin thong that tied at the throat of her beaded dress.

"I'll turn around," Clay said quickly and did so.

He had sensed it, the unexpected distance between them. Quickly, her feeling of discomfort growing, Shining Moon pulled off her buckskin dress and put on the one of homespun fabric, blue with tiny yellow flowers. She supposed it was pretty.

"I am ready," she said.

Clay turned around to face her, and he let out a low whistle of admiration as she pushed back her long, raven hair and stood before him. "Lordy, I knew you'd look good in that dress, but I didn't figure you'd be that beautiful."

His gaze searched her face, and she tried to summon up a smile but could not. Solemnly she rotated, giving him a full view of her.

"How do you like it?" he asked.

"It is—very beautiful. I am honored that you brought it to me."

"Well, you more than deserve it. I hope it makes you feel better."

"I will wear it whenever you wish."

Clay shook his head. "No, it's yours. Wear it when *you* want to."

She considered that for a moment, then said, "All right. I will put it away now since I must work and would not wish to make it dirty. But I will wear it again another time."

"Sure," Clay said, looking puzzled. "Well, I'd better get back about my business. There's plenty to do, rebuilding after the destruction of those Blackfoot and getting ready for winter." He ducked out of the tipi.

Shining Moon looked down at the dress for a long moment, then whipped it off and put on her familiar buckskins. Did Clay wish he had married a white woman? Why had he come back to the mountains, if he was not pleased with her? But if he was pleased with her, why did he want to turn her into something she was not?

They were questions with no answers, and she knew they would haunt her dreams, along with the nightmares of the past.

For the next few weeks, Clay continued to pitch in, accompanying many of the hunting parties that went out to replenish the winter supplies lost in the Blackfoot raid. He waited well back from the herds of buffalo until the hunters were in position to strike with their bows and arrows. Only after the great shaggy beasts were alerted to the presence of the hunters and had begun to run would he fire his long-barreled flintlock. He was always able to bring down at least one buffalo, sometimes two or three, before they got out of range. Aaron usually went with him and accounted for quite a few of the buffalo himself. With the help of the two white men, the Hunkpapa were able to recoup most of the losses they had suffered in the raid.

It was impossible to utilize an animal's carcass more efficiently than the Sioux did a buffalo's. Everything—meat, hide, horns, hooves—served a purpose. The women worked diligently at scraping, stretching, and tanning the hides so that new tipis could be built to replace the ones destroyed by fire. Some of the hides with the hair left on would be used as winter robes to help warm the old people and the children. The meat, not including such delicacies as the hump and the brains, which were eaten immediately, was dried and stretched into jerky, some of which was mixed with fat and berries to make pemmican. Both the pemmican and the regular jerky would last for a long time without spoiling, and they would be important staples of the winter diet.

When he was back East, Clay had heard people talk about the simple lives of the Indians. There was nothing simple about it, he thought; no matter what tribe they belonged to, Indians lived a difficult, complex existence, and everyone had to work hard if the group was to survive. He was glad to do what he could to help, and he enjoyed being among the Hunkpapa again. Despite the struggles they endured on a daily basis, they were a joyful people. In some ways, the oncoming winter months were the most joyous of all because there was little to do once the snow and the frigid winds swept down from the north except stay inside the tipis and take pleasure in one another's company. It was no coincidence that most of the children in the band were born from mid-July into early September.

Unease nagged at Clay, however. Shining Moon had *changed*.

She had tried on the dress he brought from St. Louis, but she had not smiled; she'd looked as if she was willing to wear the dress to please him but had no interest in it herself. After she had tried it on, she put it away; Clay did not press her to wear it again.

She flinched from his touch as if his hand were a

white-hot poker—not every time, but often enough to be disturbing. If he spoke to her when she did not know he was behind her, she often whirled around to face him, her eyes wide and frightened, and he had to take her in his arms and stroke her hair and murmur soft words at length before she stopped trembling. Whenever a decision had to be made, she deferred to him immediately and never questioned what he said —a far cry from the defiant, outspoken, opinionated woman with whom he had fallen in love. He still loved her as much as ever, but the changes in her made him uneasy.

At night when they shared their sleeping robes, she did not turn away from him, did not deny him what the Sioux regarded as his rights as her husband. But neither did she respond as she once had, with soft, eager cries and urgent clutchings. It was as if she were somewhere else, like the other times he had seen her drift off into a world of her own.

Clay had never been a patient, understanding man; he knew that about himself, and so he made an extra effort not to lose his temper with Shining Moon. Every so often he thought he saw a glimmer of her old self in her eyes, and that was enough to keep him hoping that one day she would fully return to him. After all, he told himself, she had endured a great deal in the past year. It was natural that she would need time to get over what had happened to her.

Winter howled down from the northlands. Christmas came, and then the new year, although Clay was not certain when either of those events occurred. Time did not mean a whole lot once the wind and snow got their grip on the land. But he was fairly sure that 1810 had arrived.

A couple of more months inched by, and Shining Moon seemed a bit better. She did not jerk away when he touched her, and when he made love to her, she sometimes held him with a fierce strength as if afraid that if she did not hang on to him, he would disappear. Every now and then, she would smile, usually when Proud Wolf was visiting and talking about the young woman called Butterfly.

Clay had to admit that his brother-in-law's predicament was amusing. As the folks in the Ohio Valley would put it, Butterfly had set her cap for Proud Wolf; she would not be turned aside from her goal. She had been flirting shamelessly with him for months now, since they had saved each other's lives during the Blackfoot raid. That had been a sign, Butterfly insisted, of the spiritual tie that bound them together. For his part Proud Wolf was at his wit's end trying to figure out what to do about her.

One day in what Clay reckoned was early March, the sheath of ice on top of the creek had long cracks in it. The next, the cracks had widened and grown even longer. The heavy snow that had blanketed the land began to melt in the glow of the sun, the ice broke up, and a breeze that was not yet warm but was definitely not cold sprang up from the south. Winter was dying.

Clay Holt looked around, saw what was happening, and said, "It's time. Time to go after McKendrick."

Shining Moon was standing in the entrance of the tipi behind him, and she let out a low cry when he uttered the name. Clay wheeled around and saw the look of sheer terror on her face. He stiffened. He had been dreading that moment, but clearly no more so than Shining Moon.

"I'll be back," he said as he stepped over to her and rested his hands on her shoulders. "You know I've got to do this. We talked about it last year, before Aaron and I took Lucy Franklin back to St. Louis."

Shining Moon shook her head. "No . . ." she choked out. "This time if you go you will not come back."

Clay's mouth tightened. He knew that Shining Moon had visions from time to time; one of them had even helped save his life the year before. Truth to tell, he had run into strange things himself out there in the mountains; he still remembered the bizarre encounter he and the Shoshone woman called Sacajawea had had with a couple of . . . spirits? . . . angels? . . . He did not know what to call them, but he and Sacajawea had run into them back during the days when he had been with Lewis and Clark, and the experience had haunted him for a long time afterward.

So he could not scoff at Shining Moon's frightened claim or ignore it completely. But at the same time, Fletcher McKendrick had spread too much evil to go unpunished. Even though Clay had never met the man, he hated McKendrick with a passion almost as deep as the love he felt for Shining Moon.

"I'll be all right. You've got to have faith."

Wildly shaking her head, she tore herself from his grip and ran into the tipi. Clay sighed and let her go. She would come around in time, he told himself. She had to. Because he was not going to let anything or anyone stop him from settling the score with McKendrick—not even Shining Moon.

He thought about what he knew of the man, who was a Scot, judging from his name. Fletcher McKendrick was in charge of the Canadian operations of a fur-trading company called the London and Northwestern Enterprise, one of the chief rivals of the Hudson's Bay Company and the North West Company. Those companies had confined their trapping and trading to the Canadian Rockies, but the London and Northwestern, through the nefarious tactics of Fletcher McKendrick, had been trying for the past year and a half to expand south into what had been known as the Louisiana Purchase when the United States obtained the vast western territories from France. First McKendrick had hired a French-Canadian renegade called Duquesne to stir up trouble between the Indians and the American trappers, hoping that the Americans would be run out so that the British could have a free hand in the mountains. When that scheme had failed, partly due to the efforts of Clay and Jeff Holt, McKendrick had boldly sent British trappers themselves across the border to construct a fort—Fort Tarrant—in American territory. The leader of that expedition had been a lunatic named Simon Brown, whose Blackfoot followers had killed Professor Franklin and nearly ended the lives of Clay, Shining Moon, Proud Wolf, and Aaron Garwood. Simon Brown had met his own death, and Clay discovered Brown's dispatch case that contained documents concerning McKendrick and the London and Northwestern Enterprise. The documents had given Clay the whole story of McKendrick's scheme, or as much of it as mattered, as well as the location of McKendrick's headquarters, a British outpost in the Canadian Rockies called Fort Dunadeen.

It was McKendrick who was ultimately responsible for the depredations of Duquesne and Simon Brown; it was McKendrick who would have to pay the price for what his agents had done. And Clay intended to see that the score was settled.

He took a step toward his tipi and stopped. As he had just reminded her, Shining Moon had known this was coming. No sooner had the survivors of the battle of Fort Tarrant recovered from their wounds than Clay had begun making plans to head north to Canada. Lucy Franklin's safe passage had to be taken care of first, of course, so by the time he and Aaron had returned from St. Louis, it had been too close to winter to make any sort of long journey.

But now spring was imminent, and it was time to put the plan into operation. Shining Moon would just have to be reasonable, Clay thought. Turning from his tipi, he headed for the tipi where he knew he would find Aaron and Proud Wolf.

Reaching it, Clay pushed back the entrance flap and stepped in, finding Aaron, Proud Wolf, Walks-Down-the-Wind, and Cloud-That-Falls sitting beside the glowing embers of the firepit in the center of the tipi. All four young men had cards in their hands, and Walks-Down-the-Wind and Cloud-That-Falls were frowning in concentration at their cards.

"Straight beats a full house, flush beats a straight, and a straight flush beats damn near anything except a royal flush," Aaron was saying. "You understand all of that? It's really pretty simple."

"Yes, simple," Walks-Down-the-Wind repeated, but his expression and tone belied his words.

"Ready to bet?" Aaron asked brightly.

Clay chuckled. "You ought to be ashamed of yourself, Aaron. And you, Proud Wolf, are you going to let your friends get took this way?"

Proud Wolf grinned up at him, a habit he had picked up from being around Clay and other whites. "We wager only shiny round stones from the creek bed. Besides, Walks-Down-the-Wind and Cloud-That-Falls wanted to learn this game called poker."

"So being their good friend and all, I figured it was my duty to teach them," Aaron added.

"You two mind what you're doing," Clay advised the novices, "else you're liable to wind up with nothing left but your breechcloths." His expression grew somber as he looked at Aaron and Proud Wolf. "Anyway, it's time to talk about McKendrick."

Aaron put down his cards without hesitation, and the cheerful expression on his face vanished. Proud Wolf also tossed in his cards. "We will play another day," he said to Walks-Down-the-Wind and Cloud-That-Falls. Uncoiling lithely, Proud Wolf stood up. "We will talk of this elsewhere," he added to Clay.

The other two young warriors looked offended, justifiably so. "Is Proud Wolf not our brother?" demanded Cloud-That-Falls. "Are you keeping secrets now?"

"This is a matter to be discussed by my white brothers and me," Proud Wolf replied.

Walks-Down-the-Wind sneered. "Perhaps you have become white yourself. Perhaps you are not even one of the people anymore."

"I am *Nadowe-is-iw!*" Proud Wolf cried, striking himself in the chest with a fist and using his people's name for their tribe. "Always will I be Sioux! But my white brothers and I have debts of our own to pay."

Walks-Down-the-Wind gestured curtly to Cloud-That-Falls, and both young men stood, tossing down their cards with disdain. "We have no wish to learn your white man's game," Walks-Down-the-Wind declared. "And you need not leave the tipi to talk to these white men. My brother and I will go elsewhere." He turned and left the tipi, pushing the entrance flap aside angrily. Cloud-That-Falls was right behind him.

"Sorry, Proud Wolf," Clay said quietly into the silence that followed the departure of the two young warriors. "I didn't mean to cause trouble between you and your friends. Anyway, there's no big secret about it. Bear Tooth knows we're going after McKendrick."

"I have talked to him and told him of my wish to go with you instead of taking part in the raid to revenge ourselves on the Blackfoot," Proud Wolf said. "Bear Tooth told me this is an honorable thing, that McKendrick must be punished for the evil he set free to walk through our land. Whenever you are ready, I will go with you."

"Figured as much," Clay said. "You're still in on this, Aaron?"

"Damn right," Aaron confirmed.

Clay motioned for them to sit again. He hunkered next to the warmth of the firepit and said, "I had to make sure that was what you still wanted before we started making plans."

"We're with you, Clay," Aaron vowed. "How're we going to do this?"

"The first couple of times we were just defending

ourselves. This time we're going to take the fight to McKendrick."

Aaron and Proud Wolf glanced at each other; then Proud Wolf turned to Clay and asked, "Canada?"

Clay nodded. "Canada. McKendrick's never seen us and probably doesn't know what we look like. I intend to get on the inside of his operation by joining a group of those trappers working for him. Once we're there and have gotten the lay of the land, we'll decide what to do next."

"As long as it involves bringing McKendrick to justice, that's all I care about," Aaron said.

Clay warned, "I won't be bringing him in and turning him over to the law. Out here on the frontier, a man's got to take care of his own fights."

"This is the way it should be," Proud Wolf said. He gave Clay a shrewd glance, then added, "And my sister? How does Shining Moon feel about this?"

"She doesn't want me to go," Clay said glumly. "I'm sure she'll tell you not to go, too."

Proud Wolf's expression was haughty. "A Sioux warrior does not let a woman dictate to him, not even his sister."

"I recollect a time not that long ago when you'd have been in real trouble if Shining Moon'd heard you say something like that," Clay said with a faint smile.

"I remember when she would have insisted on going with us," Proud Wolf said sadly. "Shining Moon is no longer herself." He looked up, and anger shone in his eyes as his gaze met Clay's. "That is reason enough to seek our vengeance on this man called McKendrick."

"Amen," Aaron said quietly.

Clay was moved by the depth of his friends' feelings. Putting his hands on his knees, he pushed himself to his feet. "It's settled, then. As soon as we've made our preparations, we'll be heading north to Canada."

"And may the Great Spirit Wakan Tanka guide us on our quest," Proud Wolf said.

Clay could not argue with that. Likely they would need all the help they could get.

Even though none of them talked much about it, the news that Clay, Aaron, and Proud Wolf were going to Canada spread quickly through the Hunkpapa village. With the end of winter drawing near, excitement was growing in the camp anyway. The spring hunts would be coming up, and, even more importantly, war parties would go out to raid Piegan encampments to the north and west. Warriors sharpened arrowheads and tomahawks. It would be a season of blood and death but also of growth and birth.

Clay almost regretted that he would miss all of it. He would have also enjoyed being part of the great gathering during the summer, when all the bands of Sioux came together for a huge buffalo hunt and celebration. But his mission of vengeance came first.

Proud Wolf, too, had concerns. He was on his way through the camp one day when Butterfly stepped in front of him, forcing him to stop abruptly. That was not a seemly thing for a young woman to do, but Butterfly had never worried much about proper behavior.

"You are going to the northlands. I would go with you," she said bluntly.

Proud Wolf stared at her, unsure for a moment if he had heard her correctly. Then he said curtly, "You cannot go," and he tried to brush past her.

With a smooth movement, she remained in front of him, still blocking his way. "I can help you with your quest." Proud Wolf regarded her with a tolerant but slightly annoyed expression and said, as if he were talking to a child, "What can you do? You are a woman."

"I am a warrior first!"

Proud Wolf stared at her, shocked at the absurdity of her statement. "You cannot be a warrior. You are female."

"Your own sister has fought at the side of her man many times. I have heard the stories."

Proud Wolf scowled. "Do not bring Shining Moon into this. You cannot be a warrior, and you cannot go with us to the northlands."

"I had a vision—"

Throwing up his hands, Proud Wolf exclaimed, "Another vision! You have more visions, Butterfly, than a buffalo has fleas."

She folded her arms across her chest and eyed him steadily. "Raven Arrow."

Proud Wolf frowned. "What?"

"Raven Arrow. It is my new name. It came to me in my vision. I will dye the shafts of my arrows as black as the raven and use them to become a great warrior and slayer of the enemy. These things the spirits have told me."

It was bad luck to mock the spirits, Proud Wolf knew, but he could not take seriously these flights of fancy in which Butterfly indulged. And he felt enough sympathy for her so that he did not want to see her hurt, as she surely would be if she persisted with her mad notion.

He looked around to make sure no one in the camp was listening to their conversation, then said slowly and patiently, "You cannot be a warrior, Butterfly, and it is foolish to talk of such things. You should concentrate on—on womanly things, like sewing and cooking. Leave the ways of the warrior to the men. Then you can be happy and stop being bothered by these strange ideas of yours."

Her expression grew darker as he spoke, and he felt a tingle of apprehension as he saw the anger in her eyes. Maybe he had made a mistake by speaking so plainly, he thought. After all, Butterfly *was* rather large and strong for a young woman. . . .

Suddenly the anger seemed to drain from her, and it was replaced on her face by a great sadness. "You are right, Proud Wolf. I will never be a great warrior. I will never be called Raven Arrow. I should forget these things. It would gladden the hearts of my parents if I turned myself toward womanly ways and married a strong, courageous warrior—such as yourself."

Proud Wolf swallowed hard, wondering if he had just gotten himself into more trouble than he had intended. Butterfly might have been laying an ingenious trap for him, even though he would have sworn she was sincere with her talk of arrows with shafts dyed black.

"I have much to do," he said quickly, trying once more to get around her. That time she let him pass, and he hurried on.

But as he left her he glanced back over his shoulder, and just for an instant he thought he saw something in her eyes—a mixture of defiance and resolve, perhaps. It was there only for an instant, and then it was gone, and Butterfly smiled sweetly at him, the expression no doubt learned from watching Shining Moon with Clay Holt in earlier days.

Proud Wolf went on about his business. But the memory of that flicker of intensity in Butterfly's eyes lurked in the back of his mind for a long time.

CHAPTER FOUR

The wind was howling outside the small log cabin, sending shivers through Josie Garwood even though a crackling blaze in the fireplace was spreading warmth throughout the room. Winters hit that part of the Ohio Valley hard, and Josie had always hated them. Just the sound of the wind was enough to make her feel chilled. She pulled up her heavy woolen shawl, cloaking her sensuous body in its folds.

Across the room from where Josie sat in an old rocking chair, her son Matthew sat on the puncheon floor and tried unsuccessfully to spin a top. The toy had been crudely carved by one of the men who came to visit Josie and given to Matthew so that the boy would take it outside on the porch and play. Many of Josie's visitors brought things for Matthew, often toys to get the youngster out of the way while they went about the business that had brought them there.

Josie was a whore. She thought of herself that way and had long since stopped trying to put any sort of different face on things. She had to provide for herself and Matthew, and there was only one thing she could do well, one thing at which she had had plenty of experience since her oldest brother, Zach, introduced her to the pleasures of the flesh so many years before.

Not so long ago really, Josie reminded herself as the wind screamed again and another shudder went through her. She was still only in her early twenties, but she felt so much older than that. Sometimes she forgot how long it had really been.

But men had no trouble discerning how young and desirable she was. Her earthy beauty, lush figure, and long black hair attracted them to her like moths to a flame.

Matthew was having difficulty with the top; displaying a six-year-old's angry lack of patience, he snatched up the toy and flung it across the room. It thudded hard against the wall near the fireplace.

"Almost went in the fire," Josie said.

"So what?" Matthew snapped. "That damn top can go to hell and burn up for all I care."

Without really thinking about it, Josie scolded, "Don't talk that way. You know it's not polite."

Of course, it did not really matter, she told herself. Matthew was a whore's child, a bastard without even a father's name to claim. He could say anything he wanted, and no matter how shocking or terrible it was, it would only be what people expected of him.

"I'm tired of winter," Matthew grumbled.

"So am I. But it'll be spring soon, and you'll be able to play outside again all day."

"While all those men are here?"

Josie felt herself redden. "That's right."

Matthew did not reply. After a moment of glaring at the floor, he got to his feet and went over to retrieve his top. A sliver of wood had broken off the toy when it hit the wall, but other than that it was not damaged. He knelt and began to spin it again.

Josie sighed. She felt the walls closing in around her. At first, after the death of her father, the cabin that had once been the Garwood family farmhouse had seemed too large and empty. With the old man gone, as well as all her brothers, Josie and Matthew had seemed to rattle around the place like pebbles in a bucket. Now, though, the shabby dwelling seemed more like a prison, and she hated its confining closeness.

So much had changed. Her father was dead, and so were her brothers Zach, Pete, and Luther. Aaron had headed west to become a fur trapper. Jeff Holt had come through Marietta the year before, and he told her of Zach's death and how Aaron had joined up with Clay Holt, who had once been the Garwood family's mortal enemy. But all that was in the past. Clay had an Indian wife, Jeff had said. *I wasn't good enough for him, but he marries a filthy squaw instead!* Josie thought, not for the first time. Her resentment seemed to be a permanent part of her now.

So the Holts had gone off to lead a life of adventure, and even her youngest brother was now a part of it. But she was stuck there in the cabin outside Marietta, with the local men sneaking up to her door to satisfy lusts they could not get taken care of at home. Josie snorted bitterly. Things had changed for the Holts and for Aaron, right enough, but not for her.

What with the sound of the wind blowing outside, she did not hear the hoofbeats or know someone was outside until a heavy fist pounded on the door. She looked up sharply, surprised. Matthew flinched, too, and his hand accidentally hit the top, sending it skidding across the floor.

"Open up in there, Josie!" a voice called over the sound of the wind. "I can see you still got a lantern lit, so I know you're there!"

"Damn!" Josie said. She recognized the harsh,

half-drunken tones of Roy Deever. He was a keelboat-man, a member of one of the crews that poled the boats up and down the Ohio River. Whenever the boat he was on docked in Marietta for the night, he came to her cabin, and if anybody else was already with her, that was just too bad. Several brutal fights had taken place when Deever ran off another customer so that he could have her to himself. But he never gave her any argument about paying, and he had never mistreated *her*, only anybody unlucky enough to be in his way.

She stood up slowly and pulled her shawl tighter around her shoulders. "Hold on, Roy," she called. "There's no need to knock down the door."

"Hell there ain't," Deever said as Josie swung the door open. "I been missin' you so bad I'm about to bust, gal." He stepped in and slammed the door shut behind him.

A tall, rawboned man with heavy shoulders and a ragged black beard, he flung his arms around Josie and pulled her tightly against him, one hand reaching down to knead the flesh of her buttocks. He kissed her, and his mouth tasted like the raw, homemade whiskey he had been drinking.

"Matthew," Josie said rather breathlessly to her son when Deever finally took his lips away from hers, "you stay out here and play, all right?"

"Sure, Ma," the boy said dully, sounding far older than his six years. He was not watching the embrace between his mother and the keelboatman; in fact, he carefully kept his eyes averted.

Deever let out a happy, drunken whoop as Josie led him into the bedroom and shut the door. He was on her in a flash, just as she expected him to be, pulling her dress away from her breasts so that he could suck on them, making her wince as his bristly beard scraped against the sensitive flesh. She made herself mouth words that had become all but meaningless to her. He had obviously been drinking heavily before he came to visit her, so Josie knew he probably would not last long. That was fine with her; the sooner it was over with, the better.

Sitting on the floor with his top, Matthew Garwood could hear almost everything going on beyond the door, which was badly fitting, with several large cracks around it. A couple of times before, he had watched through the cracks, so he knew what the strange noises were, but he did not understand why anyone would do the things he had witnessed. He knew from the way his mother talked when no one else was around, however, that she did not like what she did with the men behind that door.

He took a folding knife from his pocket and opened the blade. His mother did not know he had the knife, and he kept it hidden from her so that she would not take it away from him. He had stolen it from Steakley's Trading Post, thinking that he would learn to whittle. But now, as he listened to the noises coming from the other room, he began to slash at the top he held in his other hand, scoring it deeply with the small blade, hacking off more slivers of wood, not flinching even when he missed and sliced a shallow cut across his palm. He seemed not to see the thin line of blood that appeared.

He listened and jabbed at the top, and outside the wind continued to howl.

Roy Deever dropped off to sleep when he was through, just as Josie had expected, and while most times she would have roused him and sent him on his way, that night she let him keep snoring. He had said something that interested her for a change, and as she got dressed again, she thought about it.

St. Louis. . . . It was getting to be quite a town, according to Deever. The keelboat he was on would go all the way down the Ohio to the Mississippi and on to St. Louis before turning around. With the fur trade growing so rapidly, people were flocking to the frontier, and there was a never-ending need for supplies from back East. The keelboats were doing a brisk business, Deever had said, hauling supplies downriver and carrying furs upriver.

Josie did not care what the boats brought back from the frontier. She was a lot more interested in the westbound part of the journey.

Clay and Jeff Holt had headed west, and that was the direction Josie's brothers had gone, too. There was no reason she could not follow their example. Ever since Lewis and Clark had returned from their expedition three and a half years earlier with news of vast reaches of unsettled land to the west, folks had been heading in that direction. The frontier represented a place where people could start over, a place where they could make a new life for themselves.

Why not do the same thing herself? Josie thought.

She leaned over the bed, put a hand on Deever's shoulder, and shook him. "Roy!" she said urgently. "Wake up, damn you! Roy!"

Gradually, Deever came awake, struggling to throw off the effects of his heavy drinking and the lustful bout with Josie.

"What'd you want?" he asked blearily, sitting up in bed.

"That boat you're on," Josie said, "does it carry any passengers?"

"Sure. All the cabins are full, though." Deever summoned up a leering grin and joked, "But if you're thinkin' about travelin' downriver, I suppose we could find a bunk for you in the crew's quarters. You'd have to share, but that wouldn't be nothin' new for you, now would it?"

Josie hesitated only an instant. "I'll take it."

Deever blinked at her. "Take what?"

"That bunk in the crew's quarters. Will there be room for Matthew, too?"

"The tyke?" Deever scratched his tangled thatch of black hair. "Well, yeah, I guess we could find a place for him. Say, Josie, are you serious about this?"

"Damn right I am. There's nothing to hold me here in Marietta, and I can pay for my passage, if that's what you're worried about. I'd like to see this St. Louis you've been talking about."

"Well, I can't speak for the cap'n, but I don't figure he'd mind, specially if you was to—"

"Anything he wants," Josie said flatly. "That won't be a problem."

Deever grinned slyly. "Didn't think it would be. Might not be an easy trip, though. There's still ice in the river. Could be dangerous."

Josie wavered only slightly. She did not like the idea of exposing Matthew to danger, but she liked even less the thought of staying and continuing the life she had led the past few years. Once they got to St. Louis, maybe she could find another type of work, something that would not be such a bad influence on Matthew. It had to be hard on a boy, having a whore for a ma, Josie thought. But there was no reason she had to be a harlot for the rest of her life.

She thought briefly of selling the Garwood property first, but then she realized that with the large debt her father had left when he died, anything left over wouldn't amount to much. It wouldn't be worth the wait.

"We're going," she said resolutely. "I'll pack up tonight, and we'll be there in the morning when the boat casts off. We won't have much to take with us."

"Better make it as little as you can. There ain't much room in the cabin we use for sleepin'."

Josie gave an abrupt nod. "Get your clothes on and get out of here, Roy. I've got things to do."

Deever did not complain about being sent away for the night. As he pulled on his clothes, he said, "Sure thing, gal. Hell, I'll have you available to me the

rest of the way down the river. I ain't goin' to do
nothin' to get you angry at me now."

Josie opened the door to the other room and saw
Matthew sitting on a stool near the fire, staring into
the leaping flames. In a brighter tone than she had
managed for many months, she said, "Matthew, I've
got something to tell you. We're going to be doing
some traveling. . . ."

The trip downriver proved more uneventful than
Josie had thought it would be. The keelboat was able
to avoid the chunks of ice floating in the stream as
well as sandbars and other snags with which the captain was already familiar, so there was little danger.
Matthew seemed to enjoy sitting atop the low roof
over the cabins and watching the riverbanks slide by.
Even on days when the cold wind blew, he rode on
top of the cabins. Josie worried that he would catch a
chill, but he would not hear of going below unless it
was absolutely necessary.

That was for the best, Josie decided, since frequently she was visited by the captain or one of the
crew members, and then she had to ply her profession
again. Better to keep Matthew as far away from that
as possible.

He had not protested when she told him they
were leaving Marietta. A loner even at his young age,
he had no friends to leave behind. The other children
in the area had sometimes taunted him about his
mother and his being a bastard, even though they frequently did not understand what they were saying;
they just repeated the ugly things they had heard
their elders say.

Those self-righteous bastards back in Ohio would
have been even more scandalized had they known the
real truth, Josie thought one day as she sat on the
cabin roof with Matthew and watched the scenery
pass by. Most of Marietta's citizens believed Clay
Holt was the boy's father, even though Clay had al-

ways denied it. Josie alone knew that Matthew's father was her own brother Zach, who had met his death somewhere out on the frontier.

That was one truth it was better to keep to herself, and Josie had vowed that Matthew would never learn the real truth about his heritage. In fact, there were times when Josie herself believed that Clay was Matthew's father, simply because she had repeated the story so often.

By the time the keelboat reached the Father of Waters, as the Indians called the great Mississippi River, the last winter storms were over, and a faintly warm breeze was blowing up from the south. Soon, Josie thought, winter would be over for good and with it the life she had left behind in Marietta. From now on everything would be different for her and Matthew.

Their first sight of the city sprawled out on the west bank of the Mississippi was almost as awe-inspiring as the river itself. Josie had never seen a settlement larger than Marietta, and St. Louis would make five or six of Marietta—maybe even more. A multitude of docks extended into the water, rather than the handful in Marietta. And beyond the docks were warehouses and stores and barns and houses and even a church!

Deever came up behind Josie and rested his hands on her shoulders. "There it be. St. Louis. What do you think of it, Josie?"

"It—it's magnificent," she struggled to reply.

Shrugging, Deever said, "It's just a little frontier town. Could be I overestimated it a mite when I was drinkin'. But I hope you and the lad'll like it here."

"I know we will."

Deever leaned closer to her and said into her ear, "And I'll come see you whenever a boat brings me downriver, darlin'. Just like old times in Marietta."

Josie turned around so quickly, she surprised

him into taking a step back. The fierce expression on her face threw him even more. "No, it's not like old times, and St. Louis isn't Marietta. You'll be welcome to visit us, Roy, but that's all."

He tried to grin. "But that's what I mean. I'll visit you like I always did—"

"I'm through with that," she interrupted. "I appreciate everything you've done, Roy, but I'm going to be a respectable woman now. For Matthew's sake."

"Oh." Deever still looked somewhat confused. But he was trying to understand. After a moment he said, "I don't suppose you'd want to go down in the cabin just once more, for old times' sake?"

Josie shook her head emphatically.

"Ah, well," Deever said with a sigh, "you can't blame a gent for tryin'."

The keelboat docked a few minutes later, and Josie and Matthew waited for the other passengers to disembark before getting off. The boat's regular passengers were businessmen and immigrants headed west, and Josie knew that most of them looked down on her and her son. But all that would change, now that they had reached St. Louis. No one there knew her, no one was aware of her shameful past.

Clutching the canvas bags in which she had packed the few pitiful belongings they had brought with them, Josie and Matthew went ashore after everyone else. Roy Deever gave them a hand stepping off the keelboat, then pulled off the knitted cap he wore.

"I'll surely miss you, Josie darlin', but I hope you're happy here. Anythin' you need, you come on down here to the docks and see if I'm around."

"I'll do that, Roy," she promised. She felt a surge of gratitude toward him. True, he was a brawler sometimes, and his drinking made him surly now and then, but he had helped her and Matthew a great deal. She never would have expected him to be so kind, but he seemed to have a good heart underneath his rugged exterior. She stepped closer to him and brushed her lips across his, then said softly, "Good-bye."

"Wait a minute," Deever said quickly as she started to turn away, "what're you goin' to do now? Where will you live? What'll you do?"

"I have a little money. Enough to rent a room for Matthew and me somewhere. And then I'll find work. I was a pretty good seamstress when I was younger."

He nodded, and Josie walked away, holding Matthew's hand with her left hand and carrying their bags in her right. Deever called after them, "Good luck, Josie! So long!"

She was going to need that luck, she thought, but she was confident that everything would work out. After all, she had successfully made the biggest step of her life by leaving Marietta, and now she was in the bustling settlement of St. Louis.

What could possibly go wrong?

Josie set the wooden tray on the bar and motioned for Gort Chambers to refill the mugs with beer. The burly, bullet-headed proprietor of the place nodded and turned to one of the casks he had tapped. The casks sat on crude plank shelves behind the bar, which itself was made of several wide boards laid across the tops of empty whiskey barrels. Nobody was ever going to accuse the nameless saloon Gort Chambers ran near the St. Louis docks of putting on any fancy airs. It was as squalid a place as any Josie had seen in Ohio.

But there was an empty storeroom in the rear of the building where Chambers let her and Matthew sleep, and he even gave her a little money every now and then, in addition to the room and board. It was better than nothing.

And to think she had arrived in St. Louis only a month earlier with such high hopes, Josie mused bitterly.

The money she had counted on to last for a while vanished almost overnight. With so many people passing through St. Louis, local merchants knew they could get away with charging exorbitant prices, so food and lodging cost much more than Josie had expected. She had rented a room in a boardinghouse that was little more than a crude shack, but a week's rent had been almost as much as what she had figured to pay for a month. Basic expenses had quickly drained her funds.

Worse than that was the fruitless search for work. Josie had fancied herself a seamstress, but it had not taken long for her to realize that the quality of her work was not going to get her a job in St. Louis. For one thing, people on the frontier were more interested in utilitarian garb than finery. Josie was hopeless when it came to pushing a needle through buckskin and sewing with thread made from buffalo gut. A couple of shops hired her briefly to show what she could do, and both of those stints were utter disasters.

The man who owned the boardinghouse had not hesitated to make her and Matthew leave when their money was gone. Josie had feared that he would pressure her to sleep with him in return for continued lodging, but evidently the idea never entered his mind, gold being more important to him than lust. That was a new experience for Josie—one she was not sure she liked when she and Matthew were forced to look for another place to stay. She had always been able to rely on her earthy good looks in the past. For a week, though, she and Matthew had slept in alleys and lived on what food they could find in trash heaps. Those seven days were the most horrible of Josie's life.

There had been little hesitation on her part when someone had told her to go see Gort Chambers. The tavernkeeper needed a new serving girl, and he had hired Josie on the spot.

"You're pretty enough, I guess," he had growled.

"Just don't try to steal from me, or I'll cut your hand off."

Josie did not doubt for a minute that he would. He was a terrifying man, and she had seen him crush a man's skull with a bung starter during a brawl in the tavern.

For the past few weeks, she had served drinks in the saloon, endured the lewd comments of the customers and the hands that pawed her from time to time, and been grateful for the opportunity to work.

If only Clay Holt had married her, she caught herself thinking from time to time. Then everything would have been different. But he had turned his back on her when she had told him she was going to have his baby. Marriage to Clay would have been a way out of her miserable existence, perhaps the only way.

It was his fault, all his fault, Josie told herself.

Chambers finished refilling the mugs and said, "Take those back to the gents who emptied them." As she started to turn away, he added, "And tell that brat of yours to bring in more firewood."

Josie reluctantly agreed. Chambers had not hesitated to put Matthew to work as well, and one of the boy's primary chores was to keep the woodbox filled. A stack of cut wood sat behind the saloon, and Matthew had to carry in loads almost as big as he was. He also emptied the spittoons and slop jars and cleaned customers' boots, as well as any other filthy errand Chambers could think of. So far Matthew had done his work without complaint, although it almost broke Josie's heart to see how tired he was by the time he got to go to bed, far into the night when the tavern finally closed.

When she reached the table where four keelboatmen sat drinking and bent over to place the mugs of beer on the rough wooden surface, one of the men reached up and caressed her breasts, which were all but spilling out of the low-cut dress she wore.

"Thankee, Josie," he cackled, "for the drinks and the show, both."

She put a semblance of a smile on her face. "Enjoy them, boys."

Another man reached over, tweaked a nipple through the fabric of the dress. "Oh, we do, darlin'! Why don't you take us back to your room so's we can show you how much we enjoy 'em?"

Josie straightened, automatically holding the now-empty tray between her and the men to ward off any more crude advances. "No, thanks," she said lightly. "Mr. Chambers keeps me too busy out here, as you well know, fetching drinks for gentlemen such as yourselves."

"Well, just you keep the offer in mind," the first man said. "It's always open."

She bit back the angry retort that sprang to her lips, the harsh words telling them that pigs like them would never touch her again. If she made the customers angry, Chambers might order her to get out and take Matthew with her, and they would be back where they had started.

The problem, Josie realized as she made her way around the crowded room, was that she and Matthew had not gone far enough west. St. Louis was just as bad as Marietta—worse, since it was larger and there were more men like the four who had just tried to buy her favors. The stigma of her past had seemed to follow her from Ohio, as if it were written on her face that she was nothing but a trollop. Men sensed that about her right away.

A short while later she noticed the four keelboatmen talking to Chambers at the bar. They were having an animated discussion, and Chambers was nodding. Josie felt a shiver go through her. She had a feeling that whatever they were talking about, it would not be anything she liked.

She was right. The men went back to their table, and Chambers caught Josie's eye and motioned for her to come to the bar. When she did, he gestured curtly and said, "Put that tray down. I got something else for you to do."

"What?" she asked, knowing all too well what his answer would likely be.

"Those four gents've been drinking steady and paying good money all evening, and now they want to pleasure themselves a mite. You can take them into the back room. I can handle things out here for a while. And don't worry about the price; it's all worked out."

Coldly, Josie said, "You hired me as a serving girl, not as a harlot."

Chambers shrugged. "Same thing, ain't it? Now, go on back there; they'll be in one at a time." When he saw Josie's reluctance, he added ominously, "That is, unless you'd rather look for work somewheres else."

Josie sighed, feeling all the defiance go out of her. There was no point in fighting it any longer. She was what she had always been, and she had been a fool to try to change that.

Maybe someday, though, when she had saved enough money to move on . . . After all, Clay Holt was still out there somewhere, and he might feel differently about things now.

"I'll do it," she told Chambers.

"Good girl. And your brat still ain't brought in the wood."

Josie sighed. Leaving the serving tray on the bar, she went to the door leading to the rear of the tavern. Chambers had an office of sorts back there where he counted his money, and there was a storeroom full of beer, whiskey, and ale, as well as the empty room where she and Matthew slept. That was where she found Matthew, sitting on his blanket-covered pallet and whittling on a piece of wood. He put his knife away hurriedly, and Josie pretended not to have seen it. It was about the only precious possession he had left, and she was not going to take it away from him.

"Mr. Chambers wants you to bring in more wood," she told him, sitting on her bunk opposite him.

"But it's dark out back." The protest came reluctantly, as if he did not want to admit being frightened by the dark, even though he was only six years old.

"I know, but you've got to get the wood. And the nights are still too cold for there to be any snakes hiding in the woodpile." She paused for a second. "And when you get through, sit out in the tavern for a while. I'm going to be, well, busy back here."

"Like in Marietta?"

"Just never you mind about that," Josie replied harshly. "You run and do as you're told."

Matthew stood up and left the room without comment or even looking at her, and Josie felt like crying out and running after him. She wanted to fold him into her arms and tell him they were leaving that awful place and everything was going to be all right.

Instead, she sighed and began unbuttoning her dress.

She had had plenty of keelboatmen for customers in Marietta. They were all the same: rough, drunken brutes who used a woman with about as much feeling as they put into their jobs of poling the boats up and down the river. No, probably even less than that, she decided.

Although the experience was distasteful, it was soon over. All four men had left the room satisfied, ready to drink more of Gort Chambers's beer and whiskey. With the last one gone, Josie sat up and reached for her dress.

"No need for that." Chambers stood in the doorway, leering at her. Josie made no move to cover her nudity. It was a little late for that, after all. Chambers took a couple of coins from his pocket and tossed them beside her onto the bunk. "There's your cut. Looks like you did good."

"Thanks," Josie said hollowly. She scooped up the coins and hid them under her crumpled-up dress.

Chambers closed the door and stepped over beside the bunk, then reached down to the buttons of his pants. "You don't have to go back out there. I closed up a mite early tonight. Figured that if you're going to be working for me this way, I'd best make sure you're up to the job."

"I've never had any complaints," Josie said seductively, the old instincts taking over again. She reached up for Chambers.

Back where she had started, she thought. That was for sure.

Sometime during the next few minutes, Josie thought she heard the door open and then close softly, but she could not be certain whether she had imagined it. Not that it mattered.

Not that it mattered at all.

CHAPTER FIVE

Nothing had quite the same bitter taste as compromise, Jeff Holt thought more than once during the long, angry winter.

Melissa had pointed out, quite rightly, that they could not head west until spring, so Jeff had reluctantly agreed to remain in Charles Merrivale's house until the weather turned warm again. He might not have gone along with that suggestion had it not been for Michael, who adored his grandparents. Jeff could understand the boy's affection for Hermione, but what Michael saw in Charles was beyond him.

As for Melissa, a feeling of desperation gripped her when 1809 slipped away and 1810 marched forward. She had not minded living in Ohio when her father had decided to move there, although deep down she really preferred more civilized surroundings. But the thought of moving to St. Louis secretly terrified her. Jeff had told her that it was a bigger settlement than Marietta now, but it was still on the edge of the wilderness, and she was sure that raising Michael there would cause her endless worry.

So as the days lengthened and the air grew warmer again, Jeff's anticipation grew—and so did Melissa's apprehension.

She knew she had to do something soon, or Jeff would start getting ready for the journey west, even though she had never actually said that she and Michael would return to St. Louis with him.

One day Melissa went looking for her mother and found her in the kitchen of the large house, discussing the evening meal with the cook. Hermione took one look at her daughter's face and cut short the conversation.

"What's wrong, dear?" Hermione asked.

Melissa had not realized how apparent her anxiety was. "I need to talk to you, Mother. Can we go in the parlor?"

"Of course. Where are Jeff and Michael?"

"They've gone down to the harbor to watch the boats." In spite of her worry, Melissa had to smile at the thought of Michael's enthusiasm when she had suggested that Jeff take him to the docks. The outing would do both father and son good, as well as give her a chance to talk to Hermione in private.

When she and her mother were settled on the divan in the parlor, Melissa said glumly, "We have to do something about Father and Jeff, Mother."

"I don't see what we *can* do about them," Hermione replied with a shake of her head. "They've spoken hardly a dozen words to each other since last fall. I suppose we should be glad they haven't been at each other's throats all this time."

"No, they're not fighting," Melissa agreed, "but they're not learning to get along with each other, either. Mother, Jeff still plans to take Michael and me back to St. Louis with him."

Hermione sighed. "I was afraid of that. Your husband is a stubborn man, dear—and believe me, I know what it's like to live with a stubborn man."

"How do you stand it, Mother?" Melissa asked, leaning forward. "Does Father *ever* listen to you?"

With a dainty shrug, Hermione replied, "From time to time he does, if I express myself forcefully enough. But that's a difficult thing for me to do. I was raised to believe that a wife should always be subservient to her husband."

"Well, I can't be that way," Melissa said sharply.

Hermione patted her daughter's knee. "I know, dear. You have a streak of stubbornness yourself. You inherited it from Charles, I suppose."

Tension got the best of Melissa; she stood up and paced back and forth across the parlor. "I just don't know what to do," she said. "I don't want to move to St. Louis."

"Have you told Jeff how you feel?" Hermione asked.

Melissa shook her head. "He's so miserable here, I haven't had the heart to cause more trouble for him."

"If he forces you and Michael to go out to the frontier with him and you don't want to, he'll be causing trouble for *you*."

"But he doesn't mean to hurt us. He'd never do anything to hurt us."

Hermione took a deep breath. "All right, dear. I can see you have a dreadful dilemma facing you, and since I'm your mother, I want to help you if I can. We'll just have to put our heads together and see if we can come up with a way to make that husband of yours *want* to stay here."

"I can't think of a thing that would do that," Melissa said in despair.

Hermione patted the sofa cushion beside her.

"Come sit, Melissa," she said firmly. "There was never a man born of woman who could outmaneuver both his wife *and* his mother-in-law. Let's think about this, and I'm sure we can come up with *something*."

Jeff felt good when he and Michael returned to the Merrivale house after an afternoon at the harbor. A strong, bracing breeze had been blowing in from the sea, sweeping away a bit of the stench that normally hung over the docks. The sky had been a deep blue mirrored in the restless waves, and the sails of the boats had stood out in striking contrast. Michael had had a fine time, pointing at the boats, talking lickety-split, and asking endless questions about sailing.

"Just wait until your cousin Ned comes to visit," Jeff had told the boy. "He knows a lot about boats, and what he doesn't know, I'm sure his friend India does."

"Indian?" Michael had asked, sounding surprised. "An Indian sailor?"

"No, *India*," Jeff had repeated. "She's named after the country, and it doesn't have anything to do with the Indians out west, the ones that your uncle Clay and I knew."

"India's a *girl*?"

Jeff had quickly changed the subject. The fact that India St. Clair was female had been a secret known only to Ned, Melissa, and him. He hoped he could rely on the youngster's discretion, but given the fact that Michael was only two—well, discretion was doubtful. Jeff would have to trust to luck instead.

But not even that small slip had been enough to ruin his mood. He was carrying Michael on his shoulders as they entered the house, and the boy let out a happy laugh as Jeff swung him down to the floor. Melissa and Hermione, both of them smiling, appeared in the entrance to the parlor. They must have heard Michael's laughter, Jeff reasoned.

"Good afternoon, ladies," he said brightly.

Melissa came up on tiptoe, leaned close to him, and kissed him lightly on the cheek. "Hello, darling. Did you and Michael enjoy yourselves?"

"It was fun, Mama!" Michael said before Jeff could reply.

"It was indeed," Jeff agreed. "Michael's going to miss the docks and the boats when we head west, but there'll be plenty of other exciting things for him to see."

He caught the quick glance that passed between Melissa and Hermione, but was unsure of its significance. No doubt he would understand soon enough, he thought with a slight feeling of unease. He could tell by looking at Melissa that she had something on her mind, and he was certain it had to do with the upcoming move to St. Louis.

He supposed that he should have sat down with her and made sure that she was willing to go west with him, but once the idea had formed in his mind, it seemed to be a foregone conclusion. One thing was certain: He never could have made it through the months since the confrontation with Charles Merrivale if not for the thought that, come spring, he and his family would be leaving. That goal was the only thing enabling him to control his dislike for his father-in-law.

But if there was going to be trouble, there was no point in putting it off. "Do you have something you want to tell me?" he asked Melissa.

"Not now," she said, glancing down at Michael. "Later, perhaps."

"You're sure?"

"I'm sure."

Jeff knelt beside Michael. "You run on out back and get washed up. It's just about your suppertime."

"Yes, Papa." For all his exuberance, Michael was an obedient child. The only thing he could not seem to do was stay in one place for very long.

Jeff stood up as Michael hurried off to the rear of

the house. The servants would take charge of him and give him his supper, while the adults would wait until later for their meal. Merrivale seldom arrived home before seven o'clock and was often later than that, so dinner was usually around eight.

"All right," Jeff said, looking squarely at Melissa. "You've got something to say to me that I'm not going to like, I can tell. You might as well get it out of the way now."

"No, Jeff, let's wait—"

"Let's not," Hermione interjected, surprising both her daughter and her son-in-law with the firm tone in her voice. "You're right, Jeff, this is very important, and no, I don't think you're going to like it."

"Might as well go in the parlor and be comfortable while we're about it," Jeff muttered.

"I agree." Hermione led the way imperiously, which was a startling change. Jeff could tell that she was having to make an effort to be so forceful.

When they were in the parlor, Hermione faced her son-in-law. "Jeff, I know you and my husband don't get along, and I know that Charles can be a very difficult man to like."

Jeff gave a short, humorless bark of laughter. "That's the truth."

"Please, Jeff," Melissa said. "Hear my mother out."

"Sorry, Hermione. I didn't mean to be rude."

"I know you didn't." She managed to smile, despite the solemn tone of the discussion. "I'm well aware of the reaction Charles provokes in a great many people. But he's honestly not a bad man. He just has his own opinion about a great many things— about *everything*, I suppose—and he holds to those opinions stubbornly. It's very difficult to change his mind."

"No offense, Hermione, but you're not telling me anything I don't already know."

"No, of course not. I'll get to the point." She hesitated for an instant, then said, "I need your help, Jeff."

"My help?" Jeff blinked in surprise. "You know I'll do anything I can for you, Hermione."

She smiled again. "I'm glad to hear that. As you know, Charles isn't getting any younger."

"None of us are."

"But with his business growing so rapidly, I'm worried that he is working too hard. You've seen how he pushes himself, always staying late at the office and then working here in his study until all hours of the night"—Hermione sighed in exasperation—"and he never listens to me when I tell him he needs to rest more, of course."

For the life of him, Jeff could not see where the discussion was going, but after a glance at Melissa he kept his mouth shut. His wife's face was pale and drawn, and he figured he had better let Hermione have her say, whatever it was.

"For a time I thought that Charles's arrangement with that Mr. Hawley might take a bit of the pressure off him."

Jeff's jaw tightened.

"But Charles certainly couldn't continue working with that man after everything that happened," Hermione hurriedly continued. "So now he's trying to do everything himself again, and Melissa and I are afraid that his health is going to suffer."

"I'm sorry, Hermione," Jeff said, although genuine sympathy for Charles Merrivale was something of which he was in short supply. "But I don't see what I can do—"

"You can become Father's partner," Melissa blurted, unable to hold it in any longer. "You can help him run the business."

Jeff could not have been more surprised if there had been a clap of thunder in the parlor and lightning had struck him. He stared at Melissa, speechless.

"It was my idea, Jeff," Hermione said quickly. "I

asked Melissa what she thought, and she said you might be willing to help."

"Me?" Jeff finally managed to say. "Work with—? Oh, no! That's the—" He had been about to say that was the craziest idea he had ever heard, but he held his tongue, not wanting to hurt Hermione's feelings, since she had admitted to thinking up the scheme. Instead, he said, "I couldn't do that without staying here in North Carolina. It would mean not going back to the mountains."

Melissa put a hand on his arm as she looked up into his eyes. "I know, Jeff, and I know how much you had your heart set on that. But it would be such a help if you could. And it would mean so much to Mother and me, and to Michael—"

"What's Michael got to do with this? He'll *love* St. Louis! There're keelboats docking all the time, and folks heading west. You know how he feels about traveling. He's got that wandering foot, like all the Holts."

"There'll be plenty of time for that later," Melissa insisted. "He's just a little boy. He can see the West when he gets older, when he can appreciate it more."

"I wanted him to grow up out there. . . ."

Jeff looked at his wife and his mother-in-law and felt a mad swirl of emotions. He wanted Melissa to be happy, and he suspected this was her way of trying to tell him that she did not really want to move to St. Louis. He could respect that, he supposed, although she should have come right out and told him. And he knew that Hermione did not want to be parted from her daughter and her grandson. That was certainly understandable, too. But they had to understand how living here under Merrivale's roof grated on him, how his father-in-law's hostility toward him gnawed on his insides like a beaver on the trunk of a blue spruce. If they were going to stay permanently in North Carolina, at the very least they would have to find a place of their own.

Suddenly he laughed, surprising Melissa and Hermione, as another thought occurred to him.

"What are you laughing at?" Melissa demanded.

"Does your father know about this idea?"

Melissa glanced at her mother. "Not yet, but we're going to tell him when he gets home."

"Then there's no need to keep arguing. You'll never get him to agree to work with me."

The two women looked at each other again, and Jeff could tell that was one of the things they had talked about before broaching the subject with him. They knew Charles Merrivale even better than he did and had to be aware of how intractable he was. It would be easier to talk a maddened bull out of charging than it would be to change Merrivale's mind.

Hermione touched his arm. "If Charles does agree, will you at least give the arrangement a try, Jeff? That seems only fair."

"You're going to ask your husband to take me into his business as a partner, and you expect him to agree?" Jeff could not keep the surprise out of his voice.

"What I expect is of no consequence," Hermione said firmly. "If Charles says yes, will you agree, too?"

"Sure," Jeff said, throwing up his hands. "Why not? It'll never happen."

"What?" Charles Merrivale thundered. "What in heaven's name do you mean by even suggesting such a thing, Hermione?"

Jeff leaned back in his chair at the dinner table, patting at his mouth with his linen napkin to hide the grin spreading over his face at Merrivale's response to his wife's suggestion. Merrivale was reacting just as Jeff had expected he would, right down to his face turning a mottled brick red in anger.

"Please, Charles," Hermione said, looking flustered. "You'll wake the baby."

Michael was settled down for the night in his

bedroom upstairs, and although usually nothing could disturb him, Merrivale was bellowing like a gored bull.

"Really, Father," Melissa said sharply, "there's no need to carry on so. Mother and I just have your best interests in mind."

"I'll thank you not to tell me what my best interests are, young lady! I know them perfectly well by now." Merrivale swung around and glared at Jeff, the meal in front of him forgotten in his indignation. He demanded, "What about you? I suppose this insane plan was your idea!"

Jeff tossed his napkin down, no longer bothering to hide his amusement. "Hardly. I'd say this is the first time we've really agreed on anything. I thought it was just as crazy as you do."

"You did, did you?" Charles Merrivale snorted, picked up his glass of wine, and downed what was left of it.

Melissa said, "We're only thinking of your health, Father. The business is so successful, it's getting to be too much for you to handle by yourself."

"Is that right?" Merrivale growled. "Well, let me tell you something, daughter. The day I need help running my business from—from an unwashed backwoodsman like that—that husband of yours is the day you can put me in the ground and throw dirt on my face!"

"Charles!" Hermione exclaimed, her hand going to her mouth in shock. She stood up, trembling as she went on, "How dare you act like this, Charles Merrivale? We only wanted to help you."

"Help keep Jeff from running off to the mountains again, you mean."

"I mean no such thing!" The unexpected fire in Hermione's voice made her husband look at her in surprise. "It's true that Melissa and I don't want Jeff to leave and take her and Michael out to the frontier, but you're the one I'm really worried about, Charles.

You're not a young man anymore. You need a good man to help you run your business, and Jefferson Holt is a good man." Defiantly, she stepped over to Jeff and rested a hand on his shoulder.

Jeff looked up at her and said quietly, "Thank you, Hermione. I know you mean what you say." He glanced at Melissa. "I wish you'd just told me that you didn't want to go to St. Louis."

"You never gave me a chance to," she said. "You've had your heart set on leaving ever since last fall, and I didn't know what to do."

Jeff could hear the tortured indecision in his wife's voice, and his heart went out to her. He had put Melissa in a well-nigh impossible situation; he could see that now, but he had no idea what to do to resolve the problem. Working with Merrivale seemed out of the question.

Merrivale stood up and glared at them. "I don't wish to listen to this any longer. Dinner is ruined, and I'm going to my study."

"To work?" Hermione challenged.

"I might as well, hadn't I?" Merrivale shot back. He turned and stalked toward the door of the dining room.

Jeff could not resist calling after him, "Well, at least you didn't surprise me, Charles. I told the ladies you'd never agree to the idea."

Merrivale froze, his hand outstretched toward the knob of the dining room door. He slowly turned and regarded Jeff, his bushy white brows drawn into a frown. "What did you say?"

Jeff pushed back his chair and stood so that he could meet Merrivale's eyes squarely across the room. "I told Melissa and Hermione that you would never agree to work with me." He laughed. "I know you too well. I think you'd rather cut your own arm off first."

"Know me too well, do you?" Merrivale clasped

his hands behind his back and came toward the table. "You're an arrogant pup, you know that?"

"And you're a stubborn old man." Jeff knew the words might hurt Melissa and Hermione, but things had gone too far now. This was between him and Merrivale.

"That's the trouble with young people. Think they know everything in the world. Nothing ever surprises you, does it, Jeff?"

"Not a hell of a lot."

"Then try this." Merrivale's hand shot out. "I'm offering you a partnership in my firm. Will you take it?"

Melissa gave a startled, happy cry, and Hermione embraced her as Jeff stared in total shock and bewilderment at his father-in-law's outstretched hand. He felt as if the floor had suddenly dropped out from under him—and the worst part was he knew *he* was responsible for the unexpected turn of events. His goading had pushed his father-in-law into making the offer.

"I—I couldn't—" Jeff stammered.

"Jeff!" Melissa cried. "You promised! You said if Father agreed, you would, too!"

Charles Merrivale grinned at him, and Jeff thought he could see a glint of evil in the man's eyes. "Well, what about it, boy? Lost your stomach for trouble, have you? Because I can promise you, I'll give you plenty of it."

Feeling like a drowning man going down for the last time, Jeff abruptly reached out and clasped the hand of the man he despised above almost everyone else in the world. "I can handle anything you can come up with, old man," he growled.

Behind him, Melissa and her mother were laughing and crying, and from the way they were carrying on, Jeff thought, anyone watching would have assumed that it was a joyous occasion. But that was wrong, and the look in Charles Merrivale's eyes confirmed it.

Unless he was sorely mistaken, Jeff thought, war had just been declared.

Ned Holt scrambled up through the rigging, his lean, muscular body moving with practiced ease toward the yardarm. More than any of the other duties on shipboard, he liked being aloft with the wind and the sun in his face and the sea spread out at his feet as if he were an ancient bronzed god bestriding the oceans. Ned grinned at the thought. He had not had such romantic notions before meeting India St. Clair.

But then India was the sort of woman to put romance in any man's soul, Ned told himself. Even dressed as she was at the moment down on deck, in duck trousers and a loose blouse and a knitted cap on dark hair cropped as short as any man's, to Ned she was the most beautiful woman he had ever seen. And one thing Ned Holt had seen plenty of in his time, as he had been known to boast unwisely on occasion, was beautiful women.

He put his mind back on his work. It would not do to take a misstep and plunge ninety feet to the wooden deck below. He methodically untangled the lines that had gotten fouled and then climbed back down, landing lightly on deck as he leapt off the boom.

"Ought not to give any more trouble, Cap," Ned called to Captain Jebediah Vaughan, who stood on the bridge of the trading vessel called the *Fair Wind*. The captain, a portly, distinguished-looking figure in his blue uniform and white beard, saluted in acknowledgment.

India walked over to Ned. On board ship she was known as Max St. Clair. Ned was the only crew member entrusted with the secret of her true identity. However, he suspected that Captain Vaughan had at least an inkling that India was not the young man she pretended to be. But she was also the finest sailor on the *Fair Wind*, and Vaughan had no desire to lose a good crew member, no matter what gender.

India said firmly to Ned, her voice deep and husky and touched with a British accent, "I could tell your mind was wandering up there. You'd best be careful when you're aloft, boyo, or we'll be picking you up off the deck with buckets."

Ned leaned closer to her and said quietly enough so that only she could hear, "I love it when you talk sweet like that, darlin'."

For a second he thought she was going to punch him in the belly, and he knew from experience that such a blow would hurt. But she just rolled her eyes and turned away. Ned followed her, trotting up alongside her to say, "We'll be docking in Wilmington in a couple of hours. Are you coming to see Jeff with me?"

"I suppose I should," India replied with an off-handed shrug. "That cousin of yours is a fine gent. I was happy for him when we heard he'd found his wife after all that time."

Word of Jeff's reunion with Melissa had reached Ned and India through a cousin of the Holts by marriage, Lemuel Marsh, who was also the owner of the *Fair Wind* and quite a few other vessels. Ned had accompanied Jeff during his long search for Melissa, and when they met India, the three had become close friends. Although Ned and India had learned that Jeff had located Melissa in Wilmington, North Carolina, the ship had not put in at that port long enough to allow them to visit Jeff. Today would be different, however; the *Fair Wind* would be staying overnight.

India leaned on the ship's railing and gazed out over the waves. As Ned lounged beside her, she commented, "I'm a bit surprised Jeff is still in North Carolina. The way he talked about returning to the Rocky Mountains, I would've expected him to before now."

Ned shrugged. "I suppose he has his reasons.

Probably something to do with that pretty little wife of his.''

Glancing over at him, India asked, ''What would you do, Ned, if you wanted to go somewhere and your wife didn't?''

He laughed. ''Why, I'd just sling her over my shoulder and go anyway, of course!''

''That is *exactly* what I thought you would say.'' And with that, India stalked away, the set of her back telling Ned that she did not want him following.

Ned watched her go. Sucking on a tooth, he shook his head and chuckled sheepishly. ''Ned Holt, sometimes you're the biggest damn fool that ever sailed the seven seas.''

''Exactly what I've been thinking!'' Captain Jebediah Vaughan boomed from right behind him. ''Now, get back to work, Holt!''

''Aye, sir!'' Ned exclaimed, scrambling to find a chore that needed doing.

Jeff was looking forward to seeing his cousin Ned again, as well as India St. Clair. Having received word that the *Fair Wind* would be moored overnight, he was waiting at the docks along with Melissa and Michael for the ship to enter the harbor.

''You'll like Ned and India,'' he told Melissa as they stood watching the horizon. ''Just remember to call India Max if any of the crew is nearby. If they find out she's a woman, she'll have to stop sailing.''

''I can't imagine a young woman wanting to sail on a boat with a bunch of men, anyway. Not unless she was, well, less than respectable.''

Jeff laughed. ''I wouldn't let India hear you say that. I'd wager it would be dangerous to even imply such a thing. She's very protective of her honor. I imagine she's had her hands full fending off Ned's advances, though. My fair-haired cousin has always fancied himself a ladies' man.'' He did not mention how he and Ned had left Pittsburgh, Ned's home-town, with an irate husband in hot pursuit.

Michael was a few yards away, gazing out to sea, and he suddenly lifted a hand and pointed. "Boat! There a boat!"

His son was right, Jeff saw. The white speck of a sail was visible on the horizon, and the craft rapidly drew nearer, until it was easy to pick out the three masts of the schooner. Jeff recognized the clean lines of the *Fair Wind*, the vessel that had brought him to North Carolina the previous year.

Soon the trading ship was docking, and Jeff walked over to the end of the pier. Spotting him, Ned did not wait for the gangplank to be lowered. He vaulted to the top of the railing and leapt down to the pier, landing lightly on his rope-soled shoes. Throwing his arms around Jeff, he pounded him on the back, bellowing as he did so, "Jeff, you old mountain lion! How the hell are you?"

"Just fine, Ned," Jeff replied, disentangling himself from his cousin's exuberant embrace. "Come on, I want you to meet my wife and son."

"Can't wait," Ned said as they walked up the pier. "Lemuel told us how you found Melissa and that boy of yours. I've got to tell you, Jeff, there were times last year when I thought you never would find what you were looking for."

"I felt the same way," Jeff admitted. "But luck was with me at last." He stopped as they reached Melissa and Michael. "Ned, this is my wife, Melissa, and my son, Michael James Holt."

Melissa put out her hand, but the tall blond man swept her into a hug instead. Jeff felt a little sorry for her since this was the first time she had encountered Ned's enthusiasm.

"Mighty pleased to meet you, Melissa," said Jeff's young cousin. "I've heard a lot about you from this husband of yours."

"And—and I've heard a great deal about you,

Ned," Melissa replied rather breathlessly as he released her.

"None of it's true, I'd wager, except the good parts." Without waiting for her to respond, he turned to Michael and scooped the boy up off the dock. "Lordy, you're a big fella. Gonna be a sailor when you grow up, Mike?"

Most children would have been terrified to be snatched up by a stranger, especially one as big and boisterous as Ned Holt. But Michael just grinned at him, pointed to the *Fair Wind*, and said, "Boat!"

"Aye, that she is. Want to take a look around her?"

Michael nodded eagerly.

Ned reined in his enthusiasm long enough to look to Jeff and Melissa for permission, and Melissa said somewhat dubiously, "I suppose it would be all right. . . ."

"Go ahead, Ned," Jeff told him. "Just keep an eye on Michael. He gets into things faster'n you'd think he could."

"I'll watch the lad, I promise." By now the gangplank had been put in place, and the ship's cargo was being unloaded. Ned waited for an opening and then, still carrying Michael, hurried up the plank onto the ship.

"He's like a big child himself," Melissa said quietly, still looking a bit worried.

"That's a good description of Ned, all right," Jeff agreed. "But he's more levelheaded than he appears. He'll take good care of Michael. Ah, there's India!" He strode forward to greet a small figure in sailor's clothes who had just come onto the dock.

"Jeff!" India said, extending her hand like one man greeting another.

Jeff shook hands with her and said, "Hello, *Max*. How was the trip?"

"Just fine. Has Ned already come ashore?"

"Yes. Actually, he took my son, Michael, back on

board to show him around the ship. I suppose that
will be all right with the captain?"

"I expect so."

Melissa cleared her throat behind Jeff, and he
turned with a smile. "This is my wife Melissa. Melissa, meet"—he lowered his voice—"India St. Clair."

"Hello," Melissa said, then added in a whisper,
"I hope I don't say the wrong thing and give away
your secret, India."

"I'm pleased to meet you, Melissa," India said
with a grin. "And don't worry too much about that
other business. As long as there're no crewmen
around, I don't care what anyone calls me. Discretion
is all I ask for."

"Well, I'll certainly try," Melissa promised her.
"You're coming to dinner with Ned tonight, aren't
you?"

India frowned slightly. "This is the first I've
heard of it."

"You didn't expect to come to Wilmington and
not have dinner with us, did you?" Jeff asked. "Actually, it's my mother-in-law who's extending the invitation. She's anxious to meet both of you; she's heard
me talk so much about you."

"Well, all right," India said. "I suppose Ned and I
can be there."

"Good," Jeff said.

The three of them stood talking for a few more
minutes, until Ned reappeared at the head of the
gangplank, Michael perched on his shoulders.

Ned trotted down the plank and came over to the
others. "This is a fine lad you've got here," he said
with a grin. "Smart as a whip, he is. Full of all sorts of
questions about the ship."

"Whip!" Michael repeated, happy to have
learned a new word.

"Yes, yes, whip," Jeff said indulgently as he
reached up to take the boy down from Ned's shoulders. "Ned, we were just telling India that the two of

you are invited to dinner at the Merrivale house to-night."

"Merrivale," Ned repeated. "That's the skunk who ran off—" He stopped abruptly and looked with embarrassment at Melissa.

"Don't even think about apologizing, Ned," she told him. "We've had a great many problems in the past, but they're all behind us now, aren't they, sweetheart?"

"It would seem so," Jeff said. "In fact, Charles Merrivale and I are going into business together." He could still hardly believe that himself, but he supposed he ought to get used to it. He owed it to Melissa to give the arrangement a fair try, at the very least.

"Are you now?" Ned sounded surprised. "Well, I'm glad to hear it. Maybe that'll settle down that wild streak that's in all of us Holts."

Melissa took Jeff's arm. "I hope so."

As hard as he tried, Jeff couldn't help feeling a little . . . confined. Melissa did not want to go west, did not want him to go back to the mountains. She had a right to feel that way. And he would do everything in his power to make her happy. After being separated from her for so long and believing that he would never see her again, he had to try to make his marriage work, even if that did mean he would be stuck in North Carolina.

But he couldn't stop himself from missing the Rockies. . . .

Ned and India still had work to do on board the ship, so they went back to it while Jeff, Melissa, and Michael returned to the Merrivale house. Jeff intended to look for a place of their own, but he had not yet gotten around to it—though it was not for lack of time. The week before, he and Merrivale had signed the papers Merrivale's lawyer had drawn up, making their partnership official, but Merrivale kept putting off his son-in-law's offers to come down to the office and get started in the business. The old man was not going to make things easy, but that came as no surprise to Jeff.

That evening Ned and India arrived at the Merrivale house shortly before six. Jeff had suggested that time so they would have a chance to visit before Charles Merrivale arrived home and dinner was served. Both sailors had cleaned up, and India was dressed much as she had been when Jeff and Ned had first met her in a New York tavern, wearing high boots, black trousers, and a black silk shirt.

Melissa and Hermione were visibly taken aback by her garb, and India said quickly, "I'm sorry I don't have any dresses. I couldn't have them on the ship."

"I understand, dear," Hermione said, smiling and trying to put India at ease. "Jeff has told us all about you, so there's no need to pretend to be something you aren't. And, please, don't worry about your appearance. I think you look lovely."

"So do I," Ned said as he slipped an arm around her shoulders. India's brown eyes gleamed, her short dark hair making them seem even larger than they were. Her cheeks grew rosy from the compliment. "But I always think that, don't I, India?"

She slipped smoothly out of his embrace and let Melissa lead her into the parlor. The others followed, and for the next hour, the conversation was brisk as they caught each other up on what had been going on in their lives. Jeff left out the unpleasant details of his stay with the Merrivales out of deference to Melissa and concentrated on the joys of being reunited with his wife and the son he had not known he had. Michael was being allowed to stay up later than usual because of the company, and he sat quietly at Ned's feet, drinking in the sea stories the young man had to tell.

Charles Merrivale arrived just after seven and was polite enough when he was introduced to the visitors. He made no disparaging comments about another Holt being under his roof, and he even managed to smile a time or two as he talked to India. Jeff was surprised but gratified. Perhaps his father-in-law was going to make an effort to see that the evening went smoothly for a change.

It did. Jeff watched in astonishment as Charles Merrivale played the gracious host. Hermione must have had quite a talk with him, he thought. Whatever the cause, Jeff was grateful that the dinner proceeded pleasantly.

Afterward, however, when the group had gone to the parlor for brandy and Melissa had taken a sleepily protesting Michael up to bed, Merrivale said, "I hate to cut this evening short, but I have to go back to the office."

"Oh, Charles!" Hermione exclaimed. "Surely not. Whatever you have to do can wait until morning, can't it?"

"I'm afraid not," her husband said firmly.

Jeff took the plunge, offering, "I can go with you if you like, Charles. Maybe the two of us working together can get the chore done quicker, whatever it is."

Merrivale shook his head. "No, this is nothing you can help me with, Jefferson. I *would* like for you to think about something, however."

"And what's that?"

"How would you like to go back to Tennessee?"

"Tennessee?" Jeff repeated.

"Yes. I have a wagon train of goods going to the settlements out there, and I need an experienced man to take charge. How about it?"

Jeff felt Melissa clutching his arm, but he did not look at her as he thought about the offer. The last time he had accompanied one of Merrivale's wagon trains to the new settlements in Tennessee, he had fought bandits, the elements, and a hired killer, whose job it had been to see that he never returned to North Carolina.

Those memories flooded through Jeff's mind as he asked harshly, "Why are you asking me to go along? Intend to have somebody else finish the job Amos Tharp started?"

Charles Merrivale paled, and Melissa's fingers tightened on Jeff's arm. Ned and India looked confused, sensing the obvious tension in the room, and Hermione bit her lower lip in worry. Merrivale drew a deep breath and, making an effort to control his anger, said, "Not at all. I want you to go because you know the trail and I can trust you. And after all, you have something riding on this venture, too. Or had you forgotten that you and I are partners now?"

"I haven't forgotten," Jeff said slowly. Merrivale sounded sincere, and Jeff wondered if he had misjudged the man again.

"Besides," Merrivale went on, "I know you enjoy being out-of-doors. I thought you might like to make this trip. There'll be time enough later for you to be cooped up in an office."

There was truth in that statement, Jeff thought. He looked at Melissa for a second but was unable to read her expression. He knew she wanted desperately for him to get along with her father, but at the same time she probably would not be fond of the idea of his leaving for several weeks. Either way, he had to do what he thought was best.

"Thanks for having that much confidence in me," he told his father-in-law. "I suppose I could go. As you said, I know the trail."

"Good. It's settled, then. You'll come down to the office with me tomorrow, and we'll begin making the arrangements."

"All right." Jeff could sense the tension easing in the room. Melissa might not like his leaving, but at least he would not be gone very long, and perhaps the newfound cooperation between him and his father-in-law would continue after the journey to Tennessee was over.

Merrivale said his good-nights, then put on his hat and coat and left for his office. Jeff, Melissa, Hermione, Ned, and India spent another couple of pleasant hours before the visitors headed back to the *Fair Wind*.

Upstairs in their bedroom, Jeff put his hands on Melissa's shoulders as she sat on the edge of the bed, brushing her thick, lustrous dark hair. "Are you sure this is all right with you? Me going to Tennessee, I mean?"

"I know what you mean," Melissa replied, putting down the brush. She stood and came into his arms to rest her head against his chest. "I'll miss you terribly, and I know Michael will, too. But you'll be careful, and I know you'll come back to us."

"You can count on that," Jeff said as he stroked her hair.

"I'm just glad it seems that you and my father are going to be able to work together after all."

Jeff wanted to believe that as well, but somehow he could not bring himself to accept the idea that Merrivale's offer had been completely in good faith. The man was cunning, and he might yet have a trick or two up his sleeve.

He kissed Melissa's forehead. "We'll see. . . ."

Charles Merrivale leaned back in the big chair in his office and sipped from the glass of brandy in his hand. "Ahhh, excellent as usual, Dermot."

"It should be, at the prices I pay to have it shipped over from France." Dermot Hawley was perched on the corner of Merrivale's desk. "So Holt took the bait, did he?"

"Just as I knew he would," Merrivale replied smugly. "I didn't get to make the proposal until after I'd had to endure the company of his lout of a cousin and a rather odd trollop. However, the evening was a success, and there was really no way Jefferson could turn down the offer. After all, I was holding out an olive branch, so to speak.''

"So to speak,'' Hawley murmured. "And what do you plan to do while he's gone?''

Charles Merrivale sat up straighter and brought a clenched fist down hard on his desk. "I intend to talk some sense into that daughter of mine! It's high time Melissa realized she can't throw her life away on someone as worthless as Jefferson Holt!''

Hawley cocked an eyebrow. "It might be easier to reason with her if Holt didn't come back from Tennessee.''

For a long moment the two men looked squarely at each other; then Merrivale gave an abrupt shake of his head. "I'm not prepared to go that far, and if you keep talking like that, Dermot, I might begin to believe that those ludicrous charges Holt made against you have some basis in fact.''

"Don't be absurd, Charles. I was merely speculating, that's all.''

"Well, I prefer not to speculate in those areas. Besides, I have every confidence that Melissa will eventually come to her senses.''

"I hope so. Our silent partnership is thriving, but someday I'd like to be able to bring it back out into the open again. You know, I haven't given up on the two of us being more than business associates. I think I'd make a fine son-in-law for you, Charles.''

"That's not up to me,'' Merrivale said gruffly. "If it were, Melissa never would have gotten involved with that backwoodsman, much less married him.'' He lifted his glass again. "But I prefer to look to the future.''

"Amen to that.'' Hawley leaned over and clinked his glass against Merrivale's. "To the future—and all that it holds.''

CHAPTER SIX

It was amazing, Josie Garwood thought, how quickly a person could fall back into old habits. She hardly ever worked in the tavern as a serving girl anymore; her nights were spent in the small back room servicing the men Gort Chambers sent to her. Not that it mattered, she supposed. After all, she told herself frequently, it was not as if she had never done that kind of work before.

And Chambers paid her more than he ever would have had she not agreed to the arrangement. He took the lion's share of the money, of course—any man would, Josie told herself, under the same circumstances—but the coins she kept in a small leather pouch hidden in her room were growing in number. Someday soon there would be enough money to allow her and Matthew to move on, to find another, better place for themselves.

The worst thing about staying at the tavern was the way Chambers treated Matthew. He worked the boy almost constantly, leaving Matthew barely any time to himself. Josie had planned to teach him to read when he got old enough, but that now seemed hopeless. She simply had no time for anything like that. And if Matthew neglected his chores or did not complete them as Chambers wanted or even if Chambers just felt like it, he would beat Matthew with his broad leather belt, leaving wide, fiery welts on the boy's legs and back. Matthew suffered the abuse in silence, and although Josie's heart went out to him, she could do nothing to stop Chambers.

She had tasted the belt herself on numerous occasions. Chambers visited her bunk nearly every night when she was through with the customers, and any time she failed to perform up to his expectations, he punished her. Josie could stand such treatment—she was as accustomed to it as a person could get—but she hated for Matthew to witness her humilation.

She had been working as a prostitute again for several weeks when she took one of her rare turns at serving drinks in the tavern. Chambers liked for her to do that occasionally so that he could drum up trade for her. The tavern was only moderately busy, and Josie had hopes that her evening's work once she retired to her room would not last long.

Then the door of the smoky room banged open, and five burly men in buckskins and fur caps stomped into the tavern, talking and laughing raucously.

Josie stiffened. She recognized their kind immediately. They were fur trappers, no doubt headed west for the Rocky Mountains, since it was much too early in the season for them to be on their way back from the mountains. Besides, they had the look of men who had just gotten off a keelboat: They were well fed, their beards were trimmed, and they lacked the worn, exhausted look of trappers returning from the mountains.

But they would have one thing in common with all the other trappers she had known, Josie thought:

They would all want a woman before they left for the Rockies. A white woman. A woman like her.

She sighed. Tonight would be a lucrative one indeed for Gort Chambers, it appeared.

The trappers swaggered across the room to the bar and demanded whiskey. Chambers got busy pouring drinks, and Josie hurriedly served the ones she had on her tray. When she went back to the bar, Chambers caught her eye and then glanced at the newly arrived trappers. She knew quite well what he was instructing her to do. Just in case there was any chance the men would fail to notice her, she was supposed to get their attention and let them know that she was available—for a price.

She did that with practiced ease, sauntering past them, her hips swaying and her luxuriant black hair swinging around her face. Her posturing would have been almost laughable, she thought, if there had been anything even slightly humorous about the situation. But it was deadly serious, and it became more so when she noticed Matthew sitting on a stool in the corner. He was watching his mother, too, watching her parade before strange men so that they would be enticed to take her to the back room and bed her.

Josie swallowed hard. If she had known it would come to this when Clay Holt had turned her down, she would have killed herself, she thought.

No. She should have killed Clay. That would have been even better.

One of the trappers reached out and put a hand on her arm, stopping her. "Howdy there, little darlin'," he drawled. Judging by his accent, he was from the south somewhere. Georgia or Alabama, maybe. "Whatcha doin', sweet 'tater?"

She could not resist. "Looking at a mush-mouthed fool," she said with a mocking smile.

The trapper blinked in surprise, but his companions roared with laughter, and after a few seconds he started to chuckle, too. "Say, that's a good one. What say you and me go on back to wherever you got a place to lie down?"

Josie kept the smile plastered to her face. "That's all right with me as long as you've got the coins." She took the man's arm and started to steer him toward the back room.

"Oh, I got plenty for you, sweet 'tater," the trapper boasted.

A hand shot out, grabbed the collar of the southerner's buckskin jacket, and jerked him away from Josie. The southerner went flying into the bar. Josie gasped in surprise as the other man stepped in front of her. "Wait your turn, Perkins," the man gruffly ordered. "The lady's goin' with me first."

The trapper called Perkins was doubled over, trying to catch the breath that had been knocked out of him by his colliding with the bar. "Sure, Oren," he said. "Didn't mean to cause no trouble—"

"No trouble," Oren said without taking his eyes away from Josie. "Come on."

Long, blunt fingers folded around hers. His hand was big; in fact, he was big all over. Tall and broad-shouldered, with a thatch of black hair beneath his coonskin cap, he reminded Josie of Clay Holt. Oren's eyes were small and mean, though, his narrow gaze totally unlike Clay's direct, honest one, and his dark-stubbled jaw was heavier than Clay's. The man's grip on Josie's hand was painful as he jerked her toward the rear of the building.

When the door of the room was shut behind them, he pushed her toward the bed. "Get them clothes off," he said harshly. "I like my women buck naked."

"All right." Josie bent and grasped the hem of her dress, straightening to pull it over her head. The shift she wore under it followed. A slight tremble went through her as she saw the way Oren's dark eyes studied her body.

"Ain't no need for you to be ascared of me," he

said after a moment, his voice a low rumble. "I never been one to hurt a woman. Believe in pleasin' 'em instead."

"I'm glad to hear that," Josie said. Most men had lost the ability to frighten her, but this one was so big and powerful looking, and he had slammed that smaller trapper into the bar with such casual cruelty . . .

He stepped closer and put his massive hands on her bare shoulders. "Them boys out there are my bunch," he announced with something like pride in his voice. "We're goin' to the mountains to make our fortunes trappin' beaver."

"I-I'm sure you'll be successful."

"Name's Oren Bradley. Who're you?"

"Josie," she said, surprised. Usually the men who came to her room did not waste any time asking her name. "Josie Garwood."

"Mighty pleased to meet you, Josie Garwood." Oren jerked her toward him, and his mouth came down on hers with such bruising force that she winced for a second before she was able to make herself feign passion and return the kiss. His arms closed around her, and she had the feeling she had just been hugged by a grizzly bear. But as he kissed her, she got the impression that he was not trying to be overly rough. He was just so strong that it probably did not occur to him that he could be hurting her.

He bore her backward to the bunk and lowered her onto the thin mattress. The ropes that held it groaned under his weight as he came down on top of her. She pulled her mouth away from his and gasped, "Wait!"

"What the hell for?"

"I—can show you some things. It'll be better, you'll see."

Oren frowned. "Better'n the usual way? Hell, you'll have to prove that."

"I intend to," Josie told him, working up a smile

again. "And if you'll just . . . let me breathe, I'll
show you."

Oren rolled off her, lifting her atop him almost as
if she were weightless, and he said with a huge grin,
"All right, you just go right ahead. But I warn you,
Josie Garwood, there ain't much I ain't seen or done
or at least heard tell of. I'm from Kentucky. I done
fought Injuns and I got lightnin' in my blood and—"

Now that he was wound up, he might boast all
night if she did not stop him, Josie realized, so she
said, "Oh, shut up," and brought her mouth down on
his.

As it turned out, Oren Bradley was impressed by
her expertise, all right, but she was equally impressed
by his strength and stamina. In fact, when he finally
staggered out of the room, she would have gladly
slept off the exhausting bout she had just gone
through. But there were four more trappers, and now
that their fearsome leader had been satisfied, they
were ready for some loving of their own.

Thankfully, Chambers did not come to her room
that night. Matthew slipped in much later and
crawled onto his blanket-covered pallet. Josie was
vaguely aware that he had entered the room, but she
was too tired to even say good night to him.

Chambers was in a good mood the next day, and
Josie figured he had charged the trappers a considerable price for her favors. He gave her a quarter eagle,
and as soon as she had a chance, she hid the gold coin
with the rest of the money she had saved. Soon, she
thought, as she put the purse away, there would be
enough for her and Matthew to get out of that place.
Where they would go, she had no idea, but she felt
that any place would be better.

Then she reminded herself that it was just such
thoughts that had landed her here in the first place.

*   *   *

Oren Bradley and his companions spent several days in St. Louis, getting outfitted for their trip up the Missouri to the Rocky Mountains, and he visited Josie every night. Evidently they had pooled their money and had a considerable stake, for Oren boasted to Josie of the new traps and all the supplies they were buying. They would haul the whole lot upriver in five canoes, he told her, and when they came back, those canoes would be loaded with beaver plews. They were going to be free traders and rich men, according to Oren.

He was more likable than he had first appeared to be, and while he was more than capable of casual, brutal violence when he was crossed, he seemed to be going out of his way to be kind to her, Josie realized. That was a welcome change from men who assumed that since she was a whore, she had no feelings. She had no delusions that he was falling in love with her, but she knew he *was* growing fond of her.

The plan that sprang to her mind came from that realization.

She waited until Oren was at his most relaxed, after they had made love in the narrow bunk. Then, before he roused himself to leave, she said, "I've been thinking, Oren. How'd you and your boys like company on that trip up the Missouri?"

Oren stared at her. She was sprawled on top of him, and she had lifted her head so that she could gaze directly into his eyes. After a moment he rumbled, "What're you talkin' about, woman?"

"I thought maybe"—Josie swallowed hard and plunged ahead; if she was going to be disappointed, she wanted to get it over with quickly—"I thought maybe Matthew and I could go along with you."

"Matthew? That's the boy?" Oren had seen Matthew around enough to have figured out that he was Josie's son, but they had not been introduced.

Josie nodded. "Yes. He's mine. We want to go out to the mountains."

Oren shook his head. "Ain't nothin' out there for a woman. Damn few settlements, and them that're there are just tradin' posts, I reckon."

As she tried to fight off the despair welling up inside her, Josie said quickly, "I don't care about settlements. I never had much luck in settlements. I just want a good place to live and raise my boy."

"You won't find it in the mountains. That's rugged country out there. Ain't fit for nobody 'cept gents who're half wolf, like me."

"But the Indians live out there," Josie protested. "They have women and children."

Oren waved a hand. "They're savages. That ain't the same thing."

Suddenly Josie was overcome by a wave of frustration. She thumped a fist against Oren's broad, bare chest. "Dammit! Don't you understand? I've got to get out of here. This is no place for me or Matthew!"

"Hold on, hold on," Oren said soothingly. He sat up, moving her off him easily and then setting her down on his lap as though she were a small child. "No need to get all het up. Looks to me like you got a pretty good deal here. This place is better'n some cribs I've seen. How come you want to run out?"

She looked down at her hands. "You don't know Chambers."

Oren's eyes narrowed. "Mean to you, is he? I can do somethin' about that."

"Oh, no," she said as she caught his arm. Short of killing Chambers, nothing Oren did would stop him from mistreating her and Matthew once the trappers had headed upriver. If Oren interfered, Chambers would just resent it and take out his anger on them later. She said, "I don't want you to do anything like that."

"Then what *do* you want from me?"

"I told you, I want to go upriver. I want you to take Matthew and me to the mountains."

"You're a damn stubborn piece of baggage, I'll

give you that, Josie Garwood." He rubbed at the stubble on his jaw. "You sure you want to go?"

"Oh, yes!" She sensed that she might be on the verge of victory.

"Well . . . I reckon the boys wouldn't mind havin' company. I know I wouldn't. You'd have to do 'bout like you been doin' here, though."

"I know that," Josie said immediately. She was perfectly willing to prostitute herself, as long as it was for a good cause. She assured him, "I don't mind."

"And I can't promise we'd take you all the way to the mountains. Might find a settlement somewheres upriver and leave you there if it's a good place."

"I-I suppose that would be all right." She was confident that once the journey had begun, she would have no trouble convincing the trappers to keep her with them until she was ready to leave.

Oren hesitated a moment longer, then finally shrugged. "All right. I'm still a mite leery of this idea, but I reckon we can give it a try."

"Do you need to ask the others if it's all right with them?"

He snorted. "Hell, no. Them boys do what I tell 'em. If I say you're goin' along, they ain't goin' to argue."

Josie snuggled against him, resting her head on his chest and letting her fingers stray along his belly. "You won't be sorry," she promised in a whisper. "This will be the best trip upriver anybody's ever had."

"Yeah," Oren said, his voice suddenly husky with desire as her gentle touch aroused him. "I'm startin' to see that already."

Josie's mind wandered as she serviced Oren. Although he had agreed to take her and Matthew along, one obstacle remained: Gort Chambers. He would not want to lose such a convenient bed partner, especially one who made him so much money. Josie knew she would have to find the right moment to tell him, but she could not wait too long. Oren and his men had been in St. Louis for almost a week, and she was sure they would want to leave within another day or two.

After Oren had gotten dressed and left her room, the other men in the group visited her one by one. She made an effort to see that each one of them was well pleased with her so that they would be less likely to raise any objections when Oren told them that she and Matthew were going along with them. She was confident that none of them would complain too much.

In addition to the trappers, the tavern was crowded, and it seemed as if every man in the place wanted a crack at her. She was busy with them until well after midnight, and although she was tired and hurting by the time the final customer was through with her, her anticipation of leaving Chambers's place warded off the exhaustion and despair she normally would have felt under the circumstances. She was sitting on the bunk, dressed and brushing her hair, when Matthew came into the room soon after the last man had left.

"Hello, sweetie," she said to him with a smile, but she got nothing in return from him except his standard sullen look. He turned away from her, and she frowned in concern as he shuffled over to the pallet where he slept. She stood and stepped across the narrow room, putting a hand on his shoulder before he could lie down. Whatever maternal instincts she had told her that something was wrong. "What is it, Matthew?" she asked. "Are you all right?"

"I'm fine," he said, and tried to pull away from her. Josie held him fast, though, so that she could see his face. Despite his being tall and sturdy for his age, she was still too strong for him to resist.

Josie let out a gasp when she saw the ugly bruise that covered most of Matthew's left cheek. "My God! What happened? Did you fall?"

Even as she asked the question, she knew how ridiculous it was. There was only one explanation for Matthew's injury: Gort Chambers had done it.

"No," Matthew replied. "I didn't fall."

She knelt and gathered him into her arms, hugging him and telling him how sorry she was. He did not pull away from her, but his body was stiff and resistant. She could almost feel the anger in him.

She leaned back, keeping her hands on his shoulders. "This won't happen again," she promised.

He just looked at her, and she could see the disbelief in his eyes.

"I mean it. Chambers will never mistreat you again. And you won't have to do any more chores for him."

"He'll beat me if I say no."

"No, he won't because we won't be here. We're leaving."

There was a flicker of hope in the boy's eyes. Josie smiled, and then she stood up and told him, "You go over there and sit on my bunk. I'll find Gort and tell him we're going."

Her determination to wait until the right time had vanished. There would *never* be a right time, she realized. Whenever she told him, Gort Chambers would protest. But there was nothing he could do to stop her, really. She was not a slave, and he could not treat her like one.

She crossed to the door and opened it. A dim light was still burning in the main room of the tavern, even though the place was closed for the night, and she figured that Gort was going over his stock of liquor, something he liked to do fairly often. She called down the short hallway, "Gort, are you out there? I want to talk to you."

A moment later Gort's bulky figure appeared at the end of the corridor. "I'll be back to see you later, Josie, don't worry about that."

"I'm not worried, Gort. I just need to talk to you now."

He made a sound that was half sigh, half growl and then came toward her. "What is it?" he snapped. "I'm a busy man, you know."

"Do come in," Josie said, stepping back from the door like a high-toned lady issuing an invitation.

Chambers entered the room and looked around, glowering when he saw Matthew sitting very still on the bunk. "If it's about that bruise on the boy's face," the tavern owner said, gesturing at Matthew, "he deserved it. I told him to empty the slops jar, and the careless little bastard spilled it before he got outside."

"It was an accident," Matthew said. "The jar was heavy."

Chambers took a menacing step toward him, lifting an arm as if to backhand Matthew. He stopped and settled for glowering at the youngster before switching his gaze back to Josie. "I could've lied," he said. "I could've told you he ran into the door. You got to give me credit for telling the truth. That boy of yours is a troublemaker."

"Well, he won't make any more trouble for you, Gort," Josie said, facing him squarely and trying to control the fear she felt. "Matthew and I are leaving St. Louis."

Chambers stared at her in disbelief. "Leaving?" he repeated. "Where the hell do you think you're going?"

Josie was about to tell him about the plan to accompany Oren Bradley and the other trappers to the mountains, but she stopped herself. It might be safer if Chambers did not know where they were going.

"That's our business," she said defiantly. "I just thought you had a right to know that we're leaving, first thing in the morning." She did not know if Oren and the others were ready to leave yet, but even if they were not, she wanted to get out of the tavern and away from Chambers as soon as possible, before he hurt Matthew again.

Chambers put his hands on his hips and glared at her for a long moment, then lifted a hand and poked a finger into her right breast, hard enough to make her jump and cry out. "Listen to me, you damn trollop. You ain't going nowhere. You're staying right here, and you're going to keep on making money for me. You understand that?"

Josie swallowed hard, trying to hang on to the courage she had drawn from her outrage over Matthew's bruise. Sounding firmer than she felt, she said, "You can't keep me here. I'm not a slave or an indentured servant. I have every right to leave if I want to, and that's just what I'm going to do."

Chambers scowled; but then he gave her an ugly grin, and something shrewd and evil lit up his eyes. "What about the money you owe me?"

"The money I owe *you*?" Josie was incredulous. "If anything, you owe *me*! You've never given me my fair share of what I've brought in."

"I ain't charged you rent for this room, neither, but that don't mean you don't owe it to me. Hell, you didn't think I was letting you and the brat stay back here out of the goodness of my heart, did you?"

Josie tried to fight off the anger and shock that threatened to overwhelm her. She never would have dreamed that he would dare try something like this.

"You been working off a debt," Chambers went on, "and you're not running out on me until you make good on every damn penny of it."

"How much do you figure I owe you for this . . . *room*?" Josie asked, her voice dripping with contempt.

"Well, seeing as how the rent keeps adding up while you're working off what you owe from before" —the grin on the tavern owner's face turned into a leer—"I don't figure it'll ever be paid off, long as you can keep on doing what you been doing."

Josie felt overwhelmed with despair. Once more she had dared to let herself hope, and once more those hopes had been trampled. She was too popular, she made too much money for Chambers to let her go. And if he went to the law and told them that ridiculous story about her owing rent for a vermin-ridden hole, the authorities would probably believe him. She might even wind up in jail, and then who would look after Matthew? She had to go along with Gort, even if it meant staying—

"No!" she heard herself cry. "No! We won't stay, and you can't make us stay!" From somewhere deep inside, she had found the strength to fight.

Chambers just threw back his head and laughed. "The hell I can't," he said. "Now, get your clothes off and get on that bunk. Long as you dragged me back here, I might as well get some use out of the interruption."

He reached for her, lust in his eyes, and Josie snapped. Without her even being aware of it, a scream ripped from her throat, and she threw herself at Chambers, clawing at his eyes.

Chambers cursed and flung up an arm to ward her off. At the same time with the other arm he back-handed her on the cheek with a resounding crack.

Josie's head was jerked around by the blow, and a red haze seemed to settle in front of her eyes. She stayed on her feet, but she was too stunned to fight back as Chambers swung again and again, slapping her head back and forth. She staggered against the wall, wailing in fear and pain as she tried to lift her arms to block the blows. The tavernkeeper's lust had been replaced by a berserk rage that had him shouting curses as he struck her repeatedly.

"Filthy whore!" he howled. "I'll teach you to come at me like that, damn you!"

In her terror Josie had all but forgotten about Matthew, but a warning voice in the back of her mind told her that once Chambers had vented his rage on her, he might well turn on the boy. Matthew had already been beaten once tonight. What would an out-of-control Chambers do to him?

He might even kill both of them before he was through, Josie realized.

When Chambers swung at her again, she ducked under the blow and tried to dart past him, anxious to reach the bunk and protect Matthew. She had to get between her child and the danger that faced him. But she was too worn down by the beating she had already endured, and Chambers was too fast for her. As she went past him he gave her a shove that sent her sprawling hard onto the dirty floor beside the bunk. As she fell, Josie caught a glimpse of Matthew standing upright on the thin mattress, his face pale.

Chambers reached for her, either to pull her back to her feet to wallop her again or hit her where she lay. It hardly mattered which. She could do nothing regardless.

As Chambers bent toward her, she caught a flicker of movement above his head. She saw Matthew lean out from where he stood on the bunk, saw his hand dart forward with something that shone brightly in the candlelight. Chambers gave a strangled cry and took a sudden step backward, away from Josie and the bunk. His hands went to his throat, and his eyes bugged out in shock and pain. Josie watched in horror as Chambers pawed at the handle of Matthew's knife, its blade buried in the soft flesh of his neck.

The knife came free, and Chambers let out a gurgling scream. Blood cascaded over his chest. He stumbled back a few more steps, his body twitching this way and that. Then, as more blood flowed down the front of his shirt, his knees buckled and he fell, catching himself for an instant and then pitching forward facedown on the floor. A red puddle formed underneath him and continued to grow before a final shudder ran through his body and death claimed him.

Josie's chest heaved. She could not seem to draw enough air into her body. Her wildly racing heart set up a thundering pulse inside her skull that was almost deafening. She stared at Gort Chambers's body, then up at her son.

Matthew was looking at the corpse impassively, the only trace of emotion on his face a cold, barely discernible smile. At that moment he looked ancient, not at all like a six-year-old boy.

Forcing herself to move, Josie grasped the bunk and pulled herself into a sitting position. She made herself lean over and grab Chambers's wrist and search for a pulse she knew she would not find. She was right. She dropped the wrist, letting it thud to the floor. He was dead, no doubt about that.

"We've got to get out of here."

She had no idea where the words had come from, but she knew she was right. If the law would have taken Chambers's side over the so-called rent she supposedly owed him—and she was convinced it would have—then certainly no one would believe her if she said that Matthew had killed Chambers to protect her and himself. She would be accused of killing him in a dispute over her work, no doubt. She would be blamed; whores always got the blame.

Trembling, she got to her feet. Matthew still had not moved. Josie lifted him off the bunk, turning him so that he could not see the body, and walked across the room. She reached under a loose floorboard—Chambers had never discovered her hiding place, although she was certain he had looked for it—and pulled out the pouch full of coins. She had nothing else except a few clothes for herself and Matthew, which she gathered up and tied into a bundle. Then, steeling herself, she picked up the bloody knife that Chambers had dropped on the floor as he died and shoved it into her dress pocket.

"Come on," she said, taking Matthew's hand to

lead him out of the room where the stench of death already hung in the air.

He looked up at her. "Where are we going, Mama?"

"We . . . we'll find Oren," Josie replied, forcing her sluggish brain to work. "He'll help us. He was going to take us to the mountains, anyway. He and his friends can just leave a bit early. I want to be out of St. Louis before morning."

She was assuming a great deal, she knew. Oren and the other trappers might not be willing to leave just yet. But she was sure Chambers's body would be found the next day, and she wanted to put as many miles as possible between her and the city before then.

The trappers were staying in a small hotel near the river; Josie remembered Oren telling her that much. Clutching Matthew's hand, she led him out of the tavern and through the streets. The moon was almost full, creating enough light for her to find the hotel, a sturdy log structure of two stories. A lamp was still burning inside, so she rapped sharply on the door.

It was opened by an elderly woman carrying a lantern. "What d'ye want?" she demanded.

"I'm looking for a man named Oren Bradley," Josie answered, squinting as the light from the lantern struck her full in the eyes.

The old woman studied her for a minute, contempt growing on the wrinkled and weathered face. "We don't let your kind in here," she said at last. "The men who stay here can go somewheres else for the likes of you."

Josie felt frustration welling up, mixed with the terror that still stretched her nerves almost to the breaking point. "You don't understand—"

"I understand, all right, and I got no truck with cheap baggage like you." The old woman glanced down at Matthew. "And dragging a child around with you whilst you try to drum up business! Ain't you got no shame?"

Anger took hold of Josie. She reached out and closed her hand over the old woman's bony upper arm. "I don't care what you think!" Josie yelled as she shook the hotelkeeper and brought a cry of pain from her. "I just want to see Oren Bradley!"

A shutter on the second story of the building opened, and a surprised voice called down, "Josie? Is that you?" Oren sounded sleepy and more than a little hungover, but his voice was about the sweetest sound Josie had ever heard.

She released the landlady's arm and stepped back to look up at him. "Oren!" she cried. "Can you come down here? I have to talk to you!"

"Right now?"

"Oh, please." Josie swallowed. "It's very important."

"All right, all right," Oren grumbled.

When he closed the shutter, the elderly landlady shook a trembling finger at Josie and threatened, "I'll send for the constable! I'll have the law on you, you slut!"

Josie tried to ignore her. With all the trouble she might already be in, a few threats from a querulous old woman meant little to her.

Oren emerged from the hotel a few minutes later, and he shooed the old woman inside impatiently before turning to Josie and asking, "What's all this about?"

In a quiet voice, she said, "Chambers is dead."

"Dead?" Oren repeated in surprise.

"He lost his temper when I told him I was leaving, and he started hurting me. I—I thought he might beat me to death."

"So you killed him instead." Oren did not sound shocked.

Josie shook her head, then looked down at Matthew, who seemed to be paying scant attention to the conversation.

The big trapper let out a low-pitched whistle. "Most folks wouldn't believe that. They'd think you did it."

"I know. That's why Matthew and I have to get out of St. Louis now, before morning."

"And you expect me and the boys to take you?"

"We had a deal," Josie said, putting a hand on Oren's arm. "We'd just be starting a bit earlier than we expected."

He rubbed his jaw. "You sure you're tellin' me the straight of this?" he demanded.

"It's the truth, I swear."

"Some folks wouldn't take the word of a gal like you, but I reckon I will." He nodded curtly as he reached a decision. "I'll roust out the boys. There's a good moon tonight; we ought to be able to see well enough to paddle. We'll put a few miles 'tween us and St. Louis afore mornin'."

"Thank you, Oren. Oh, God, I don't know how to thank you."

He grinned, his teeth gleaming in the moonlight. "I reckon we'll think of a way," he said, chuckling. "Hell, I never liked that Chambers fella, anyway."

Josie felt relief washing over her. Oren would take care of things, would handle everything from here on out. She and Matthew would leave St. Louis behind them. No constable would pursue them into the wilderness, not over the death of a man like Gort Chambers.

The other trappers had been understandably grouchy about being shaken out of their beds and told they were leaving for the mountains immediately, but they had cooperated. None of them wanted to cross Oren Bradley. After dressing quickly, they had loaded their gear in the canoes and headed north along the Mississippi. Josie and Matthew rode with Oren.

By dawn the canoes had reached the parting of the rivers and swung northwest into the Missouri. Nothing was in front of them now but frontier, Josie thought as the sun rose over her right shoulder. Nothing out there but new beginnings.

New beginnings and a man named Clay Holt.

PART II

There is nothing relating to the Indians so difficult to understand as their religion. They believe in a Supreme Being, in a future state, and in supernatural agency. Of the Great Spirit they do not pretend to give any account, but believe him to be the author and giver of all good. They believe in bad spirits, but seem to consider them rather as little wicked beings, who can only gratify their malignity by driving away the game, preventing the efficacy of medicine, or such petty mischief. The belief in a future state seems to be general, as it extends even to the Nodowessies or Sioux, who are furthest removed from civilization, and who do not even cultivate the soil. It is known, that frequently when an Indian has shot down his enemy, and is preparing to scalp him, with the tomahawk uplifted to give the fatal stroke, he will address him in words to this effect: "My name is Cashegra. I am a famous warrior, and am now going to kill you. When you arrive at the land of spirits, you will see the ghost of my father; tell him it was Cashegra that sent you there." He then gives the blow.

—JOHN BRADBURY "Travels in the Interior of America 1809–1811"

CHAPTER SEVEN

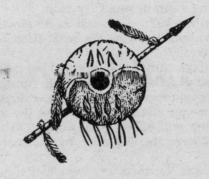

No people on earth discharge the duties of hospitality with more cordial good-will than the Indians.

—JOHN BRADBURY "Travels in the Interior of America 1809–1811"

As Clay Holt made his preparations for leaving the Hunkpapa Sioux village, a frigid blast blew down out of the mountains, and a dusting of white coated the plains and the foothills to the west—a reminder that winter did not die easily in this part of the country. Clay was not fooled by the change in the weather, however; spring was still on the way, and he, Aaron, and Proud Wolf would need to leave shortly to reach the Canadian border in time for the year's prime trapping season.

That goal was made easier by Bear Tooth, the

chief of the Hunkpapa band. Although some of the band's horses had been lost in the Blackfoot raid the previous fall, a few of the wild stallions that roamed the hills had been captured and broken for riding during the winter months, thus replenishing the herd. As Clay and the others got their gear together for the journey, Bear Tooth came to the tipi shared by Clay and Shining Moon and greeted the white man by saying, "I bring a gift to you, Clay Holt."

"I am honored," Clay said as he emerged from the tipi, without knowing yet what Bear Tooth was referring to.

Bear Tooth turned and gestured behind him, and Clay looked past the chief to see three young warriors leading horses toward the tipi. "These three fine ponies are for you and Proud Wolf and the one called Aaron. They will speed your journey to the north lands to avenge the evil done by the man McKendrick."

Clay was touched by the chief's generosity. Horses were important to the Sioux and becoming increasingly so. The Shoshone, who lived to the west, had horses, had in fact provided mounts for Clay and the other members of the Corps of Discovery when the Lewis and Clark expedition made its way across the area. Some of the other tribes also had a few horses, but none of them had taken to the idea like the Sioux, who seemed to have a special rapport with the animals.

"You have my thanks, Bear Tooth," Clay told the chief. "These horses will allow us to reach Canada in plenty of time to do what we need to do."

"They are yours to keep when you return. Ride them proudly."

Clay stepped over to the horses. One was a pinto, with contrasting areas of black and white on its hide. Another was a chestnut, a fine-looking animal. The third horse was a rangy, long-limbed dun, a rather unprepossessing mousy color except for a strip of darker hide down the center of its back. Of the three it was the least impressive, but as Clay reached up and patted its shoulder, he sensed something, an almost instant bond between him and the animal. The dun might not look like much, Clay thought, but he would have wagered that it could run all day when it had to.

Bear Tooth sent for Proud Wolf and Aaron, and the two young men were just as impressed as Clay had been by the chief's gift. Aaron selected the chestnut as his mount, while Proud Wolf seemed to have the same natural affinity for the pinto that Clay had for the lineback dun.

Clay had planned to take only as many supplies as they could carry on their backs, even though the gift of the horses would allow them to take more. The weight of heavy packs would more than offset the benefits of extra provisions. There would be plenty of game along the way to provide fresh meat, so the main things Clay and his companions would need to take along were adequate supplies of powder and shot.

Aaron and Proud Wolf took their horses back to the tipi they had been sharing for a few days, ever since Proud Wolf's falling out with Walks-Down-the-Wind and Cloud-That-Falls. Clay used the rope bridle on the dun to tether it to a bush beside his tipi, then turned to see Shining Moon standing in the entrance of the dwelling. She had not come out when Bear Tooth brought the horses, and now she barely spared a glance for the dun.

"That was very considerate of Bear Tooth," Clay said as he waved a hand at the horse. "It'll be a lot easier now for us to get up to Canada in time."

"You rush to death like a young brave blinded by visions of glory," Shining Moon said, frowning.

Clay bit back an angry response. "I'm in no hurry to die. But there's such a thing as justice, and that Scotsman's badly in need of some. Besides, if somebody doesn't put a stop to McKendrick, he's just going to keep on stirring up trouble down here. A lot of folks have already died because of him. I'd like to think that nobody else will."

"A dream," Shining Moon said. "A pretty dream."

Clay sucked air through his teeth. "I'll be back, dammit," he growled, stepping closer to her. "I told you that before."

She met his gaze and asked, "When will you leave?"

Clay looked up at the sky for a moment, judged the weather to be clearing and warming again, then said, "In the morning. We'll ride north in the morning."

Shining Moon nodded curtly and went back into the tipi. He did not try to stop her.

The rest of the afternoon was spent sharpening knives and tomahawks, filling powder horns and shot pouches, cleaning rifles and pistols, and packing a supply of pemmican in case game was scarce in places. That evening the villagers enjoyed a feast prepared by the women, and songs and dances asking favor of the spirits as Clay, Aaron, and Proud Wolf prepared to begin their journey. In a long, solemn prayer chanted by Bear Tooth, the Great Spirit, Wakan Tanka, was asked to guide and protect them.

Clay sat by the big fire in the center of the village, basking not only in its warmth but in the warmth of the Hunkpapa Sioux as well, thinking that only one thing marred his decision to pursue McKendrick: Shining Moon had not left their tipi to take part in the celebration.

Was she was so angry at him that he ought to sleep elsewhere tonight? he wondered. He considered the idea, then angrily discarded it. Shining Moon was his wife, and he was damned if he would let her run him off. He would roll up in his buffalo robes on the far side of the tipi from her if that was what she wanted, but at least they would spend this last night under the same shelter.

As Clay slipped away from the fire, he glanced over at Proud Wolf and Aaron, who were caught up in the excitement of the singing and dancing after the feast. Neither of them saw him leave. He returned to his tipi—finding the quiet in that corner of the village a marked contrast to the center of the village—pushed back the entrance flap, and stepped inside.

The flames in the firepit had burned low, leaving only a faint reddish yellow glow. Clay placed his flintlock rifle on one of the buffalo robes spread out on the ground and then tossed his coonskin cap beside it. He glanced over at the figure on the far side of the tipi, lying motionless, wrapped in a buffalo hide. He said nothing as he put his pistols, his knife, and his tomahawk beside the rifle and the cap. Then he took off his belt and pulled the buckskin shirt over his head. The cool air inside the tipi was bracing as it hit his bare skin.

The figure in the buffalo robe shifted slightly, then rolled over. Shining Moon peered up at him in the dim light. "I did not know if you would come," she said softly.

"I still live here," Clay said. "But if you want me to get out, just say so." Despite his earlier resolve, he decided he would leave rather than cause another argument.

Shining Moon sat up and let the robe slip away from her. She was nude, and in the firelight her smooth skin seemed to glow. She looked solemnly at Clay. He felt his pulse start to race as his gaze strayed down the graceful lines of her neck, over the roundness of her shoulders, and down to her thrusting breasts. Her nipples stood out against the dark brown circles around them, hard with urgency and desire.

"Do not go, Clay Holt," Shining Moon whispered.

As much as every fiber of his being wanted to go

to her, possess her, love her, he had to know what she meant by the invitation. He took a deep breath and asked, "Do you mean for me not to leave tonight—or not to leave at all?"

"You will do what you must do," she answered without hesitation. "But for this night, and this night alone, stay with me."

"Yes," Clay murmured as he came to her and dropped to his knees to take her in his arms. His mouth found hers, and as her arms went around him, her fingers clutched at his back, drawing him down into the warmth of the buffalo robe. His lips trailed down her throat, his tongue tasting and exploring. She gave a soft cry as it flicked one of her nipples, then left a burning trail on her skin.

He drew the robe tighter around them. They were warm all night long.

Clay woke early the next morning and slipped out of the tipi while Shining Moon still slept. He drew his capote tighter around him against the predawn chill and looked around the peaceful camp. He would miss this village, these people. There was no way of knowing how long he and the others would be gone; he had no real plan other than settling things with McKendrick, and that might take all summer. If he and Aaron and Proud Wolf did not rejoin the Hunkpapa by the time winter came again, they might have to hole up somewhere until spring, which meant it could be as much as a year before Clay saw Shining Moon again.

He drew a deep breath and shook his head. He had come too far, had endured too much, to change his mind now. Shifting his gaze to the north, Clay mused that McKendrick was up there somewhere . . . waiting.

A faint noise behind him made him turn. Shining Moon stood there, just outside the tipi, her face unreadable. She stepped closer to him and put her hand on his arm.

"I know," she said, and for the first time he thought he saw true understanding in her eyes. "I know what you must do, and my love and my prayers will go with you."

Overcome by emotion, Clay crushed her in his arms for a long moment, then stepped back. He brushed her hair away from her face, his hand lingering on her chin. "Time to get going. I'll wake Aaron and Proud Wolf."

They were already awake, Clay found when he reached their tipi. In fact, they were dressed and standing outside. A young woman stood in front of Proud Wolf, and Clay recognized her immediately as Butterfly.

". . . would be no trouble to you," Clay heard Butterfly saying, and he knew she was still trying to talk Proud Wolf into taking her with them.

"I have told you before, Butterfly," Proud Wolf said haughtily, "you are a woman, and this is a task for men. Go back to the tipi of your parents, before they see that you are gone and begin to worry."

Butterfly was almost shaking with frustration, Clay saw. Stepping beside her, he said gently, "We've got a long way to go, Butterfly, and there's bound to be trouble before we come home again. Proud Wolf just wants what's best for you."

She turned to face him, an anguished look on her pretty, young face. "Why does no one ask *me* what is best for me? What about my visions? I am to be a mighty warrior known as Raven Arrow!"

"Well, maybe you will be, one of these days," Clay said. "But that's for the future to bring."

Butterfly looked from Clay to Proud Wolf to Aaron. She saw the same resolution on all of their faces. She made a small anguished sound and hurried away.

"Females," Proud Wolf said fervently when she was gone. Clay and Aaron both chuckled.

"Don't worry, Proud Wolf," Aaron told him. "I suspect Butterfly'll still be waiting for you when we get back."

"That, my friend, is what I am afraid of." Proud Wolf shook his head slowly, then turned to Clay. "We are ready to depart?"

"I reckon we are."

Proud Wolf had painted his mount for the journey, sketching several medicine symbols on the white part of the animal's hide. On the pinto's white face, Proud Wolf had drawn a black ring around one of its eyes, making its appearance even more distinctive.

The horses apparently sensed something was afoot because they were quite frisky as they were being saddled. A short buffalo-hide blanket went on their backs first, then a saddle made from a buckskin pouch stuffed with dried grass and decorated with beads and quillwork. Rawhide straps were tied to the saddles and cinched around the horses' bellies. The arrangement was similar to leather saddles Clay had seen back in the Ohio Valley, but these were even more comfortable for both rider and horse.

After the horses were saddled, bedrolls were draped behind the saddles and lashed down, along with small packs carrying extra powder and shot as well as salt and pemmican, and some plain jerky and fried cakes made from corn mush. The travelers would eat well for a few days, at the very least. The horses also carried waterskins, although finding water would likely not be a problem during the trip: Innumerable small creeks flowed down to the plains from the mountains, which would be to the west for the entire journey. Clay intended to stay on the prairie for the most part, since they could make better time on the flatlands, but when they were far enough north, they would veer into the high country and begin looking for Fletcher McKendrick.

Canada was a big place, Clay reminded himself as he tightened a cinch on the dun. They would need to have luck riding with them as well. He had a feeling that McKendrick would be somewhere close to the border. The Scotsman probably planned to have his men make another foray into American territory in the spring. It was apparent from events in the past two years that expanding the operation of the London and Northwestern Enterprise across the border was McKendrick's main objective.

This year a surprise would be waiting for McKendrick, Clay vowed.

The entire village was awake by the time the three men were ready to ride. Bear Tooth clasped hands with each of them and said to Clay, "You ride with the prayers and the hope of the people. May the Great Spirit lead you."

"Thank you, Bear Tooth," Clay replied. "The memory of you and your people will keep us strong in times of trouble."

The chief briefly embraced Proud Wolf. "You have been like my own son. Sometimes foolish, sometimes a great trial, but always loved."

Proud Wolf swallowed hard. "I will make Bear Tooth and all of my friends proud of me."

Walks-Down-the-Wind and Cloud-That-Falls came over to him and extended a fine beaded quiver filled with arrows. "We made these for you," Walks-Down-the-Wind said. "May they fly true and slay your enemies."

Visibly touched by the overture of reconciliation, Proud Wolf reached around his neck and lifted off two leather thongs with small pouches attached to them. Handing each of his friends one of the pouches, he said, "I leave a part of myself with you in hopes that you will wear these medicine bags until I return."

"This we will do," Cloud-That-Falls promised. He and Walks-Down-the-Wind took the pouches and slipped the thongs over their heads.

Clay looked around. He saw no sign of Shining Moon, and he felt a surge of disappointment. He had hoped that she would come to say farewell to him, but perhaps they had already said the only farewell that really mattered.

It was time to leave. Aaron and Proud Wolf swung up on the chestnut and the pinto and settled into their saddles. Clay hesitated, hoping that Shining Moon would put in an appearance. But she did not come out of their tipi again, and he sensed that she was not going to. He put his foot in the rawhide loop that served as a stirrup and mounted the dun.

Clay looked at Aaron and Proud Wolf, then took a deep breath. "Let's go."

There were no cries of farewell, no revelry as the three of them rode out of the village. Silently the Hunkpapa band watched them leave, and Clay looked back only once. He saw her then, as the sun rose over the low line of hills to the east. Its rays touched her hair and her face as she came out of the tipi to look northward. In that instant he felt the bond between them, as strong as ever, as tangible as if a rawhide rope tied them together. "Good-bye, Shining Moon," he whispered, and he seemed to hear her say *"Farewell, Clay Holt."*

Then he turned his gaze to the north and rode on.

Behind them, at the edge of the Hunkpapa village, Shining Moon watched the three figures on horseback dwindle into nothingness, and then she looked down at herself. Her hands went to her abdomen and pressed lightly against it. *You are here, Clay Holt,* she thought, *and as long as I have the child you have left behind, I will have a part of you as well. . . .*

When Clay returned to the village, he would have a son. She was sure of it.

They covered over fifteen miles the first day, maybe closer to twenty, Clay thought. When he and

Aaron had been in St. Louis, escorting Lucy Franklin on the first leg of her journey home, he had gone to the courthouse and found maps of the Louisiana Territory to study, in preparation for going north after McKendrick. Borders were an uncertain thing out on the frontier, but he had estimated that Canada was about four hundred miles north of the stretch of the Absarokas where Bear Tooth's band had their village. If he and his companions could average close to twenty miles a day, he thought that they would reach the border in about three weeks.

Those estimates were close enough for what he had in mind, Clay decided. After three weeks on the trail, they would swing to the northwest, into the mountains. Any fur trappers they encountered in that vicinity would likely be working for McKendrick.

The horses proved their worth immediately, covering the miles in a ground-eating lope that was easy on their riders without tiring the animals too much. Clay and the others camped for the night on the bank of a small stream and dined on a couple of rabbits brought down by Proud Wolf's arrows. The arrows made by Walks-Down-the-Wind and Cloud-That-Falls did indeed fly true, and Proud Wolf was beaming as he retrieved the shafts.

The second day the men traveled even farther than the first. The weather was cooperating; there was a brisk, cool breeze, and the sky was relatively free of clouds except for some high, puffy ones that held no threat. They could have pushed the horses and covered even more ground, but that would drain the mounts of strength and stamina that might be needed later. By being prudent, and with plenty of grass and water each night when they stopped, they saw to it that the horses were fully recovered by the next morning.

Two more days passed. During the journey Clay, Aaron, and Proud Wolf had seen only a couple of other riders, both of whom turned out to be Sioux from other bands. They kept a close eye out for the tribal enemies of the Sioux—the Crow, the Arikara, and the Blackfoot—all of whom roamed the plains at times. Clay intended to avoid trouble if at all possible. He did not want their mission endangered by a skirmish with hostile Indians.

Despite having seen no one except the two friendly Sioux, an uneasy feeling grew stronger in Clay with each mile that passed. If he had not known better, he would have sworn they were being followed, but when he sent Aaron and Proud Wolf on ahead and circled around to check their back trail, he found nothing. When he rejoined the youths, he could tell they were curious about where he had gone, but he kept his suspicions to himself. As far as he could tell, there was nothing to worry about.

Since leaving the village, they had taken turns standing watch at night. That night Clay was especially alert as he stood guard, and he told Aaron and Proud Wolf to pay particular attention, too. The night passed quietly, however, and the prairie was peaceful the next morning as they started northward again.

Trouble came without warning. As the three riders were moving through a broad, shallow valley, several mounted Indians came racing out of a grove of spruce at the far end of the valley. Clay spotted them immediately, and although they were too far away for him to distinguish the markings on their clothes and faces, he knew they were not friendly—not the way they were racing toward the three travelers. Out here on the frontier nobody came at you that fast unless they had hostile intentions.

Clay pointed out the attackers to his companions, then swung the dun toward the mountains and dug the heels of his moccasins into the horse's flanks, urging it into a gallop. "Come on!" he called to Proud Wolf and Aaron. "We'd better find a place to shield us!"

For a second Clay had considered trying to outrun the enemy, then abandoned the idea. The approaching Indians had several riderless horses trailing from lead ropes, and during a long chase, they could switch mounts and keep their horses fresher than the ones their would-be victims were riding. Their only chance was to find a place from which they could defend themselves and make the attackers pay a high enough price to drive them away.

The horses responded, racing over the gently rolling plains and actually increasing the distance between them and their pursuers. That gap was only a temporary one, Clay knew, but perhaps it would last long enough to allow them to find a good spot to make their stand.

Clay's gaze swept the landscape ahead. They were galloping toward the mountains, which jutted up from the prairie with few foothills in that area. Clay spotted a line of thicker brush that marked the course of a creek flowing down from the heights, and at the base of the steep slope where the stream entered the plains was a cluster of boulders, which had tumbled down probably decades or even centuries earlier. Pointing, Clay called to the others, "Head for those rocks!"

He veered the dun to take a straighter course toward the boulders, then cast a glance over his shoulder at the pursuing Indians. They were still a good distance behind. Clay had a feeling they might be Arikara, but the distance was still too great to be sure.

It hardly mattered, he thought. An Arikara arrow could kill just as easily as one fired by a Blackfoot or a Crow.

He would have preferred that the boulders not be so widely spaced; the large gaps between them made it easier for hostile arrows to penetrate the ring of stone. Racing the dun through one of the gaps, he then dropped from the horse's back and landed running with the Harper's Ferry rifle clutched tightly in his left hand. He let the dun go, hoping the horse would have the sense to stay out of the line of fire and not go too far.

Proud Wolf and Aaron dismounted on the run, too, and each of them picked a boulder to use as cover. Clay primed the lock on his rifle with powder and nestled the curved stock against his shoulder as he dropped to one knee beside the large rock. He waited a couple of moments until the attackers were within rifle range, then settled the bead of the flint-lock's sight on a buckskin-clad chest and pressed the trigger. The rifle boomed, spewing flame and smoke from its muzzle as its charge ignited.

Aaron and Proud Wolf fired at almost the same instant, the sound of the three shots blending together in a huge roar. When the powder smoke cleared, Clay saw that two of the attackers had been shot off their horses.

That still left eight or ten attackers—more of them than Clay had originally thought. It was a good-sized raiding party, and they would not discourage easily.

But Clay and his friends would not die easily.

He reloaded smoothly and quickly. As he did so three shots sounded from the attackers, but none of them came anywhere close. The attackers had only old trade muskets, Clay surmised, weapons famous for their lack of accuracy. And the attackers had fired from the backs of their galloping horses, the worst possible platform for shooting.

Finished with his reloading before the others, Clay lined up his second shot and fired. The Indian in his sights clutched a shattered shoulder, but he managed to stay on the back of his mount.

They were Arikara; they were close enough for Clay to be sure of that now. They were also close enough to bring their bows and arrows into play and were considerably more accurate with the war bows than the old muskets. Clay had to duck back behind the rock to reload as arrows rained around him.

Aaron fired again, then Proud Wolf, but when Clay edged out from the boulder far enough to line up his third shot, he saw that none of the Arikara had fallen since the first two. And the war party was closing fast now. It was going to be almost impossible to keep them from overrunning the rocks.

His expression grim, Clay pressed the trigger again and saw a third warrior go spinning off his horse. At least one more of the bastards would not get to celebrate a victory, he thought.

Then from the corner of his eye, he caught a flickering movement. Something black shot through the air, and one of the Arikara let out a shriek and tumbled off his horse as an arrow buried itself in his chest. Clay had no idea where the shaft had come from, but an instant later, a second attacker died, silently this time as another black arrow took him in the throat and flipped him backward off his pony.

The Arikara were in pistol range now, and Clay leaned his rifle against the boulder and jerked out the brace of North and Chaney pistols he carried tucked under his belt. He cocked them and held them ready as the attackers charged the boulders. The pistols boomed one after the other, and the shots took down two more of the Arikara.

At the same time Aaron Garwood fired his pistol, and the ball tore through the arm of one of the warriors. The wounded Arikara screamed in pain and defiance and flung himself off his horse, landing on Aaron and driving him to the ground. With his uninjured arm the Indian lifted his tomahawk for a killing blow.

Proud Wolf struck first, thrusting his knife into the Arikara's back. As the attacker slumped, Proud Wolf tore his blade free and turned to meet the charge of two more riders. He had his knife in one hand, 'hawk in the other.

Clay dropped his pistols and pulled out his own 'hawk, but before he could use it, two more of the mysterious black arrows thudded into their targets, spilling two more Arikara to the ground with fatal wounds. The arrows had been fired with such force that the heads passed completely through the warriors' bodies.

That left only one of the warriors, who suddenly seemed to realize that he had ridden into a hornet's nest. He whirled his horse around and started to flee, but Clay threw his tomahawk, the finely balanced weapon revolving a couple of times in the air before the blade thudded into the back of the Arikara's head, splitting his skull. The man fell to the ground, limp as a cloth doll.

Incredibly, Clay, Aaron, and Proud Wolf—with some help from an unknown source—had not only fought off the Arikara raiders, but killed them all as well. Clay was breathing hard, and his pulse was racing, but he felt a fierce exultation as he looked around at the sprawled bodies. A civilized man probably would not feel so good about witnessing such carnage, let alone participating in it, he told himself.

But then, a civilized man would not last very long out on the frontier.

Proud Wolf walked over to one of the bodies and grasped the black shaft of the arrow that had killed the man. He pulled it free from the corpse and held it up in front of him, staring at it in bewilderment. He looked at Clay and said, "Who . . . ?"

The answer to that question came to Clay as he remembered a few incidents he had witnessed in the Hunkpapa village. "You ought to know better than anybody," he told Proud Wolf. A glance at Aaron told Clay that he had figured it out, too.

After a moment Proud Wolf's eyes widened. Shaking his head slowly, he said, "No. It could not be *her*. . . ."

"Proud Wolf!" a female voice cried, and a buckskin-clad figure emerged from a nearby clump of waist-high grass and ran toward the boulders. "Proud Wolf, are you all right?"

"Butterfly!" Proud Wolf exclaimed with dismay.

She stopped short, an injured look on her face, and then gestured at the arrow he still held in his hands. "Raven Arrow," she said sharply. "My name is Raven Arrow, as you should know better than anyone."

A war bow was clutched in her hand, and a quiver of arrows with black-dyed shafts was slung on her back. She wore high moccasins, buckskin leggings, and a buckskin shirt without the fancy bead-and quillwork that usually adorned a Sioux woman's clothing. A buffalo-hide cape was draped around her shoulders, and her long black hair was pulled back into a single thick braid. She wore a sheathed knife on her belt and carried a tomahawk as well. The young woman was clothed as a warrior, and from what he had seen of her ability with that bow, Clay judged that she had the necessary skills, too. She did not bat an eye as she looked at the sprawled bodies of the men she had just killed. They were Arikara, and, more importantly, they had been trying to kill the man she loved.

Proud Wolf threw the arrow he held to the ground and glared at Butterfly. "You followed us. We told you that you could not come with us, and still you followed us."

"It would appear that it is a good thing," she said with a meaningful glance at the dead warriors.

"Saved our hides, sure enough," Aaron put in. "But where in blazes did you come from, Butterfly?"

Clay wondered if she would correct Aaron, too, about her name, but she merely sighed and said, "I have been watching you. My horse is over there." She pointed to a clump of trees about a hundred yards distant.

Clay frowned in thought. "You've been staying *ahead* of us."

"Only a little. I moved past you when you camped the first night, circling a good distance around your fire. After that I stayed even with you, or slightly ahead, but I was careful to stay out of your sight."

"You did a good job," Clay told her with admiration. "I sensed that somebody was watching us, but I figured they were on our back trail. When I doubled back and didn't find anybody, I reckoned maybe I was getting soft in the head."

She stifled a laugh. "I was lucky. You would have found me soon, I know."

Coldly, Proud Wolf said, "You ignored our wishes. You have acted in a very unseemly manner, Butterfly. You should go home now."

She turned toward him, her face darkening with anger. "Are you blind? I killed four of those warriors! I saved your life!"

Proud Wolf folded his arms across his chest. "A true warrior does not rely on a woman to save him. He lives or dies by the strength of his arm and the keenness of his eye. You have dishonored me."

With that, he stalked away.

Butterfly stared after him, a mixture of anger and amazement on her face. When she started to follow him, Clay moved quickly in front of her.

"Hold on," he told her quietly. "No point in arguing with him when he's got his back up like that. Better let him calm down first."

"Besides, Butterfly," Aaron said, "Clay and me, we're grateful as all get-out for what you did. Aren't we, Clay?"

"That's right." Clay looked again at the trees where Butterfly had said her horse was hidden. "You must've crawled all the way over here to keep those Arikara from seeing you."

"That is correct. I saw what was happening and knew that I could not help you unless I took them by surprise. I stayed as low as I could in the grass."

Low enough, Clay thought, so that neither he and his companions nor the Arikara had noticed her approach. That lack of attention had cost some of the raiders their lives.

Butterfly looked at him intently. "Are you going to send me back to Bear Tooth's village?"

Clay rubbed his jaw as he mulled over the question. "The village is a far piece," he said after a moment. "I wouldn't feel right about sending you off that far by yourself. And we can't afford the time it'd take to escort you back there."

Hope lit up Butterfly's eyes. "You mean you will let me go with you?"

"I reckon we don't have much choice in the matter," Clay said with a wry chuckle. "Must've been pretty frightening, being out here by yourself like that."

"A warrior is at home wherever he—or she—is."

"If you come along," Clay warned, "you'll have to look out for yourself and keep up with us. We can't be slowing down for you."

Butterfly nodded eagerly. "Do not concern yourselves with such matters. I will be no trouble to any of you."

"In that case, we can give it a try."

She looked as if she wanted to thank him effusively, but with a visible effort she confined herself to a stoic nod. "You will not regret this decision, Clay Holt."

"I hope not," he replied. Then, gesturing toward Proud Wolf, who stood stiffly with his back to the others some fifty yards away, Clay added, "Question now is, who's going to tell *him?*"

"I can—" Butterfly began.

"Better let me," Aaron cut in. "He might take it better that way."

Butterfly reluctantly agreed, and as Aaron started toward Proud Wolf, Clay said to the young woman, "Let's go fetch your horse."

Aaron walked out to join Proud Wolf wondering why the young Sioux warrior was so upset. All the evidence pointed to Butterfly being a valuable addition to their party.

Proud Wolf had evidently heard him coming, for he turned. Looking disdainfully over at Clay and Butterfly, he asked, "Is Clay sending her home?"

"No. She's coming with us."

Proud Wolf stared at him in disbelief. "Have the spirits made Clay Holt lose his senses?"

Aaron shrugged. "Looked to me like she'll be pretty good to have around. She sure handled herself all right during that battle with the Arikara."

"But—"

"What's the matter with you, Proud Wolf?" Aaron interrupted. "As far as I can see, Butterfly's awfully capable, not to mention awfully pretty. Why don't you want her around?"

Proud Wolf's jaw tightened in anger; then he drew a long breath and let it out slowly. "For years Butterfly has looked at me as a young woman looks at a young man she wishes to court her," he explained.

"You mean she's had her eye on you."

"That is right. Since we were children, she has babbled about her visions and how one day she and I will be married. But at the same time . . ." Proud Wolf hesitated, and it was evident that what he had to say was very difficult for him. After a moment he continued. "Butterfly was always bigger and faster and could do more things than I could. When we were young, I thought that someday I would catch up with her, but as you can see"—he looked down at his slender frame—"I am smaller than all the other warriors, and that is bad enough. But to be smaller than a female like Butterfly . . . it is a thing of shame."

"Now, hold on a minute. You may not be as large and as strong as the other men in your band, but you've done more, had more adventures, killed more enemies, than any of them. Hell, since you and me

joined up with Clay, we've been all over this territory
—farther'n anybody else in Bear Tooth's village."

Proud Wolf slowly replied, "In my head I know
these things are true. But in my heart . . . I look at
Butterfly, and these things do not dwell in my heart. I
look at her, and once again I am small and slow and
weak, just as when we were children."

"Well, I'm truly sorry to hear that, but it doesn't
change anything. Clay won't send her home by herself, and we don't have the time to take her. So she's
got to go with us."

Proud Wolf slumped in grudging acceptance. "I
will not go against Clay Holt, my brother and my
friend. But I hope we do not all regret this decision in
the future."

"Me, too. And don't worry, I won't say anything
about what you told me. We're friends, and all that's
just between you and me."

Proud Wolf put a hand on Aaron's shoulder.
"You are my friend, and that is *why* I spoke so freely."
He glanced at Clay and Butterfly, who were returning
from the trees, Clay leading Butterfly's pony. "There
is no one else in the world I would tell this to, but—
Butterfly frightens me."

Aaron tried hard not to smile. "Maybe you'll get
over that once we've all traveled together." He did
not say it, but he was thinking that Proud Wolf was
lucky to have a woman like Butterfly interested in
him. "Come on, let's go catch those horses of ours."

Leaving the fallen Arikara where they lay, they
headed north again, four riders now instead of three.

CHAPTER EIGHT

Before the Indians had any intercourse with the whites, they made the heads of their arrows of flint or horn stone. They now purchase them from the traders, who cut them from rolled iron or from hoops.

—JOHN BRADBURY "Travels in the Interior of America 1809–1811"

The tall, red-haired man sat on the cabin roof of the keelboat as its crew poled it up the Missouri River. The boat had left St. Louis only a couple of days earlier and so far had not proceeded very far up the broad river after leaving the Mississippi. Large chunks of ice floated down it, down from hundreds of miles upstream, where the thick coating of ice that formed on the Missouri every winter was only now beginning to break up. It was really too early in the season for a keelboat to be attempting the journey, but the vessel's captain had it loaded down with supplies for the forts and trappers on the frontier and stood to make a healthy profit by being the first trader of the year to head upriver. That was worth taking a few chances.

The red-haired man drew his thick coat tighter around him. He was the only passenger, and he could have gone belowdecks to the tiny cabin where he slept, but the sun was shining brightly, and that warmed him somewhat. He wanted to see the landscape drifting past on both sides of the wide, shallow river, even though it was for the most part only a grassy, treeless plain, changing little as the miles rolled past.

Thomas Brennan did not care. God had led him to this land, and it was beautiful to him. He smiled as he looked from side to side along the riverbanks.

One of the keelboatmen, a burly, bearded man with an ugly knife scar across the bridge of his nose— a souvenir from a brawl in a waterfront tavern— walked past from front to back along the ledge that ran the length of the boat, poling the craft. Glaring at the red-haired man, he demanded, "What're you smirkin' at?"

"I'm not smirking at anything, friend." A faint tinge of a brogue remained in his voice, even though his parents had left Ireland and come to America when Thomas Brennan was but a babe.

"Well, I don't like the way you're looking at me," the keelboatman growled as he halted to scowl at Brennan.

One of the crewmen behind him objected, "Move along, Quint. You're holding us up."

Quint half-turned and snapped, "Shut your damn mouth! I don't like this fella, and I got a right to tell him about it."

"If I've offended you, Mr. Quint, all I can do is offer my apologies," Thomas Brennan said sincerely.

Quint narrowed his eyes and stared at Brennan. "How about if I just throw you off this here boat and make you swim all the way up the Mizzou?"

Thomas Brennan glanced at the captain, who stood behind the cabin with the long rudder gripped in his hands. He doubted that the captain would step in to put a stop to Quint's harassment. The boatman had not particularly wanted to take along a passenger in the first place, but Brennan had offered him a good enough price so that he could not turn it down.

Turning his attention back to Quint, Brennan said, "I've paid for my passage on this boat, and 'twould not be right for you to put me off without good reason. Besides, 'twould not be Christian to strand a poor pilgrim out here in the middle of nowhere."

"Don't go singin' psalms to me, boy!" Quint thundered. "And I'll show you what's right or not. You're going for a swim!" He gripped his pole with one hand and reached for Brennan with the other.

But the red-haired man slipped to the side and avoided Quint's grasping hand. His own fingers closed over Quint's wrist as he half-rolled off the cabin roof and landed lightly on the ledge. Before any of the other crewmen could even think about interfering, Brennan jerked Quint around and bent his arm up painfully behind his back. With a hard shove he sent the keelboatman flying off the ledge. Quint's arms and legs windmilled as he fell; then water flew high in the air as he landed in the river with a great splash.

Brennan was breathing hard, but not from exertion. He was horrified at what he had done. His brawling days were supposed to be long behind him, and he had not been in a serious fight since he had heard the calling and devoted himself to the Lord's work. Now, as Quint broke the river's surface to the accompaniment of raucous laughter from the other keelboatmen, Thomas crossed himself, offered up a short but heartfelt prayer, and jumped in after his opponent.

Brennan was instantly soaked through, his boots and coat threatening to pull him down to the bottom. He fought against the pulling weight and stroked over to the floundering Quint. Grasping one of the man's flailing arms, he called out, "Don't worry, I've got you!"

Quint twisted around, bellowed, "You!" and jabbed a short punch into Brennan's face. He fell back, losing his grip on the keelboatman. Quint yelled, "Stay away from me, damn you! I can swim!"

Choking and coughing from the water he had swallowed in surprise when Quint hit him, Thomas Brennan decided to take the man at his word. After all, it made sense that someone who made his living on keelboats would know how to swim. He oriented himself and paddled back to the keelboat, pulling himself aboard just a couple of seconds before Quint followed suit a few feet away.

As Quint gasped for breath, he rolled over and reached toward his belt, but the captain called out from the stern, "Leave that knife alone, Quint! I'll have no killing on this boat."

"But, Cap'n," Quint protested as he pushed himself awkwardly to his knees, "you saw what this bastard did to me! You *all* saw it!"

"Still and all," the captain said firmly, "I'll not have you knifing a man of God on my vessel. Kill him on your own time, if you must."

"Man of God?" Quint stared at Brennan, who had pulled off one of his boots and upended it to let some of the water drain out.

Father Thomas Brennan looked up at him with a grin and pulled his coat open enough for Quint to see the large crucifix dangling from his neck. "Father Thomas Brennan. I should have introduced myself to you sooner, Mr. Quint. I hope to get to know all of you men before our journey's over."

"A priest!" Quint exclaimed, sputtering even more than he had when he fell into the river. "Nobody told me—"

"It's all right, Mr. Quint," Father Brennan said as he emptied the other boot. "Our little altercation was as much my fault as it was yours. I never should have allowed myself to lose my temper. Before I found God, I'm afraid I was a rather hotheaded lad."

Quint climbed to his feet and held out a hand to the priest. "Come on, Father. We'd better get down below and out of these wet shirts 'fore we catch our deaths. If you don't have another one yourself, I got a spare I can lend you."

Father Brennan suppressed a shiver. The wind that blew over the deck of the boat *was* bitingly cold, especially considering their wet garb. He took Quint's hand and let the man haul him to his feet.

"Quint," the captain called as they started belowdecks, "the time we've lost because of you will be taken out of your wages for this trip. So maybe you'll think twice before starting another fight."

"And I'll make sure I'm not pickin' on some priest," Quint muttered, drawing a grin from Father Brennan. As they went down the short flight of steps in the center of the boat that led to the cabin, Quint added, "Pardon me for asking, Father, but what the devil is a priest doing going up the Missouri like this?"

"You said it yourself, Mr. Quint. The Devil." The priest swept an arm toward the landscape in front of them. "He's out there just as sure as he's anywhere else, and I'm going west to fight him. I'm going to bring the Word of God to the trappers and the savages and anyone else I can find out there."

Quint shook his head skeptically. "That's wild country, mighty wild. You're goin' to have a hard fight in front of you, Father."

"It won't be the first one, my friend," Father Brennan said. "Not the first one at all."

* * *

Spring had always been one of Shining Moon's favorite times of year, but this season was different. With Clay gone, she felt more alone than she ever had, even though she was surrounded by her people. Her days were busy, and she was grateful for that. Many tasks needed doing as the Hunkpapa prepared for the great buffalo hunt that would take up much of the summer. Shining Moon helped repair the tipis after the ravages of winter as well as make arrows for the hunters to use, traditionally a man's task but one at which she excelled.

A war party went north to Blackfoot territory, the leader one of Bear Tooth's subchiefs, a warrior and medicine man called Stalking Panther. The villagers were convinced that Stalking Panther and his men would avenge the Blackfoot raid of the previous autumn and bring honor and glory to the Hunkpapa— as well as more horses, it was hoped.

Shining Moon paid little attention to the talk of raids and vengeance. The nightmares she had suffered so frequently during the months Clay Holt was in St. Louis had faded while he was with her again, and though she had feared they would return and perhaps be worse than ever when he left again, she remained untroubled by dreams for th most part. But she felt his absence keenly and longed for the time when she would once again hear his voice and feel the touch of his hand. She knew she had not been a good wife to him after his return from St. Louis, and the regret she felt gnawed at her.

As the weather warmed even more, the tipis were taken down and carried away by the women, and the entire village was moved closer to the Big Horn River, in the valley to the east of the Absarokas. Soon the great herds of buffalo would come again, Bear Tooth told his people, and there would be much feasting and celebrating.

One day soon after the village had moved, Shining Moon sat cross-legged in the tipi where she now slept alone. A buckskin pouch sat in front of her, and she stared at it with a particular intensity. Finally, after looking at the pouch at length, she reached out, opened it, and removed the dress that Clay Holt had brought her from St. Louis. It was still neatly folded, untouched since she had first put it away because she could not bring herself to wear it.

Now she stood and shook the dress out, holding it up in front of her. The garment was lovely, there was no doubt about that, but when Clay had given it to her, her only thought was that he wished she were white, not Indian. He had regretted marrying her, she had decided, and he wanted to make her more like a white woman.

She knew now that she had been wrong. Clay Holt was a good man, an honest man, a straightforward man. He had bought the dress for her because he thought it was pretty, and he had given it to her because he hoped she would like it. She was sorry that she had never worn it for him after that first time.

After carefully placing the dress on the ground, she took off her buckskin dress, then slipped on the one Clay had given her, tugging it down and then buttoning it up. The fabric felt strange to her. So different from buckskin or even doeskin. She ran her hands over it. It made her feel better, as if Clay were somehow closer to her when she wore it instead of hundreds of miles away on a vengeance quest from which he might never return.

For the first time in weeks, a faint smile touched Shining Moon's lips. She would wear the dress until Clay Holt returned safely to her, she vowed.

Her fingers went to her long black hair. Gathering one side of it, she began to braid the raven strands. The smile was still on her face.

Shining Moon had just finished braiding her hair when another woman from the village looked in through the entrance of the tipi and announced excitedly, "More white men are coming—in a boat this time!" Then she noticed what Shining Moon was wearing and gaped at her in surprise.

Shining Moon ignored the reaction. The other villagers were just going to have to become accustomed to seeing her like that.

She walked out of the tipi and joined the rest of the villagers hurrying to the river. Although spring was just beginning, several white men had already passed through the area, some on horseback and others on foot, all bound for the mountains where the creeks teemed with beaver. Over the past few years, white trappers had become a common sight on the frontier. Most were friendly, and some even adopted Indian ways and lived with Indians during the winter months. Still, newcomers were a curiosity, especially ones who arrived in a keelboat like the one being poled along the Big Horn toward the Hunkpapa village.

Shining Moon and many of the other villagers had seen keelboats before. Her first sight of one was when she had accompanied Clay to Manuel Lisa's fort soon after they had met. And a keelboat had carried Clay's brother Jeff away from the mountains when he returned to Ohio to see his wife. Often they carried trade goods as well as passengers, and the Hunkpapa always had pelts with which to barter. The arrival of a boat was cause for celebration.

Shining Moon did not particularly feel like celebrating, but she was interested in the newcomers. Perhaps Jeff Holt would be among them; Clay had expected his brother to return long before now.

Joining the other women on the bank of the river, Shining Moon scanned the faces of the men on the keelboat. None looked familiar. They were all typical keelboatmen, rugged, bearded, and dangerous looking. Except for one man, she noted, a man who was clean shaven and who had thick red hair under his knitted cap. He looked as strong as any of the keelboatmen, but he was not wielding one of the long poles. He had a large canvas drawstring bag slung over his shoulder, and although it appeared to be rather heavy, he stepped ashore nimbly as the bow of the keelboat nudged the bank of the river.

Bear Tooth and several warriors were waiting, well armed with muskets and bows just in case the strangers proved to be unfriendly. The Hunkpapa were willing to give these white men the benefit of the doubt, but they were not foolish. Bear Tooth regarded the red-haired man solemnly as the stranger smiled and said, "Greetings, Chief. We come in peace, and I certainly hope you know what I'm saying."

"I speak the white man's tongue," Bear Tooth informed him. "If you truly come in peace, then you and your friends are welcome. I am called Bear Tooth, and these are my people."

"I'm Father Thomas Brennan. The captain and his men here wish to trade with you, and I come to bring you the Word of God."

A priest! A stir went through the villagers as they realized what the stranger was. The ones who understood English translated for those who did not, and within moments everyone gathered on the shore of the river knew the identity of the man with red hair.

The Hunkpapa had seen priests before, although all the messengers of God who had visited that area in the past had been French-Canadian Jesuits. In fact, a Jesuit priest had taught Shining Moon and Proud Wolf to speak not only English, but French several years earlier, before they met Clay and Jeff Holt. None of the priests had stayed in the mountains for long, however, and the last one to come had been killed by a band of hostile Crow warriors.

This man was certainly not a French-Canadian. He had a trace of an accent that Shining Moon could not identify, and he had bright red hair, which was rare. He shook hands with Bear Tooth in the manner of white men, and as he did so, his coat fell open to reveal a large cross on a golden chain. It seemed to be the symbol of his calling, rather than the hooded black robes all the other priests had worn. Except for the cross he was dressed as the keelboatmen were, in sturdy, functional clothes and thick boots.

The captain and his men piled off the boat and carried out crates, kegs, and bags of the goods they wished to trade for pelts. Many of the items were pretty, such as the brightly colored glass beads and bolts of cloth, while others were useful: steel hunting knives and tomahawks, whetstones, muskets, iron arrowheads, salt and tea and coffee and tobacco. The Hunkpapa gathered around eagerly to look over what the white men had brought, and soon the air was filled with the sound of spirited bargaining led by the captain and Bear Tooth.

Father Brennan took no part in the trading. Instead, he wandered away from the edge of the riverbank, looking around at the nearby tipis. Shining Moon watched him, finding him more interesting than the bartering; he must have felt her gaze on him because he turned to look directly at her. His eyes were a dark green, almost brown, and they widened slightly at the sight of an Indian woman in a white woman's dress.

The priest started toward her, and for a moment Shining Moon's impulse was to turn and run. She did not want to confront this white man. Although there was little physical resemblance, the priest reminded her of Clay Holt. There was something in the way he carried himself. Shining Moon wanted to move, but her feet seemed rooted to the spot.

"Hello," he said as he stopped in front of her and lowered his bag to the ground by his feet. "That's a very nice dress you're wearing. I didn't expect to see such way out here."

"On an Indian, you mean," she said, her voice stronger and calmer than she had expected it to be.

Father Brennan shrugged. "I have to admit, I'm

more used to buckskins on your people. Obviously we're not the first white men you've ever seen."

"No. My husband is white. He gave me this dress."

"Oh. Well, that explains it." He held out his hand. "I'm Father Thomas Brennan."

Shining Moon did not take his hand but instead folded her arms across her chest. "I am called Shining Moon," she said reluctantly.

"Pretty name," he said with a grin, not seeming offended by her refusal to shake hands. "I guess you heard me telling your chief that I'm a priest."

"I heard. What are you doing here?"

He seemed slightly surprised again. "Why, I've come to establish a church," he said. "Why else would I be here? The Lord led me here."

For a long moment Shining Moon did not say anything. Then she repeated, "A church?"

"Yes, for your people and for mine, too. I'm told there are a great many trappers in the mountains." He waved a hand toward the Absarokas.

Shining Moon nodded. "That is right."

"Well, they need a place to worship and to receive the Sacraments, don't they? I intend to build that place." There was strength and determination in his voice.

"We worship in our own way; we pray to our own gods," Shining Moon said tightly.

"Of course you do. Still, 'tis my duty to bring you the Word." Thomas bent over, unlaced the top of his bag, and reached inside. He brought out a small glass vial of colorless liquid. "And to bring you this, as well."

Shining Moon's eyes narrowed. "What is that?"

"Have you heard of smallpox?"

A shiver went through Shining Moon. She was well aware of the smallpox epidemics that had raced through some tribes, all but destroying them. Many Indians believed the disease was a curse brought upon them by the coming of the white men, and in a way that was true: The white men had indeed brought smallpox to the frontier with them. But Clay had explained to her that it was only a sickness. There was nothing mystical about it—but it was deadly all the same. So far Bear Tooth's band had been lucky; they had been spared such a grim visitation. However, Shining Moon and all the other Hunkpapa lived with the knowledge that such a disaster might one day befall them.

"I know of this thing called smallpox," Shining Moon told the priest. She gestured at the vial he held. "What does it have to do with that?"

"This is what the doctors call a vaccine," the priest explained as he held up the vial so that the sunlight caught the liquid within. "It's made from cowpox, and it causes a sickness that isn't nearly as bad as smallpox. But once you've had the cowpox, you'll never get the other. It's medicine, you understand, to keep your people from getting sick."

Shining Moon understood about good medicine and bad medicine, although she suspected the white man used the word to signify something slightly different than the Sioux did. But the meanings were close enough for her to grasp what he was talking about. She asked, "This—medicine will protect us?"

"That's right, and I've plenty of it for all of your people and any of the other tribes who want to be protected. Will you help me spread the word about this, Shining Moon?"

"Why do you ask this thing of me?" she demanded. "This is *your* concern, a white man's concern."

Father Brennan shook his head. "It's important to all of us, white and Indian alike. And you can help save some lives."

Shining Moon hesitated, then said, "I will consider this thing. Now I must go."

She started to turn away, but the priest put out a

hand to stop her, without actually touching her. "Will you come to the church once it's built?"

"I—I do not know." A feeling of unease, almost panic, was growing inside Shining Moon. She had no idea why she felt that way, except possibly because Thomas Brennan was the first white man she had talked to since Clay had left. She had never been very comfortable around white men, with the exceptions of Clay and Jeff Holt and Aaron Garwood. All the others made her nervous, and so did this priest. Again she turned to leave, and she did not hesitate.

"I'll be looking for you," Father Brennan called to her retreating back.

She did not respond.

When she reached her tipi, she looked toward the river. The trading was still going on, and the priest was moving among the villagers now, no doubt informing them of his plans to save their souls and protect them from the dreaded smallpox. Shining Moon needed nothing else to disturb her or to stir her emotions into a wild confusion these days. She already had enough to concern herself with, just getting through the days until Clay Holt returned.

She wished the man called Father Brennan would get on the boat when it left and never come back to her village.

Father Thomas Brennan had no intention of leaving. He had looked around at the Hunkpapa village and known right away that it was where he was meant to be. The village was large and well populated and located in the center of the region where the various bands of Sioux roamed. It was where the Lord intended for him to carry out the work that had brought him to the frontier. He was sure of that.

The encounter with Shining Moon had convinced him even more. He had seen the intelligence in her eyes. She was well respected in the village, he learned over the next few days as he talked to Bear Tooth and some of the other leaders of the band. She was married to a man named Clay Holt, Bear Tooth told the priest. Holt had come to the mountains as a trapper and explorer, but he had become a staunch friend and ally of the Hunkpapa. He was away from the village right now on an errand. Bear Tooth was reticent about the details of Holt's journey, and the priest did not press the chief about it. He was just grateful that Clay Holt had broken the ground for him, convincing the Hunkpapa that some white men could be trusted, could even be friends with the Indians.

All during the trip up the Missouri River, Father Brennan had been looking for the right place to establish a church, and now that he had found it, he threw himself into the work with all the fervor he could muster, which was considerable. There was an ax in his pack, and the day after the keelboat had left, heading up the Big Horn, he hiked to a site a quarter mile upstream, a clearing surrounded on three sides by a lazy bend of the river and on the fourth by a dense forest. There he began cutting down trees. The Hunkpapa watched him curiously as he felled the trees and stacked the logs and then went back to cut some more.

That went on for several days. He had pitched a tent by his stack of logs and slept there at night. His meals consisted of jerky and hardtack he had brought with him, washed down by river water. To the priest, the clear, cold water of the Big Horn might as well have been the sweetest wine he had ever drunk. The air was clean and bracing, and he rose each morning with a prayer of thanksgiving for having been led here.

The nights were different. The nights were when the doubts came.

As much hard physical labor as he was doing during the day, he should have slept like one of the logs he would soon use to build the church. Instead, he was frequently restless, tossing and turning inside the small tent, dozing off only to wake suddenly, eyes wide with terror. Finally, long after midnight, exhaustion would claim him, and he would get just enough rest before dawn so that he could rise and get back to work.

But he did ask himself if the nightmares would ever go away. He had prayed about them, but still they came to him. . . .

He was in a small room, and a stench in the air made his nose burn and his eyes sting. Tears ran down his face. He flinched at loud noises assaulting his ears, and then the smell became even worse, more acrid and biting. Smoke . . . a lot of smoke, then more tears and red dancing shadows. And it wasn't fair because he was only a wee lad, and now the flames of hellfire were licking about his feet, and even though he was a sinner, it was not fair—

Father Brennan awakened with a gasp and saw morning sunlight slanting into the tent through the opening. The nightmare had come even though he usually slept soundly during the last hours of the night. But he had slumbered on past dawn, and the dream had seized the opportunity to grip him again.

Movement at the tent opening made the priest sit up abruptly. "Who's there?" he asked quickly. He had no weapons, no gun or knife, and he had left the ax outside the night before. But he was more curious than afraid. After years of relying on the Lord to protect him, he was not going to start becoming fearful now.

"I—I am sorry," a familiar voice said from outside. "I did not mean to disturb your sleep, Father. But when I did not see you, and then I heard noises coming from your tent, I thought perhaps you were sick."

The priest felt a warm flush of shame wash over him. He reached for his boots, pulled them on, and

stepped out to see Shining Moon standing there, looking slightly incongruous but very pretty in the blue
dress with tiny yellow flowers on it. She had witnessed his struggle with the demons of memory, and
now they were both embarrassed.

"It's all right," he told her with a smile, hoping to
put her at ease. "I needed to be up and about the
Lord's work, anyway."

"You are not ill?"

"Not at all." He hesitated, then added, "I was
just having a nightmare."

"Yes. An evil dream. I know them well."

He felt a touch of surprise. She seemed so self-
possessed, he would not have thought nightmares
would plague her. Out of habit he said, "If there's
anything I can help you with, anything you'd like to
talk about, t'would be my pleasure."

"My dreams are my own," Shining Moon said
stiffly. "Besides, you were the one shouting."

"That's true." Again he paused. She had seemed
to leave a question unspoken, and he thought that
perhaps if he was more open with her, she would feel
more comfortable talking to him later on. "When I
was a boy in Boston, there was a fire in the building
where my family lived. It burned to the ground, and I
was the only one who lived through it."

"Your entire family died in the fire?" Shining
Moon asked softly.

"Except for my baby brother. He had already
starved to death. Those were hard times."

"And now the memories sometimes haunt you
like evil spirits."

He smiled sadly. "I suppose you could say that.
But enough of my troubles. What brings you here,
Shining Moon? I've been hoping you'd pay me a
visit."

She gestured at the stack of logs that had been
growing daily. "We have seen you cutting down the

trees, but we do not understand why you are doing this. Are you going to build a fort like Manuel Lisa?"

Father Brennan laughed and shook his head. "I'm no fur trader. I told you when I first arrived that I intend to establish a church. I'll build it out of logs."

Shining Moon looked confused, and the priest suspected he knew why. The Sioux made their dwellings out of buffalo hides, tipis that could be taken down and moved almost at a moment's notice. It was difficult for them to comprehend the idea of building something as permanent as a log structure unless it was a fort.

"This—church," Shining Moon said, hesitating slightly on the unfamiliar word, "will you use it for protection if the Blackfoot or the Crow come?"

"I'd rather invite them in to worship with me."

Now she was looking at him as if he had lost his mind. "You should make thick shutters for the windows and cut slits for rifles. If you invite the Blackfoot or the Crow to join you, they will gladly do it. Then they will kill you."

"I don't think so."

"This God of yours must be a powerful spirit."

"The most powerful of all."

"I hope for your sake you are right." She sounded dubious. Then she looked at the logs again. "You can build this church by yourself?"

"I can if I have to. But it would be easier if some of your people would give me a hand."

"I will speak to Bear Tooth. Some of the young men could help you carry the logs from the woods."

"Anything you can do to intercede on my behalf will be most appreciated," Father Brennan said sincerely. "The Lord never turns away those who want to help do His work, and I follow His example."

"I will speak to Bear Tooth," Shining Moon said again, and then she started to leave.

Father Brennan stopped her by saying, "Shining Moon, why did you come here this morning?"

To his surprise she smiled, something he had not seen very many of the Indians do. "I hear the other women talking, as well as some of the men, and they think you are—not right in the head. Touched by the spirits, they say. But I talked to you the day you came to our village, and I know this is not true. I suppose I wanted to know more about you and why you are doing these things. And I want to know about the— the cowpox. I do not want the sickness to come to my people."

He felt a surge of excitement. It was important to win over some of the Indians, not only to his religious message but to his medical one as well. Only with their help would he be able to convince the tribes that they should be inoculated against the disease.

"I'll explain it to you as best I can, Shining Moon. I'm not a physician, remember. But when my bishop in Boston sent me out here, he made arrangements with the hospital there for me to bring a supply of the vaccine with me. I was instructed on how to administer the medicine, too, and I can teach you." Father Brennan heard the excitement in his own voice as he spoke. He sensed that that morning marked the true beginning of his work here.

"I . . . would like to learn," Shining Moon said slowly.

The priest grinned. The hand of the Lord had led him here, and now, with the friendship of one young woman, his real work could begin. It was, perhaps, somewhat short of a miracle, but it was a good start.

CHAPTER NINE

J eff Holt reined in his horse and called over to the
driver of the wagon team next to him. "Take them
on to the wagonyard, Barney. I'll let Mr. Merrivale
know that we're back."

The driver lifted his reins in acknowledgment.
"Sure, Mr. Holt." He grinned and added, "It was a
good trip, wasn't it?"

"Yes, it was," Jeff agreed. "A very good trip."

In more ways than one, Jeff thought. He pulled
his horse aside and watched the long line of wagons
lumber by, headed for the wagonyard on the outskirts
of Wilmington, North Carolina. When all the big can-
vas-covered vehicles were past, Jeff sent his horse can-
tering down the road toward the main part of town
and the harbor.

Six weeks had passed since Jeff left Wilmington
with the wagons bound for the settlements in Tennessee. He knew the route well from riding it with the
wagon train led by Amos Tharp, and with his frontiersman's instincts, having covered the ground once,

he had no trouble retracing the path across the Piedmont Plain and over the Blue Ridge Mountains into Tennessee's Great Valley. Along the way the wagons had stopped at the farm of a family named Crockett, where the last train had spent a night on the previous trip, and Jeff had enjoyed seeing Davy again. The garrulous backwoodsman had told them the Cherokee were peaceful at the moment, and that had proven true. They had encountered no trouble along the way from Indians or from bandits, either. In fact, after the problem-plagued journey Jeff had made to Tennessee the first time, this trip seemed rather uneventful. They had found a market just waiting for the goods the wagons carried, and Jeff sold them for a healthy profit. He wished he could have come up with some sort of cargo to bring back with them rather than making the return trip with empty wagons, but that had not worked out.

He still had a few things to learn about being a businessman, Jeff thought, but so far the arrangement between Merrivale and him had gone better than he had expected. Of course, it had helped matters that the two of them had been hundreds of miles apart for most of the past six weeks.

Jeff wore buckskin trousers and a homespun shirt, and his old wide-brimmed brown hat shaded his eyes as he rode through Wilmington toward Merrivale's office. His Harper's Ferry rifle was slung in a fringed sheath from his saddle, but he had not used the weapon during the journey except to bring down a couple of wild turkeys. He had enjoyed seeing the mountains of the Blue Ridge again. While not nearly as majestic as the Rockies, they did remind him of the western high country where he had lived with his brother Clay.

Clay. His brother had to be wondering what had happened to him, Jeff thought. One of these days, regardless of how the partnership with Merrivale worked out, he was going to get out to the Rockies and join up with Clay again. It was destined to be that way. After all, they were brothers.

Jeff had no doubt that Clay was still alive. Above all else, his brother was a survivor.

As he passed the street to the Merrivale house, he felt an almost physical tugging. His longing to see Melissa and Michael was so great that it almost overwhelmed him. But he was determined to make the arrangement with Charles Merrivale work, for Melissa's sake if nothing else, and so he kept riding toward the office. He would report to Merrivale first, then go home to his wife and child. That was what Merrivale would do, had their positions been reversed, Jeff sensed.

He arrived at Merrivale's office near the docks. Before dismounting, he looked out over the curving sweep of harbor protected by the peninsula that ended at Cape Fear. A number of boats were moored in the harbor, but he did not recognize any of them at first glance. Later he would have to take a closer look and see if one of them was the *Fair Wind*. It would be good to see Ned and India again, too, if they happened to be in port.

Jeff swung down from the saddle, looped the reins around the rail in front of the building, then went up the steps to the entrance. His hand was on the doorknob when he paused and looked back over his shoulder at the buggy tied next to his horse. Something was familiar about it.

Shrugging, Jeff opened the door. Some of the clerks sat at their desks, their quill pens scratching on the papers in front of them, while others hurried back and forth to the open shelves where the ledger books containing all the company's records were kept. Jeff smiled. Scurrying around like mice, they were. He was glad he did not have to spend his days like that; he preferred being out in the sun, seeing the sights and breathing fresh air.

One of the clerks came out of Merrivale's office,

blanched when he saw Jeff, then ducked back in and closed the door behind him. Warning Merrivale, no doubt, Jeff thought with a grin. The clerks knew about the partnership arrangement, but they also knew about the long-standing hostility between Merrivale and Jeff, and old habits were hard to break.

Jeff's long-legged stride quickly carried him across the room. He grasped the doorknob and swung the door open. A smaller door led from Merrivale's private office into the alley behind the building, and it was swinging closed as Jeff stepped into the room. Merrivale was sitting behind his large desk, and the clerk was still there as well, so there must have been someone else in the office, Jeff reasoned. He vaguely wondered who it had been, though it hardly mattered. All he wanted to do was check in with Merrivale and then head home as fast as his horse would carry him.

"Hello, Jefferson," Merrivale grunted as he looked up, not appearing surprised by Jeff's arrival. Nor would he be, Jeff thought. Merrivale knew that if things had gone smoothly, the wagon train would be returning to Wilmington at any time.

Jeff nodded curtly. "Hello, Charles. The wagons are back safely. I sent them on to the yard."

Merrivale picked up a small letter opener and began toying with it. "Good," he said heartily, and Jeff thought he was sincere. "You can go now, Jenkins," Merrivale told the clerk, who hurried out without saying anything. Looking at Jeff again, Merrivale went on, "Any trouble along the way?"

"None at all." Jeff reached down inside his shirt and pulled out a small leather bag that was looped around his neck. He removed his hat long enough to slide the rawhide thong over his head. The bag clinked when Jeff tossed it on the desk in front of Merrivale. "There's more there than what we agreed the goods were worth. The folks in Tennessee were glad to get them."

Merrivale's eyes lit up as he reached for the bag and opened the drawstring. He upended the pouch and the coins and currency inside spilled out onto the desk. "Very good," he said as he pawed through the money. He looked up at Jeff. "I suppose you want your share now."

"No, you total it all up first and get it entered in your books. I'll let my share carry over for a while."

"You mean you want to put your profits back into the company?" Merrivale's voice reflected his surprise.

"I'm no businessman, but that seems to me the smartest thing to do right now."

Merrivale scooped up the money and began putting it back in the bag. "Very well."

If he had expected a thank you, it looked as though he was going to be disappointed, Jeff mused. But that was all right. It was unreasonable to expect Charles Merrivale to come around all at once or quickly.

"Well, I'll be heading to the house now. I just wanted to let you know that we got back safely and didn't have any problems along the way."

"All right."

Jeff hesitated, then added, "I saw a buggy outside that looked familiar. Did you have a visitor a few minutes ago, Charles?"

"Just one of my suppliers," Merrivale said casually. "We had just concluded our business. Perhaps you've seen his buggy here before."

"And who would that be?"

"Ah . . . his name is Artemus Johnson."

Jeff mulled over the name. "No, I can't say as I know him. But I suppose I will. With us being partners and all, I'll get to know all of your associates before too much longer."

"Yes, I suppose so."

Merrivale seemed uncomfortable, so Jeff said to him, "See you at supper," then went out to the street to unhitch his horse. The buggy was gone, of course. He mounted up and turned the horse toward the Merrivale house, heeling into a trot that carried him quickly through the busy streets.

Jeff frowned in thought. Charles Merrivale's behavior had seemed rather suspicious. Jeff suspected that when the clerk had carried the news of his arrival into the inner office, Merrivale had had his visitor quickly leave by the rear door so that Jeff would not see him. The only possible reason for that was Merrivale did not want Jeff to know who the visitor really was. . . .

His jaw tightened and his hand clenched on the reins. *Dermot Hawley!* That had to be the answer. Hawley had been in Merrivale's private office.

His anger rising, Jeff breathed deeply and told himself to calm down. Hawley's presence did not have to mean anything. After all, they had been partners in the past, before Melissa had insisted that her father not do business with the man, and perhaps Hawley had just stopped by to see if the situation had changed. Or perhaps he was just cleaning up some old business. Or maybe it had just been a social call. The fact that Hawley had been there did not have to mean that he and Merrivale were plotting against Jeff.

But no matter how much Jeff wanted to believe that, he could not quite bring himself to accept the idea. Hawley had been his enemy from the day he had met the man—even before, apparently—and Jeff did not expect that to change. He was going to keep his eyes and ears open for any sign of treachery. That would be only wise.

A few minutes later he reined up in front of the big whitewashed house and dismounted quickly. Thoughts of Dermot Hawley disappeared as he rushed up the walk to the porch and opened the door. His next order of business, Jeff told himself fleetingly, would be to look for a place that he and Melissa and Michael could call their own.

One of the maids was standing in the hallway, and she exclaimed, "Mister Jeff!"

"Hello, Arabella," Jeff said with a grin. "Are my wife and son home?"

"They surely are!" Arabella returned his smile. "You go on and set yourself down, Mister Jeff. I'll fetch them for you."

That was unnecessary. Melissa appeared at the top of the staircase and cried, "Jeff!" Gathering up her skirts, she ran down the stairs to the foyer.

Jeff flung his hat on the console table by the wall and met Melissa partway up the staircase. He took her into his arms and kissed her with all the passion that he had been storing up for a month and a half. It was not as it had been before, finding her after they had been separated for two years—but six weeks had been plenty long enough. Jeff reveled in the sweet warmth of his wife's lips and the softness of her body pressed against his.

"Pa!" a young voice cried from behind him, and Jeff forced himself to break the kiss and turn to look at his son. Michael was coming in from the parlor, holding Hermione Merrivale's hand, but he pulled away from his grandmother and ran to Jeff, who bent to sweep him up into a bear hug.

"Oh! Be careful with him, Jeff," Melissa cautioned with a happy laugh. "You'll squeeze the stuffing out of him."

"Not hardly." Jeff chuckled. He ruffled Michael's sandy hair and kissed the boy's cheek. "What have you been up to while I was gone, little one?"

"Waiting for you to get home!" Michael answered. "Will you take me 'sploring?"

Jeff laughed. "One of these days we'll go exploring all over the place," he promised. "Where did you learn about that, anyway?"

"Mama says Uncle Clay is a es—explorer." Michael struggled a bit with the word before getting it out, but Jeff thought he was doing a fine job. It seemed as if the boy was speaking a little clearer each day. And he was growing like a weed, tall and sturdy for a child not quite two and a half years old.

"That's right," Jeff told him. "Your uncle is an explorer, all right, and someday we'll go see him. But right now we have to stay here in North Carolina and help your grandfather with his business. Is that all right with you?"

Michael shrugged grudgingly. "I guess so."

Jeff looked over at his mother-in-law. "Hello, Hermione. How are you?"

She smiled warmly at him and gave him a kiss. "I'm just fine. We've been expecting you back, Jeff. It's so good to see you."

"Was there any trouble?" Melissa asked. "It wasn't like last time?"

"Not at all. The trip went very well. I've already gone by your father's office and delivered the proceeds to him."

"Was Charles satisfied with the results?" Hermione asked.

"He seemed to be." Jeff decided not to say anything about the unseen visitor who might have been Dermot Hawley. No point in upsetting Melissa and her mother. However, later on, when he had an opportunity, he would have a private talk with Merrivale about the matter. If they were to be partners, they could not go around keeping secrets from each other.

Still holding Michael, Jeff went into the parlor, flanked by his wife and mother-in-law. Hermione sat down in her favorite rocking chair while the others sat on the long divan, Michael settling down between Jeff and Melissa. The boy was bubbling over with questions about the trip, and Jeff could tell that Melissa and Hermione were curious, too, so he spent the next hour telling them about the journey to Tennessee and back. Arabella brought in some lemonade that had been cooling in the root cellar, and Jeff sipped gratefully from the glass as he talked. He could have used something stronger, but the Merrivales allowed only wine and brandy in their house, which were served only with meals or after-dinner cigars for the men.

After a while Hermione said, "I'm sure the two of you wouldn't mind a little time alone, so why don't I take Michael out to the kitchen with me for a bit? We can help Cook with dinner, can't we, Michael?"

"I want to stay with Mama and Pa," Michael protested.

Hermione stood up, came over to the divan, and took his hand. "Come along," she said firmly. "Grown-ups can't spend all their time with children, you know, just as children can't spend all their time with grown-ups."

Still complaining, Michael let her lead him out of the room, and Jeff called, "We'll play later, Michael. That's a promise."

That seemed to mollify the youngster. Jeff grinned as he turned to his wife. "The lad doesn't want to take a chance on missing anything."

"He reminds me of you and your brother," Melissa said. "He's certainly got that Holt restlessness about him."

"Born in the blood," Jeff said with a laugh. He slid an arm around Melissa's shoulders, and she moved over to nestle against him. It felt good to be back, good to have his wife in his arms again—almost good enough so that he could put his concerns about Merrivale and Hawley out of his mind.

Almost, but not quite.

"Something strange happened at your father's office," Jeff said after a few moments of silence. He intended to tell Melissa how Merrivale's visitor had ducked out of the office and ask her if she had ever heard of a man named Artemus Johnson—keeping his suspicions about Hawley to himself for the time being.

But before he could go on, Melissa sat up straight and faced him directly. "You and Father didn't have a fight, did you?" Her voice was tight.

"No, but—"

"Please don't be upset with him, Jeff. He only has my best interests at heart, mine and Michael's, and anyway, after all this time, I don't pay that much attention to him when he starts talking about you."

Jeff stiffened. He had assumed that with the partnership had also come a truce. But from the way Melissa was talking, that had not held true. "So, your father's had a lot to say about me, has he?"

"No, not at all," Melissa said quickly. Too quickly, Jeff thought. "Every now and then he just talked a little about the trip to Tennessee. About how he hoped it was going well, things like that."

"I see," Jeff said slowly. As much as he hated to think that Melissa would lie to him, he did not believe what she was saying. His unease about the entire situation increased. Just what had been going on in North Carolina while he was gone?

He doubted if he would get an honest answer from Melissa, not right now, and to press the issue would just ruin his homecoming. He put his arm around her again and drew her head down on his shoulder.

"I'm just glad I'm back here with you and Michael."

"And we're glad to have you back." She tilted her head up. "Jeff . . . Mother's watching Michael, and it's still hours until dinner. We could go upstairs for a while."

Jeff had to grin. "How forward of you! You've turned into quite a hussy, Mrs. Holt."

"You *have* been gone for six weeks, Mr. Holt," Melissa said, her voice taking on a throaty tone that Jeff knew very well.

He kissed her again and murmured, "That sounds like a fine idea. In fact—"

Without warning, he stood and hefted her over his shoulder. Melissa let out a cry of surprise, then pounded him on the back and said sharply, "You put me down, Jefferson Holt!"

"But I thought—"

"You're *not* going to carry me up to the bedroom draped over your shoulder like a sack of flour. I'll walk beside you, as a wife should, or I'll not go up with you at all."

Feeling sheepish, Jeff quickly put her down. "Didn't mean to offend you. I guess I got carried away."

Melissa smiled. "Well, it's nice to know I can still have that effect on you." She leaned against him, kissed his chin and the line of his jaw, then took his hand and said, "Come on."

Grinning, he headed for the staircase with her right beside him. "Always glad to accommodate."

Yes, it was good to be home again, Jeff thought as they started up the stairs. There might still be problems, but Melissa made it all seem worthwhile. He hoped Hermione kept a close eye on Michael and did not let him go exploring upstairs. At least not for a while.

The sun had not yet set when Jeff came out of the room he and Melissa shared and sauntered over to the second-floor landing. A window there overlooked the harbor and Cape Fear beyond. Jeff stretched, grimacing when his bones popped, and looked out at the harbor and the masts of the ships riding at anchor. He was tired, but it was a good weariness. He and Melissa had made love twice, the first time fast and eager and full of fire, the second time slower, more tender and loving. They had sated the need that had built up while they were apart, and now Melissa was dozing in the bedroom, snuggled down in the quilts of the four-poster bed.

Jeff had not felt like sleeping. Leaving Melissa

there to nap, he had slipped into his clothes and out of the bedroom, to go downstairs and join Michael and Hermione in the kitchen, if they were still there.

A soft footstep behind him made him turn. Arabella stood there, a stack of clean linens clutched in her arms, and she was looking at him with a hesitant expression.

"What is it, Arabella? You look upset."

"I don't know if I should be talkin' to you 'bout this, Mr. Jeff," the young woman said. "It ain't good for a colored gal to go messin' in white folks' business. I seen too many get whipped for doin' that."

"Nobody's going to whip you, at least not without coming through me first. And that's not too likely."

Arabella smiled shyly. "No, sir, I don't suppose it is."

"So if something's bothering you, you just tell me what it is, and I'll see what I can do about it."

"Well . . . it's about you, Mr. Jeff."

Jeff was surprised. "Me?"

"You and Mr. Merrivale and the things he's been sayin' 'bout you whilst you was stopped, gone."

Jeff's suspicions came back to him in a rush. Melissa's inadvertent hint that her father had been talking about Jeff during the wagon train trip had just been confirmed by Arabella. He asked tightly, "What has Mr. Merrivale been saying?"

Arabella's eyes widened. "You mean Miz Melissa ain't already tol' you?"

"I wouldn't be asking you if she had, now, would I?"

Tightening her grip on the linens, Arabella started past Jeff. "I best be puttin' these away," she muttered. "Don't you pay no mind to my ravin's, Mr. Jeff. I get these spells sometimes and don't rightly know what I'm sayin'—"

"Arabella!" Jeff's sharp voice stopped her. "You can put those things away later. Right now I want you

to tell me what Merrivale's been saying about me and
to whom."

"Lawsy, Mr. Jeff, I don' know if I ought to—but I
suppose you got a right to know what's been goin' on
behind your back." The maid took a deep breath.
"Mr. Merrivale, he's been talkin' to Miz Melissa 'bout
every day, tellin' her how she ought to divorce you
and marry that Hawley fella instead. Says you ain't
never goin' to amount to nothin' and how you
wouldn't even have a job if he didn't give you one."

Jeff felt anger welling up inside him, but he
fought to constrain it. In a low, controlled voice, he
asked, "That's what Merrivale says about me, is it?"

"And—and other things. Like how you ain't a
good daddy to little Michael and such. That man
purely don't like you, Mr. Jeff. But I do, and I don't
think it's right for him to be runnin' you down to
Miss Melissa, even if he is her daddy. He sure do like
that Dermot Hawley, though."

The anger was threatening to flare into rage now.
"And what do you think about Hawley, Arabella?"
he forced himself to ask.

"Me?" Clearly she was surprised that her opinion was being sought. But she said, "I don't like him.
He looks at me like he figgers I'm some sort o' play-
pretty and one day he'll have his way with me." She
snorted contemptuously.

Jeff's hands balled into fists. "Hawley comes
here?"

"Sometimes late at night, when Miz Hermione
and Miz Melissa done gone to bed. I had to let him in
a time or two when he come callin' on Mr. Merrivale.
They go into the study and talk for a long time."

Jeff patted the young woman on the shoulder
and said with genuine appreciation, "Thank you for
telling me about this, Arabella."

"I hope I didn't just cause a whole heap more
trouble," she said, her brow creasing with concern.

"Nothing that wouldn't have come about sooner or later anyway. You did what was right."

Jeff's plan to join Hermione and Michael downstairs was forgotten now. He went back into the bedroom for his jacket. He intended to settle things with Charles Merrivale once and for all.

"Is that you, Jeff?" Melissa murmured sleepily as he entered the room.

"Yes, it is," he said, his voice strained.

Melissa sat bolt upright. "What is it? What's wrong?"

"Who said anything's wrong?"

"I know you, Jeff. You sound angry and upset."

"I've got good reason to sound that way. Your father's been trying to talk you into ending our marriage so that Hawley can have you, hasn't he?"

Melissa said softly, "Oh, my God . . ."

"Apparently you were afraid to tell me, but you must have known I'd eventually find out. This partnership with your father is nothing but a sham. He never intended for it to work. He only agreed to it so that he could send me to Tennessee and have a free hand in trying to poison your mind against me." Jeff stood up. "For all I know, he's succeeded."

Melissa jumped out of bed, heedless of her nudity as she grasped his shoulders tightly and turned him to face her. "Jefferson Holt! Do you remember what we were doing a few minutes ago? Did I act like anyone had poisoned my mind against you?" Her dark hair was tousled, and her face was flushed with anger. She was as lovely as Jeff had ever seen her.

He felt a sudden burst of contrition. "I'm sorry, Melissa. When I found out some of the things your father's been saying, I lost my head."

"Mother told you, didn't she?"

He shook his head. "I haven't talked to your mother. If you have to know, it was Arabella who warned me, and I wouldn't take it kindly if she was punished as a result."

"You know me better than that, Jeff." The anger on Melissa's face faded away to be replaced by shame. "I should have told you myself. I intended to, but I was so happy to have you home again, and I didn't want to spoil that just yet."

Jeff put his hands on her bare shoulders and looked squarely at her. "I'm glad you didn't tell me. I'm glad we had the time together this afternoon. But now I've got to settle this. It won't do any good to let it fester."

"What are you going to do?" she asked anxiously.

"Your father will still be at his office. I'm going back down there to have a talk with him."

"You've confronted him before," Melissa reminded him. "It's never done any good."

Jeff's body slumped. She was right, of course. Charles Merrivale always got his way by one method or another. But maybe this time—his head lifted—maybe this time would be different.

"There's only one thing we can do," he said to Melissa. "The thing I knew we needed to do a long time ago. We've got to leave."

"For St. Louis?"

"I honestly don't know. We can decide that later. I don't want to drag you anyplace you don't want to go. But we've got to get out of this house and away from your father. That's the only way we'll ever have any peace."

She sighed. "You're right, I know."

"You'll go along with me on this?" he pressed. "You and Michael will move out with me?"

"Of course. We're a family. We have to stay together."

Jeff felt a surge of hope. Despite what he had learned about Merrivale and his continuing association with Hawley, with Melissa standing beside him, he was sure he could handle her father. He reached for his jacket.

Her hands tightened on his arm. "What are you doing?"

"Going to tell your father what we decided. There's no need to wait."

"But—but I thought you'd agreed not to go down there! We can talk about it when Father gets home—"

"Not this time. I don't want Michael hearing any of this. Better to get it out of the way now." He leaned over and kissed her lightly on the forehead. "You start getting ready to leave. First thing in the morning we'll find someplace else to live, even if it's just a rented room."

"But, Jeff—"

He shook his head, cutting off her plea. He was not going to be turned aside again. "I'll be back soon," he said and left the room before she could stop him or say anything else.

His heart was pounding as he went downstairs and picked up his hat from the table in the foyer. Casting a glance toward the kitchen, he told himself that he ought to go say good-bye to Michael and Hermione—but then Hermione would want to know where he was going, and the whole argument might get started all over again. Besides, he did not want to delay long enough to give Melissa time to get dressed and come downstairs.

Clapping his hat on his head, he opened the door and went out. His horse had been stabled by one of the servants, but it took him only a few minutes to go and saddle it up. He rode toward the harbor at a fast trot. This was one confrontation with Charles Merrivale that he was actually looking forward to having.

CHAPTER TEN

Some instinct made Jeff Holt approach Charles Merrivale's office by a side street so that he could look down the alley that ran behind the building. He stiffened in his saddle. Parked there, its horse waiting patiently in the traces, was the same buggy Jeff had seen earlier. Turning his mount, he rode slowly down the alley.

There was no window in the rear wall of Merrivale's private office, only the narrow door. Halting his mount several yards away, Jeff slipped down from the saddle and approached quietly on foot so that no one inside would hear him. When he was in front of the door, he leaned closer and put his ear against it. He could make out the hum of a low-voiced conversation, and although he could not distinguish any words, he knew to whom the two voices belonged: Charles Merrivale and Dermot Hawley.

So Hawley was inside at that very moment, Jeff

thought. He almost wished he had his pistol, or even his knife, but he had been so anxious to confront Merrivale that he had left the house unarmed, a rarity for him. On the other hand, maybe it was a good thing he did *not* have a gun. If he did, he would have been hard put not to kill Hawley. From what he knew of the man, he would not have been surprised if Hawley was the true mastermind behind the plan to turn Melissa against him.

Jeff lowered his hand to the doorknob and tried it. It turned slowly. Taking a deep breath, he shoved the door open, stepping into the room as the door banged against the wall.

Merrivale and Hawley, who stood on the other side of the room, turned sharply and stared in surprise at Jeff as he strode in. Hawley's beaver hat sat on the desk, and both men held glasses of brandy. A cigar smoldered between the fingers of Hawley's other hand. It was a very friendly scene, indeed; the dissolution of their partnership was certainly as much of a sham as was the arrangement between Jeff and Merrivale.

Jeff did not say anything; he just glared at them. They had been caught red-handed, and there was not a lot that could be said. But finally Merrivale asked coldly, "What are you doing here, Jeff?"

"I came to see you about the things you've been saying to Melissa about me," Jeff replied, his voice equally icy. "You're still trying to turn her against me, just as you've done all along."

The older man shrugged in the face of the accusation, not bothering to deny it. "I've merely told Melissa the truth, which is that she and Michael would be much better off with someone like Dermot."

"Not someone *like* him. You've been talking about Hawley himself."

Hawley murmured, "I *am* in the room, too, Holt. Do me the consideration of not speaking about me as if I'm not present."

"Shut your damn mouth," Jeff snapped. "This is between Charles and me. You're just an incidental."

Hawley's lips tightened angrily, and Jeff figured he had struck a nerve. But as he had said, he had come to see Merrivale, and that was all that was important at the moment.

Merrivale smiled faintly. "Bursting in on your partner and accusing him of all manner of wrongdoings isn't very good business, you know. Why don't you run on home, Holt? I'll have another errand for you soon. I'm thinking about sending some wagons down to Georgia."

"Take them yourself. Our so-called partnership is over."

Charles Merrivale shrugged again. "Well, that's your decision to make, isn't it? Although I'm sure you'll find some way to blame me for it and try to make me look bad to my wife and daughter. You always do."

Hearing the note of bitterness in Merrivale's voice, Jeff realized he was wasting his time. The man was genuinely convinced of the validity of his stand; to his way of thinking, Jeff was nothing but an interloper, someone trying to steal away the affections of his family. The man's mind was so twisted that there was no hope of compromise.

"I'm not going to argue with you," Jeff said wearily. "It's all over. I'm taking Melissa and Michael, and we're leaving."

"Over my dead body!" Merrivale barked. He put his half-empty glass of brandy on the desk and squared his shoulders. Pointing a finger at Jeff, he ordered, "Get out of my office right now. You're no longer welcome here, and you're no longer welcome in my home."

"My wife and child are there. You can't stop me from getting them."

"The hell I can't! Leave immediately, or I'll summon the authorities."

Jeff was so angry that his head was spinning. He stared at Merrivale's taut, flushed face. "We were going to leave in the morning, but I can see now we can't wait even that long. We'll be gone by the time you get home. And if you never see Melissa and Michael again, it'll only be what you deserve!"

Whirling around, he took a step toward the rear door.

He did not reach it. With a roar of rage, Charles Merrivale lunged for him, grabbing his shoulder and whirling him around. Jeff was taken by surprise. His previous confrontations with his father-in-law had been filled with harsh, angry words, but they had never turned physical. The surprise slowed down his reactions long enough for Merrivale to drive a punch into his belly.

Gasping for breath, Jeff saw Merrivale's other fist looping toward his head, and he threw up an arm to block the blow. He then jabbed his fist into Merrivale's solar plexus. The man turned pale and staggered back a step.

Balancing himself, Jeff sent an uppercut into Merrivale's jaw. The older man was solidly built, with plenty of strength, but Jeff was a young man in his prime with the strength and vitality that sprang from a frontier heritage and a vigorous outdoor life. The powerful punch that Jeff threw caught Merrivale flush on the jaw and sent him flying backward to crash against the door leading to the outer office. The latch gave under the impact, and Merrivale spilled through the door as it was knocked open.

Jeff went after his opponent without hesitation, tackling Merrivale as he tried to get back to his feet. The two men sprawled on the floor between a couple of desks, where several of the clerks had been working. The clerks scrambled to get out of their chairs and reach a position of safety—and a good vantage point from which to watch the fight.

Although Jeff and Merrivale traded punches, the

younger man maintained his clear advantage. But he had forgotten about Dermot Hawley. He had just landed a blow on the side of Merrivale's head when something smashed into the back of his own head, knocking him to his hands and knees. From the feel of the blow, Jeff deduced that the weapon had been Hawley's walking stick. He shook his head, trying to clear it, but before he could do so, Merrivale scrambled upright and launched a kick. It took Jeff in the side and spilled him back to the floor.

Merrivale kicked Jeff again and again. Jeff tried to block the kicks, but Merrivale had become a madman, gripped by an insane rage. One of those kicks was liable to crack his skull, Jeff realized, and he knew he had to get up unless he wanted Merrivale to stomp him to death.

The sudden blast from a pistol put an abrupt end to the fight. Hawley stepped up behind Merrivale, caught his arms, and pulled him away from Jeff as several men strode into the building from the street. Jeff rolled over, blinked his eyes, and focused on the newcomers enough to see that one of them wore a badge pinned to his coat. He had a pistol in his left hand that had smoke curling from the barrel, and in his right hand the man gripped another pistol. The men behind him were armed as well. Jeff realized the leader was the local constable, and the men with him were no doubt his underlings.

"What the hell's going on here?" the lawman boomed. "Somebody came running down the street and said folks were killing each other in here." He leveled his unfired pistol at Jeff. "You there! Don't try anything!"

"Constable Tolbert—arrest that man!" Merrivale demanded, pointing at Jeff. "He burst in here and attacked me."

"Is that true, mister?" the constable asked. "You can stand up while you answer me, just do it nice and easy."

Somewhat unsteadily, Jeff got to his feet. He rolled his shoulders, shook his groggy head, then said, "That's a lie, Constable. I was on my way out of here when Merrivale jumped me."

Charles Merrivale glowered. "That is absolutely untrue."

Jeff wanted to jump Merrivale again. "Listen, old man," he said hotly, "you'd better tell the truth and stop meddling in my life, or you're going to be damned sorry!"

"Settle down!" the constable said sharply. Faced with conflicting stories, he looked around at the clerks. "Anybody here see how the fight started?"

Jeff figured the clerks would lie and back up their employer's story, but, surprisingly, there was no response except a general shaking of heads. Apparently Merrivale was the kind of man who inspired fear but little loyalty among his workers.

"I saw what happened, Constable," Dermot Hawley spoke up.

Jeff had a sinking feeling. If Hawley could help get Jeff thrown in jail on charges of assault and disturbing the peace, it would solidify his position with Merrivale even more.

"You're Mr. Hawley, aren't you?" the constable asked. When Hawley confirmed that he was, the lawman continued, "Thought I recognized you. Well, what about it? Who threw the first punch?"

"I'm afraid that dubious honor falls to my friend Charles," Hawley said smoothly. "Everything happened the way Mr. Holt said."

Merrivale stared at Hawley, clearly feeling shocked and betrayed. Jeff was no less surprised. He knew that Hawley hated him and had tried to have him killed. Why in blazes would Hawley stand up for him?

"I'm sorry, Charles," Hawley said to Merrivale, "but I have to tell the truth, after all. I can't lie to the constable, as much as I might like to." He turned to

the lawman and added, "For what it's worth, Mr.
Merrivale was provoked by Mr. Holt, provoked very
severely. I'd say there were extenuating circumstances."

"Yeah, I suppose so," the constable said. He
tucked his empty pistol beneath his belt, then rubbed
his jaw in thought. He looked at Jeff and asked
harshly, "What about it? You going to press charges,
mister?"

As appealing as the idea of Charles Merrivale behind bars was to Jeff, he knew he could not do that.
Melissa and Hermione would never forgive him. "I
don't want Mr. Merrivale in jail," he said after a few
seconds. "Let's just let it end here."

"All right with me," the constable said. "But you
get on out of here and don't come back and cause any
more trouble, Holt. Because if you do, no matter who
throws the first punch, I'll be hauling you to jail."

Jeff nodded curtly. He picked up his fallen hat
and strode to the front door. Never mind the more
convenient rear door. He did not even want to look at
the man again. He would circle around to the alley for
his horse.

Then he would ride back to the house and do
what he should have done months ago: He would
gather up his family, taking only what they could
carry with them, and leave. They could send for the
rest of their things later, when they had found a place
to stay. There was no point in postponing things even
one minute longer. He hoped Melissa would not argue with him, but one thing was certain: He would
not spend one more night under the same roof with
Charles Merrivale.

Melissa and Hermione were in the parlor when
Jeff returned to the house, and they looked up with
anxious faces when he strode in.

"It's over," Jeff announced woodenly. "We're
leaving, Melissa—tonight."

Hermione's hand went to her mouth, and she exclaimed, "No!"

Jeff looked at her and tried to summon up a comforting smile, but he failed miserably. "I'm sorry, Hermione. I really am. But Melissa and Michael and I just can't stay here anymore."

"What happened down at Father's office, Jeff?" Melissa asked.

"We . . . came to blows."

"Oh, no!"

"I'm sorry about that, too. For what it's worth, I didn't strike the first one. I was trying to leave when things got, well, confused. A lot of hard words had been exchanged, and Hawley was there, the two of them drinking brandy. Things got out of hand, I'll admit that. I didn't mean for it to happen. Then the constable came—"

"The constable?" Melissa gave a brief, humorless laugh. "Oh, Jeff, what has it come to?"

"What it's come to is that we're leaving right now."

"But you can't!" Hermione protested. "We haven't even had dinner yet. Cook is giving Michael his supper right now. You can't just leave."

"Your husband's fixed it so that we don't have any choice." Jeff looked at Melissa, who was biting her bottom lip. "You're going along with me on this, aren't you, Melissa? You said you'd back me up."

"I know, but I was hoping you'd work things out with Father. I hoped he would understand that he had to stop trying to bully all of us into giving him his way."

Jeff snorted. "Your father's never going to understand anything. You couldn't beat sense into that man's head with a singletree."

Hermione stood up and drew her shoulders back stiffly. "I'll thank you not to talk about Charles like that, Jefferson. After all, he is still my husband, and I love and respect him."

"I know you do, Hermione. Frankly, I don't see how, but—"

"Jeff!" Melissa said angrily. She stood up and came toward him, her eyes blazing. "Stop it right now! You come in here bragging about how you've been in a brawl with my father—"

"I wasn't bragging, dammit!"

"And then you want me to go out to the kitchen and jerk Michael out of his chair while he's in the middle of eating and drag him out of here, when you don't even have any idea where we would go! We may well wind up sleeping on the street tonight, if you have your way!"

"I've slept under the stars many times," Jeff muttered. "It never hurt me."

"You're not a young child!"

Jeff heaved a sigh. It was all going wrong. Quietly he asked, "What do you want from me? Do you want me to stay in the house of a man who hates me, who'd like nothing better than to see me dead? He's never forgiven me for marrying you, Melissa, you know that. And he's never forgiven me for not getting killed when I was out in the Rockies with Clay, either."

"I-I know," she said, sounding as wretched as he felt. "But you said we wouldn't leave until the morning."

"And you were hoping that would give you time to talk me out of it. To give your father one more chance. How many 'one more chances' do I have to give him, Melissa? He's never going to change."

"Are you?" she asked, her voice little more than a whisper.

Hermione remained silent. Some things had to be settled between husband and wife.

Jeff stared at Melissa for a long moment, seeing the mixture of love and pain in her eyes and knowing that it was mirrored in his own. He was not able to answer her question.

"I'll go with you," she said, "in the morning. That was what we agreed upon."

"You're right," Jeff said heavily. "But I won't stay here tonight. I'll sleep in the stable out back."

"That's your choice." From the wounded look on her face, though, it was clear that Melissa did not like that solution.

Neither did Jeff, but he was not going to change his mind. It would not be so bad, he told himself. The weather was warm, and there was plenty of straw in the stable to make a soft bed. He turned and left the parlor.

After going upstairs to get his knife and his pistol, he fetched his horse from the front of the house and led it around to the stable. There he unsaddled the animal, put it in a stall, and gave it some water and grain. That done, he stepped to the wide double doors and gazed at the house across the yard. He sighed. He had half-expected Melissa to follow him, but she had not. Jeff could not decide if he was glad or disappointed.

The sun was going down. He had not eaten since noon, but even hunger would not make him go back into the house. He knew he was being stubborn, but he did not care.

Evening settled over the city. Jeff sat on a three-legged stool, hunched forward, his hands clasped between his wide-spread knees and his head drooping. He had made an unholy mess of everything, he told himself. Since he had left the Rockies, in fact, luck had been running against him. They might have all been better off if he had not found Melissa.

But then he would never have known Michael. And Michael had filled a hole in his life that he had not even been aware was there. It was a big gap to be filled by such a little boy, but somehow Michael James Holt managed to do it just fine.

Jeff smiled. Maybe things would work out after

all. As long as he and Melissa and Michael were together, there was a chance. . . .

"I brought you something to eat," Melissa said
from the door of the stable. Jeff's head jerked up in
surprise. He had been so lost in thought that he had
not heard her coming. If she had been a Blackfoot
warrior, he thought wryly, he would be dead now.

"Thanks," he said, standing up to take the tray
she carried. In the fading light he could see a plate of
fried chicken, along with some biscuits and a little
bowl of honey. "Looks awfully good."

She smiled awkwardly, and it was evident that she
felt the wall between them just as much as he did.
"Michael loves fried chicken," she commented as Jeff
sat down on the stool and balanced the tray on his
knees.

"Something else he inherited from his pa." Jeff
managed a grin, then picked up a drumstick and took
a bite of the spicy, crispy chicken. He followed it with
a biscuit dipped in the honey.

The food was good, and despite—or perhaps because of—all the emotional turmoil he had been
through that day, he was hungry, and he ate swiftly.

"Michael was disappointed that you weren't inside to tell him good night when I put him to bed. But
I told him you were doing some important work out
here."

Jeff smiled. "Thanks. You know I don't want to
upset him."

"I know. You're a good father."

"But I haven't been around as much as I should
have been."

"Well, that was hardly your fault, was it?" She
crossed her arms, took a few steps across the straw-
littered floor, then turned around abruptly. "This is
all wrong, Jeff. You and I shouldn't be fighting about
this. You're my husband, and I love you, and I should
go wherever you want to go without complaining.
After all, the Bible says a wife is supposed to leave her

parents and cleave to her husband. You reminded me of that recently."

"Maybe. But that doesn't mean you have to stop loving your parents, and it doesn't mean you stop trying to get along with them. Hell, Melissa"—he set the empty tray aside and stood up—"I never meant to cause any trouble. I just want to be with my wife and boy and not have somebody trying to ruin everything all the time."

"What about the mountains?" Melissa studied him intently in the dim light.

"I miss the mountains," Jeff admitted. "I miss Clay and Shining Moon and even Aaron Garwood. But I wouldn't trade them and the mountains for you and Michael."

"Oh, Jeff," she whispered. She came into his arms and buried her face against his chest. "I'm sorry, so sorry."

"So am I," he told her, holding her tightly.

"I'll go with you in the morning, wherever you want to go. We'll make our own life, and we'll be happy."

He nodded, gripped by emotions so strong that he did not trust himself to speak. Finally he was able to say, "It'll be all right. I promise it will."

"I know," she said softly.

Jeff wasn't sure how long they stood embracing, drawing strength from each other, but full darkness had long fallen when suddenly a light at the stable doorway startled him. Hermione stood there holding a lantern, and she had a worried look on her face.

She summoned up a weak smile and said, "I hate to interrupt. It looks like things are all right between the two of you again."

Melissa turned to face her mother, and Jeff put his arm around her shoulders. "They will be," he said. "Sorry everything got so complicated, Hermione."

"So am I. And I'm afraid there's another complication."

Suddenly Jeff felt wary. "What's that?"

"Charles hasn't come back from the office. You . . . you didn't hurt him badly, did you, Jeff?"

Jeff shook his head emphatically. "I swear to you I didn't. He'll have a few scrapes and bruises, same as me, but nothing worse."

"Then I can't figure out where he might be." The worry in Hermione's voice was plain to hear.

"Father always works late, Mother, you know that." Despite the reassuring words, however, a note of concern was evident in Melissa's voice as well.

"I know, but I have a bad feeling about this. I think something is wrong."

"He was all right when I left, Hermione, just shaken up some from the fight. But no more than I was. And his friend Hawley was there. I'm sure if anything was wrong, you'd have heard by now."

"You're right. I'm being a worrisome old woman. Nonetheless, I think I'll have Bart hitch up the buggy. I'm going down there to see about Charles."

"I'll go with you, Mother," Melissa said immediately. "You shouldn't be out this late by yourself."

Jeff felt himself in a quandary. Although the idea of seeing Charles Merrivale again was exceedingly distasteful, he did not like the idea of Hermione and Melissa driving down to the docks, whether they were together or not. That could be a rough area after dark, especially for a couple of women. He wavered for a moment longer, then said, "Neither one of you needs to go down there."

"But, Jeff," Melissa protested, "if Mother's worried—"

"I'll go," he said.

"Oh, no," Hermione said. "I couldn't ask you to do that after everything that's happened."

"I wouldn't be going on account of Charles. I'd be going so that I can ease your mind, Hermione, and yours, too, Melissa. That's well worth the time and trouble." He reached for his saddle. "Won't take me but a few minutes."

"Are you sure about this, Jeff?" Hermione asked.

"I'm sure," he told her as he carried the saddle into his horse's stall.

Melissa followed him into the stall and put a hand on his arm. "Thank you," she said softly. "I'm sure Father is all right, but—"

"But it won't hurt to check," Jeff finished for her.

In fact, Jeff thought that Merrivale's habit of working late was a bit risky. He often had considerable sums of money on him when he left the office, and there were thieves who would cut a man's throat for a few paltry coins. At the very least, by going down there, he could give Merrivale an escort home.

Besides, it would doubtless annoy the man no end to have *Jeff* come to make sure he was all right.

That thought made Jeff grin. He quickly finished saddling the horse and rode out of the stable. Glancing back briefly, he saw the two women standing there in the pool of lantern light looking after him, worry on their faces.

A dull ache throbbed behind Charles Merrivale's eyes, but he forced himself to ignore it and concentrate on the ledger spread open before him. It had been a hellish day. First there had been the fight with Jeff Holt, then the argument with Dermot Hawley. Hawley had stunned him by failing to back up his story to the constable, and when the authorities were gone, Merrivale had angrily demanded to know why Hawley had betrayed him.

Hawley had coolly deflected Merrivale's complaints, saying that he had not wanted to be caught in a lie in case any of the clerks had had the temerity to contradict Merrivale's claims. That explanation had sounded lame to Merrivale, but it had not surprised him. Hawley had become difficult to handle in recent weeks, pushing him more and more to get rid of Jeff so that Melissa would be free to marry again. Deep down, Charles Merrivale suspected that Holt's story about Hawley trying to have him killed during the first trip to Tennessee was true. The man was involved with several shady characters, and the more Merrivale learned about Hawley, the more he was convinced that not only was a business partnership with him ill-advised, but also he was certainly *not* the man for Melissa. If Jeff Holt had not been so damned infuriating, bursting in with his accusations, Merrivale might have told him as much.

Merrivale sighed. It was too late for such things. The rift between him and Jeff could never be repaired. As for his misgivings about Dermot Hawley, they could wait until a later date to be dealt with.

Merrivale pulled out his pocket watch and opened it. It was after eight o'clock. He snapped the watch closed and stood up. After putting away the ledger, he got his hat from the rack beside the door. He was usually home by now, and he hoped that Hermione was not worrying about him. Settling his hat on his head, he turned down the wick on the lamp and walked to the rear door. His carriage was parked just outside.

He took a deep, ragged breath. He wondered if Melissa and Michael were still at home or if Jeff had taken them away as he had threatened. He loved his daughter, despite her headstrong ways, and although he might have gruffly denied it if asked, his grandson meant more to him almost than life itself. The boy was a wonder, smart and courageous and full of exuberance. Being around Michael almost made Charles Merrivale feel young again.

And Jeff wanted to take the lad thousands of miles away into the godforsaken wilderness!

Merrivale shook his head as he stepped out of the building and shut the door behind him, hearing the latch click. He would do everything in his power to prevent Jeff from separating him from his grandson.

He started toward the carriage but had taken only a couple of steps when a tall, well-built figure loomed out of the darkness. Merrivale stopped short, surprised by the man blocking his way.

"I thought I'd find you here," a familiar voice said.

"What the hell are *you* doing here?" Merrivale demanded.

His only answer was a fist that came whipping out of the darkness to crash into his face.

The blow was so forceful that it knocked off Merrivale's hat and drove him several steps backward, and he was so stunned by the attack that he could not even utter a cry. The assailant came after him, hitting him over and over, driving him to his knees. Merrivale gasped for breath and tried to get up, tried to see where his attacker had gone.

The man was behind him, he realized when a hand grabbed his thick white hair. His head was jerked back, causing him to gasp with pain.

Merrivale knew he had to do something, had to fight back somehow, but all his strength seemed to have deserted him. He thought about Hermione and about Melissa, and he thought about Michael. Then something that felt icy and blazing hot at the same time was drawn across his neck, and he knew his throat had just been cut.

The fingers loosed their cruel hold on his hair.

Merrivale felt sudden warmth flood down the front of his body. He tried to talk, to call out Hermione's name, but nothing came out except a strangled croak. The light in the alley, already dim, faded even more. Charles Merrivale's eyes slowly slid shut.

He fell forward in a pool of blood. His fingers moved a couple of times against the dirty surface of the alley, and then he was still.

*　　*　　*

It was after nine o'clock by the time Jeff entered the parlor of the Merrivale house again after putting his horse up. He had sworn that he would not set foot in the house again except to collect his wife and son and be on his way, but he had no other choice.

He paused in the parlor doorway, frowning when he saw Melissa and Hermione stand up anxiously from the divan. They were alone.

"Where is he?" Hermione asked. "Isn't Charles with you?"

"I figured he was already here," Jeff said.

Melissa asked, "You mean he wasn't at the office?"

Jeff shook his head. "When I got there, the place was dark and all locked up. Nobody was there. His carriage was gone. There was no sign of anyone."

Hermione, her voice trembling now, said, "I knew something was wrong, I just knew it!"

"Hold on," Jeff said. "We don't know that anything's happened."

"Then where is he?" Melissa asked, the fear in her voice an echo of Hermione's. "He always comes straight home from the office. He never goes anywhere else."

"Maybe he had trouble with his carriage," Jeff suggested. "A broken axle perhaps."

"Did you see him anywhere along the way, or the carriage?" Hermione asked.

Jeff frowned. "Well, no, but—"

"I think we should send for Constable Tolbert," Melissa said.

Jeff was not fond of the idea of facing the lawman again, but perhaps Melissa had a point. It might be better to get someone who knew how to handle such matters looking for Merrivale.

"I'll fetch him," he said, and turned toward the door.

Heavy pounding sounded on the door, and one of the servants hurried down the hall and opened the door before Jeff got to it. A burly figure brushed past the maid, and Jeff recognized the man. He had last seen him that afternoon in Merrivale's office.

"Constable Tolbert!" Jeff exclaimed. "I was just about to go looking for you."

"I'll just bet you were, Holt," the lawman said, glaring at Jeff.

The sarcastic comment confused Jeff, but Hermione and Melissa emerged from the parlor before he could ask the constable what he meant.

Hermione asked, "What is it, Constable Tolbert? Is there some trouble?"

Tolbert took off his hat. "Yes, Mrs. Merrivale, I'm afraid there is."

Hermione caught her breath, and the color drained from her face. "It's Charles, isn't it?"

"I'm afraid so. A couple of my men found him a few minutes ago. He was . . . well, this is hard to say."

"Tell us, dammit," Jeff grated.

Tolbert glared at him for a second. "He was found floating in the harbor down by the docks. His throat was cut."

Hermione clapped her hands over her mouth, muffling her scream. Her eyes rolled up in their sockets, and her knees buckled.

Jeff acted instinctively, hurrying to Hermione to catch her under the arms and keep her from falling. He heard a metallic click and looked over to see the constable pointing a cocked pistol at him.

"Step away from that poor woman right now, blast you!" Tolbert ordered. "You've already done enough harm to this family, Holt!"

"What are you talking about?" Jeff demanded. He glanced at Melissa. She was as pale as a ghost, horror and grief etched on her face, but at least she did not seem to be on the verge of passing out.

"I'm arresting you for the murder of Charles Merrivale," Tolbert said.

"No!" Melissa cried. "No, Jeff wouldn't do such a thing!"

"A good half dozen people saw Holt fighting with your father this afternoon, ma'am," the constable said, keeping his gun trained on Jeff. "I heard him threaten Mr. Merrivale with my own ears. It makes sense that he's the one who did it."

"That's crazy!" Jeff said. Ignoring the threat of Tolbert's pistol, he helped his half-conscious mother-in-law back to the parlor and onto the divan. Melissa sat beside her mother, clasping one of Hermione's hands with both of hers.

Jeff turned to glare at the constable. "I didn't kill anybody," he snapped.

"Oh? You've been here all evening, have you?"

"No, as a matter of fact, I rode down to Merrivale's office a short while ago to look for him. We were worried about him." Jeff hated having to admit that he had been in the vicinity of the office, but the truth was bound to come out. He certainly could not expect Melissa and Hermione to lie for him. And no Holt would hide behind the skirts of a woman.

"Worried about him, eh?" Tolbert said. "Looks like somebody had reason to worry about him, all right."

"I tell you, I didn't kill him." Jeff could hear the desperation edging into his voice, but he could not help it.

With his free hand the constable gestured toward the knife sheathed at Jeff's hip. "You've been a back-woodsman, from what I hear. You carry that hunting knife just about all the time, don't you?"

Jeff reached for the knife and slid it slowly from the sheath so that Tolbert's finger would not get too jumpy on the trigger. He reversed the blade and held the hilt out toward the constable. "Take a close look at it. You won't find any blood on it."

Tolbert took the knife but barely glanced at it. "That doesn't mean a thing. You could have cleaned the blood off. If you were quick enough, you might not have gotten much on the blade, and if you stood behind Merrivale, you wouldn't have gotten any on your clothing, either."

Jeff swallowed hard and glanced at the front window and at the doorway. He felt as if a war party of Blackfoot or Arikara were closing in around him. The web of evidence against him might not be very strong, but it was still enough to ensnare him.

"I didn't do it," he said again. "I didn't like Merrivale, but I didn't kill him. I wouldn't do that."

"That's for somebody other than me to decide," Tolbert said. "Will you come along peacefully?"

"No!" Melissa sprang up. "You can't take him to jail!"

"Got to, ma'am. He won't hurt anybody else, I can promise you that."

"Let's just get on with it," Jeff said, barely recognizing his own voice.

Tolbert held out his free hand. "Give me that pistol."

"It's not loaded," Jeff told him as he carefully drew out the pistol and handed it to the constable. The lawman tucked it away, then stood back and gestured with the barrel of his own weapon.

"You're being smart, Holt. I've got more men outside, so don't give us any trouble. We'll clap the irons on you, put you in a wagon, and take you down to the jail."

A shudder went through Jeff, but he allowed Tolbert to take him outside. He looked over his shoulder and said firmly to Melissa, "You stay here and take care of Michael and your mother, you hear?"

"But, Jeff—"

"They'll need you, Melissa. Please." He managed a small smile. "Don't worry. This will all get straightened out in no time."

He wished he could believe that.

Melissa hesitated, then nodded, and he knew she

would be all right. There were reserves of strength in her that had never been tapped, Jeff sensed, and she would be needing them in the days to come.

Most of what happened after leaving the house was a blur to him. He vaguely remembered having the irons put on his wrists, and then he was shoved roughly into the back of a wagon and driven several blocks to a large, ugly stone building. The only saving grace to the whole incident was that since it was night, few people were on the streets to gawk at him. He was hustled into the jail and then led down the corridor of a cellblock. The door of a cell was opened, and he was shoved inside.

"You behave yourself, Holt," Constable Tolbert said. "Things will go a lot easier if you do." Then he slammed the iron-barred door.

Jeff felt panic well up at the sound, but he forced himself to calm down. It had been hard enough for him to leave the wide-open spaces of the frontier and head back east to find Melissa. Now he was caught in a trap himself, just like a beaver in a cold mountain stream.

CHAPTER ELEVEN

Something about new country, Clay Holt thought as he reined in the rangy dun, sang to a man's heart. To sit on a good horse at the top of a ridge like the one he had just crested and look out across forty or fifty miles of new territory was a special feeling, a feeling that had first driven him to go west with Lewis and Clark and then to return later.

It would be all right with him if he never went back East again. There was plenty to see out here. He would not mind taking another glance at the Pacific Ocean, and he had heard about some desert lands down south, where the Spaniards lived, that might be worth taking a look at one of these days. Yes, plenty to see.

But a small matter of vengeance had to be taken care of first.

"Think we're in Canada yet?" Aaron asked as he let his chestnut mount move up alongside Clay's horse.

"Have been since yesterday, I reckon," Clay replied.

"Really? You didn't say anything."

"I wanted to be sure first," Clay said. "But we've made good time and come a fair distance north. We're bound to be across the border by now."

Proud Wolf and Butterfly rode up to join them, Proud Wolf on his pinto and Butterfly on the sturdy little bay mare she had ridden from the Indian village. "Those are mighty mountains," Proud Wolf said as he looked at the peaks to the west. "But not as mighty as those of the Sioux."

Clay smiled. Like most youths, it was hard to get Proud Wolf to admit to being impressed by anything.

The ridgeline on which the four riders sat ran north and south and overlooked a narrow valley where a river flowed. On the other side of the river were the mountains, and as Clay looked to the north, he could see where the valley joined the peaks and became a canyon that wound among them.

"There's our road," he said, pointing to the canyon. "And now we'd better get down off this rise. We've been standing out against the sky too long as it is."

They started down the slope into the valley, out of view of any enemies who might spot them. And up there in the north country, Clay mused, there were nothing *but* enemies, as far as they were concerned.

The journey north had gone well, and the foursome had not run into any trouble after their skirmish with the Arikara war party. They had come across other Indians but always managed to see them first and get out of sight. They had encountered no white men at all.

When they reached the river, they paused to refill their waterskins and to let the horses drink. Clay knelt on the bank, scooped up some of the water in his cupped hands, and swallowed it. It was icy cold from the snowmelt. He looked at the trees along the riverbank and saw the tooth marks on their trunks and on the fallen ones hanging half over the river—a sure sign of plenty of beavers. A shadow flitted over the stream, and he looked up to see an eagle winging high overhead. Somewhere off in the distance a bull elk bugled.

Despite what Proud Wolf said, this country was every bit as good as the land on the other side of the border. A man would never go hungry in such a place. What motivated somebody like Fletcher Mc-Kendrick to keep spreading out where he had no right to be, when all this wonderful country was right here?

Clay shook his head and stood up. He would never understand the greed that drove some men, the need to have more and more, whether they could ever make use of it or not. But there was no point in troubling his brain over it. McKendrick just had to be stopped.

They mounted up and rode on, following the river as it curved toward the mountains. The terrain climbed rather steeply where the valley entered the mountains and became a canyon. When they got up a bit higher, Clay knew, they would be in prime beaver country, and any trappers they ran into would likely be working for McKendrick. Or so he hoped, anyway.

Butterfly talked eagerly about everything she saw, and Proud Wolf listened with an expression of pained tolerance. During the first couple of weeks of the journey, he had tried riding so that Clay and Aaron were between him and Butterfly, but she had been so persistent, circling to join him wherever he went, that he had finally given up.

Clay and Aaron both liked Butterfly. She rode from dawn to dusk and never complained, she did

her share of the work, and she could bring down a
rabbit on the run with one of those black arrows from
her bow. She reminded Clay of a younger version of
Shining Moon—at least, the way Shining Moon had
been before her ordeal at the hands of Simon Brown's
Blackfoot henchmen.

Clay hoped his wife was all right. As much as he
would have liked to have her with him, for the time
being she was better off with Bear Tooth and the rest
of her people. Only time would tell whether she
would heal or not; however, that very knowledge was
frustrating for a man like Clay Holt, who was accustomed to facing his enemies and having it out with
them. Whatever was wrong with Shining Moon, it
was an enemy he could not shoot or wrestle or take a
tomahawk to.

For the next three days, Clay and his companions
rode higher into the mountains, following the river
canyon. Sometimes the path was so narrow there was
barely room for their horses to walk alongside the
stream. The heavily forested walls of the canyon rose
nearly straight up, right at the shoulders of the riders.
The nights were still cold, but the days were warm,
and the beavers were busy. Often Clay heard the
crash of a tree from somewhere up or down the canyon and knew that another beaver family would eat
well on the sticky pulp underneath the bark. He saw
dozens of lodges in the stream, the water flowing
white and swift around them. A man with a good set
of traps could take a fortune in pelts out of this country, Clay thought, and once again he wondered why
McKendrick and men like him could not be satisfied
with what they had.

Neither Clay nor Aaron had shaved since leaving
Bear Tooth's village, and their beards were both full
now, which considerably altered their appearances.
Aaron's was a sandy color, several shades lighter than
his brown hair, and Clay's was the same midnight
black as his hair. Despite being only in his late twen-

ties, Clay already had streaks of gray in his beard, and his features had grown craggier from the hardships he had endured over the past couple of years. When he saw himself in the surface of the stream, he realized that he looked considerably older than he really was. But that was all right with him; the changes in his appearance would help keep him from being recognized if they happened to run into anyone who had been down below the border and might have seen him during the run-in with Brown, or Duquesne before him.

Late in the afternoon of the fourth day after entering the mountains, Clay spotted a finger of smoke curling into the sky. It was still several miles ahead, but he pointed it out to his companions, and they all rode more carefully.

"Better hush now, Butterfly," Clay told the chatty young woman. "Voices can carry up and down these canyons, and we don't want anybody listening in on anything they don't need to know. The sound of the horses' hooves on the rocky ground will do enough to announce our presence."

She nodded and fell silent, not bothering to remind him, yet again, that she preferred the name Raven Arrow.

When the smoke was only a quarter mile or so ahead of them, Clay motioned a halt and spoke softly to the others. "All of us need new names, except you, Butterfly, just in case McKendrick's heard of us under our real names. I'll go by Hogan. Aaron, how about Carson? Proud Wolf—"

"In honor of my chief, I will be Bear Claw," Proud Wolf said.

"Sounds fine," Clay said. "I was about to tell you to pick a name for yourself because I hadn't thought of one. Is Carson all right with you, Aaron?"

"One name's as good as any, I suppose. You think McKendrick might know who we are if he heard our real names?"

"It's possible. I think all of Brown's men died in the showdown with him, but some of Duquesne's men could've gotten away and made it back up here. No point in taking a chance. That was one of the reasons I grew this beard."

"I wasn't with you when you took on Duquesne, so no one would know me, anyway," Aaron pointed out. He grinned. "I don't mind the beard, though. It makes me look a mite older, don't you think?"

"That's not always a good thing," Clay said dryly. He looked at the young woman. "Butterfly, you'd best give Proud Wolf your bow and arrows, and that knife and 'hawk you're carrying, too."

"Why?" she asked, looking startled by the request.

"Anybody we run into up here won't understand about your being a warrior," Clay explained. "They'll come closer to believing the story we'll tell them if we say you're some sort of servant."

Butterfly frowned, and Clay knew she did not care for the idea. But then she suggested, "I could pretend to be Proud Wolf's woman."

"No," Proud Wolf said immediately.

"It'll be better if they think you're a slave," Clay said quickly. "Now, give Proud Wolf your weapons."

Grudgingly, Butterfly handed over her bow and arrows, then the knife and tomahawk. Proud Wolf tied the bow to his saddle so that it looked like a spare and stowed the knife and the tomahawk out of sight. Then he slung the quiver of black-dyed arrows over his shoulder. He looked particularly well armed, but Clay hoped the Canadians would not think anything of it.

"Come on, let's go see who's making that smoke," Clay said. "Looks like a campfire."

They rode ahead slowly through the twists and turns of the canyon. Clay had his long rifle balanced on the saddle in front of him, holding it just behind the lock so that he could pull back the cock and prime it in a hurry if need be.

Gradually the canyon widened until it was some two hundred yards across. The river ran down its west side, leaving a large cleared area to the east. Clay abruptly pulled his horse to a stop, motioning for the others to follow suit. He had spotted movement through the trees. Slowly, he walked his mount up to the edge of the woods and looked out across the clearing that was covered with short grass and dotted with occasional bushes.

Near the river a half dozen tents were pitched in a rough circle with a campfire in the middle. What looked like an antelope haunch was spitted over the flames, and Clay could smell the savory scent of cooking meat even from that distance. Several men in buckskin trousers and linsey-woolsey shirts moved around the camp. All of them were bearded; some were bareheaded, while others wore knitted caps. Canoes were pulled up onto the bank of the stream near the tents, and Clay could see a dark, irregular shape in each of them that he knew had to be a stack of pelts. These men were trappers, all right.

Aaron, Proud Wolf, and Butterfly moved up beside Clay. "What do we do now?" Aaron whispered.

"Ride ahead slowly and easily," Clay said. "Keep your hands in sight, and don't make any quick moves. Judging from the number of canoes, I'd guess there are likely to be ten or twelve of them, so they've got us outnumbered. But there won't be any difficulty if we handle this right."

With the heels of his moccasins, he urged the dun into a walk and cautiously emerged from the cover of the trees. The others were behind him, Aaron next in line, followed by Proud Wolf and then Butterfly. Clay was confident that Aaron would not say anything to cause trouble with the Canadian trappers, but he wished he could be as sure about Proud Wolf and Butterfly. Proud Wolf sometimes let his heart do the talking instead of his head, and Butterfly was a far cry from the docile servant she was pretending to be.

They could do nothing except go ahead, however. The trappers had already spotted them, and Clay faintly heard them calling out to one another, warning that strangers were on their way into camp.

Clay kept his horse moving slowly and steadily until he was within fifty feet of the closest tent. More men had come out from the canvas shelters, and he counted them quickly, coming up with a total of ten in the party. He reined in, signaling for the others to do likewise.

"Hello, gents," he said to the trappers in a distinct voice. "We saw your fire back apiece. That's a fine-looking haunch of antelope you've got cooking."

One of the trappers said, "You're welcome to join us. Climb down from your horses."

The words could have been taken as an order or even as a veiled threat. All of the trappers were well armed. However, no hostility was evident in the spokesman's voice. He was soft-spoken, with a trace of an accent, which Clay supposed was British. He certainly was not French.

Clay swung down from his saddle and gave the spokesman a friendly smile. "Name's Ray Hogan," he said, then jerked a thumb at Aaron and added, "This is my partner, Carson. George Carson." He ignored Proud Wolf and Butterfly. White men greeting each other out here would only concern themselves with their own introductions, leaving any mention of Indians until later, if at all.

"I'm Clive Chamberlain," the Englishman said. "Nice to meet you men. Americans, aren't you?"

Clay's smile widened. "That's where we hail from, all right. But we're in no hurry to get back there, are we, Carson?"

"Nope," Aaron said.

"The climate got a bit warm for us," Clay explained, hoping that he was not overplaying his role.

But he wanted the Canadians to think that he and his companions were at least a little on the wrong side of the law.

"Well, it should be cool enough up here for just about anyone," Chamberlain said with an answering smile. He waved toward the campfire. "Sit down. We've some tea brewing." As the other men relaxed and went back to what they had been doing, Chamberlain added almost as an afterthought, "You have some Indians traveling with you."

"The boy's been scouting for us. Calls himself Bear Claw."

Chamberlain looked closer at the two Hunkpapa Sioux and exclaimed, "I say! One of them is a girl."

"Yep, her name's Butterfly. We traded with some Crow for her on the way up here. She's Sioux, like the boy, and I think he took a fancy to her."

Proud Wolf kept his face neutral, but Clay knew that he would have something to say later about that remark.

Chamberlain grunted in acceptance of the story, and when the visitors were seated by the fire, he poured tea for Clay and Aaron. Clay had never been overly fond of tea, but evidently the trappers did not have coffee. He sipped the strong, bitter brew and indicated his appreciation.

"You have the look of frontiersmen," Chamberlain said after a moment. "Done much trapping?"

"You might say we've been up the creek and over the mountain a few times," Clay replied dryly. "Trapped the Yellowstone and the Big Horn, seen the Great Falls, and been up the Marias. We've been all over that country down yonder, so we thought we'd come up here for a while and see what it looks like. So far we like what we see."

"Thinking about staying, are you?"

Clay shrugged. "Could. Nothing to hold us down there." He decided it was time for him to ask some of the questions. "Are you gents free trappers, or do you work for one of those big fur companies?"

One of the other men had squatted on his haunches nearby to pour himself a cup of tea, and he laughed and said, "We ain't bloody Nor' Westers, if that's what you mean."

Clay recognized the reference to the North West Company and cast his mind back over what he had learned about the Canadian trapping operations from talking to Manuel Lisa and other fur traders back in St. Louis.

"You're a bit far south for Hudson's Bay men."

If Clive Chamberlain sensed that Clay was probing, he gave no sign of it. "We work for the London and Northwestern Enterprise, trapping out of Fort Dunadeen, about forty miles back up this stream. Heard of it?"

The London and Northwestern Enterprise was Fletcher McKendrick's operation. Luck had brought Clay and his companions to the very spot they needed. Clay kept his elation hidden, but it took all the self-control he possessed.

"Nope, I don't know it," he said, his voice casual.

"It's a good outfit," Chamberlain went on. "The pay's fair, and a man can make a good living trapping for them."

"Aye," one of the other men said, "if ye dinna cross McKendrick. Lord help ye if ye do, the way he's been acting the past year or so."

"That'll be enough of that, Alec," Chamberlain said sharply. "Mr. McKendrick's got his own problems, just as we all do." The man looked at Clay and the others again. "McKendrick runs the enterprise. He's a hard man, as Alec here implied, but he'll not do wrong by anyone who hasn't done wrong by him."

Clay knew that was not true; McKendrick had harmed countless people through sheer greed in trying to expand into American territory. Carefully, he asked, "Do you suppose this McKendrick fellow could use more trappers?"

"Come with us and ask him yourself," Chamberlain invited. "We've all the pelts we can carry on this trip, so we're heading back to the fort in the morning. You're welcome to travel along with us. Your horses ought to be able to keep pace with our canoes."

"We might just do that," Clay said noncommittally, not wanting to appear too eager.

"Suit yourselves. The offer stands open."

Clay gave his thanks.

A few minutes later the antelope haunch was ready, and the men used their hunting knives to hack off pieces of it. Chamberlain invited the visitors—the two Indians, as well—to join them, and they did so eagerly, enjoying the meat with its strong, smoky flavor.

While they were eating, Aaron asked Chamberlain, "Have much trouble with Indians around here?"

The Englishman shook his head. "Mostly Blackfoot in these parts, and they get along with us. McKendrick is always generous in his trading with them at the fort, so they don't want to drive us out. Most of their hostility is reserved for you Americans across the border."

"I've heard plenty about Blackfoot raids down there," Clay said.

"Have you ever had any trouble with them yourself?" Chamberlain asked.

"Nope. We've gone our own way. Bear Claw there is a Sioux, so of course he just naturally doesn't care much for Blackfoot."

"Ancient and ancestral enemies," Chamberlain said with a nod and a smile for Proud Wolf. "How well I understand, young man."

Stern faced, Proud Wolf said, "Bear Claw hates Blackfoot."

"But you can put up with them if we go to this

fort Chamberlain told us about," Clay said sharply. "Can't you?"

Proud Wolf hesitated, then gave a reluctant nod.

Clay gave Butterfly a sidelong glance. She had been silent since they joined the group of Canadian trappers, and he could tell that her discretion was not coming naturally. But so far she had been fine, and he hoped that would continue.

He went on quickly, "Me, I'd just as soon get along with redskins, no matter what tribe they are. I came out here for hides, not to fight."

"There are certainly plenty of hides to be had," Chamberlain commented. "This land is teeming with beaver. Although I've heard that the country south of here is even better."

That was not necessarily true, Clay thought, but he said, "There's plenty of beaver down there, you're right. But that doesn't do you much good when you've got people on your trail. Now, this Canada— why, a man could get lost in it."

"Many men have done exactly that, my friend," Chamberlain said in a quiet voice, and Clay wondered if the Englishman was one of them. Who knew what secrets lay in the man's past? Out here, folks never asked too many questions about a person's background.

Darkness had fallen, and it was taken for granted that the visitors would spend the night at the trappers' camp. After everyone had eaten, the men brought out a jug of rum, and Clay and Aaron shared a drink with them. The jug was not offered to Proud Wolf, and Clay would not have let the young man accept if it had been. It was all right in the view of the Canadians to trade rum for hides when Indians brought pelts to their fort, but they were not eager to share their *own* jug with a "redskin."

The travelers spread their robes a bit away from the tents, and Clay told Butterfly in a low voice to put hers next to his. She was an attractive young woman, and he did not want any of the trappers getting ideas about her during the night.

As they settled down for the night, Butterfly whispered, "I still think it would have been better for me to be Proud Wolf's woman."

Clay just grinned and rolled over to go to sleep. Whether Butterfly thought so or not, so far everything was going just fine.

The next morning the Canadian trappers set out early, pushing off their canoes and paddling upstream when the sun was still below the tops of the pine trees. Setting off with them, the travelers rode alongside the stream, keeping the trappers in sight. Both groups stopped to take their midday meal together, and Chamberlain informed Clay that the canyon narrowed and became impassable for horses a few miles farther on.

"You'll have to cross the river and climb a trail on the west side to a pass," Chamberlain said, sketching the route in the sandy riverbank. "And I'd suggest crossing at this point because the river deepens considerably in the narrows. The trail will swing east again on the other side of the pass and rejoin the river. We'll be camping for the night at a spot about ten miles beyond that."

"We'll find you," Clay said.

After everyone had eaten, the riders crossed the river, which was about four feet deep and some twenty feet wide at that point. Clay had no trouble spotting the path they were supposed to use, and with good-byes on both sides, the two groups parted company.

Now that they were alone again, they could let their guard down, and Aaron said, "What do you think, Clay? Did they believe what you told them yesterday?"

"They seemed to. But I reckon we'll know before the day's over."

"How's that?"

Clay turned in the saddle to look at the other three. "If they didn't believe our story, then likely they've sent us off into a trap. If we don't run into any trouble before we meet up with them again this evening, we can figure they've accepted us."

"What will we do when we reach this Fort Dunadeen?" Proud Wolf asked.

"Join up with McKendrick, if he'll have us. We'll have to bide our time. We can't just go in there shooting, or we'll all wind up dead. But when the right moment comes, that's when we'll hit him—hard."

The trail wound higher into the mountains. They followed it to the pass Chamberlain had mentioned, the air growing thinner as they climbed. From the top of the pass, they could see a magnificent sweep of territory, the mountains, valleys, and canyons laid out before them like a gigantic canvas on which a master painter had poured out all of his talent and soul. Clay was awestruck by the sight.

Almost reluctantly, they pushed on. A couple of miles to the east Clay could make out the canyon where the river ran, and the trail wended gradually in that direction. The sun started setting before they reached the canyon again, and Clay hoped they could catch up with the trappers before nightfall. He urged the dun into a faster gait, and the others followed suit.

Out 'of the blue Proud Wolf said, "Butterfly should spread her robes beside mine tonight."

Clay glanced at him in surprise. Aaron and Butterfly were looking at the young warrior, too.

"What makes you say that?" Clay asked.

"I have been thinking. She is supposed to be our slave, and she should not give all of her attention to only one of us. Besides, you yourself told those trappers that I had taken a fancy to her.'"

Clay turned away to hide his grin. Proud Wolf was jealous, he realized, even though there was absolutely no reason to be. Proud Wolf had to know that, too; after all, Clay was married to his sister. But still, he had a point.

Turning back, Clay said, "That's good thinking. Butterfly, spread your robes with Proud Wolf's tonight."

"I will do as you say," Butterfly replied demurely, but Clay could tell she was quite pleased with the idea.

Chuckling, Clay hoped that Proud Wolf's suggestion would not land him in more trouble than he could handle.

The sun had set, and dusk was settling rapidly when Clay spotted the campfire built beside the river by the trappers. He and his companions pushed on into the growing darkness until they were near enough for him to call out, "Ho, Chamberlain! It's Hogan!"

"Come ahead!" the Englishman called back.

The travelers rode up to the fire, and Clay swung down from his mount, saying, "Figured I'd better warn you. I didn't want you taking shots at a bunch of strangers riding in on you out of the dark."

"That's true enough," Chamberlain agreed. "You can't be too careful in this country. It's still wild, after all."

Proud Wolf had brought down a deer with a well-placed arrow a few hours earlier, and it was draped across the rump of his pinto. Clay slapped the carcass and said, "We brought some supper, since you fellows shared with us last night."

"That's excellent," Chamberlain said, "since we're out of fresh meat ourselves. Enough for all, eh?"

"More than enough," Clay said heartily.

After cooking deer steaks over the flames, they ate, then turned in for the night. Butterfly spread her robes next to Proud Wolf's, as they had agreed, and Clay thought the young woman was lying closer to Proud Wolf than she had to him the previous night.

Only a narrow strip of sky was visible at the top of the narrow canyon, but that band of black was studded with countless brilliant stars. As Clay looked up at them he figured that they had covered over twenty miles that day. Chamberlain had said that Fort Dunadeen was forty miles upriver. That meant with a good day of traveling tomorrow, they would reach the fort.

And for the first time, Clay would lay eyes on the man he probably hated more than anyone else on earth.

The now-shallow river widened as they rode alongside it the next day, and so did the valley through which it ran. The travelers made good time, just as Clay had hoped they would. He and his companions were able to keep the canoes of the trappers in sight almost continuously.

At midday they paused briefly to eat, then were soon on their way again. The trappers had been out for two weeks, working the river and the creeks that fed into it, spending long days in the icy water setting and checking their trap lines, and they were more than ready to get back to the fort and enjoy a short rest before starting out again. Clay and his friends shared that eagerness to reach the fort, but for a vastly different reason.

Late in the afternoon, as the valley broadened even more and the mountains on both sides fell back into ranges of lower hills, Fort Dunadeen came into view. Although still about a half mile away, Clay could see the fort clearly. It was a rambling compound of log buildings surrounded by a high stockade fence with a double gate in its front wall and a smaller gate in the rear. Watchtowers rose at each corner of the stockade. The gates were open at the moment, and just beyond the fort, several men were cultivating fields, apparently getting the ground ready for planting. The inhabitants of the fort no doubt prided themselves on their self-sufficiency, just as most American trappers did. Smoke rose from inside the fort, probably from a cookshack.

The canoes had drawn slightly ahead of them, so the trappers would reach the fort first. Chamberlain would, of course, immediately tell McKendrick about the Americans they had encountered, but that was to be expected. All the travelers could do was ride in and hope they would not find themselves facing flintlock muzzles.

The trappers reached a stretch of river where the bank fell away to a sandy slope, and Clay watched them ground the canoes there, pulling them well up on the grassy shore. Men from the fort, spotting them coming, were there to meet them with whoops of welcome and slaps on the back. Then they escorted them into the fort.

"Keep riding," Clay said to his companions. "We'll know soon what's going to happen."

As they drew nearer, he noticed men in each of the watchtowers. Even though this was Blackfoot country and McKendrick's men were friendly with the Blackfoot, only a fool would fail to take precautions so far from civilization. And Fletcher McKendrick, for all of his other failings, was no fool. Clay was sure of that.

Under the watchful eyes of the sentries, the foursome rode up to the fort. Clay drew rein in front of the open gates and waited. Fort Dunadeen was laid out much like Fort Tarrant, Simon Brown's headquarters, he noted. Along the rear wall of the fort was a long bunkhouse that ended in a makeshift tavern. To one side were several sturdy-looking, windowless buildings that no doubt served as warehouses. Tons of collected pelts could be stored there until keelboats came downriver to pick them up and start them on their long journey to Montreal, the center of the Canadian fur-trading industry. In the middle of the stockade was a large building that surely housed the offices of McKendrick and his clerks as well as quarters for them. On the other side of the fort were small storehouses for supplies such as traps and food, and tucked away in one corner was an even smaller building that was probably the powder magazine, Clay judged. He took special note of it, then turned his attention to the building in the center of the fort.

A group of men stood on the covered porch that ran along its front. One of them was the lean, bearded Chamberlain. Some of the trappers from his group were with him, while the others had already headed for the bunkhouse and the tavern. A couple of men who looked like clerks were nodding and taking notes as Chamberlain talked to them, probably relating the success he and his men had had on their trip. Off to one side stood a man in a long coat, his arms crossed; he was listening intently to Chamberlain's report. Clay focused on him, taking in the big hands, the ruddy face, the thatch of curly, graying red hair. Without having to be told, he knew who the man was.

Fletcher McKendrick.

McKendrick looked toward the riders waiting at the gate and lifted a hand, stopping Chamberlain in midsentence. He gestured toward the visitors and said something, and Chamberlain nodded. McKendrick stepped down from the porch and started toward the gate, Chamberlain following along beside him. Chamberlain motioned for Clay and the others to come in.

"This is Mr. Hogan and Mr. Carson from America," Chamberlain said when the visitors approached. He introduced them to Fletcher McKendrick.

McKendrick folded his arms across his chest. "Aye." He looked up at Clay as the big frontiersman halted his horse. "Chamberlain tells me ye might be interested in doing some trapping for the London and Northwestern Enterprise. I'll be glad to talk to ye about it. There's rum in the office if you'd care to have a drink while we're talking."

Clay dismounted and faced McKendrick. It was hard for him to believe that after all the weeks, all the miles, he now stood a couple of feet away from his quarry.

Forcing a smile, he said, "Sounds like a good idea."

McKendrick stuck out his hand. It was large, freckled, and blunt-fingered, with hair on the knobby knuckles. "I'm Fletcher McKendrick. Pleased to meet ye, Mr. Hogan."

Without hesitation, Clay stepped forward to shake the hand of the man he had come to kill.

CHAPTER TWELVE

There was no doubt about it now. Shining Moon had been sure from the very morning that Clay had ridden north to Canada; now, after two months, it was a certainty.

She was with child.

Her pregnancy was not the only development along the Big Horn River. Father Thomas Brennan's church had gone up rapidly with the assistance of the young men from the Hunkpapa Sioux village, including Proud Wolf's friends Walks-Down-the-Wind and Cloud-That-Falls. Although the Hunkpapa did not share the white man's religion, Bear Tooth had grown to like Father Brennan and encouraged his people to help the priest whenever possible. For his part, the priest repaid the villagers with his medical knowledge. It took some convincing by him and Shining Moon, but most of the Hunkpapa finally agreed to be inoculated against smallpox. Shining Moon set the example, allowing the priest to make the small cut on her arm through which the cowpox vaccine was introduced to the body.

His medical training was quite limited, although Father Brennan was able to help treat the minor illnesses and injuries that were common among the villagers. Their shaman was none too happy about that at first, but as Father Brennan questioned him about the various herbal remedies and ancient healing rituals, he gradually lost his hostility toward the priest. Father Brennan doubted that he would actually convert many of the Hunkpapa to Christianity, but at least he had become a friend to them and helped them, and the way he saw it, that was doing God's work as well.

If the Indians were not totally receptive to his message, some of the trappers who passed through the area were. More and more white men were coming to the mountains, some free trappers, others agents of the big fur trading companies in St. Louis. When the priest held services and said mass in the small log chapel on the banks of the river, usually a half dozen or more buckskin-clad men were in attendance. Despite the rugged terrain and vast distances involved on the frontier, word of such things spread through the high country with surprising speed.

On a Sunday morning in late spring, Shining Moon walked from the village toward the church. She heard singing coming from within the sanctuary, and although to ears accustomed to the songs of the Hunkpapa the white man's hymns sounded shrill and monotonous, she had to admit that the trappers attending the service sang them lustily. Just as they did everything else, she thought wryly. It was common among the white men to spend six days drinking and fighting, then stumble into the church on the seventh day to beg forgiveness for their sins—before going out and starting the cycle all over again.

Shining Moon slipped inside the door at the rear of the church and watched with interest as Father

Brennan conducted the service. She had no intention of leaving her religion for his; the Great Spirit, Wakan Tanka, guided and protected her. Even after she had been raped and brutalized by the Blackfoot, she did not question why it had happened, assuming that one day, either in this life or the next, she would understand. But she enjoyed listening to the priest chanting the odd-sounding words—the liturgy in Latin, he had explained. He wore a long black robe now most of the time and looked more like the missionaries who had come to the land of the Sioux in the past, but there was a strength and vigor about him that said he could have outdone any of the trappers if he had chosen to follow that path.

As she sat on a rough-hewn bench at the back of the room, Shining Moon's thoughts drifted northward toward Canada. She wondered where Clay was, what he was doing, whether he was all right. She thought about her brother, Proud Wolf, and her parents, dead since she and Proud Wolf were children. Her hands went to her stomach, which had not yet begun to swell to announce that she was with child.

It was good that the family was growing, she thought. The child within her was a part of Clay, and so she would have him with her as long as she had the child. In time the baby would grow, would become a young man or a young woman, and would move on. But wherever that child went, Clay Holt and Shining Moon would go with it, and that thought brought a smile to her face. She moved her hands down, smoothing them over the fabric of the dress Clay had brought her from St. Louis.

Perhaps one day she and Clay and the child would go to this place called St. Louis. It had to be a huge and wondrous city, bigger than any of the Sioux villages she had seen. She had heard Clay and Aaron speak of it, and she felt a growing curiosity. She wanted to see its wonders for herself. She was sure Proud Wolf would want to go, too.

The nightmares no longer plagued her, and she seldom thought of the torment she had endured as a captive at the hands of the Blackfoot. She had put that behind her at last, but it left her a changed person. Never again would she be the simple Hunkpapa woman whom Clay Holt had married.

The dress she wore was proof enough of that. She had grown to like it and preferred to wear it instead of her buckskins. Even without her vow to wear the dress until Clay returned, she would have preferred it. She sometimes wore her long dark hair loose now, instead of braided in the manner of Hunkpapa women. She was not white—she would never be white, of course—but she had decided that the ways of the white women were not all bad.

Actually, she had never even seen a white woman except Lucy Franklin, so she did not know much about them. . . .

"I hate to disturb you, Shining Moon—"

Her head lifted as the gentle voice spoke to her.

"—but the service is over," Father Brennan went on. "You look like your mind strayed a bit during my sermon." His tone was rueful. "I suppose I'll have to try harder."

"No, it was fine, Father," she said quickly. The priest was her friend, and she did not want to hurt his feelings. "But there is much on my mind these days."

She was about to tell him of her pregnancy, as she had almost told him several times. But now, as before, she stopped herself. Being with child was a private matter, and she could not bring herself to tell Father Brennan when Clay himself did not yet know. Of course, as her condition became more apparent, the priest would become aware of it, but for the time being she wanted to keep that secret for herself.

As she stood up she looked around and saw that the church was empty except for the priest and her. She hadn't even noticed when the trappers had left. They would go back to their trap lines now. Some would return for the next service and some would not, but there would be others, newcomers to the territory, who would take the places of those who did not come back.

Shining Moon and Father Brennan left the church, and she enjoyed the warmth of the sun on her face as they emerged. However, no sooner had they stepped outside than something in the river caught her eye. A keelboat was coming. It was piled high with goods, more supplies than Shining Moon had ever seen in one place before. A squat, black-bearded man wearing a broad-brimmed hat that shaded his face stood beside the captain of the boat. The man pointed toward the shore, and the captain swung the rudder, skillfully grounding the vessel against the low riverbank moments later.

The bearded man jumped nimbly ashore, then strode toward Shining Moon and the priest. "Greetings," he called out in a booming voice. "A man of God, I see. Glad to meet you, Father." He stuck out his hand as he approached. "Malachi Fisher's my name, and that's my store back there on yonder boat."

Father Brennan shook hands with the newcomer, then said curiously, "What do you mean, that's your store, Mr. Fisher?"

"Just what I said, Father." Fisher put his hands on his hips and looked around. "I loaded up everything in my trading post back in Pennsylvania and brought it out here to the wilderness to start anew. Civilization and mercantilism go hand in hand, you know. There be many trappers hereabouts?"

"Quite a few," the priest replied with a nod.

"Well, I can outfit 'em without 'em having to go all the way back to St. Louis." Fisher gestured at the clearing beside the church. "Fisher's Trading Post, that's what I see right there. Best trading post 'tween the Shining Mountains and the upper Missouri. *Only* trading post, I figure."

"I'd say you're right," Father Brennan said, grinning.

"You've got no objection to me moving in next to your church, do you, Father?"

"No objection. If anything, you'll draw more trappers as well as more of the natives." An enthusiastic light shone in the priest's eyes at the thought of his newfound flock growing.

Shining Moon was following the conversation, even though Malachi Fisher had directed none of it at her. Now he turned to her, lifted his hat momentarily, disclosing a bald pate, and said, "Good day to you, missy. Got something for you." He reached into his pocket and took out a small hand mirror. He caught her wrist and pressed it into her palm. "There you go. Hope you enjoy it."

"Thank you," Shining Moon said softly. She had seen enough mirrors carried by various traders not to be frightened of them, even though some of her people still harbored the suspicion that the reflecting glass stole the soul of whoever peered into it.

Fisher began walking around, taking deep breaths and waving his arms about. Finally he stopped and said, "Ah, that mountain air! Bracing, it is." He turned toward the boat and called, "You can start unloading, Captain. This is where I'm going to stay."

"We'll be glad to have you, Mr. Fisher," Father Brennan told him as the keelboatmen began carrying crates of goods off the vessel and stacking them on the bank. The Hunkpapa had turned out to watch the arrival of the boat, of course, and now they looked on with great curiosity as the unloading proceeded.

Fisher turned back and asked the priest, "What's the name of this settlement of yours, Father?"

"Well, I never really—" Father Brennan stopped short, looked thoughtful for a moment, then said in a firm voice, "New Hope. The settlement is called New Hope."

"Fisher's Trading Post, New Hope, Louisiana Territory," Fisher mused. "I like it!"

So did Shining Moon. She put her hands on her stomach and repeated the words to herself.

New Hope.

Josie Garwood leaned back in the canoe and held Matthew tighter against her. The canoe plunged ahead through the boiling rapids, seeming as if it were about to leap out of the water. Josie held back her urge to scream. After everything she had been through over the past few years, it seemed ridiculous to panic over a little white water.

But she was frightened, as frightened as she had been back in St. Louis when she had thought that Gort Chambers might beat her to death.

The canoes carrying Josie, Matthew, and the trappers led by Oren Bradley had encountered rapids before on the journey, but none this rough. During the long weeks since they had left St. Louis, they had paddled up the Missouri to the point where the great river of the north joined the Yellowstone, then followed the Yellowstone to its junction with the Big Horn, where the fort built by Manuel Lisa stood. Men at the fort had told the travelers about how good the trapping was along the Big Horn and in the Absarokas to the west. Oren had decided to push on farther, and the group had left the fort and headed southwest along the Big Horn. When they had trapped all the beaver they could carry, they would return to the fort, Oren decided, and sell the pelts to Lisa's men.

Josie had thought about staying at the fort. It had grown into something of a settlement, with quite a few outbuildings around the original stockade. There were even a few women there, most of them whores like herself who had somehow wound up out on the frontier. They probably all had pitiful stories, she had thought, same as she.

But when she had broached the idea to Oren while they were still camped alongside the fort, he had turned ugly. "We brought you and the boy this far," he had said. "You can stay with us awhile longer."

He had been drinking, and Josie did not want to cross him. He had taken to slapping her now and then, but only when he was drunk. And she could understand why he did not want her to leave: She handled most of the cooking for the group, and if anybody got hurt, she could patch up most injuries. Nary a night went by when at least one of the men, and usually more than one, did not share her blankets. She was pretty handy to have along, she thought.

But enough was enough. She had gone out west to start a new life with Matthew, not to be a camp follower to a bunch of greasy trappers.

There would be another settlement farther along the river, she had told herself when they left Lisa's fort. Somewhere . . .

That had been a few days before. Then they had run into these rapids, and for an hour now the canoes had been bucking and lurching, carried along by the fast-flowing stream. The current was so swift that the men were exhausted from paddling into it. And it seemed that for every six inches of progress they made, the river threw them back a foot.

Spray splashed over the sides of the canoe, drenching the occupants. Josie and Matthew huddled against the stack of supplies in the center of the canoe. Oren was up front, and one of the other trappers sat in the back. Finally Oren lifted his paddle from the racing water.

"Head for shore, dammit!" he shouted to the other trappers. "Let the current carry you. We'll never get anywhere this way."

He was right. Even a pilgrim like Josie could see that trying to make headway against the rapids was a hopeless task. But Oren was a stubborn man. They had paddled their way through the other rapids they encountered, and he had thought they could do it again.

When the canoes were on the shore, Oren confronted the men, all of them soaked through to the skin and looking like half-drowned rats. "We'll have to portage," he said bitterly. "Start gettin' the gear out of the canoes. Josie, you and the boy'll have to help."

Josie nodded. She and Matthew would carry as much as they could. She just hoped the rapids were not too long. Toting the canoes and their contents overland was not going to be an easy task.

The trappers got the canoes unloaded, and the cargo was divided up among the men, who slung the packs on their backs. Josie took two of the packs herself, Matthew one. Then the canoes were picked up, one man at each end, and the portage got under way. At least the terrain was fairly flat, Josie thought, and made for easy walking.

The rapids were a good three miles long, and the sun had almost set by the time the group reached the end of the white water. Oren ordered them to make camp. Gratefully Josie lowered her packs to the ground and then helped Matthew with his. He was pale and exhausted, but he had not once complained. That was typical of him. He had little to say of late.

But he watched everything that went on, and she suspected that he even watched as the trappers took her at night. Remembering what had happened in St. Louis, she sometimes wondered what went on behind those cold, dark eyes of his.

But most of the time she did not really want to know.

For one of the few times during the journey, none of the men came to her blankets that night. They were all too tired from the portage. The extra rest was more than welcome to Josie, and she slept well.

In the morning they moved on. Once past the

rapids, the Big Horn was broad and placid, and the day's travel went much more smoothly.

It was midafternoon when one of the men in the lead canoe turned and called back to the others, "There's something up ahead!"

Josie and Matthew were in the second canoe. Fearing that the man had spotted some more white water, she leaned to the side and peered forward. Her eyes widened in surprise when she saw the buildings on the shore about a quarter mile ahead.

The most prominent one was a large log structure on a point of land formed by a long curve of the river. Something was on top of it, something that Josie realized with a shock was a cross. The building was a church.

Not far away from the church was a sprawling log building, with a wide porch along its front. A sign of some sort was attached to the roof over the porch, and as the canoes drew closer Josie was able to make out the crooked letters daubed in red paint on a raw plank: Fisher's Trading Post.

Set farther away from the riverbank and scattered around the clearing that ran some five hundred yards back to a stretch of woods were a half dozen or more canvas shelters and cabins in various stages of construction. Washing was hung out to dry in front of some of them. Josie felt a surge of relief go through her. She had hoped that they would find another settlement somewhere up the river, and sure enough, they had.

At that moment she stiffened with resolve. She was leaving Oren and the other trappers. It was surely the last settlement, the last chance she would have. That tiny outpost of civilization, surrounded by hundreds of miles of untamed wilderness, would be her home, hers and Matthew's.

She wondered if it had a name.

"Put in to shore!" Oren boomed the order to the other canoes. "We'll pay these folks a visit."

Josie knew what he was thinking. They were running low on rum, and the trading post might have some.

As the canoes slid in to shore the trappers jumped out and pulled them up on the bank. Josie and Matthew stepped out of the one in which they were riding. She glanced at the porch and saw a short, thick-bodied man with a dark beard emerge from the store and stand on the porch with his hands on his hips. His head was bald except for a fringe of hair around his ears. He lifted a hand and waved in greeting to the visitors.

At the same time a priest in a black robe came out of the church and started toward them, trailed by a dark-haired white woman. No, Josie realized as she looked closer, the woman was wearing a white woman's dress, but she was an Indian. There was no mistaking the coppery skin and the angles of the face.

The priest had a long, energetic stride, and his thick, red hair was ruffled by the wind. He was smiling broadly as he came up to the trappers. "Welcome to New Hope. I'm Father Thomas Brennan."

"New Hope, eh?" grunted Oren. "That the name of this place?"

"That's right."

"Didn't know there was a settlement out here."

"It hasn't been here long. I established the church a couple of months ago, and Mr. Fisher began his trading post only a few weeks ago." He grinned. "The building was erected with remarkable speed, thanks to the efforts of a great many people. And once word spread that a church and a store were here, other people began arriving almost daily."

Oren looked around and rubbed the back of his hand across his mouth. "Looks like a fine place," he said, but Josie could hear the insincerity in his voice. He did not care anything about this settlement except for what it could provide him: rum and supplies and a possible market for the furs he and his men could bring in. The man at the trading post would probably pay less for the furs than Lisa's agents up at the fort, but on the other hand, if they sold their pelts here, they would not have to carry them all the way back up the Big Horn. Josie could almost hear those thoughts going through Oren's head as he went on, "Good trappin' around here?"

"Very good," Father Brennan replied. "Some of the men who've come here have said they want to make this their home. They can trap in the mountains and leave their families here."

"What about Injuns?" Oren glanced pointedly at the Indian woman wearing the yellow-flowered dress.

"The Hunkpapa who live a short distance away along the river are quite friendly," the priest said. "And the rest of the Sioux tend to leave us alone. However, we do have to be on the lookout for raids by the Blackfoot and the Crow. So far, though, they haven't bothered us."

"Glad to hear that," Oren said. "Reckon we'll prevail on your hospitality for tonight and stock up on a few things, since there's a tradin' post here. Didn't expect to find no store like this."

"You're welcome to stay as long as you wish. The community can always use new citizens."

The place must have been pretty desperate if it welcomed trappers and whores, Josie thought. She saw the Indian woman looking curiously at her, and the priest had sent a few glances her and Matthew's way, too. She smiled at the Indian woman; it would not hurt to make a few friends among the savages, she supposed. But her warmest smile was reserved for the priest. If she was to be successful in her attempt to leave Oren's group, she would need influential friends.

And priest or no priest, she had never met a man yet who did not react at least a little to her smile.

Father Brennan turned to her and said, "Hello. Welcome to New Hope."

"Thank you, Father. Matthew and I are glad to be here."

"Your son?" He looked down at the boy but got no reaction from Matthew, whose face might have been carved in stone for all the emotion it revealed.

Josie rested her hands on Matthew's shoulders. "Yes, Matthew is my son. My name is Josie."

"I'm very glad to meet you." The priest looked over at Oren and commented, "That was quite courageous of you, bringing your wife and child out here like this."

Oren burst out laughing. "She ain't my wife, and that sure ain't my whelp, Father." He shook his head. "Nope, they're just travelin' with us, I guess you could say."

"I see."

There was a faint look of disapproval in the priest's eyes as he glanced again at Josie and Matthew. He had to know now what she was, and she could not expect him to like it. She could have killed Oren for opening his big mouth. Of course, for the priest to help her leave the group of trappers, he would have had to know the truth sooner or later, but it would have been nice to have a man like that respect her, even if only for a little while.

Father Brennan moved along to introduce himself to the other men, and the Indian woman came over to Josie and Matthew. "I am called Shining Moon," she said.

"Glad to meet you," Josie replied, running her fingers through her tangled black hair. A part of her hated for another woman to see her looking as dirty and bedraggled as she was, especially when that woman was as pretty as Shining Moon. She went on, "I'm Josie, and this is my boy Matthew."

"I am pleased to meet you."

She spoke English awfully well for an Indian, Josie thought. She had probably known quite a few trappers as well as the priest. The way Josie had heard

it, many of the trappers in the Rockies wintered with
Indian tribes, taking a squaw for a wife during the
cold months, then leaving her behind. Shining Moon
could well have had two or three white "husbands."

"Are you and your son going to stay here while
your man goes to the mountains?" Shining Moon
asked.

Josie felt her pulse speed up. She had been wondering how to introduce the subject, and now Shining
Moon's curiosity had given her the perfect opening.
"I'd like to stay," Josie quickly said, making sure her
voice was loud enough for Oren to hear.

He heard, all right. He turned toward her and
growled, "You're travelin' on with us. We'll stay here
tonight, but then we're movin' on."

The owner of the trading post had sauntered
over, his hands in the pockets of his apron, and several other men—trappers, by the looks of them, who
had probably come out of the mountains for a short
break—had wandered up to greet the visitors as well.
With the same instinct for survival that had carried
her thus far, Josie sensed that the time and place were
right for her to make her move.

"Matthew and I are staying," she said defiantly
to Oren. "I never said I'd go all the way into the
mountains with you."

"Hell you didn't," he snapped, drawing a frown
from Father Brennan.

"You're not my husband. You can't force me to
go with you." Josie struggled to keep her voice calm
and level. Losing her temper now might backfire on
her. She looked at the priest and Shining Moon, letting them see the desperation in her eyes. "I came out
here to *find* my husband."

The lie had sprung into her mind with no advance warning, but once it was out of her mouth, she
knew she had to keep going. From the sympathetic
expressions appearing on the faces of the settlers of
New Hope, she had chosen the right tack. She contin-

ued hurriedly, "He's a trapper, and the last letter I had from him said he was coming to this area. He was supposed to send for us, but we never heard from him again. I-I have to find him."

There never was a whore who was not a born actress, Josie thought as she saw the way they were all swallowing the story. Even Oren frowned in confusion. "You never told me any of that," he said.

She looked down as if contrite. "I was afraid you wouldn't help me come out here."

"Then that story you told me back in St. Louis . . ." Oren's frown deepened, and Josie held her breath, praying that he would not say anything about Matthew killing Gort Chambers. "That wasn't true?"

She shook her head. "I had to appeal to your sympathy, Oren. I was just so worried about my husband."

He knew, of course, that she had been working as a prostitute at the tavern owned by Chambers, but that did not mean the story she was telling now was false. Plenty of so-called soiled doves had had husbands at one time or another. A woman on her own, especially one with a child, did what she had to do to survive. Even a man as thick-skinned as Oren Bradley could understand that, Josie hoped.

"You can't hold this woman against her will," Father Brennan said into the silence.

Murmurs of agreement came from the storekeeper and some of the other men standing around watching the confrontation. Shining Moon was looking at Oren, and anger glittered in her eyes.

"You should've told me, Josie," Oren finally muttered. "I didn't know nothin' about this husband of yours. But I reckon it wouldn't be right for us to make you go on with us."

Josie fought the impulse to heave a great sigh of relief. Clearly Oren did not like the idea of her leaving his group, but he was not willing to go against the priest and the other settlers. For that matter, he would not want Shining Moon to hold a grudge against him, either, not when she could likely cause trouble for him and his men with her whole tribe.

"You can stay here, and we won't bother you no more," Oren went on. "Come to think of it, maybe we can help you find that man of yours, since we're goin' up in the mountains. What's his name, anyway?"

Josie blinked. She had not been expecting that question and had not gone that far in figuring out her story. So she said the first name that came into her mind, repeating a variation of the lie she had told many times before.

"His name is Clay Holt."

Shining Moon heard the words come out of the white woman's mouth, but for a few seconds her stunned brain refused to comprehend them. Then, when what she had just heard began to penetrate, her throat seemed to close as if a large stone had been lodged in it. She gasped for breath while blood hammered in her head.

Father Brennan stepped quickly to her side as the others looked on curiously. Shining Moon was vaguely aware of the woman called Josie staring at her in surprise at the reaction her words had provoked.

"Help me back to the church," she whispered to Father Brennan as he took her arm. Her eyes pleaded with him not to say anything. He knew, of course, of the relationship between her and Clay, but even he did not know the full extent of her shame: She was carrying the child of a man she had considered her husband but who was really married to someone else —a white woman.

That was why Clay had brought her the dress, she suddenly realized as she stumbled toward the church with the priest supporting her. Clay had wanted her to be more like Josie. Josie would be beautiful in such a dress, Shining Moon thought.

She could feel the stares of the others following her. None of the recently arrived settlers knew about Clay yet; they and the Hunkpapa had kept a respectful distance from each other. Father Brennan was the only one who knew, and if Josie stayed away from the Hunkpapa village, as she was likely to, then Shining Moon could keep the knowledge from her until the right moment came to reveal it.

She was in such pain and turmoil, though, that she could not even think about when that right moment might be. As she and Father Brennan entered the church, Shining Moon realized that her pain was not only in her heart, but in her body, too. She clutched her stomach and sank gratefully onto one of the benches.

This was not like the sickness that came to all women who were with child. Shining Moon could deal with that feeling. This was different; this was a pain deep inside her. She took several shuddery breaths and tried to use her will to bring the pain under control.

"I'm sorry, Shining Moon," Father Brennan said as he sat down beside her and gently took one of her hands in his. "I know that must have been an awful shock to hear about Clay that way. But I'm sure there's some sort of mistake or misunderstanding—"

"No!" she said sharply. "There is no mistake. You heard her. Clay Holt is her husband."

"Did he ever say anything about having a wife back East?"

"No. . . ." A memory cut through the pain, which was subsiding somewhat now. Shining Moon's head lifted. "He did speak of a woman once. Her name was Josie. She had a child, and Clay told me that she had spread lies about him being the father. He—he said that he would not marry her, that she did not speak the truth." She looked bleakly at the priest.

"I think now that she did. I think she spoke the truth."

"We don't know that," Father Brennan said, but he sounded as unconvinced as Shining Moon felt. There was no doubt in her mind that the woman who had just come to New Hope was that same Josie and that the boy with her was Clay's son. The resemblance was not strong, but the boy had the same dark hair and eyes. It was close enough, Shining Moon thought. It had to be true.

"Please," she said quietly, looking down at the floor again, "do not speak of this to the woman. Do not speak of it to anyone."

"A man with my calling is used to keeping confidences," the priest said with a sad smile. "I've told you about how I hear confessions and can never speak of them to anyone else. I'll regard this the same way."

"Thank you, Father."

"But there's more to it than being surprised by what Josie said," he pressed. "You were in pain out there, physical pain. What's wrong, Shining Moon? Are you ill?"

She took another deep breath. He was her friend, the only one she could confide in. And now, with her faith in Clay Holt shattered by the revelation she had heard, she needed someone like that.

"I am with child. Clay's child." A hint of bitterness crept into her voice, but she could not help it.

"Well," Father Brennan said after a moment, "that makes things even more complicated, doesn't it? But I'm sure everything will work out fine, Shining Moon. When Clay comes back from Canada, the two of you can sit down and have a long talk and straighten this whole thing out."

"Yes," she murmured. When Clay Holt came back from Canada—*if* he came back from Canada— they would have a great deal to talk about, indeed.

CHAPTER THIRTEEN

Feeling as bleak as he ever had in his life, Jeff Holt lay on the hard bunk, his arms cushioning his head, and let his gaze roam around the cell. He had been in the jail less than twenty-four hours and already knew every inch of his surroundings, every ugly detail. But there was nothing else to do, so he looked around the cell again.

The walls and the floor were stone, and being so close to the sea, moss and lichen had grown freely, giving the cell a dank smell not unlike that of the hold of a ship. The ceiling was made of thick wooden planks, and moss grew on it as well. The door and the front wall were a latticework of iron bars set firmly in mortar. A small, barred window sat high on the rear wall so that enough air passed through the cell, but it carried with it the effluvium of the nearby docks, a smell Jeff had never gotten used to. The only item of furniture in the room was the iron cot he was lying on, its bare mattress so thin as to be almost nonexistent. There was one blanket with which Jeff could cover himself, a ratty flannel thing that once might have had color but had faded to an ugly gray. Under the far end of the bunk was the slops bucket, and the stench from it blended with the odors coming in through the window to create a truly sickening smell.

His home, Jeff thought grimly, until the authorities came to their senses and realized that he had not killed Charles Merrivale. And to think he had been upset about staying at the Merrivale house!

He heard the heavy wooden door that led from the jail to the cellblock open, and footsteps echoed off the stone floor of the corridor outside his cell. A couple of other prisoners inhabited the place, and Jeff found himself hoping that someone was coming to see one of them, rather than him. He was in no mood for visitors, especially since there was only one person it was likely to be.

"Somebody to see you, Holt," Constable Tolbert said harshly.

Jeff sat up and swung his legs over the side of the bunk, feeling his heart sinking. Just as he had feared, Melissa stood there in the corridor, looking small and frail next to the burly constable.

Jeff stood up and said tightly, "You shouldn't have come."

"I had to," she said, her voice so soft he could barely make out the words.

Tolbert pointed a finger at Jeff. "You behave yourself now, laddie. I'm going down to the other end of the hall, but I'll be keeping an eye on Mrs. Holt, so don't either one of you even think about passing anything back and forth. You won't do your husband any good by trying to help him break out of here, ma'am."

"Don't be ridiculous," Jeff snapped. "Melissa's not going to do any such thing, and I'm not going to try to break out. I'm innocent."

The lawman just grunted and turned away, and Jeff listened to his footsteps slowly recede. Hearing a scraping sound, Jeff knew Tolbert had pulled up a stool to sit on at the end of the corridor while Melissa was visiting.

She was dressed all in black, and her large bonnet and veil shielded most of her face. He could make out her features well enough, though, to see that her face was drawn and her eyes were red and swollen.

"You've been crying," he said. "The funeral was this afternoon, wasn't it?"

"I came here directly from the cemetery," she replied as she raised her veil. Her voice became stronger as she said, "I sent Mother home with the servants after the service was over. But I had to see you, Jeff. I have to know."

He knew what the question would be, and he also knew she had to ask it.

"Did you kill my father?"

"No," he answered without hesitation. "I swear on my life that I didn't, Melissa."

He would not have thought it possible that she could be any paler, but her face drained of what slight color it had left, and she sagged toward the barred door. Jeff reached for her—

"Get back! Get back, dammit!" Tolbert bellowed as he ran down the corridor. He caught Melissa's arm and held her up as he drew his pistol with the other hand and waved it at Jeff, who moved back a couple of steps and lifted his hands halfway into the air.

"Put that pistol away, blast it!" Jeff exclaimed. "Couldn't you see she was faint? I just didn't want her to fall and hit her head."

"All right, all right," Tolbert muttered. He stuffed the pistol back beneath his belt and asked solicitously, "Are you all right, ma'am?"

Melissa seemed to have regained some of her composure. "I-I'll be fine, Constable. I was just a bit dizzy for a moment."

"Maybe you'd better sit down."

Melissa shook her head at the suggestion. "No, I'm all right. I'll be fine, I assure you. I have my breath back now."

"Well . . ." Tolbert released her arm and slowly walked away. "Just you be careful now, ma'am, and don't upset yourself," he called. "Jail's no place for a distraught woman."

Melissa waited until Tolbert had reached the other end of the corridor, and then she looked intently at Jeff and said, "I had to know. I was sure in my heart, but I had to ask you directly and hear you deny it."

"I understand," he said quietly. "Sometimes I tell myself the same thing over and over, just so I'll stay convinced of it, too."

"But if *you* didn't, then—"

"Who?" Jeff finished for her. "That's what I asked myself all last night and all day today."

"My father was a businessman. He had enemies."

That was probably an understatement, Jeff thought, but again he kept silent. Charles Merrivale had been a ruthless man and not above doing whatever he deemed necessary to get his way, as had been demonstrated time and time again where his son-in-law was concerned. Probably dozens of people, perhaps more, had had a grudge of some kind against the man.

But were any of those grudges strong enough to lead someone to slit Merrivale's throat?

The constable had reluctantly answered some questions for Jeff earlier in the day. Merrivale's purse had been found on him, full of gold coins, which meant that robbery had not been the motive for the murder. That left hatred and revenge.

Both of which it would seem that Jeff had plenty.

Tolbert had been uninterested in Jeff's denials, telling him to wait until he was in court to spin his lies. That response had been enough to indicate that Jeff was highly unlikely to get a fair hearing in Wilmington. Merrivale was a respected, successful, influential member of the community. To most of the citizens of the town, Jeff Holt would be nothing more than a crude backwoodsman with a penchant for violence.

Jeff had smiled sardonically at that thought. Back home in the Ohio Valley, Clay had been the one with the reputation for hotheadedness. Jeff had always been the peacemaker, the one who would rather turn aside trouble with talk than meet it with fists or steel.

Well, that had changed, too.

He said to Melissa, "The law will prevail. The constable and his men will find out who really killed your father."

Even as he spoke them, the words sounded hollow. And Melissa recognized them for what they were—a lie—for she leaned closer to the bars and whispered, "The constable isn't going to find anything. He's convinced you're guilty, and I heard enough talk at the funeral to know that the whole town feels the same way."

"What about Hermione?"

"I don't know," Melissa admitted. "She doesn't want to believe that you—that you could do such a thing, but she knows how much the two of you fought."

"I just wanted to be together with my wife and my son," Jeff said, feeling miserable. "That's all I ever wanted."

She started to lift a hand, then stopped, and Jeff knew that if Tolbert had not been watching, she would have reached out to him. He nodded, his eyes on hers, to let her know that he understood.

After a moment of silence he asked, "What about Michael?"

"All he knows is that his grandfather is dead. He

doesn't know how or why, and I'm not going to tell him."

Jeff sighed. "That's wise. Has he asked about me?"

"Of course. He's upset because you aren't with us again. He asked where you had gone, and I told him you had to stay somewhere else for a short time, but that you would be back soon."

"I wish that was true, but—"

"It will be," Melissa said emphatically. "You will be home soon. But if you'd like, I can bring Michael down here to see you."

"No!" The word ripped out of Jeff. He shook his head forcefully. "Don't bring him down here ever! I won't have him seeing me like this."

"You're sure?"

"Swear to it, Melissa." His hands tightened on the bars, but he was not even aware of grasping them. "Swear you won't bring him."

"All right, I promise." Melissa's face was filled with grief as she forced the words out.

Jeff realized what a strain she was under. "You'd better go," he said, his voice quieter and calmer now. He wished he had not lost control, even for a moment. "There's nothing you can do to help me. Just take care of Michael and Hermione—and yourself."

"I will." She choked back a sob and brought a handkerchief from her pocket to dab at her eyes. "Do you think the constable would—would let me kiss you good-bye?"

"I don't give a damn what he thinks," Jeff said. He reached through the bars, took hold of her arms, and leaned toward her. Their lips met, brushing together for a few precious seconds before the quick footsteps of the constable sounded again.

"All right, that's enough," Tolbert insisted, but he did not sound as upset as he had earlier. "You'd better leave now, ma'am."

"I can come back, can't I?" Melissa asked as she turned to face him.

"I suppose you can. Come along now." Tolbert took her arm and led her away.

Jeff watched them until the cellblock door had closed behind them; then he heaved a sigh and went back to the bunk. He sat down, his body sagging, head drooping into his hands. A shudder ran through him.

Finally, after several minutes, he lay back, and as he stared up at the moss-encrusted ceiling, the same despondent thought that had pounded at him many times before plagued him again: Melissa and Michael would have been better off if he had never come back from the mountains.

Melissa leaned against the cushions of the carriage seat and closed her eyes, fighting back her tears. The thought was almost impossible to contemplate, but she realized now that Jeff would have been better off if he had never come back from the mountains and found her and Michael.

But he had, and none of the things that had happened in the last year could be changed.

The driver leaned around from his seat and asked through the carriage window, "Take you home now, Miz Holt?"

Melissa started to say yes, then thought about facing that big house, which seemed painfully empty with both Jeff and her father gone. The servants would take care of her mother; Hermione was in good hands. And Michael would be all right, too.

"No," she told the driver on the spur of the moment, letting her impulses take over, "I want to go to my father's office."

"But, Miz Holt—"

"Just do as I say," Melissa snapped, and as the words came sharply from her, she realized she sounded a little like her father. That thought made fresh tears roll down her cheeks.

The carriage lurched into motion and rolled through the streets of Wilmington, taking only a few minutes to reach the office building next to the large warehouse where Merrivale had built his empire. As the vehicle rolled to a stop, Melissa steeled herself for the ordeal that lay ahead of her. Someone had to deal with the thriving mercantile business her father had started. The store itself had a competent manager and could continue to operate much as before. But someone had to oversee the purchasing and shipping of goods, and Hermione Merrivale was certainly in no shape to do it.

The driver hopped down from his seat and opened the door of the carriage, and Melissa stepped out, hoping that the nervousness she felt was not too evident. She had absolutely no experience when it came to running a business, but she could at least look over the operation and try to gain some understanding of it. She owed her father's memory that much.

"Please wait," she said to the driver, then went up the building's steps to the landing. She did not intend to be inside for very long, just long enough to look over the books.

She took a key from her bag and unlocked the front door. The business was closed that day, of course, and the employees would report for work the next morning. Melissa intended to be there when they did, just as her father had always been. As she swung the door open, she kept her eyes averted from the funeral wreath that was hung there to mark her father's passing.

She stepped into the large front office with its angled writing desks, where the clerks did their work, and the shelves containing the firm's ledgers, then started across the room toward the door of her father's private chamber. Something about the room struck her as odd, and she stopped. It took her a moment to figure out what about the office had bothered her; then she noticed that several of the ledgers were protruding slightly from the shelves, and others had been pushed in more deeply than their neighbors. Her father had always insisted that the ledgers be uniformly lined up on the shelves, and the clerks had been meticulous about doing just that. Now it looked as if someone had pulled down some of the ledgers and been careless in replacing them.

Melissa had never been a stickler for neatness, but she could not imagine any of the clerks being that careless, not when her father might have fired them for doing such a thing. She was frowning in puzzlement at the shelves when she heard a faint sound coming from somewhere in the building.

She stiffened at the realization that she was not alone. She heard the sound again and was able to pinpoint its location: It was coming from inside her father's private office.

For a second or two, Melissa thought about going outside and sending the carriage driver to fetch the constable. But then her resolve strengthened. If she was going to take over her father's business, she was going to have to learn to deal with the problems involved. She would confront this interloper herself, whoever he was. Taking a firm grip on her purse, she marched across the room and threw open the door that led into what had been Charles Merrivale's office.

A man was crouched behind the desk in the center of the room, going through the contents of the drawers. As Melissa flung the door open, he straightened immediately, his hand darting under his coat. He grunted in surprise at the sight of her standing there.

Melissa was no less surprised to see him, but she maintained her composure and forced herself to ask, "What are you doing here, Mr. Hawley?"

Dermot Hawley visibly relaxed, evidently not

considering Melissa to be a threat. He took his hand out of his jacket, trying to make the gesture inconspicuous. Melissa noticed it, however, and she had no doubt that Hawley had been reaching for a small pistol concealed under his coat.

"I could ask you the same thing, my dear," he said smoothly. "Unless I'm mistaken, your poor departed father's funeral was this afternoon. I would have expected you to be at home with your mother following the service."

"Obviously," Melissa said crisply as she stepped closer to the desk. "You thought no one would be here and you would have free rein to riffle through Father's desk. And I am not your dear," she added pointedly.

Hawley shrugged. "More's the pity. And you're wrong about what I'm doing here. I'm not riffling through your father's desk."

"Oh? Then what are you doing?"

"Merely looking for information. I thought I should familiarize myself with your father's current dealings if I intend to help you and your mother in this time of need."

"What?" Melissa could not keep the surprise out of her voice.

"I *was* Charles's partner at one time, you know. I assumed you would need someone to help straighten out his business affairs, and what better man for the job than myself?"

Hawley was as bold as brass, Melissa thought; she would give him that. But she found herself despising him and his smooth answers.

"You thought you would take over, now that he's dead, is that it?"

"All I want to do is help." Hawley gave her a sad smile, as befitted the occasion.

Melissa's anger grew to the point where she could barely contain it. Standing before her, smiling so blandly, was the man who had tried to have her husband killed, who had helped poison her father's mind against her marriage, who had been behind all the trouble that had plagued her for so long—and now he had the audacity to claim that he was only here to help!

"I think you had better leave," she said, her voice low and quivering slightly.

"Of course, if that's what you want, Melissa. Perhaps I *was* rushing things a little. I'll come back in a day or two and start going through Charles's records—"

"No!" Melissa cut in, her voice sharp. "You don't understand, Mr. Hawley. You're not welcome here."

He shook his head. "No, I don't understand. You and I used to be such good friends, Melissa, and you and your mother need someone to help you with this business."

"Not you." Melissa could no longer keep the scorn out of her voice. "You're no longer a partner in this business, Mr. Hawley, and you never should have been. My father was wrong to trust you."

"Now see here—" Hawley began.

"No, *you* see! I don't want you here. You've caused nothing but trouble for my family ever since we met you. Now, get out, and don't ever come back!"

Melissa was trembling. Standing up to someone in that manner was totally foreign to her, especially someone as charming yet forceful as Dermot Hawley. In the past she might have fluttered her hands and let him do whatever he wished. But no more, she vowed. Things were going to be different now. She had no choice but to be strong.

"Are you sure you mean that?" Hawley asked, his voice cold.

"I do," Melissa declared. "You have no right to be here, and I want you to leave before I have to summon the authorities."

"You'd do that, too, wouldn't you?" Hawley muttered.

"You'll find out if you don't get out of this office."

Hawley reached for his hat, which was sitting on the desk, and gave her a snide look. "I see I've underestimated you, Melissa. You've changed—and not for the better, I fear. You may regret throwing me out of here. You may need a strong shoulder to lean on in the days to come, what with your father dead and your husband in jail charged with his murder!"

No longer trembling out of consternation, Melissa was now shaking with rage, and she fought to keep from slapping Hawley's face. "Get out!" she hissed.

He stalked over to the rear door and wrenched it open. But he could not resist a parting comment. "The day may come when you want my help. We'll see who's so high and mighty then!"

With that he left, slamming the door behind him.

Melissa stood there for a moment, feeling tremors of anger and indignation go through her. They were followed by a wave of helplessness. She was taking on too much, a part of her insisted; she was not capable of putting her father's business affairs in order. Hawley was right; she would have to have help.

But then she stiffened. She said aloud, "I *can* do it. I *will* do it. I *have* to do it. There's no one else."

She took off her bonnet and her veil and dropped them on the desk as she went behind it. The center drawer was still open, the one Hawley had been pawing through. She saw the corner of a ledger sticking out from under a pile of papers and extricated the book as she sat down in her father's chair. Opening the ledger, she saw that the dates on the first entries were recent, and flipping to the last page that had any figures on it, she took note of the date: the day her father died. Her eyes misted with tears, blurring the inked figures on the page before her. Those were the last entries her father would ever make.

Melissa wiped her eyes. There were things to do, she told herself sternly. Emotion had no place in the world of business. Charles Merrivale had taught her *that*, if nothing else in his life.

She blinked away the last of the tears and began studying the ledger, turning the pages toward the front. There was a lot to learn. . . .

Two days later, wearing no bonnet or veil but a dark gray dress as was appropriate for a woman in mourning for her father, Melissa stood on the pier and watched as men carried crates of cargo from the hold of a ship that had docked a short while earlier. A cargo manifest in hand, she checked off each item as it was unloaded. Having found the manifest in her father's desk and seeing from the date on it that the ship carrying the cargo was expected to arrive that day, she had been at the pier when the vessel sailed around Cape Fear and into the harbor.

Wagons were waiting on the street at the end of the dock, and as soon as all the cargo was unloaded and verified, the wagoners would take over. The crates would be loaded and taken to one of the Merrivale warehouses that now belonged to Melissa and her mother. Some of the goods would be used as stock for the mercantile store, while the rest would be sold at wholesale prices to other merchants. The clerks in her father's office had filled Melissa in on the usual procedures, and she decided to adhere to them for the time being, until she could study the situation and determine if any improvements needed to be made.

If any of the clerks objected to working for a woman, none of them had shown it. They were probably glad to be out from under her father's iron-handed supervision, Melissa thought, although they would never dare admit such a thing. She could not

hold such feelings against them, knowing all too well
how difficult a man Charles Merrivale had been. As
long as the clerks did their jobs, that was all she asked
of them.

The warehouse workers and the freighters were a
different story, however. They were much rougher
types, and she had sensed some definite resentment
when she had appeared at the warehouse and issued
the orders to come to the docks and pick up the cargo.
No one had openly defied her, however. She hoped
that in time they would come to respect her.

Of course, if any of the men did not wish to work
for her, that was their option. She could hire others to
take their places. But she hoped it would not come to
that.

So far, Melissa had taken to the business world
better than she had expected she would. Her innate
intelligence, which had never really been challenged,
had responded eagerly to the task of making sense of
Charles Merrivale's business dealings. She had
quickly learned to decipher the system her father
used to denote sales and purchases, profits and losses.
She found his shipping schedules, his contracts with
other companies, all of his records going back to
when the family had returned to North Carolina from
the Ohio Valley. She even found documentation of
Dermot Hawley's involvement in the business, and
she was shocked at the extent of it. For a time Hawley
had been almost an equal partner in Merrivale's various enterprises. Hawley's involvement had shrunk,
however, and finally disappeared almost entirely
from the records; Melissa knew that that reflected her
insistence to her father that he have no more dealings
with the man.

She suspected that Hawley had still been more of
a silent partner than the records indicated, however,
but that no longer mattered. He now had nothing to
do with the business, and that was the way she intended for it to remain.

By throwing herself into the work, she had helped keep her mind off Jeff's tragic predicament, although she had visited him in jail each of the past two days. During those visits, the sight of her beloved husband behind bars had made her confidence sag dangerously. Being locked up was eating away at Jeff, she could tell, and he was already growing gaunt and haggard. His trial was not scheduled to begin for another couple of weeks, and Melissa hated to think of what continued captivity would do to him in that time. But he maintained his innocence and that the trial would bring out the truth.

Melissa believed him, and she wanted to believe that the trial would clear his name. However, what little evidence there was pointed directly to him as her father's killer. There was every likelihood that he would be found guilty of the murder and sent to prison—or even hung.

A shudder went through her as that thought crossed her mind for what must have been the thousandth time. She forced it away, ordering herself to concentrate on the business at hand. The cargo was almost unloaded now.

"Melissa! Is that you?"

The loud voice made her start in surprise. Clutching the cargo manifest tightly against her, she turned quickly to see who had called her name. She sighed and relaxed when she saw the tall, muscular, sandy-haired man in sailor's clothes coming toward her. A considerably smaller, dark-haired figure strode along easily beside him, and Melissa recognized the young woman who masqueraded as a young man so that she could be a sailor.

"Ned!" Melissa called out, trying to make her greeting cheerful. "And Max. How good to see both of you again. When did you get into port?"

"Early this morning," Ned Holt replied with a grin as he came to a stop in front of her.

"Hello, Melissa," India said. "How are you?"

"Not very well, I'm afraid," Melissa said quietly.

"Where's that cousin of mine?" Ned demanded boisterously. "And what are you doing down here at the docks? I'm surprised you're not home with that youngster of yours."

"My mother is taking care of Michael these days. It gives her something to do. She needs to keep busy, and so do I." She held up the manifest. "I'm working now, you see."

"But why?" India asked. "I'm surprised your father allows such a thing."

Melissa could not keep the truth from them, nor did she want to. Ned and India were her friends, and Ned was Jeff's cousin. They deserved to be told what had happened.

"Terrible things have happened," she began. "My father is dead—murdered. And Jeff is in jail. The authorities say he's the murderer."

Both Ned and India gaped at her for a moment, even India's cool self-possession shaken by such unexpected news. Ned reacted first, bursting out, "But that's crazy! Jeff wouldn't do a thing like that!"

"I know," Melissa said. "I believe he's innocent."

"Why don't you tell us the whole story?" India suggested. "If it's not too painful, that is."

"It is," Melissa said, tears filling her eyes, "but you should hear it anyway." She hurriedly gestured at the stacks of crates. "Just let me finish checking this cargo so my men can start loading it on the wagons and take it to the warehouse. Then I'll explain."

Melissa could tell that Ned and India were barely containing their impatience as she finished her business. Finally, however, the cargo was loaded. When the wagons were rolling toward the warehouse, Melissa turned to her two friends.

"Come with me back to the office," she suggested.

As the three of them walked along the bustling streets, Melissa told Ned and India what had happened. Ned wanted to know how the constable could have made such a foolish mistake as to arrest Jeff, but Melissa could hear the doubt in his voice. India, always level-headed, asked searching questions about what had gone on before Charles Merrivale's death, and Melissa told them about the series of confrontations between Jeff and her father that had finally ended in a physical battle.

"Constable Tolbert heard Jeff threaten Father that very afternoon," Melissa said. "So it's no wonder that he immediately thought of Jeff when—when Father's body was found."

"It's still ridiculous," Ned snorted. "Jeff wouldn't kill somebody just because of an argument. He was the one who was always trying to get *me* to calm down and be less hotheaded."

Melissa smiled ruefully. "I know. But Jeff is in jail. He's supposed to have his trial in two weeks, and I fear he'll be found guilty."

"It doesn't look good," India admitted. They had reached the office building, and as they went inside, the young woman looked around at the clerks, busy at their work. She asked, "You're running the business now, Melissa?"

"That's right. Someone had to. Mother doesn't have a head for business, or so she says; anyway, she doesn't want to come down here. It reminds her too much of Father. But she's glad to take care of Michael for me. She needs something to do with herself—just as I do."

"Mighty big operation for one woman to head up," Ned commented as they went on into the private office. He frowned in thought and scraped a thumbnail over the light-colored stubble on his jaw. "Maybe you could use a hand, Melissa."

She smiled at him as she closed the door. "Are you volunteering, Ned?"

"I wouldn't mind a little change of scenery. Don't get me wrong, I love the sea and sailing," he added with a quick glance at India. "But Jeff is family, and since he's in trouble, I figure I ought to help out. I probably speak the language of those stevedores and warehouse workers better than you do."

"Well, I appreciate the offer, but I wouldn't want to take you away from your berth on board the *Fair Wind*."

"Nonsense," India said crisply. "There's no reason we can't stay here awhile to help you out, then find an opening on the crew of another ship. Captain Vaughan will understand."

"You intend to stay, too?" Ned asked in surprise.

"Yes. Far more needs to be done than just running a mercantile business, however. It's much more important that we help Jeff."

"How can you do that?" Melissa asked.

"It's quite simple, actually," India said. "I believe Jeff is innocent, and there's only one way to prove that."

"Of course," Ned said with a grin and a nod.

Melissa felt a surge of hope, even though she had told herself that that was one emotion she could not really afford. She said, "Do you mean—?"

"I mean the three of us are going to discover the identity of the real killer," India St. Clair said, "whatever it takes."

CHAPTER FOURTEEN

Misfortunes do not flourish particularly in our path—they grow every where.

—from Sioux burial oration, as quoted in
JOHN BRADBURY's "Travels in the Interior
of America 1809–1811"

Clay swung the heavy pack of furs out of the canoe he had been paddling and onto his shoulder, then started toward the open gates of Fort Dunadeen. Behind him, Aaron and Proud Wolf hefted their own bundles of pelts out of their canoes and carried them toward the stockade.

Three weeks had passed since the Americans had arrived at the fort. McKendrick had agreed almost immediately to hire them as trappers, and they had gone out on their first trip within days. Butterfly had stayed at the fort to help with the washing and cooking, and although she had concealed the reaction well, Clay knew she had been quite chagrined at being given that job. He hoped that during the time he, Aaron, and Proud Wolf had been gone, Butterfly had done nothing to jeopardize the chances of success in their mission.

Clay had also feared that leaving Butterfly at the fort might tempt some of the Canadians to take advantage of her, but he could not have objected without drawing Fletcher McKendrick's curiosity. And for the time being, Clay wanted to blend into the background of the fur-trapping operation as much as possible.

The Americans had gone along with a half dozen other men and Clive Chamberlain, who was again in charge of the party, and Clay had gotten to know the Englishman fairly well during the time they were trapping. Subtle questioning in the guise of campfire talk had elicited some pertinent information about the London and Northwestern Enterprise.

Clay had learned, for one, that McKendrick was under considerable pressure from the firm's owners in England to make it a success on the same level as the North West Company and the Hudson's Bay Company. Clay had doubts that that was even possible, considering what giants those two companies already were. But the pressure on McKendrick explained why he was so determined to expand the trapping operation south into American territory. Only by going there would the Scotsman have even a chance of succeeding.

Chamberlain had also explained that McKendrick's hatred for Americans had grown to an almost irrational level, fueled by the failure of his first two schemes to claim American territory for the London and Northwestern. Hatred for Americans or no, McKendrick was still a canny businessman, and that was why he had hired Clay, Aaron, and Proud Wolf. Even though his gaze was starting to turn southward again, he could not afford to neglect efforts north of the border, and Clay and his companions were experienced frontiersmen.

Besides, it probably gave McKendrick some sort of perverse satisfaction to be using Americans to trap Canadian furs, Chamberlain had commented to Clay in an unguarded moment.

The Western Canadian headquarters of the London and Northwestern had originally been at a British military post known as Fort Rouge, but it had been moved to Fort Dunadeen the previous year. It was the central collection point for the far-flung network of trappers working for the company, and the warehouses at the fort were already bulging with pelts ready to be shipped to Montreal.

That information had particularly caught Clay's interest. The pelts in those warehouses represented a sizable investment for the London and Northwestern. If something were to happen to them—and to the supplies that were also stored at the fort—it might strike a veritable death blow to the company, putting it out of business for good.

Short of going to England and hunting down every one of the owners, that was the best Clay could hope for as revenge for the deadly schemes hatched by McKendrick. And as for McKendrick himself, Clay had decided that if he could put the company out of business and hold McKendrick accountable for his crimes, the debt of honor that had brought him to that northern land would be paid.

The only question remaining was when to strike.

Carrying the furs into the warehouse, Clay found the building even more chock full than it had been when he and the others had left. Some of the other trapping parties must have come in with pelts of their own, he thought. The bundles were stacked nearly to the ceiling in some places. Clay, Aaron, Proud Wolf, and the other men added theirs to the huge piles, then left the warehouse. Most of the men headed for the tavern at the end of the bunkhouse, ready for a cup of rum.

Chamberlain clapped Clay on the back as they emerged from the building. "Come along with me," the Englishman suggested. "I'll make my report to McKendrick, then we'll get a drink."

Clay hesitated; he had been trying to avoid McKendrick as much as possible until the moment came for the showdown, since it was extremely difficult for him to control his emotions around the man. It might look suspicious, though, if he turned down Chamberlain's offer, and besides, he genuinely liked the Englishman, which was something that Clay had not expected. He had come to realize that not all of the men north of the border were the fiends he had imagined them to be. Some, like Chamberlain, were honest, hard-working trappers much like the men Clay had known in the American Rockies.

"All right," Clay agreed. He turned to his companions. "Carson, you and Bear Claw go on without me. I'll join you shortly."

Aaron said, "Fine." But he and Proud Wolf stopped in their tracks when Butterfly emerged from the bunkhouse and eagerly ran toward them.

Clay paused, hoping she was not so happy to see them that she would shout out their real names. But she restrained her enthusiasm, at least enough to keep her wits about her.

"Bear Claw!" she cried as she came up to Proud Wolf. Before he could get out of her way, she had her arms around him and was hugging him with all the passion of a woman who had not seen her man for three months, rather than three weeks.

Proud Wolf looked stunned when she finally let him go, and as Clay followed Chamberlain, he chuckled over the expression on Proud Wolf's face, thinking that the young man might as well give up. Butterfly was a determined young woman, and sooner or later she was going to get what she wanted.

McKendrick stepped out onto the porch of the headquarters building to greet Chamberlain, and Clay carefully kept his expression neutral as he nodded to the Scotsman. Chamberlain told McKendrick about their successful trip and informed him of the number of pelts they had brought in, a figure that was written down by the clerk who had followed McKendrick onto the porch.

When Chamberlain was through with his report, McKendrick looked over at Clay and asked, "How about ye, Mr. Hogan? How do ye like working for the London and Northwestern Enterprise?"

"Just fine, Mr. McKendrick," Clay said. "Seems like you've got a good bunch of fellows working for you."

"Aye, that they are. And since ye and Mr. Chamberlain seem to get along so well, I've got in mind to team the two of ye on a wee project I've been thinking about. I'll tell ye about it later."

"Fine with me," Clay said with a nod, hoping he sounded enthusiastic enough.

McKendrick waved a hand at them and grunted in dismissal, and Chamberlain headed for the tavern. Clay fell in step beside him. When they were out of earshot of the headquarters building, Chamberlain said fervently, "Bloody hell!"

"What's the matter?" Clay asked, surprised by the man's vehement reaction.

"I know what *project* McKendrick is talking about. He's going to send men down into America again, and this time he wants me to be in charge of the party."

Clay frowned. He would have to pretend ignorance. "I thought you had to stay on this side of the border."

"We're supposed to, but McKendrick's got a bee in his bonnet about expanding the operation into the American Rockies, especially since the dividing line is somewhat in dispute, anyway. But I'm damned if I want to be part of starting another war between the Crown and you Yanks. No offense meant by that, Hogan. It's just that I had two older brothers who were grenadiers during the War of Rebellion, and neither one of them came back alive from the colonies."

"I'm sorry," Clay said, and meant it. "My pa fought in that war, too. He always said a lot of good men on both sides got killed because the politicians never could figure out a way to settle things without fighting. But he figured it was our right to be free, and in the end there was only one way to do that."

"I suppose I have to agree," Chamberlain said. "I hold no grudges against the Americans. I just don't want to cause any more trouble by going across the border. We have plenty of beaver up here."

That was true in one way but untrue in another, Clay thought. There were certainly more beaver in these Canadian streams than the trappers of the London and Northwestern could ever catch, as long as the number of men was as small as it was now. But as more and more trappers came into the area, eventually the scales would tip in the other direction. The company would have to spread out if it was to survive. And with the Hudson's Bay Company and the North West Company competing elsewhere, the only way to go was to the south, into American territory.

Clay suddenly realized that the Revolution had not settled everything, not by a long shot. Regardless of the outcome of his own quest, many problems still existed between America and England. But the two countries' grievances would be settled in embassies, not a frontier fort in western Canada. The stakes here were smaller, more personal than those that had caused the war—though no less deadly.

Clay and Chamberlain went up the three wooden steps to the porch of the tavern. Proud Wolf and Butterfly were sitting on rough-hewn chairs down at the end of the porch, talking earnestly in low voices. Butterfly still wore a big smile on her face, and Proud

Wolf did not look too displeased by her company, Clay thought. Maybe the young man was finally realizing that there were worse things in the world than having an intelligent, pretty young woman in love with you—a hell of a lot worse things.

He and Chamberlain entered the tavern, and Clay spotted Aaron standing at the bar. The room was a rough square, with the bar along the left-hand wall, adjoining the bunkhouse, a massive fireplace on the right-hand wall, and the area in between scattered with tables. The men who had just come in off the trapping expedition were mostly lined up at the bar, enjoying cups of rum being poured for them by a barrel-chested bartender, although a few were sitting at the tables. One table was occupied by three Blackfoot warriors in a state of advanced drunkenness. There would probably be a fight before the night was over, Clay thought as he glanced at them.

But that was not his concern. At the moment he intended to enjoy a drink with Chamberlain, then turn his mind to the problem that still awaited him: trying to decide when to make his move against McKendrick and the company. He wanted to do it when not quite as many men were at the fort; that a pursuit would ensue once he and his companions had taken their vengeance was inevitable, and Clay wanted to cut down the numbers as much as possible. He was confident that if he and his friends could get their hands on their own mounts and scatter the few remaining horses at the fort, they could outdistance anyone who came after them.

Chamberlain signaled for rum, and the two men were served. While Clay drank, he thought about the kegs of gunpowder stored in the powder magazine. If he could plant a few of them inside the warehouses and manage to blow them all up at the same time, the explosions and the resulting fires would probably destroy the whole fort and all the pelts stored inside it.

It was an agreeable idea.

He heard a chair leg scrape on the puncheon floor behind him but paid little attention to the sound. Unsteady footsteps became increasingly louder, and abruptly someone bumped his shoulder. He looked over to see one of the Canadian trappers, a gray-haired man with a gaunt, scarred face, leaning past him and trying to get the bartender's attention. The man idly glanced in Clay's direction, then looked again, this time frowning and blinking owlishly.

"Don't I know you, mate?" the trapper asked in a voice thickened by rum.

An icy shock of recognition ran through Clay, but he managed by great effort to conceal it. He did not remember the man's name, but the trapper had been one of Duquesne's lieutenants. Clay would never forget the merciless men who had been his captors, when he was a prisoner in Duquesne's camp two years earlier.

But he replied in a calm voice, "I don't think so, friend. I haven't been up here very long."

"American, ain't you?"

Clay nodded. There was no point in trying to conceal a nationality that was already known by many at the fort, including his drinking companion, Chamberlain.

The drunken man shook his head, then rubbed his stubbled jaw. "Would've sworn I knew you," he muttered. Then he turned and went back to trying to get another cup of rum from the bartender.

Clay felt relieved and gratefully sipped his own rum. After the man got his drink and headed to a table for more solitary drinking, Chamberlain leaned over to Clay and asked, "So old Cyrus thought he knew you, eh?"

"Is that his name?" Clay said casually. "Yep, he thought he knew me from somewhere, but I've never seen him before."

"Poor Cyrus." Chamberlain's expression was sympathetic. "He hasn't been right in the head, you know, ever since he went down across the border with Duquesne."

"I don't know as I've heard about that."

"It's not a pretty story," Chamberlain said. "I'll tell you about it someday. Cyrus was hurt down there, and he's never been the same since. He was a good man once, one of the best, but now we have to keep an eye on him constantly whenever he goes out with us. I try not to take him in my group, when I can avoid it."

Clay went along with that sentiment. He hoped to avoid Cyrus if at all possible. No sense in jogging the man's memory any more.

He downed the rest of his rum, and as the fiery liquor warmed his stomach, he said to Chamberlain, "I think I'll head over to the bunkhouse and catch up on some sleep. It's been a hard couple of weeks."

"Amen to that. I'll talk to you later, then."

"Sure," Clay agreed. He caught Aaron's eye and jerked his head toward the door. Aaron finished off his drink and joined Clay.

Their path took them right by the table occupied by Cyrus. Clay would have preferred not getting that close to the man again, but circling around would have drawn even more attention. He kept his head averted as he strode past the table toward the door. At least he did not have to worry about Aaron being recognized, he thought. Aaron and his brother, Zach Garwood, had not arrived in the vicinity of Manuel Lisa's fort until after all the trouble with Duquesne was over.

The two of them reached the entrance, and Clay started to breathe easier. He was about to step out onto the porch when a voice rose in high-pitched excitement behind him.

"Holt!" Cyrus cried, standing up so quickly that his chair fell over behind him with a crash. "By God, that's Clay Holt!"

When he heard the shouted words, Clay's first

impulse was to freeze, but he forced himself to keep walking out to the porch as if Cyrus's cry had nothing to do with him. But he hissed under his breath to Aaron, "Get Proud Wolf and Butterfly and take off!"

"But—"

"*Do it!*"

Aaron kept walking, motioning curtly to Proud Wolf as he did so. Out of the corner of his eye, Clay saw Proud Wolf and Butterfly get up from their chairs at the end of the porch and go to join Aaron as the young man headed across the stockade yard. Clay veered in the other direction, hoping to draw any pursuers after him and away from his companions.

He heard voices and rapid footsteps behind him, then a hand grabbed his shoulder. He stopped and turned to confront the wild-eyed Cyrus, who jittered around nervously, bouncing from one foot to the other.

"It's Clay Holt, I tell you," Cyrus insisted at the top of his voice. "It's Clay Holt!"

Behind Cyrus, Clive Chamberlain and some of the other men had emerged from the tavern. Clay saw them watching him curiously and said in a loud voice, "What the hell do you want, old man? I told you I don't know you."

Cyrus gave a cackling laugh. "But I know *you*. You're Clay Holt, and Mr. McKendrick's posted a reward for you. And now it's mine, all mine!"

Clay looked past Cyrus at Chamberlain. "I don't want to hurt this old fool," he said harshly, "but I may have to if he doesn't stop bothering me. Explain to him who I am, Clive."

"You've got the wrong man, Cyrus," the Englishman said patiently. "This fellow's name is Hogan, not Holt."

"He's Clay Holt, I tell you!" Cyrus pointed a quivering finger at Clay. "I saw him when Duquesne had him prisoner, 'fore he killed poor ol' Nick and Donnie. He's Clay Holt!"

Clay saw doubtful expressions forming on the faces of Chamberlain and the other trappers. He said coldly, "This old man is insane."

"Cyrus always did have a good memory for faces," Chamberlain said slowly. "I don't know if he's right this time or not, but we'd better go talk to McKendrick about this."

His muscles tensing, Clay stood rooted to the spot as Chamberlain came toward him. He had heard how McKendrick felt about the man who had ruined the first two efforts to expand into American territory. Cyrus's accusation would likely be enough for McKendrick. The Scotsman could order him executed out of hand, just on the off chance that he might be Clay Holt. And, of course, in this case McKendrick would be right.

A quick glance told Clay that Aaron, Proud Wolf, and Butterfly had almost reached the gates. The guards were paying no attention to them; their curious gazes were focused on the confrontation in the center of the fort. Clay steeled himself. The moment turned out not to be of his choosing after all, but, nonetheless, the time had come to make his move.

He lunged forward, lowering his shoulder and slamming it into the chest of the startled Chamberlain. With a quick movement Clay pulled the Englishman's pistol from beneath his belt. As he thumbed back the cock, Clay pulled out one of his own pistols with his other hand. Leveling the weapons at the group of trappers in front of him, he said sharply, "Stay back, all of you, and keep your hands away from your weapons! I don't want to kill anyone but McKendrick!"

"My God!" Chamberlain exclaimed. "You *are* Clay Holt!"

"In the flesh," Clay said with a menacing smile. He backed up slightly so that he could see both the gate and the men he was covering with the pistols. He saw that Aaron and Proud Wolf had followed his lead and were covering the sentries with their rifles. With a nod to Chamberlain, he went on, "Let's go see Mc-Kendrick, just as you said."

Although the situation was bad, Clay still had hopes it could be salvaged. But he had not counted on the madness of Cyrus. With a sudden squall of rage and hatred, the old man launched himself at Clay, jerking a knife from his belt as he leapt.

Clay fired one of the pistols instinctively, and a small ball thudded into Cyrus's chest. The insane light faded in the man's eyes to be replaced by the glaze of death.

Chamberlain immediately lashed out with the butt of the rifle he was carrying, striking Clay's wrist and sending the loaded pistol spinning away. The other men surged forward with a howl, smelling the reward promised by McKendrick the way a wolf smells blood. Collecting himself, Clay grabbed his tomahawk and swung it in a wide circle, smashing in the skull of one of the men.

He hoped Aaron, Proud Wolf, and Butterfly had the sense to try to escape. As if in the far distance, he heard guns blasting. Completely surrounded as he was, he could swing the 'hawk freely with assurance that he was hitting his enemies, and for a few barbaric seconds, blood showered around him, until something slammed into his forearm and made his fingers go numb. The 'hawk slipped away from him.

Then they were all on him, overwhelming him with their number. Fists pounded into him, and he felt himself going down under the onslaught. He tried to twist away from the men holding him, but there were too many of them. He saw a rifle butt coming at his face and jerked his head to the side, but the blow still grazed him. Lights exploded behind his eyes. The rifle butt rose and fell again, and this time Clay was too groggy to try to dodge the blow. It landed with a solid thud.

That was the last thing Clay Holt heard or felt for a long time.

A war raged inside Proud Wolf's breast as he raced toward the forest outside the fort. Every instinct in his body told him that he could not abandon his friend and brother-in-law, Clay Holt. But his head told him that Clay's only real chance for survival was if he and Aaron managed to stay free so that they could strike back somehow against Clay's captors.

When the fight had begun, Proud Wolf and Aaron had both opened fire on the sentries in the watchtowers, cutting down the men in the observation posts at the front of the fort so that they could not fire on Clay. However, with their guns empty, the two young men had no choice then except to flee. Proud Wolf had seen Clay go down under the press of the attacking trappers. The young warrior hoped that the Canadians would want to keep Clay alive for McKendrick to deal with; that would give him and Aaron time to come up with a plan to rescue Clay.

Proud Wolf threw a glance over his shoulder, expecting to see Butterfly right behind him, but he discovered with a surge of fear that she was not there. In fact, he did not see her anywhere.

Stopping short, he called, "Butterfly!"

Someone had already climbed to the top of one watchtower and was firing at them. The ball missed Proud Wolf by inches.

"Come on!" Aaron yelled from a few feet away. "We've got to get out of here!"

"Butterfly is not here!"

"Somebody must've grabbed her when we lit out from the fort." Aaron winced as another shot blasted from the other watchtower and thudded into a nearby tree. "We'll get her when we go back for Clay. Now, let's get into the trees, before they cut us down!"

Proud Wolf knew his friend was right. Standing there in the open would accomplish nothing except getting them both killed. He turned and ran toward the forest, although every fiber of his being wanted to go the other way, toward the fort and Clay and Butterfly.

She had to be all right, Proud Wolf thought as another rifle ball whined past his ear. She just had to be. . . .

Butterfly crouched at the rear corner of the bunkhouse, her breath rasping in her throat and her pulse pounding inside her head. Although she had fought in the battle against the Arikara war party, that had not been like this. Never had she experienced fear like that which gripped her now.

She had hesitated when the fight broke out between Clay Holt and the trappers, and one of the men had run over to grab her just as Aaron and Proud Wolf began their dash out of the fort. Butterfly had not wanted to abandon Clay in the first place, and when the trapper had caught hold of her left arm and seemingly tried to jerk it out of its socket, her warrior's instincts took over. She slid the knife at her waist from its sheath and plunged it into the man's chest. Then, before he could react, she ripped the blade free and stabbed him again. His grip on her arm slid away as blood began to well from the wounds. Butterfly darted past him and started for the gates, but some of the men were swinging them closed, so she headed for the bunkhouse.

No one came after her. She reached the long building and ducked around its corner as more men climbed into the watchtowers and fired after the fleeing Proud Wolf and Aaron.

Butterfly sent up a prayer to the Great Spirit, asking Wakan Tanka to watch over Proud Wolf and protect him from the Canadians' lead balls. She was glad he and Aaron had got away, and she hoped they had the sense to keep running once they reached the forest.

She knew better, however. They would be coming back for Clay—and for her, too.

When they came, she would be ready to help them. There was much killing to come, and she would do her share.

But she had to subdue her fear. She closed her eyes for a moment, willing the terror to go away. She was a warrior, she told herself, not some frightened girl.

She was Raven Arrow.

And when she stood up from her crouch, straight and tall once again, it was Raven Arrow who strode along the rear of the bunkhouse, not Butterfly.

Proud Wolf had kept her bow and her arrows, since a slave such as she was pretending to be would not be so well-armed. But she knew which room in the log bunkhouse was his. There were windows in the rear of the rooms, and she made her way to the one opening into Proud Wolf's quarters. Its shutter was open, since the weather was warm, and she had no trouble levering herself through the opening and into the room. It took only seconds for her to find the quiver of black arrows and the bow that leaned against the wall in a corner. She slung the quiver onto her back and hefted the bow. It felt good in her hand as she wrapped her fingers around the smooth wood.

Many men would die that day, she thought. And if she died, too, then she would meet the Great Spirit standing tall and proud, as a warrior should.

The cold water hit Clay in the face like a blow from a fist. He came back to consciousness sputtering and shaking his head, water dripping from his beard. A wave of dizziness struck him, and he would have fallen forward if he had not been tied to one of the support posts of the headquarters building porch.

A face was thrust within inches of his own, and Fletcher McKendrick growled, "Awake now, are ye, Holt?"

Clay lifted his head, even though it felt as if it weighed a hundred pounds, and glared at the Scotsman. "You son of a bitch," he said flatly.

"Ah, now that's more like it! We're not pretending anymore, are we? You're Holt, I'm McKendrick, and all we really care about is seeing the other one dead. 'Tis the right of it."

McKendrick had summed it up well, Clay thought as his brain began to function again. No need for pretense now. Revenge drove both of them, stripping away all other considerations.

"Why don't you go ahead and kill me?" Clay looked around. Chamberlain and several of his trappers stood on the porch; others were in the stockade yard behind him. "The odds are all on your side. Get it over with."

McKendrick raised a finger. "Not just yet. Your friend and that Indian scout are out there in the woods somewhere, and I'm going to sit back and wait for them to return for ye."

Clay snickered. "They're long gone by now. They won't come back for me."

"That's what you'd like for me to believe, I'm sure. But we'll just wait awhile and see."

McKendrick was right, Clay knew. Aaron and Proud Wolf would never desert him, even it was the smart thing to do. They would at least try to rescue him—and that loyalty would lead them right into McKendrick's trap.

But there was another card yet to be dealt, Clay realized. McKendrick had not said anything about Butterfly. Clay did not know if she had escaped with Proud Wolf and Aaron or if she was still somewhere inside the fort. Either way, she could be important. McKendrick, Chamberlain, and the others considered her nothing but a slave and no danger; therefore, she might be able to take them by surprise.

It was a slim hope but one of the few he had left.

"I think we'll leave ye for a while," McKendrick

went on, "so you'll have time to think about all the havoc you've caused. Ye came damn close to ruining me, Holt. Ye destroyed Fort Tarrant and with it all the pelts collected there by Simon Brown and his men. Destroyed them, too, by God. But our fight is over now, and I've won. One of these days the London and Northwestern Enterprise will stretch all over those mountains you and your bloody Sioux have tried so hard to protect. 'Tis a kindness ye won't be alive to see it, wouldn't you say?"

With that McKendrick turned on his heel and stalked into the headquarters building. The other men dispersed, except for Chamberlain, who came over to stand in front of Clay and shake his head sadly.

"I never thought it would come to this," the Englishman said. "You shouldn't have come up here, Holt."

"I didn't have much choice in the matter. A debt of honor had to be paid. I don't suppose you'd know about things like that, though."

"You'd be surprised, my friend," Chamberlain replied softly. "You'd be surprised, indeed."

Then he went into the building, too, leaving Clay alone on the porch.

He strained against the rawhide bonds holding him fast to the post, but they were cruelly tight. Knowing there was nothing he could do for the moment, he relaxed as much as he could. McKendrick was leaving him out here like a staked goat, he thought, trying to draw in Aaron and Proud Wolf. The Scotsman was underestimating them, however; the idea that they would waltz right in and try to free him was ludicrous. They would set up some sort of diversion.

But McKendrick had the men and the guns, and no matter what Proud Wolf and Aaron did, the odds would be against them.

And where was Butterfly?

Clay stood there, his muscles cramping painfully,

for a length of time he could not even estimate. The blows to his head had left him with a pounding ache inside his skull, and his face was bruised and crusted with dried blood. His arms and shoulders screamed with agony from being pulled back so tightly behind him. Only his hands were free of pain; they were numb from the rawhide thongs cutting into his wrists. A part of Clay's mind wanted to let his head sag forward again, to let unconsciousness claim him so that at least the hurting would stop for a while.

But somehow he kept his eyes open, and he was still alert when the smell of smoke suddenly drifted to his nose. He blinked and lifted his head slightly, trying to determine the source of the smoke. The smell was getting stronger by the second.

"Fire!" shouted a man in one of the guard towers.

Clay twisted his head and looked to the south side of the fort. A pillar of black smoke rose not far from the stockade fence. The wind was out of the south, and even though the trees around the fort had been cleared when it was built, the grass would still burn, and when the flames reached the log wall, it would catch fire, too. What was more, the powder magazine was right inside that wall.

Despite his predicament, Clay smiled.

Guns cracked outside the fort, and one of the sentries plunged down from his tower with a scream that was abruptly cut off by the thud of his body against the hard ground. The smoke was thickening, and it stung the eyes as the wind carried it over the fort. Men boiled out of the headquarters building and the bunkhouse. A forest fire was one thing backwoodsmen feared above all else.

Proud Wolf and Aaron had come up with one hell of a diversion, all right, Clay thought.

McKendrick and his men ran toward the gates. "Get water from the river!" he bellowed. "We've got to get that fire out before it reaches the walls!"

More was at stake now than revenge. If the powder magazine went up, the warehouses full of furs would undoubtedly be destroyed along with everything—and perhaps everyone—else at Fort Dunadeen. Even if McKendrick lived, it would be the end of his career. It would mean disgrace for him, and the owners of the London and Northwestern Enterprise would break him like a rotten branch under the foot of a bear. Although Clay's physical pain had hardly lessened, he had to grin as he watched McKendrick racing around frantically, directing the firefighting operation.

Some of the men had grabbed up buckets to scoop water from the nearby river, but as they dashed through the gates, shots rang out, and the men fell to the ground. That drove the other men back, despite McKendrick's howls of fury.

Clay strained at his bonds again. He could see the orange glow of the flames right outside the stockade wall now. In a matter of moments, it would be too late to save the fort.

A buckskin-clad figure vaulted lithely onto the far end of the porch and raced toward him. "Butterfly!" Clay exclaimed.

Her knife flickered as she reached him and sliced through the thongs around his wrists. As his arms came loose from the post Clay stumbled forward, then caught himself. His hands were so numb that he almost dropped the pistol that Butterfly thrust into them.

"I took it from one of the men," she said. "I am sorry there was no time to get another."

Clay hefted the gun in his tingling hand. Feeling in the form of pain was returning to his fingers; it was the most welcome pain he had ever felt.

"That's all right. Let's get the hell out of here! Head for the back wall!"

They turned, and as they did so, Clay spotted Proud Wolf and Aaron dashing in through the open gates. Each of them held a pistol, and the weapons belched smoke and flame as they fired, sending two more of the trappers spinning off their feet. Most of the trappers were panicking now because the south wall of the stockade was ablaze and sparks were falling on the roof of the powder house, its wooden shingles beginning to smolder.

Clive Chamberlain leapt onto the porch and trained a pistol on Clay. "Stop, Holt!" he cried.

Clay twisted and brought up the pistol he carried, feeling a split-second of regret as he pressed the trigger. Chamberlain fired at the same time, the two explosions blending into one. Clay saw the Englishman rock back as the ball struck him in the chest. In the same instant he felt a giant hand slap at the outside of his thigh, and knew he had been hit, too. He fell to one knee.

Beside him Raven Arrow was firing her bow as fast as she could notch arrows. The black-dyed shafts whipped around the stockade yard. Several of the trappers screamed, staggered, and went down with arrows through them. Proud Wolf and Aaron were fighting their way across the yard, the Hunkpapa using his tomahawk to clear a path and Aaron slashing from right to left with his long, heavy hunting knife. The trappers were not putting up much of a battle; they were more interested in getting out of the fort before the stored gunpowder blew up.

Clive Chamberlain was still alive, even though blood welled from the wound in his chest as he lay on the porch. He looked at Clay and blinked. Kneeling, Clay feebly tried to push himself back up on his wounded leg. He knew he would never find out what had brought the Englishman to the Canadian wilderness, and in the end it was of no real consequence. They had almost been friends, but fate had made them enemies.

Suddenly, as Chamberlain's eyes went glassy with death, Fletcher McKendrick materialized.

"Holt!" McKendrick thundered as he started along the porch toward Clay. He held two pistols, both of them cocked. "Your time has come, Holt!"

The gun in Clay's hand was empty, and his leg would not work. He saw his death striding inexorably toward him. McKendrick lifted the pistols.

But McKendrick's shout alerted Raven Arrow. She whirled around and, in a fluid movement of arms and shoulders, gripped the bow, pulling back one of her arrows and releasing it a second before McKendrick pulled the triggers of the pistols. The arrowhead slammed into the Scotsman's right shoulder, the impact twisting him to that side. His pistols boomed.

The ball from the right-hand gun went harmlessly into the ground. The shot from the left-hand gun struck Raven Arrow in the belly.

Proud Wolf was less than ten yards from the porch. "Noooo!" he screamed when he saw Raven Arrow stagger backward, dropping her bow and clutching her midsection. Blood welled between her fingers. She fell. Proud Wolf covered the distance between him and McKendrick in a couple of bounds as the Scotsman struggled to right himself. McKendrick looked up in time to see Proud Wolf's tomahawk coming at him, and then the heavy stone weapon crashed against his head, driving him to the floor of the porch.

Clay finally pushed himself to his feet as Proud Wolf pounded along the porch to kneel beside Raven Arrow's body. The young warrior slid his arms underneath her, and even though she was larger than he, Proud Wolf picked her up as if she weighed nothing.

Aaron appeared at Clay's side, his face grimy with powder smoke and bleeding from several cuts. He caught Clay's arm to support him and said urgently, "We've got to get out of here! That powder's going to blow!"

There were too many trappers and too much

chaos in front of the headquarters building for them to reach the main gate, Clay judged. "Out the back!" he said, then hustled along, with Aaron helping him. Proud Wolf managed to keep apace with them, despite carrying Raven Arrow.

The smoke was almost too thick for them to see where they were going. One man tried to stop them, but Aaron plunged his knife into the luckless trapper's chest and shoved him aside. When they reached the rear gate, Aaron kicked it open, and they stumbled through, coughing and wheezing, eyes watering from the smoke.

What sounded like the largest clap of thunder in history slammed against Clay's ears, and the force of the explosion drove him and the others forward. Debris rained around them. They fell, got to their feet, and limped on, Proud Wolf still cradling Raven Arrow's body in his arms. Another huge explosion sounded behind them, but this time they were far enough away so that the concussion did not knock them off their feet. Clay turned and saw that all of Fort Dunadeen was ablaze.

It made a fitting funeral pyre for McKendrick, he thought, and then he and Aaron staggered after Proud Wolf and moved ever deeper into the woods.

How long they trudged through the forest Clay could not have said, but he knew they had to have traveled several miles from the fort. Finally, however, Proud Wolf came to a stop and gently lowered Butterfly to the ground. Clay sat down with Aaron's help and leaned back against the trunk of a pine.

Proud Wolf knelt beside the young woman and brushed back a strand of black hair that had fallen over her face. She stirred slightly and let out a low moan.

Proud Wolf leaned over her and said urgently, "Butterfly! Butterfly, can you hear me?"

Her eyelids flickered; then she looked up at him and said in a weak voice, "Raven Arrow. . . . My name is . . . Raven Arrow. . . . I am . . . a warrior."

Proud Wolf was crying unashamedly as he picked up her hand and pressed it to his lips. "Raven Arrow," he whispered. "So shall you be known. The Sioux will sing songs and tell tales of Raven Arrow, the greatest of warriors. This I swear."

"The . . . greatest of warriors," she repeated with a smile that turned into a grimace of pain. When she could speak again, she asked, "And the . . . the beloved of Proud Wolf?"

"The greatest of warriors and . . . and the beloved of Proud Wolf," he agreed, his voice choked with grief.

"It is . . . about time. . . ." She let out a great sigh with the words, and a tremor ran through her body. A few feet away, Clay bit back a curse, and Aaron's head slumped forward, his shoulders shaking with silent sobs.

Proud Wolf still held Raven Arrow's hand. Gently he placed it on her breast, crossing it with the other one. Then he stood, looking through the forest toward what had been Fort Dunadeen. Smoke was still visible.

"I will take you home to our village, Raven Arrow," Proud Wolf said. "You will have a warrior's burial."

Clay looked down at his leg. There was a bloody gash in the thigh of his buckskin trousers, but he could tell now that the pistol ball had not penetrated. It had ripped a painful furrow in the flesh of his leg— a messy wound but not a serious one, as long as it was cleaned and bound up with a poultice on it to draw out any festering.

No, he thought, the only serious injuries he and Aaron and Proud Wolf had suffered were the wounds to their souls. They had gotten their revenge on McKendrick, but at the cost of Raven Arrow's life as well as the lives of Clive Chamberlain and other men who had never done any harm to them. Somehow the retribution was not nearly as satisfying as Clay had thought it would be.

He wondered if it ever was.

Not far from the burning fort, a man lay facedown on the ground, dirt in his mouth, nose, and eyes. Pain, impossible pain, gripped him. His skin was charred until it was almost crisped in places, and the broken shaft of an arrow protruded from his shoulder. On his forehead was a huge gash that had bled heavily, but the heat of the fire had dried the blood, crusting it over his eyes. He whimpered and moaned and finally managed to lift a hand so that he could paw feebly at his eyes. After several interminable minutes filled with agony, he had scraped away enough of the dried blood so that he could open them.

He saw nothing but grass and dirt and the trunks of trees and something shining that he determined was sunlight on the river. He moaned again and tried to drag himself toward the water. Even though the flames were now behind him, he felt as if he were still on fire, and he longed to plunge himself into the cool stream.

An inch··· ... six inches ... a foot. ... Slowly, the burned man crawled and pulled himself along until he reached the bank, and then he slid down through the grass and mud into the river. He screamed as the water touched his raw flesh, but then the coolness enveloped him, and the pain eased a little. He lay there with only his face out of the water, clinging to a root jutting into the water just below the surface to keep from being pulled under. The sunlight faded and night fell.

And then Fletcher McKendrick came out of the water and muttered a name, the name of the man he was going to kill. He would have his revenge on that man and everyone close to him. It might take a long

time, given his injuries, but McKendrick drew
strength from the rage that burned within him more
fiercely than the fire that had destroyed Fort
Dunadeen. He would have his vengeance, and it
would be terrible to behold. He whispered the name
again.

"Clay Holt."

PART III

I shall be wrapped in a robe, (an old robe, perhaps) and hoisted on a slender scaffold to the whistling winds, soon to be blown down to the earth—my flesh to be devoured by the wolves, and my bones rattled on the plain by the wild beasts.

—From Sioux burial oration, as quoted in JOHN BRADBURY's "Travels in the Interior of America 1809–1811"

CHAPTER FIFTEEN

I reckon we were due some good luck after everything
that's happened, Clay Holt thought as he looked
across a clearing in the woods and saw several
horses grazing on the far side. Feeling far stronger
after a decent night's sleep, he had decided to scout
around for game before they started for home. He had
not expected to be that lucky. He recognized his own
lineback dun, as well as Proud Wolf's pinto and
Aaron's chestnut. Three other horses from Fort
Dunadeen were grazing with them.

Clay stood stock still for a long moment before
emerging from the trees. All the horses had been kept
in a small pole corral inside the fort, and Clay guessed
that during the battle, spooked by the smoke and the
shooting, the horses had kicked down the corral fence
and raced out of the stockade, unnoticed amidst all
the chaos. Apparently most of them had survived and
stayed together.

If he could capture the horses, the trip back
would be much easier, that was for certain.

He stepped out of the forest, and the dun immediately raised its head, staring at him with its nostrils flared. The other horses did likewise, some of them shying nervously as the man walked slowly toward them.

"Take it easy, boy," Clay called softly to the dun in a soothing voice. "You remember me. You know I won't hurt you."

He limped slightly from his leg wound, which he had cleaned with river water. He had used a poultice of mud and dried leaves on it, then bound it tightly. The leg was still stiff and painful, but not so bad that Clay could not force the ache out of his mind most of the time. Aaron and Proud Wolf were both in better shape, at least physically, although Proud Wolf was devastated over Raven Arrow's death, which Clay and Aaron both felt keenly, too. The young woman had given her life to help save theirs, and none of them would ever forget her. But for the time being, Clay had to ignore his grief just as he ignored the pain in his leg.

He lifted a hand and kept talking to the dun, and it now seemed to recognize him. But would it be willing to submit to him again after tasting freedom? Clay sensed that if he could win over the dun, the other horses would follow.

The dun shied a little and blew menacingly through its nose, but it calmed down and stood motionless as Clay approached it. He reached out and rubbed its head, then patted its flank. The horse nudged against him companionably. A grin broke out on Clay's face, and he patted the big animal some more.

"We're still partners, aren't we, boy?" he asked.

He started back to where he had left Aaron and Proud Wolf. Looking over his shoulder, he saw that after a second's hesitation the dun was following him. The other horses trailed along behind the dun, which had apparently become the leader of the herd.

A few minutes later Clay found Proud Wolf and Aaron hacking down saplings with their knives. Nearby was the body of Raven Arrow, which Proud Wolf had laid out and arranged carefully. Clay saw that the young warrior had unbraided his long black hair and hacked it off crudely with his knife, a gesture of mourning among the Sioux.

"We cannot take Raven Arrow with us back to her village," Proud Wolf said sadly. "The miles are too many."

Clay nodded. "I know. I figured you'd realize that, but I wanted to let you do it in your own time."

"She will be buried here, near the destroyed stronghold of our enemies so that her spirit may glory in their destruction."

"And because it's a mighty pretty place," Aaron added, sweeping his arm to take in the magnificent landscape around them.

Clay said, "I think she'd like that," and then he pitched in to help erect the scaffold of poles on which Raven Arrow's body would be laid to rest.

When it was complete, Proud Wolf took the paint he had made that morning from crushed berries and gently painted Raven Arrow's face, as a warrior should be decorated on entering the Land of Many Lodges. He placed her quiver of arrows beside her, along with her bow. It was good that a warrior be well armed in the life beyond life.

"She should be wrapped in the hide of the buffalo," he said, "but there are no buffalo here and no time to hunt them down. Raven Arrow will understand."

"I'm sure she will," Clay said quietly. "Are you ready, Proud Wolf?"

With a nod, Proud Wolf reached down and took hold of the corpse, and with the help of Clay and Aaron, he lifted it to the top of the scaffold, then lashed it to the structure using rope fashioned out of plaited strips of willow bark.

He went over to the pinto Clay had retrieved with the other horses. Raven Arrow's bay was not among them, so once again the next best thing would have to do. With a swift stroke of his knife, he cut the horse's tail off, making the pinto scream in pain and rear up. Remarkably, it did not run away. Proud Wolf would have said that it sensed the honor in what had just been done. The young warrior used a piece of his buckskin shirt to bind the stump and stop the flow of blood.

That done, he solemnly carried the tail to the scaffold and secured it tightly to one of the posts, then nodded with satisfaction. In the afterlife Raven Arrow would have her bow, her arrows, and a good horse. No warrior could ask for more. As he stepped back, Proud Wolf lifted his head to the sky and began to chant, the words rising in a mournful wail that sent shivers down the backs of the two white men. No matter how much time he spent with the Sioux, Clay thought, there would always be a boundary that could not be crossed at a time like this. He offered up a silent prayer of his own, a prayer that Raven Arrow's spirit would find peace.

Finally Proud Wolf's chanting ended. After a length of silence, he said, "It is ended. The spirit of Raven Arrow has entered the Land of Many Lodges." Looking older than his years, he turned to face Clay and Aaron. "It is time for us to leave."

Clay nodded. Their mission had been accomplished, and it was time to go home.

Father Thomas Brennan was soundly sleeping, but the pounding on the door of the church dragged him up out of slumber. He swung his legs off the bunk in his small room at the back of the church and rubbed his eyes. In a matter of moments, he had thrown on a shirt and trousers and slipped his feet into his moccasins. The pounding continued, and as he walked out into the sanctuary he called, "Just a minute! I'll be right there!"

The door was unlocked, of course; he believed that the doors of a church should never be barred except in an extreme emergency. But whoever was outside did not want to enter uninvited. The priest swung the door open and found an Indian youth from the nearby Hunkpapa village standing there. He recognized the boy as the one called Cloud-That-Falls.

"You must come," Cloud-That-Falls said urgently without giving the priest a chance to speak. "It is Shining Moon. She calls your name."

The priest stared at the young Indian in the moonlight. "Shining Moon," he repeated. "Is she ill?"

"She screams in pain inside her tipi. Yesterday the shaman went to the mountains to seek the guidance of the spirits. You must come."

Father Brennan did not bother to go back for his robe. Stepping out of the church, he said, "Take me to her. Quickly!"

The young Hunkpapa broke into a trot as he headed toward his village, but the priest, with his long-legged stride, had no trouble keeping up. Along the way he passed the tents and cabins of the still-growing community of New Hope. The glow of lanterns was coming from some of them, including the cabin where Josie Garwood and her son were now living.

Acting on impulse, Father Brennan said to Cloud-That-Falls, "Wait a moment, please." He went to Josie's cabin door and knocked; a few seconds later it opened, and Josie peered out. She looked surprised when she saw the priest standing there.

She had probably been expecting someone else, he decided, then warned himself not to be too uncharitable in his thoughts. But there was no denying the fact that in the weeks she had been here, Josie had become quite popular with some of the men in the settlement. Too popular, as far as the priest was concerned, especially since she claimed to be a married woman.

But right now he had another, more pressing concern. "Something is wrong with Shining Moon," he said without preamble. "Will you come with me?"

Josie peered at him. "Is she sick?"

"I'm not sure." He wondered if Shining Moon had told Josie that she was with child. The two women had become friends of a sort, but Father Brennan doubted Shining Moon would have confided that secret to Josie. He went on, "All I know is that something's wrong, and I think it might be a good idea to have a lady with me when I visit her."

Josie gave him a wry smile. "I don't know as I fit that description, but I'll come." She reached back into the cabin for a shawl that she wrapped around her shoulders. "Matthew's sound asleep, so I suppose he'll be all right."

"I'm sure he will be, and if there's any problem, Mr. Fisher is close by. We had better hurry." Cloud-That-Falls was getting impatient, Father Brennan saw.

Nodding, Josie came out of the cabin, and together they followed the anxious Hunkpapa. The village had moved again, and it was now a good three-quarters of a mile away from New Hope. Father Brennan knew that Josie had never been to the village —the whites and the Indians tended to keep a respectful distance from each other—and he could tell that she was growing nervous as they came in sight of the tipis.

"These Indians aren't—aren't savages, are they?" Josie asked in a low voice.

"Not to us, not so far. As long as we treat them decently, I expect they won't be."

"Shining Moon's been a good friend since I got here," Josie said worriedly. "Lord, she's sat and listened to me ramble for hours about living back in the Ohio Valley."

No doubt because Shining Moon was trying to

learn more about Clay Holt, Father Brennan assumed. He was trying to understand how the man she had loved and committed herself to could be married to someone else and never tell her.

Before they even reached Shining Moon's tipi, they could hear the cries coming from inside. The priest felt fear tickle his spine, and he muttered a heartfelt prayer for strength. It would take a terrible ordeal to coax such cries from Shining Moon, who was perhaps the strongest woman he had ever known. He pushed through the crowd of Indians gathered around the tipi, then ducked down and pushed aside the flap of hide over the entrance. Josie followed him inside.

The tipi was illuminated by flames from the firepit, revealing Shining Moon lying curled in a ball on a buffalo robe, her hands clutched to her belly. Beads of sweat covered her face, and although her eyes were open, there was no recognition in them as the priest knelt beside her. She was too far gone in pain to know him. Blood stained the lower half of her buckskin dress.

"Son of a bitch!" Josie exclaimed harshly. "Sorry, Father. Do you know what's going on here?"

"I have an idea," he said. "Shining Moon is with child—"

"Not anymore," Josie cut in. "She's lost it."

The priest's face was bleak. "Yes, I suspected as much. And if we don't do something, she may bleed to death." He stood up. "You stay with her while I get some moss. It's the best thing to stop the bleeding."

"Better hurry, Father," Josie said as she knelt beside Shining Moon and took hold of one of her hands. "You hang on, gal. It's me, Josie. Your friend Josie, remember? It's going to be all right."

The priest hurried out into the night and started issuing orders to the worried members of Bear Tooth's band. He heard Josie repeating her confident words over and over, and he prayed that she was right.

* * *

The cry flew from Clay's mouth before he could stop it. He sat bolt upright, his eyes wide open, but he was not seeing the moonlit night around him. Etched in his mind was the image of Shining Moon, screaming in agony and calling his name as she sank in a bottomless pool of fire and blood.

A hand came down hard on Clay's shoulder, causing him to cry out again. Then a familiar voice said urgently, "What is it, Clay? What's wrong?"

A great shudder shook Clay as he lifted his hands and buried his bearded face in them. He shook his head for a moment, then raised it and gave a heavy sigh. His heart was still pounding wildly, his pulse ringing like hammer blows inside his skull, but his wits were slowly starting to return to him.

"Damn it, Clay—" Aaron Garwood began.

Clay looked up at his friend standing over him. It must have been Aaron's watch, for Proud Wolf was sitting up on the ground a few feet away.

"I'm all right, Aaron," Clay said, "but something's wrong, sure enough. Something has happened to Shining Moon."

"My sister?" Proud Wolf asked. He leaned toward Clay intently. "You had a vision of Shining Moon?"

"A dream, I guess. I reckon you could call it a vision." Clay shuddered again. "It sure seemed real enough."

"What was this vision?" Proud Wolf demanded.

Clay hesitated before answering. He hated to even think about the horrible images; however, he supposed Proud Wolf had a right to know. But it still took an effort for Clay to get the words out.

"There wasn't that much to it," he said hesitantly. "I just saw Shining Moon, and she was in some sort of—pit, I guess you'd call it . . . and she was sinking into this pool of fire, and at the same time the pit was full of blood. . . ." Clay shook his head. "I know it doesn't make any sense, but there it is."

"It was a vision," Proud Wolf said, awe in his voice. "Shining Moon is in great danger. Perhaps she is even dead."

"No!" Clay's voice was sharp. "She may be in danger, and something terrible may be happening to her, but she's not dead. I'd know it if she was."

Clay breathed deeply and willed himself to stay calm. After being on the frontier for several years, it did not occur to him to discount the nightmare as simply a bad dream. While he did not share all the beliefs of the Sioux, he had witnessed too many strange things to scoff at any of their notions. He himself had had visions before, and Shining Moon had told him of a time when her visions had helped her pull him back from the brink of death. Some people might say that such things were only superstitious hogwash, but Clay Holt knew better.

He stood up, looked at the sky, and saw by the grayness in the east and the way the stars were fading from sight that morning was near. He would have been awake soon anyway, even without the nightmare.

"No point in trying to get any more sleep. We'll get ready to travel and make an early start of it."

They had eaten the last of their fresh meat the night before, and until they came upon some game again, they would have to make do with the roots, berries, and nuts they could find. It was not very appealing fare, but a man could live on it for a while, anyway.

In the five days since they had left the ruins of Fort Dunadeen, they had covered a lot of ground. Clay was not sure if they were over into American territory yet, but if they had not reached it already, they would soon. That morning was no different from the others; they ate a quick breakfast, looped the crude bridles they had fashioned from plaited bark strips on the horses, then rode bareback south, leading the spare horses with additional tethers made of the same crude ropes as the bridles.

Clay kept them moving at a brisk pace. They had followed the river out of the mountains and were now riding over plains covered with lush grass. The north country's brief summer was in full bloom, and wildflowers waved in the prairie wind. Even though the nights were still cool, the sun was warm, almost hot, during the day. He should have been enjoying this trip, Clay thought—after all, McKendrick was dead, and they were on their way home—but too much had happened. First Raven Arrow's death, and now the vision of Shining Moon in danger, which stayed vividly with him throughout the day.

Late in the afternoon he led his companions back into the foothills in search of a good place to camp, and along the way they scared up a small herd of deer. Clay took aim with his rifle and fired only once; their powder might run out before they reached their destination, so each shot had to count. One of the does plunged to her knees when Clay fired, then collapsed onto her side and kicked out the last of her life. Aaron was already off his horse and headed for the fallen deer, knife in hand ready to dress the carcass.

Clay found a good campsite nearby, at the base of a rocky bluff that jutted out from a foothill. They gathered wood and soon had a small fire lit using Aaron's flint and tinderbox. Hacking off haunches of venison, they impaled them on sharpened sticks and roasted them over the flames. After not eating anything since that morning, and then only some berries and roots, the aroma of the cooking meat was delicious agony.

However, not even fresh meat could take Clay's mind off the nightmare he had had, and as he chewed the tender, savory venison, his mind insisted on drifting back to that hellish vision. With an angry shake of his head, he told himself to stop making things worse.

They were heading for home as fast as they could, and there was nothing else he could do.

Except pray that Shining Moon was all right.

Since a part of him dreaded falling asleep again, fearful that another dream would come to him, he took the first watch. Aaron would take the second watch, then Proud Wolf. After the other two had rolled up by the embers of the campfire and gone to sleep, Clay paced around the camp, rifle in hand. Time seemed to drag by. The horses were calm, which meant that no wild animals were nearby, and they had seen no Blackfoot since leaving Fort Dunadeen. Still, they had let the fire die as darkness fell rather than keep it stoked through the night, so as not to attract any unwanted attention.

Reluctantly Clay woke Aaron when he judged by the stars that his portion of the night's watch was over.

"Any trouble?" Aaron asked quietly.

"All's quiet."

"Good," Aaron grunted. "Hope it stays that way."

Clay lay down on his back and looked up at the sky, part of it cut off by the bluff looming above. He had always thought that few things were prettier than a brilliant array of stars sparkling against the pitch-black sky, but that night the stars seemed to call down a warning to him. Something was wrong, something bad, and he could not do a damn thing about it.

He fell asleep without even realizing it, a deep, dreamless slumber. He might have been surprised and gratified by that fact the next morning—except that all hell broke loose.

Clay was jolted awake by a harsh rumbling sound, followed by several crashes and a scream. He came up off the ground with his rifle gripped tightly in his hands, but there was nothing for him to shoot at, only thick clouds of dust that burned his eyes and made him cough. With a feeling of dread, he realized that he and his companions were caught in the middle of a rockslide. From the sound of it, half of the overhanging bluff was coming down on them.

Someone bumped into Clay, and he reached out to grab an arm. Unsure if he had hold of Aaron or Proud Wolf, he shouted, "Come on!" and broke into a run toward what he hoped was the open plain next to the bluff. If he was turned around and was running directly into the path of the avalanche, they were doomed.

The gray predawn light showed that the air was becoming clearer, however, and the rocks smashing down around them became fewer. As Clay continued away from the base of the bluff, he saw that Proud Wolf was beside him.

"Where's Aaron?" Clay yelled over the dwindling rumble of the avalanche. He remembered the screams he had heard and had a cold feeling in his belly.

Coughing from the dust, Proud Wolf shook his head. "I-I did not see him. I was standing watch when the rocks began to fall. One of them hit me in the back and knocked me down, and when I got up you were here, pulling me out of danger."

Clay halted and swung around to face the bluff. The rocks had stopped falling, and the morning breeze was carrying away the clouds of dust particles. He thought about the huge mudslide that had nearly taken his life the year before; this avalanche had been much smaller, but it was just as deadly. He prayed that Aaron was all right.

"Come on," Clay shouted as he headed back toward the place where they had camped. "We've got to find Aaron."

Hurrying toward the site of the disaster, he mentally cursed himself for choosing this spot. But when he had decided to camp here the previous evening, he had looked the bluff over carefully, making sure there were no precariously balanced rocks above them. As far as he could tell, there was no reason for the rock-slide to have occurred.

But it had.

As he approached the camp, Clay shouted, "Aaron! Where are you, Aaron?"

A faint moan answered him, and Clay felt a leap of hope. At least Aaron was not already dead, buried by the falling rocks. A weak voice said, "Over here . . ."

Clay bit back a curse when he spotted Aaron. Only the upper half of the young man's body was visible. The lower half was buried by a jumble of small rocks on top of which rested a large boulder. Clay placed his rifle on the ground, then put his shoulder against the massive rock.

"Hang on, Aaron," he muttered, throwing all his strength into moving the boulder. "We'll get you out of there."

"Better . . . hurry," Aaron gasped. "I can't . . . feel my legs . . . anymore." He gave a grim snicker. "Could be that's a . . . blessing."

Proud Wolf joined Clay, and together they pushed the boulder that was pinning Aaron down. Grunting and straining with the effort, they finally shifted the big rock slightly. They shoved again, and it shifted some more. Aaron cried out in pain as the boulder moved.

"Sorry," Clay muttered automatically. He and Proud Wolf shoved again, and this time the boulder abruptly slid off the mound of smaller rocks, tumbling several feet to the side before it came to a stop. Instantly, Clay and Proud Wolf began tossing aside the smaller rocks, uncovering the lower part of Aaron's body.

His legs had taken quite a beating, Clay saw immediately. The left one was broken, the shinbone poking through the ripped buckskin breeches. The right leg was more than broken; it was crushed almost beyond recognition.

"Good Lord," Clay breathed involuntarily as he saw the extent of the injuries.

"Bad?" Aaron asked.

"Bad enough." No point in lying to him, Clay thought. Aaron was smart enough to know what was going on, even through the haze of pain that had to be enveloping him. Clay went on, "Both your legs are broken."

"You better—you better just leave me here."

"No!" Proud Wolf exclaimed. "We had to leave Raven Arrow behind. We will not leave you, my friend."

"Couldn't travel with two broken legs," Aaron insisted. "Couldn't ride a horse—not like this."

That reminded Clay of the horses, and when he looked around he was relieved to see that all six of them were standing a couple of hundred yards away on the prairie, grazing peacefully. The animals were routinely hobbled at night, but they could have drifted off a bit in search of better grass. Luckily they had not been near the base of the bluff when the rock-slide began.

"You won't have to ride," he told Aaron as he knelt beside him. "We'll make a travois to carry you."

"That'll slow you down—a heap," Aaron objected.

Clay shook his head stubbornly. "Like Proud Wolf said, we're not leaving you. You might as well get used to the idea."

"But Shining Moon—"

Clay's expression was grave. "Whatever's wrong, there's nothing I can do about it. Now, listen to me, Aaron. Proud Wolf's going to hunt up a good-sized stick, and you're going to bite the hell out of it while I splint these legs, understand? Because I can promise you it's going to hurt."

Aaron looked up at Clay, gratitude on his face. "I understand," he whispered.

Proud Wolf found a stick for Aaron to bite down

on, and Clay got busy trying to force the broken bones back into place—or at least some semblance of the way they had been. The left leg was the worst in one way because it was less severely damaged and therefore was more acutely sensitive. Aaron screamed in agony as Clay worked the jagged end of the protruding bone back through the torn muscle and sinew. No bones were sticking out of the right leg, but from the way it looked, Clay had a feeling that it was shattered in a dozen places or more. He straightened it out as best he could and lashed several branches to both legs as splints. Proud Wolf had done a good job of cutting and trimming the branches. Clay hoped he had done as good a job of setting the bones.

Once the splints were in place, Clay tore strips from Aaron's ripped breeches and bound them tightly around both legs to stop the bleeding from the numerous wounds. That was all he could do. He wished he had a bottle of whiskey for Aaron. The young man was going to need something for the pain, which was going to get even worse once the shock fully wore off.

Proud Wolf was hacking down more saplings to build a travois that could be pulled behind one of the spare horses. Clay patted Aaron reassuringly on the shoulder, then joined Proud Wolf in constructing the crude sled. In the absence of rawhide or rope, they used plaited grass and willow bark to lash the framework of the travois together and to fashion a harness for fastening the sled to a horse.

When they were done, they discovered that Aaron had passed out. For one awful moment Clay thought his friend was dead, but then he discerned the rising and falling of his chest. Trying not to jolt him around too much, they carefully lifted him and placed him on the travois. Aaron tossed his head back and forth a little and moaned, but he did not regain consciousness.

"It's probably best that he's unconscious," Clay said as he and Proud Wolf got their horses ready to

ride, "what with the kind of pain he'd be feeling if he
were awake."

The sun was up by now, but neither man felt like
eating breakfast. They wanted to get away from that
place. The avalanche was over, and Clay did not expect it to start again—but then he had not expected
any sort of rockslide in the first place. Better to get out
on the open prairie, he thought. They would stop
later, cook some of the venison they were taking with
them, and eat then. Maybe Aaron would wake up and
feel like eating, too.

They mounted up and were about to be on their
way when Proud Wolf stared up at the bluff and
frowned. "Those rocks should not have fallen."

"Nope," Clay agreed, "but once they started,
there was no stopping them."

"But why did they start?"

Clay shook his head. "Don't know. It doesn't
make sense. I reckon we've just got some bad luck
following us around."

Or something else, he thought as he heeled the dun
into motion, leading the horse that pulled the travois.

A couple of days passed, and nothing else unto-
ward occurred. The travelers were moving slowly
now, since every bump and jolt of the travois sent
pain shooting through Aaron's battered, broken body,
but they covered ground steadily, heading due south.
Clay kept them well away from the mountains, not
wanting to risk any more mysterious avalanches.
They rode through the buffalo grass on the prairie,
over gentle hills that rolled like the waves of a seemingly endless ocean.

Aaron seemed a bit stronger, Clay thought. They
had given him most of the venison; an injured man
needed all the fresh meat he could get to fight off the
effects of his injury. Proud Wolf felled some sage hens
with his arrows, so they had plenty to eat.

Another week and they would be getting close to

the territory inhabited by Bear Tooth's band of Hunkpapa Sioux, Clay thought. Before that, they might run into other bands of Sioux, although that was somewhat unlikely; Bear Tooth's band ventured farther west and north than most of the tribe.

On the third day after the avalanche, Proud Wolf spotted a small group of riders far in the distance, and Clay quickly hustled them into a buffalo wallow where they could hide. The riders did not come close enough for Clay to positively identify them, but he felt certain they were Blackfoot.

He and Proud Wolf did not have enough powder to fight off an attack, so they would have to rely on stealth. As they rode they constantly scanned the horizon on all sides, alert for any sign of trouble.

Another few days went by, and on the second one, they spotted more Indians in the distance and had to lie low again, this time by pulling the horses down on their sides and stretching out in the tall grass for several hours while the sun beat down on them and the bugs chewed on them. It felt pretty miserable but better than having your scalp decorating the lodge pole of some Blackfoot warrior's tipi, Clay decided.

Aaron was now feverish and incoherent, and Clay did not like the way both of his legs were swollen and pressing against their bindings. He had heard of men who had had badly injured legs cut off rather than risk death from blood poisoning. However, he did not think he could stand to live that way, and he was not about to make such a choice for Aaron—not to mention that even attempting such a thing out here in the middle of nowhere would be tantamount to killing him; there was no way he would survive it. All they could do was take him back to Bear Tooth's village and hope that the medicine man could do something for him.

They were riding along with the mountains some miles off to the west when Clay glanced in that direction and saw smoke rising into the air. Not the thin spiral from a campfire of buffalo chips, but large gray-ish black billows.

"What the hell?" he muttered.

Proud Wolf saw the smoke, too, and tensed as he pulled back on the pinto's bridle to bring the horse to a halt. "I have seen such smoke before. It looks like a prairie fire."

Clay's jaw tightened. He had heard about prairie fires, but he had never seen one. He knew they could whip across dozens of miles in no time, destroying everything in their path. This one was a long way to the west, but the wind was from that direction, and it would drive the flames before it as it swept down from the mountains and across the plains. Already he could faintly smell smoke.

"Let's go," he told Proud Wolf. "We'll have to travel faster."

He glanced back at the travois carrying Aaron as he urged the dun into a trot. The faster pace would be hard on the injured man, but they had no choice. Either they had to get out of the path of the fire or be consumed by it. Luckily the grass was still green in most places, and that would slow down the progress of the blaze.

Now was not the time to panic, Clay told himself. Their only hope was getting the right mixture of speed and stamina out of the horses. Galloping madly across the plains would be a good way of hitting a prairie dog hole and breaking a horse's leg. Then they would be in really bad shape. With that in mind, Clay rode as fast as he could without being reckless, his gaze constantly shifting from the ground in front of him to the prairie fire coming toward them.

Even over the pounding of hooves, Clay heard the curses and cries of pain coming from Aaron and knew that the faster pace was sheer torture for the young man. Better that than being caught in the fire, however. Clay did not slow down.

The fire advanced inexorably, and soon Clay and Proud Wolf could see the orange flames licking at the base of the smoke cloud. The blaze was less than a mile away now, crawling toward them like some sort of monster. Clay pushed the dun harder, shutting his ears to Aaron's screams.

Suddenly Clay spotted a line of thicker vegetation up ahead, which cut across the terrain at an angle. That had to mark the course of a creek, he thought. And that could prove to be their salvation; a creek might not stop the fire, but it should slow down the advance long enough for Clay and his companions to get out of the path of the flames. At least that was what Clay hoped. He dug his heels harder against the flanks of the dun and tightened his grip on the lead rope of the horse pulling the travois.

"Make for that creek!" Clay shouted to Proud Wolf, who nodded in understanding and urged more speed out of the pinto. They swung their horses more in a direct line toward the stream.

Now speed was all that mattered. The leading edge of the fire was only a few hundred yards away. The air was thick with smoke, and Clay's hands and face stung from the smoldering ashes that pelted them, carried ahead of the fire by the wind. Clay knew that the ashes could cause the fire to spread across the creek, but the water would certainly impede the encroaching inferno.

The creek was broad and shallow, just what Clay had hoped to see. He twisted on the dun's back and called to Aaron, "Hang on, you're about to get wet!" Then the horses were pounding down the gentle bank of the stream and into the water. Their hooves churned up the pebble-strewn bottom.

And then they were across. Clay looked back at Aaron, still lashed securely to the travois. He could not tell if Aaron was conscious or even still alive, but they had to put more distance between themselves and the blaze before they could stop and check. He waved Proud Wolf on.

Looking back after they had ridden a couple hundred yards, Clay saw that the fire was still burning fiercely on the other side of the creek but did not seem to be advancing. He breathed a little easier but kept going until they had put a good mile between themselves and the stream. Then, pulling the dun to a halt, Clay turned and studied the fire again. Black smoke was still billowing up, but it was far in the distance now.

"We did it," he said to Proud Wolf as he swung down from the dun. He hurried to the travois and knelt to check on Aaron.

The young man was still breathing, and Clay felt a wave of relief wash through him. But the bandages around his legs were stained with fresh blood in places, the bouncing around having reopened some of Aaron's wounds. They needed to push on now, to put even more distance between them and the flames, but as soon as they stopped for the night, Clay would have to unwrap the legs and take a look at them.

"Will he be all right?" Proud Wolf asked.

Clay shook his head in uncertainty. "I don't know. He's unconscious, and it doesn't look very good. But we'll do what we can for him as soon as we've stopped for the night. Right now we've got to keep going, to be on the safe side."

Proud Wolf hesitated, then asked, "Clay, what started that fire? There was no lightning; the sky is clear."

Clay had wondered about that himself, although there had been no time to ponder the question during their flight. Just like the avalanche a few days earlier, the prairie fire should not have happened.

"Looks like we've got bad luck following our trail," he said as he mounted the dun again. That was not a good answer, and both of them knew it.

He glanced to the north. Could somebody be

back there, somebody who had started both the avalanche and the fire in hopes of killing them? Somebody who hated them enough to want them dead?

Clay took a deep breath. There was one answer that should have been impossible, and he did not even want to think about it. The name resounded in his mind anyway.

Fletcher McKendrick.

CHAPTER SIXTEEN

What is passed, and cannot be prevented,
should not be grieved for.

—from Sioux burial oration, as quoted in
JOHN BRADBURY's "Travels in the Interior
of America 1809–1811"

Thomas Brennan pushed aside the entrance flap
of Shining Moon's tipi and stepped out into the
midday sun. It was warm and felt good on his
face. He was smiling a little, pleased with the way the
visit had gone. Shining Moon was still weak from the
ordeal she had endured a couple of weeks earlier, but
her strength was steadily returning. The melancholy
that had gripped her for a time after the loss of her
baby seemed to be easing, too, and the priest hoped
that he had helped by comforting her when she

needed someone. Comforting the grief-stricken was part of his job, after all.

But it was different with Shining Moon. She was his friend, perhaps the best friend he had ever had.

It had come as a surprise to him, that he would become so close with an Indian—and an Indian woman at that. He sometimes felt uncomfortable with that part of the relationship, but then he chided himself for such thoughts. He was a priest, after all, sworn to God, and Shining Moon was a married woman. At least, she had *believed* she was married to Clay Holt. Father Brennan sighed at the thought. Shining Moon had survived the loss of her child, but the confrontation with Clay was yet to come—assuming that he returned to the Hunkpapa village one day.

New Hope was still growing, and as the priest walked back to the mission, he passed some of the evidence of that growth. Just within the last week a man named Budd Spenser had arrived and begun building a blacksmith shop. Malachi Fisher and the other men in the community were pitching in to help him, and the shop was going up quickly. Spenser was already shoeing some of the horses belonging to the trappers. The idea of shod horses struck the Indians as ludicrous, but that did not prevent them from coming over to watch in curiosity as Spenser went about his work, clad in just trousers and a thick leather apron, his muscular bare arms and shoulders bulging as he fired the forge and swung his massive hammer. There might not be much call for a blacksmith out here yet, except to make traps, but the more people who came to the mountains, the more necessary Spenser would become.

Progress, Father Brennan thought. More people, more need for the accoutrements of civilization. Looking beyond the settlement at the as yet unspoiled wilderness, he was not sure progress was always such a good thing. But there was no stopping it once it started.

He went into the church. It would be time soon
for evening prayers, and he was sitting on one of the
benches that served as pews, his head down and his
Bible held in his hands, lost in meditation, when he
suddenly became aware of shouting outside. He lifted
his head and listened, hoping it was not the beginning
of some new trouble.

He rose and hurried out of the church and saw
two men on horseback riding along the riverbank toward the mission. They were leading several other
horses, one of which was pulling a travois with a man
strapped onto it. Several men from the settlement
were walking alongside the riders, talking with them.

The men on horseback were both striking-
looking figures. One was white, although his skin was
tanned to such a degree that he could have passed for
an Indian had it not been for the black beard on his
craggy face and his piercing blue eyes. The other man
was a young Indian warrior, and something about
him struck the priest as being familiar, even though
he was sure he had never seen him before. They were
obviously bound for the church, and Father Brennan
hurried forward to meet them.

The bearded man gave a curt nod as he drew his
mount to a halt. "You're Father Brennan?" he asked.

"That's right."

"These gents tell me you can do some doctoring.
We've got a hurt man with us."

Thomas went over to the travois and knelt beside
the injured man as the bearded fellow and the young
Indian dismounted. The injured man was white, too,
with a tangled thatch of brown hair and a full beard.
His legs were splinted and wrapped in bandages, and
the man's flushed face was contorted with pain as he
thrashed his head from side to side, muttering inco-
herently. Father Brennan felt his forehead and grimaced.

"How long has he been feverish like this?"

"Off and on for a couple of weeks," the tall,

bearded man replied. "The fever broke a few times, and we thought he was getting better, but then it would take him again."

"What happened to him?"

"He got caught in an avalanche. His legs were crushed under rocks. Broke the left one clean but really tore up the right one. Both of them are festering."

Thomas leaned closer to the bandaged legs, sniffed, and grimaced again. "I'd say so. Let's get him inside."

He looked around and saw Fisher, Spenser, and several other men standing nearby, watching. "Malachi, you and Budd help us carry him. You other men, push a couple of benches together to form a table."

They all did as they were instructed, and the injured man was carried into the church and placed on the makeshift table.

"We've got to get these bindings off," the priest said. He turned to the bearded man. "Give me your knife."

The man took the blade from its sheath and handed it to the priest, who carefully cut the braided bark thongs that held the bandages in place. Although he tried not to put too much pressure on the swollen flesh beneath the wrappings, the injured man cried out in pain. Once the bindings were loose, Father Brennan handed back the knife and then began to unwind the bandages, which he now saw were buckskin strips. The putrid smell grew worse as the bandages were unwrapped.

The splints underneath were still in place, and Father Brennan left them where they were. If the man's legs had been broken two weeks earlier, the bones would have already started to knit back together if they were going to, and he did not want to disturb that progress. But that left the terrible wounds in the flesh, most of which were necrotic.

He looked up at Fisher and asked, "Malachi, can

you go over to the Hunkpapa village and fetch Soaring Owl? I'm going to need some help with this."

Before Fisher could reply, the young Indian said, "I will bring Soaring Owl."

"You know the shaman?" Father Thomas asked in surprise.

"Of course I know him. The Hunkpapa Sioux are my people. I am Proud Wolf."

The priest recognized the name immediately. He exclaimed, "You're Shining Moon's brother!" He swung toward the bearded stranger. "Then you must be—"

"I'm Clay Holt. You've got the advantage of me," he went on, still surprised that a priest would be out here in the wilderness near his adopted people's village.

But then, his homecoming had been filled with nothing but surprises so far. He had never expected to find white men's cabins in this valley, let alone a church, a trading post, and a blacksmith shop. The place had gotten downright civilized in the months he and Aaron and Proud Wolf had been away!

The priest was continuing his examination of Aaron's legs, and he said distractedly, "My name is Father Thomas Brennan. I've heard a great deal about you, Mr. Holt, from Shining Moon and the others in Bear Tooth's village."

Clay's breath caught in his throat. It had taken all his willpower to stop first at the church and seek medical attention for Aaron rather than rush on to the Hunkpapa village in search of Shining Moon. The dreadful vision he had experienced had not returned, but the memory of it was strong. He owed Aaron the best care he could provide, however, and when the trappers he and Proud Wolf had run into farther up the valley had said that there was a priest who knew something about medicine, Clay had known they would have to stop at the church first.

While they were waiting for Proud Wolf to come

back with old Soaring Owl, the Hunkpapa shaman, Clay thought he could at least find out if Shining Moon was all right. He asked the priest, "You know Shining Moon?"

"Indeed, I do. I visited her earlier today, in fact, and left her only a short while ago."

"Then she's all right?" Clay heard the anxiousness in his own voice.

"Physically, she's all right, although she's still rather weak, of course."

"Of course? What do you mean, of course? Weak from what?" Clay asked sharply. "What's wrong with her?"

The priest hesitated as if unsure whether to say anything else, but then he told Clay in a somber voice, "She was with child, but she lost the baby a couple of weeks ago. For a while we thought we were going to lose her, too."

Clay stiffened. He felt like a gigantic fist had just slammed into his gut. A *baby*? *His* baby? The world seemed to spin crazily, and he sank onto one of the benches.

"I—I didn't know," he said after a long moment.

"Shining Moon suspected it before you left for Canada, but she was going to surprise you when you came back." Father Brennan paused once again, then added, "She was always sure you would be coming back. She wouldn't allow anyone to even speculate otherwise."

The sour taste of pain and loss welled up in Clay's throat. He was trembling inside and out, and his thoughts were a jumble. He felt relief that Shining Moon was still alive, mixed with grief for the child of whose existence he had not even been aware. It must have been horrible for Shining Moon, he thought, to have gone through yet another ordeal, and this time he had not even been around to help her through it.

But evidently this priest, this man Brennan, had been here to comfort her. Clay looked up at him. He was wearing a priest's robe, but other than that he looked more like a mountain man himself, with his tall, brawny build and his broad shoulders.

Clay mentally winced. There was no call for thoughts like the ones trying to insinuate themselves into his mind. He trusted Shining Moon, trusted her fully and completely, and even though she had changed since the run-in with Simon Brown's Blackfoot the year before, she was still the same virtuous woman he had married.

"I'm sorry to hear about what happened," he said heavily, "but thank God Shining Moon is still alive."

"Amen to that. I know she'll be very happy to see you again, Mr. Holt. I take it your mission in Canada was successful?"

Clay looked up. "She's told you a lot, hasn't she?"

"We're friends," the priest said simply, as if that explained everything. "Did you find that man McKendrick?"

"We found him. Burned the bastard's fort down around him. But we lost a great warrior named Raven Arrow, and we may lose Aaron here as well."

"Raven Arrow," Father Thomas repeated. "I don't believe I know the name."

There was no time to explain because Proud Wolf rushed into the church leading Soaring Owl, the elderly Hunkpapa medicine man. The old man's back was bent, and his face was wrinkled with age, but there was still a power and a vigor in the way he carried himself. Together, he and the priest examined Aaron's legs, the man of God and the shaman talking in low voices as they bent over their patient.

Walks-Down-the-Wind and Cloud-That-Falls had accompanied their friend Proud Wolf back to the church, and the three young men stood talking a few feet away. Soaring Owl looked up and spoke sharply to them in the Sioux tongue, and the young warriors hurried out to find the roots and moss that he wanted. The shaman and the priest had agreed that something had to be done to draw out the cause of Aaron's fever. To Soaring Owl, that cause was evil spirits, while Father Brennan considered it to be a matter of unclean, gangrenous flesh. Either way, the results were the same, and so was the treatment.

Over the next half hour they cleaned the wounds as best they could with whiskey fetched from Malachi Fisher's trading post, then packed moss around them, as Clay had done. The delirious Aaron howled in pain during the procedure and tried to thrash around, but Clay and some of the other men held him down. When clean bandages had been wrapped around his legs, he was given a tea brewed up by Soaring Owl from the roots gathered by the young men.

"It is all we can do," Soaring Owl said as Aaron slipped into a groggy sleep brought on by the tea. "Now we must pray over him, Bren-nan, you to your God and me to the Great Spirit, Wakan Tanka."

Clay half-expected the priest to berate the old man for being a heathen, but evidently he was more tolerant of other's beliefs than most of the religious leaders Clay had run into over the years. It was an incongruous sight, the priest and the shaman praying together to different gods, but maybe it would improve Aaron's chances.

Can't hurt, he told himself, offering up a brief, silent prayer of his own.

Then he decided that he had waited as long as he could. Catching Proud Wolf's eye, he gestured with his head toward the door of the church. The two men walked outside. Clay looked in the direction of the Hunkpapa village, although the tipis were not visible from where they stood.

"Did you see Shining Moon when you went to fetch Soaring Owl?" Clay asked Proud Wolf anxiously.

The young man shook his head. "I did not take

the time. But Walks-Down-the-Wind and Cloud-That-Falls have told me disturbing news."

"I've heard about the child," Clay said, his haggard face bleak. "I need to go to her now."

Proud Wolf caught his arm. "The loss of the child was the source of your vision. The night it happened was the same night the dream visited you."

"I halfway figured that already. The priest said Shining Moon almost died, too."

He went to the dun and swung up onto its back. Proud Wolf mounted the pinto, and side by side they rode toward the village, their impatience growing as they came within sight of the tipis.

Clay spotted the tipi he had shared with Shining Moon, recognizing it from its markings. He rode straight to it, perfunctorily returning the Hunkpapas' greetings he and Proud Wolf received. Now that they had returned from Canada, the story of their exploits would soon be the stuff of songs and legends. Eventually the undertaking would be glorified almost beyond recognition. Clay, of course, knew it for what it really was—a grim, gritty business that had cost more than one innocent life—but the Hunkpapa could make of it whatever they wanted to, he supposed. All he cared about now was Shining Moon. As he reined in his horse in front of the tipi, the flap over the entrance was pushed back, and a woman with black hair wearing a blue dress stepped out. Clay's heart beat faster. He started to call out to her when she stood up, revealing her face, and he realized she was not Shining Moon. But he recognized her with a shock like a sudden hard blow to the chest.

Josie Garwood!

For a moment he doubted his eyesight—Josie was back in Ohio, at the old Garwood place near Marietta. Then he doubted his sanity because she was sure enough standing right in front of him, and that just could not be!

She looked surprised, too, but her lips quickly

curved into a smile. "Hello, Clay," she said, and the voice was the same one he remembered, low and throaty and having whatever it was that made a lot of men go crazy when they heard it. Not him, though. Never him. He was one of the few young men back home who had been able to resist Josie's charms, which had always seemed to make her want him that much more.

"Josie?" he said as he stared down at her from the back of the dun. "It's really you?"

"Didn't expect to see me here, did you?"

Before Clay could answer, the tipi's entrance flap was pushed back again. A woman stepped out, and in a voice that meant more to Clay than Josie's ever could said, "Josie? Who are you talking—"

Shining Moon stopped speaking as she straightened and looked up to see Clay and Proud Wolf sitting on their horses. For a long moment Clay just looked at her, drinking in the sight of her. She was as beautiful as ever, although her face was a bit thinner and paler. She stepped toward him, raised a hand, and whispered, "Clay. . . ?"

"I said I'd be back," he answered huskily. With that, he swung his leg over the back of the dun and dropped to the ground. She was in his arms as soon as his feet hit the dirt. Her head lifted to his, and he kissed her, a brief but intense melding of lips that sent tremors through both of them. Then she pressed her face to his chest, and he was content just to hold her for a long time.

But not long enough, for she suddenly drew away from him, and as he looked down into her eyes in surprise he saw the anger flashing there. He said quickly, "I'm sorry, Shining Moon. I didn't know about . . . about the baby. I should've been here."

"There was no way for you to know," she said tautly. "But you could have told me about Josie."

Josie? What the hell was she talking about? As Clay blinked in surprise and confusion, Shining Moon slipped out of his embrace and threw her arms around her brother, welcoming Proud Wolf home.

Clay glanced at Josie and said in a hard voice, "You've got some explaining to do."

Her smug smile just widened. "I'd say *you're* the one with the explaining to do, Clay Holt. Shining Moon and me are good friends now, and you ought to tell her why you ran off and left a wife and a child back in Ohio and never told anybody out here about me and Matthew."

"*Wife?*" he hissed. "Dammit, Josie, I never married you!"

"That's not what folks around here think," she said in a low voice as she sidled toward him. "They think you're a no-good son of a bitch who deserted your family."

For one mad moment he wanted to kill her, wanted to wrap his fingers around her throat and close that lying mouth forever. Her lies were the reason he had come west in the first place, lies that he had slept with her and fathered her son.

But if he had not joined up with Lewis and Clark, he might never have come to this country, and then he never would have met Shining Moon. So in a strange way, he realized, he owed Josie a debt of gratitude. He took a deep breath and brought his raging emotions under control.

"Listen, I don't know how you got out here, but you're going to tell the truth for once in your life," he said coldly. "You're going to tell Shining Moon and everybody else that I'm *not* your husband and never was, and I'm *not* that boy's father."

"Why, Clay, is that any way to talk about little Matthew? After all, he's your only child." Josie shot a glance at Shining Moon, who was still talking to Proud Wolf. "And the way things have been going around here, he's likely to be your only child, too."

Again he felt a surge of murderous rage. How dare she talk that way about Shining Moon's loss?

That was just like Josie, twisting everything around so that it would work to her advantage.

"We'll talk about this later," he said, knowing that if he didn't get away from Josie soon, his iron-willed control was going to snap. "Right now, if you want to see your brother again, you'd better get over to that church."

"Aaron?" Anxiety etched lines in Josie's forehead. "He's at the church? What's wrong with him?"

"He's hurt bad. I don't know if he's going to make it or not."

"Oh, my God!" Her hands went to her mouth, and Clay thought he saw some genuine concern in her eyes. Josie and Aaron had always been close. Without another word she turned and ran toward the river and the church.

Aaron, Clay thought. Aaron could confirm that he and Josie had never been married and that Matthew was not his son. Clay did not know if Aaron wanted the identity of Matthew's father revealed, but regardless, what was important was that Shining Moon be convinced there was nothing to Josie's story of being married to Clay.

But Aaron could not tell Shining Moon about any of that until he regained consciousness. *If* he regained consciousness. Clay needed no reason other than friendship to hope that Aaron pulled through, but under the circumstances he could not help but pray even harder for the young man's recovery.

He turned back to Shining Moon and Proud Wolf just as Proud Wolf was saying, "I must go to Raven Arrow's parents and tell them of the way she died and how we buried her with a warrior's honor."

Clay saw tears on Shining Moon's cheeks; Proud Wolf must have earlier explained about Raven Arrow's death. One more innocent life stolen by the hand of Fletcher McKendrick, Clay thought.

He just hoped that McKendrick was really dead and that all his victims had been avenged. But after the mysterious, nearly fatal events during the journey back from Canada, Clay was no longer so sure of that. True, nothing else had happened after the prairie fire he and his companions had so narrowly avoided, but as Proud Wolf had pointed out, the fire and the avalanche could not be explained.

Clay pushed the thought away. McKendrick had been badly hurt in the battle at Fort Dunadeen. Even if he had survived the explosion and fire and trailed them for a while, he was probably dead by now. And if he was not, he could not strike at them in the middle of Bear Tooth's village.

Putting his hand on Shining Moon's arm, Clay said, "Things have changed a lot around here since we've been gone."

She looked at him, brushing back the long black hair hanging loose around her shoulders, and nodded. She was wearing the blue dress he had bought for her in St. Louis, and despite her pallor and thinness, he thought he had never seen her looking more beautiful. Separation would do that, he supposed, but there was more to it than that. All the pain she had been through of late had given her face more character, turning a lovely woman into a truly beautiful one.

But at what price? Clay asked himself.

"All things change," she said, and he could not read the meaning on her face or in her voice.

Proud Wolf reached over and clasped Clay's wrist. "I will go now to the home of Raven Arrow's father and mother, and then I will go to the mountains."

Clay looked at the youth with confusion. "To the mountains? Why?"

"There is much I must think about. Raven Arrow's death, the loss of the child that would have been born to you and my sister, the terrible thing that has happened to my friend Aaron. . . . I must seek the guidance of the spirits so that I may know what these things mean."

Clay understood. Proud Wolf had been a staunch ally, but now that they were back home, he had to deal with his own pain and grief. For Proud Wolf that meant going off into the high country to be alone with his feelings, and Clay could appreciate that need. He felt a little of it himself.

He clasped Proud Wolf's wrist hard and said quietly, "Good-bye, my friend, my brother. We will meet again."

Proud Wolf released Clay's arm, then turned away. Clay watched him go, his back straight, showing none of his inner turmoil.

"He is truly a man now," Shining Moon said softly, "and more proud than even his name would indicate. Sometimes I miss the happy young boy who was my brother."

"We all have to grow up, and that means we go through a lot of pain." Clay wanted to put his arm around her shoulders, but a certain tenseness in her bearing told him the gesture might not be welcome. He went on, "Shining Moon, we must talk about Josie."

"Your wife?"

Clay bit back an angry response and instead said quietly but firmly, "She is *not* my wife. Never has been, never will be. I swear that to you."

Shining Moon lifted her head, and her gaze met his. She studied his eyes at length, then said, "You have never lied to me, Clay Holt, and if what you say now is true, then I must believe you. Josie is not your wife."

Clay felt a surge of relief that he had finally gotten through to her. Then he realized that her response had come too easily. She might say the words, but she did not mean them, not fully anyway. Deep inside she was still unconvinced. And Lord, when he thought about what she had been through the past few months—to lose a child, to have her world turned upside down by the arrival of a stranger, to have her

faith in the man she had believed in shaken to its core
—no wonder she could not readily believe him. She
might have a hard time ever believing anything again.

"We'll talk of this another time," he said, putting
his hands on her shoulders and brushing his lips
across her forehead. "I'll tell you all about Josie and
her son, and when Aaron gets better, he can tell you
about her, tell you the truth about her. The truth's not
very pretty, Shining Moon, but it's certainly not what
you were told."

For a long moment she did not look at him. Then
she raised her eyes again and said softly, "I am glad
you are home, Clay Holt. Come into the tipi and
smoke a pipe and tell me of many things."

That sounded good to Clay, damned good.

Josie knelt beside Aaron, staring in horror at his
haggard face and his bandaged limbs. Looking up
into the solemn faces of Father Brennan and Soaring
Owl, she asked, "He's going to be all right, isn't he?"

Father Brennan shrugged and spread his hands.
"I wish we could tell you, Josie. Your brother is very
seriously hurt. We've done what we can for him, and
now we just have to wait and pray."

"Put trust in Great Spirit," Soaring Owl said in
his awkward English. "Will either heal boy or take
him to Land of Many Lodges."

The frustration Josie felt made her want to shout
at both men with their useless answers. Her brother,
her only living relative except for Matthew, was lying
before her more dead than alive, and all they could do
was mouth platitudes. She wanted to slam her hands
on the bench and scream, to grab Aaron by the shoulders and shake him and tell him to get well.

But she would not do any of those things.

Aaron muttered something in his delirium, but
Josie could not make out the words, not even when
she leaned closer to him. It was nonsense, all of it. She
sighed and stood up.

Then a thought occurred to her, and her forehead creased in a frown. As long as Aaron was either unconscious or incoherent, he could not tell anyone the truth about the nonexistent marriage between his sister and Clay Holt. Clay could deny it up one way and down the other, could deny that he was Matthew's father, but Josie knew from experience that once a lie had taken root, it was extremely difficult to kill. No matter what Clay said, some people would believe the worst and would always think deep down that she was telling the truth, that Clay really was her husband. Nearly everybody in Marietta had accepted as gospel her claim that he was Matthew's father, and there had been no more proof of that than there was of the alleged marriage. But if her own brother stood up and called her a liar and said there was no truth in her story, then most folks would see her for what she really was.

So, Josie thought, should she pray for Aaron's recovery? Or would she be better off if his tenuous hold on life just slipped away?

"Josie," Father Brennan said, breaking into her reverie, "did you talk to Clay Holt?"

She took a deep breath. "Oh, I talked to him, all right, Father. I don't think he was very happy to see me."

"What about Shining Moon?"

Josie smiled faintly. "I don't think *she* was very happy to see *him*."

The priest sighed and slowly shook his head. "The last thing that Shining Moon needs right now is something to upset her more," he said sternly. "I hope you'll be discreet about this matter, Josie."

She felt a surge of anger. He wanted to protect his precious Shining Moon, even if it meant everybody else could go to hell. She knew how he felt about the Indian woman; Josie had seen that look in the eyes of plenty of men in the past. Father Brennan might deny it, might not even realize it, but his feelings for Shining Moon were not as holy and pure as he expressed.

At the same time Josie felt kind of sorry. Shining Moon had been a good friend to her, and it was too bad she had to be hurt more. But Josie was not going to turn back now.

"Oh, I'll be discreet, Father, but that doesn't change things. Clay Holt's my husband, and I won't give him up without a fight."

And may the best woman win, she added silently, because she sure as hell knew who *that* was going to be.

CHAPTER SEVENTEEN

The close confines of the cell were maddening, and after being in jail for a week, Jeff Holt was surprised he had not yet lost his mind. But there was still at least a week to go before his trial, he reminded himself grimly as he was led out into the large yard behind the jail, shackles binding his wrists and leg irons fastened around his ankles.

A high stone wall ran around the yard, and once a week Constable Tolbert allowed the prisoners to go outside and shuffle around for a half hour or so. Jeff appreciated that. He was no expert on jails, but he had the impression that most prisoners were left locked up all the time, that the only fresh air and sunlight they ever got was what little came through the small windows in their cells.

The number of prisoners had grown during the week that Jeff had been incarcerated. Besides him, a half-dozen men were inside the walled yard. They all seemed to be acquainted because they stood talking in a tight group on the other side of the yard. That was fine as far as Jeff was concerned; he had no desire to know them. He shuffled around the yard awkwardly because of his leg irons. He was the only prisoner accorded that dubious "honor" because he was the only one charged with a crime as serious as murder. He imagined the other men were in jail for such things as theft, brawling, and unpaid debts. Those were the usual crimes in a city like Wilmington, although around the docks the possibility always existed that someone would be knifed, either in a fight or in a robbery.

Or have his throat slit for some other reason, Jeff thought, like Charles Merrivale.

He leaned against the stone wall and squinted against the bright sunlight. It seemed especially brilliant, and was painful to his eyes, after having spent a week in the gloom-shrouded cell. He glanced around. Deputies armed with pistols stood in the rear door of the jail and in every corner of the yard. If any of the prisoners tried to get away, they would be cut down without hesitation, Tolbert had warned.

Lifting his manacled hands, Jeff rubbed at the week's growth of beard on his face—an appropriate accompaniment to his filthy shirt and trousers. He was glad Melissa was not here to see him. He felt like a caged animal, and he probably looked and smelled like one, too.

A sudden burst of loud voices broke into Jeff's musing. He looked up to see that the prisoners across the yard were involved in a brawl. The odds seemed to be heavily uneven, as five of the prisoners were gathered around the remaining man, raining punches and kicks on him. Two of them had pinned the hapless prisoner's arms while the others delivered the blows.

Jeff straightened away from the wall and watched the battle. The guards seemed to be doing the same thing: watching. All of them had their hands on the butts of their pistols, but none of them made a move to help the prisoner being set upon by the others. Jeff assumed that they figured that whatever happened to the man was no more than what he deserved; otherwise, he would not have been in jail in the first place.

With a roar of anger, the prisoner flung his arms out and threw off the two men holding him. He slammed a punch into the jaw of another man, but then one of the remaining men drove a vicious punch into the small of his back, staggering him. He caught his balance and elbowed one of the grapplers, but then one of the others leapt on his back, forcing him to his knees.

If the man went down, Jeff knew, the others might kick him to death before the deputies intervened. And regardless of who the prisoner was or what he had done, Jeff hated to see such an unequal battle. Acting on impulse, he shuffled as quickly as he could across the narrow yard.

One of the prisoners had his fists clasped together and was about to club the back of the other man's neck. Jeff reached him just as the blow began to fall. Forming a loop with the chain between his wrists, Jeff swung it up and over the head of the prisoner, then jerked back. The man staggered against him, unable to follow through with the blow. Jeff tightened the pressure of the chain against the man's neck.

One of the other prisoners saw that he was interfering in the fight and let out an indignant curse. He swung a fist toward Jeff's head, but Jeff jerked the man he had hold of around so that that man took the blow. The man went limp, with the chain around his neck the only thing holding him up. Jeff released him,

flipping the chain up and letting the unconscious man
fall to the ground.

He raised his arms to block a second punch, realizing as he did so that he might have gotten into
deeper trouble than he had expected. With his wrists
chained together, it was difficult for him to strike
back. All he could do was fend off the blows and start
backing up. That strategy did not work, either, because his feet immediately got tangled up with the leg
irons, and he fell over.

The man who had been attacking him pulled
back his foot to launch a kick. But Jeff acted first, putting his feet together, swinging them around, and
snapping a kick of his own that drove his bootheels
into the man's stomach. The man went pale, doubled
over, and stumbled off to the side.

Jeff rolled and planted his hands on the ground,
then shoved himself upright again. The odds were
down to three to two now, but those three were still
pounding the hell out of their original victim. With a
shout of rage, Jeff tackled one of them from behind,
catching the man in the small of the back with his
shoulder. As the man went down, Jeff landed on top
of him and brought his fists down on the back of the
man's head. The man went limp.

Just as Jeff looked up, a kick caught him in the
chest, knocking him backward and stunning him. The
man who had kicked him came scrambling after him,
foot upraised as he set himself to stomp Jeff in the
face. Jeff knew he would not be able to mount a coun-
terattack in time to save himself.

Before the foot could fall, the brawny, black-
haired man whose plight had gotten Jeff into this battle to start with slammed a fist into the mouth of the
last man and knocked him into the one about to grind
Jeff's face under his heel. As they staggered, Jeff managed to roll away, and when he came to his feet again,
gasping for breath, he gathered the chain into a loop
once more. He had not wanted to use the chain as a

weapon for fear of injuring his opponents too badly, perhaps even killing them, but the fight had gone on too long, and he had taken too much punishment. He wanted to end it now. He stepped forward, swinging the chain, and slashed it alongside the skull of one of the men. The impact sent the man sprawling to the ground with a moan.

The black-haired man disposed of his last opponent with a blinding combination of punches that rocked the man's head from side to side before dropping him unconscious.

Although bleeding from several cuts, the prisoner grinned as he turned to Jeff and stuck out a knobby-knuckled hand. "I'm beholden to you, my friend," he said, "and Terence O'Shay always pays his debts."

Jeff grinned back at the man and took his hand, meeting the nearly bone-crushing force of the clasp with equal strength of his own. "I'll remember that, but I'm not sure when you'll get a chance to return the favor. I may be in here for a while."

"A man in jail always needs a friend. If you hadn't come to me aid, those spalpeens would've beaten the bejeysus out of me."

"What was that all about, anyway?" Jeff asked.

Before O'Shay could answer, Constable Tolbert came into the yard, a double-barreled flintlock shotgun clutched in his hands. "What the hell's going on out here?" he roared at his men.

The only answers they gave him were sheepish grins.

Tolbert swung toward the big Irishman. "Brawling again, were you, O'Shay? That's what got you in here in the first place. Or don't you remember that?"

"I remember, Constable," O'Shay said. "But 'twasn't me who started this fight. These gentlemen scattered around the yard took a dislike to me, something to do with a friend of theirs who got his head busted in a fight a few weeks ago at Red Mike's."

"By you, I suppose. And I suppose that one wasn't your fault, either," Tolbert said. He turned to the deputies again. "Well, don't just stand there! Haul this lot inside and put them back in their cells. If they can't come outside without causing trouble, maybe we'll just do away with this practice."

Jeff spoke up. "It really wasn't O'Shay's fault, Constable. The five of them jumped him without warning. I saw the whole thing."

The lawman's eyes narrowed as he looked at Jeff. "And what about you, Holt? What's your part in all this?"

With a shrug, Jeff said, "Five against one didn't seem like fair odds to me. I couldn't stand by and watch them beat this man to death—the way your deputies seemed intent on doing."

Tolbert's face, already flushed with anger, darkened to an even deeper shade of red, but Jeff couldn't tell if the anger was directed at him or the deputies who had stood idle during the brawl. Jeff had a feeling they were in for a severe dressing down, at the very least.

"So you jumped in to help O'Shay?" Tolbert said after a moment. "I wasn't aware that the two of you were friends."

"I didn't even know him until a few moments ago," Jeff said.

"Aye," O'Shay said in his booming voice. "Helped me out of the goodness of his heart, he did. And I'll not forget it."

"Funny thing for a murderer to do," Tolbert muttered; then he jerked the barrels of the shotgun toward the rear door of the jail. "Back inside, the both of you. I'll figure out later whether or not to lodge any additional charges against you."

Terence O'Shay seemed unperturbed by that prospect, and under the circumstances the idea of being charged with brawling did not particularly frighten Jeff, either. He and O'Shay walked back into the jail side by side, with Tolbert behind them, prodding them with the shotgun. The deputies had already taken the other men back to their cells.

"Better have the doctor come over and take a look at that lot," the constable called to one of his underlings as an afterthought. "Make sure they're not damaged too badly."

O'Shay gave Jeff one more grin, then Tolbert shoved him through an open door into a cell. Jeff's cell was two doors farther down the corridor.

When the door had clanged shut, Jeff asked, "Aren't you going to take these manacles and leg irons off?"

"You can wear them awhile. Maybe they'll teach you to think twice before jumping to the aid of somebody like O'Shay."

"Nobody deserves to get pulled down by a pack of wolves like that," Jeff replied, his voice cold.

Tolbert frowned at him. "You're a strange one, Holt. You don't turn a hair at slitting Charles Merrivale's throat, but you won't stand by and watch a fight because the odds are too uneven. Must come from living out in the wilderness so long instead of in a civilized place."

"You call this civilized?" Jeff asked, and then he began to laugh for the first time since he had been locked up. He slumped onto the bunk and ignored Tolbert's glare as he continued to laugh. Finally, the constable stalked off.

Well, Jeff thought with a final chuckle, if civilization meant locking up an innocent man and letting a killer go free, this place sure fit the description.

That evening, when one of the jailers brought Jeff's supper, two others were with him, and they stood outside the cell with pistols trained on Jeff while the first man quickly unlocked his shackles and leg irons, then scuttled back out of the cell.

The jailer gave Jeff a sullen glare and said, "Constable Tolbert told us to turn you loose from them things. Said you'd been punished enough for causin' that trouble this afternoon."

Jeff did not bother correcting the man. They knew full well he was not responsible, but he no longer gave a damn, just as he no longer cared if the constable or his men believed that he was innocent of Charles Merrivale's murder. Melissa believed him, and that was all that mattered—that and the hope that a jury would also believe him. But it was only a faint hope.

"You got a visitor," the jailer added.

Jeff looked up sharply. Melissa had not come to see him for several days, at his request. Her visits were too painful for both of them. He would see her again at the trial, and that would be soon enough, he had told her. So who could be visiting him?

The jailer locked the cell door, and the other two men relaxed a little, lowering their pistols. One of them motioned toward the end of the corridor, signaling whoever was down there to come ahead. Jeff was not prepared to see his cousin Ned come striding into view, a big grin on his face.

"Hello, Jeff," Ned said heartily. "Looks like you got yourself in a spot of trouble."

Jeff stood up and extended his hand through the bars. As Ned clasped it firmly, Jeff said, "You could say that, my friend. It's damned good to see you, Ned. When did you get back into port?"

"A couple of days ago. India and I came in on the *Fair Wind*, but this time we stayed behind when the ship sailed again."

"Why? I thought you were both happy sailing under Captain Vaughan's command."

"Oh, we were, but we had more pressing business here. You see, we ran into Melissa on the docks and she told us about this trouble you're in."

Jeff felt his face turn hot with disgrace and anger "There's no truth to the charge. I didn't kill Charles Merrivale."

Ned waved a hand. "Hell, I know that. That's why India and I decided to stay on for a bit. We're giving Melissa a hand with running the business." He lowered his voice so that the deputies who had retreated to the far end of the corridor couldn't hear him. "And we're going to find out who really killed Merrivale so that we can clear your name."

Jeff frowned. It was good to know that Ned and India were helping Melissa with the business, but the three of them did not need to be running around trying to discover the identity of the killer. That could lead them into trouble, and the last thing he wanted was for Melissa to be in danger.

"I'm not sure you should do that," he said slowly. "You might run into some folks who wouldn't take kindly to being investigated."

Ned laughed. "That's what we're hoping."

Knowing that under the circumstances it was useless to argue with Ned, Jeff changed the subject. He just hoped that Melissa would have enough common sense to stay out of trouble; she had to know that it would only make things worse for him if anything happened to her.

"You say Melissa's running her father's business?"

"And doing a good job of it, too, even before India and I got here to pitch in. I guess it's *her* business now, hers and her mother's."

Jeff clung to the bars of the cell door. "I'm glad you're here to help her, Ned. She'll need to be strong, especially with the trial coming up."

"How do your chances look?"

"Not good," Jeff said with a doleful shake of his head. He filled Ned in on the details of Charles Merrivale's murder, or at least as many of them as he had learned from Constable Tolbert, and the conclusion that Tolbert had drawn: Jeff Holt was the killer.

Ned said, "That's the story going around town, too. Seems that a lot of people knew of the bad blood 'tween you and Merrivale, and plenty of them even claim to have heard you threaten the man at one time or another."

"That's always the way it is," Jeff said bitterly. "Folks say they know more than they do. Like my pa told me about the Revolution: If as many men who claimed to have been at Bunker Hill had really been there, the British wouldn't have won the day."

"Well, you'll win your day of freedom," Ned insisted. "India and Melissa and I will see to that."

Once again Jeff felt a strong sense of misgiving. Anyone who could so coldly slit a man's throat was a dangerous enemy, and the idea of Melissa trying to hunt down such a killer made him fearful. Even Ned and India, who were highly capable of taking care of themselves, might have set themselves too difficult a task this time.

"Maybe you should leave this to the law," Jeff suggested. "Melissa's already been through enough."

"Do you think the law's going to find the real killer when they've got you already locked up in jail?" Ned challenged.

"Well, probably not, but—"

"Don't you worry about us, Jeff." Ned reached through the bars and clapped a hand on his cousin's shoulder. "We'll have you out of here in no time."

One of the jailers called out, "Back off, down there, before you get thrown behind bars, too, mister!"

"All right, all right," Ned said as he stepped away from the barred door. "No need to get yourself in an uproar." He grinned at Jeff and added, "I'll be back to see you. Don't lose faith, now."

"I'll try not to."

Not that he had had much faith to start with, he thought as he watched Ned stroll down the hall and out of the cellblock. It seemed that from the first, fate had conspired against him. Every attempt he had made to close the gap of hostility between him and Merrivale had ended in disaster.

He went back to his bunk, lay down, and stared at the ceiling. Then he heard a sudden "Hsst!" Looking up in surprise, Jeff decided that the sound had come from down the hall. The hissing noise was repeated, and Jeff stood up and went to the door of his cell.

"What is it?" he called in a low voice.

"Go to your drain," came the soft reply.

Jeff looked at the drain, covered by a grate, in the center of the cell. Every cell had a drain, and each morning the slops jars were emptied into them, then flushed with pails of water. Jeff knelt beside the drain and wrinkled his nose at the smell coming from it; however, a hoarse whisper also seemed to issue from the grate.

"Are you there, Holt?"

Jeff was quite sure the voice belonged to Terence O'Shay. "I'm here," he replied in a whisper of his own as he leaned closer. "Is that you, O'Shay?"

"Aye. We can talk this way without Tolbert or his lackeys being any the wiser."

Jeff couldn't help smiling. Trust a man like O'Shay, who had evidently been in quite a bit of trouble in his life, to know all the ins and outs of being in jail.

"What about the other prisoners? Can't they hear us, too?"

"They're all on the other side of the corridor, so they've got a separate drainpipe running under their cells. We're the only ones over here. 'Tis safe, I assure you."

Jeff accepted the explanation. "What do you want, O'Shay?" he asked.

"I heard what you were telling that visitor of yours, about how you're supposed to've killed your father-in-law. Merrivale, that's the name, ain't it?"

"That's him."

"Charles Merrivale?"

"That's right. What about him?"

"Just seems I've heard the name before. Something to do with some business I was involved with a while back."

Jeff wondered how a brawler like O'Shay could have anything to do with a respected businessman such as Charles Merrivale. Aware that he might be treading on delicate ground, he asked, "What business was that?"

"Well, seeing as how this is just between you and me, one of the gents I done work for had some goods he needed to dispose of. Goods that maybe wasn't his to begin with, if you know what I mean."

"Go on," Jeff said tightly.

"So this gent says he knows somebody who'll sell the goods for him. Not around here, mind, where word of the plan might get back to them that didn't need to know about it, but in some of them new settlements over in Tennessee."

A pulse began to throb in Jeff's temple. "Did you say Tennessee?"

"Aye. And the man who was going to sell the stuff for my boss was named Merrivale."

Jeff's hands clenched into fists. Merrivale had been dealing in stolen property! Some, if not all, of the goods Jeff had taken to Tennessee with the wagon train had been stolen. It was so obvious, now that he looked at events from this new angle. But had Merrivale been aware that he was selling stolen goods? It was possible that Merrivale had been a dupe, too, as Jeff had been.

Leaning close to the drain again, Jeff whispered, "Maybe I shouldn't ask this, O'Shay, but who were you working for?"

"Well, normally gents in my line of work keep their mouths shut about such things. . . ." O'Shay hesitated for a moment that seemed maddeningly long to Jeff. "But if you hadn't helped me when that bunch jumped me this afternoon, they'd have hurt me bad, maybe even killed me. And like I told you, Terence O'Shay's a man who pays his debts. . . ." He paused again. "Hawley is the gentleman's name. Dermot Hawley."

The answer came as no surprise to Jeff, but he needed to hear it from O'Shay himself. And with that answer, like the blinding flash of the sun rising, came the truth: Charles Merrivale had been a stubborn, hateful man, but he was not a criminal. Jeff was convinced of that, as much as he might have liked to believe otherwise. Which meant that Hawley had been playing Merrivale for a fool all along, using Merrivale's mercantile business to dispose of ill-gotten goods. It made sense, and to Jeff the theory had the rock-steady feel of truth.

But there was one more question to answer, and Jeff asked it. "Did you ever hear Hawley say anything against Merrivale?"

"Only that he thought the old man might be getting suspicious of him and that he was tired of Merrivale dragging his feet on everything else. Said he knew how to take care of that."

Jeff closed his eyes and sighed. Dermot Hawley had killed Charles Merrivale. He had witnessed the fight between Jeff and Merrivale on the afternoon of the murder, and he knew that the clerks in the office had seen the confrontation as well. It would have seemed like an acceptable gamble to a man like Hawley. With one stroke of a knife blade, he could both dispose of a troublesome partner and, knowing that Jeff would probably be blamed for the crime, clear the way to begin courting Melissa, once Jeff had been convicted and either hung or sent away to prison for the rest of his life. Hawley no doubt expected to take over the business as well as Melissa. A multitude of rewards with one stroke.

Jeff leaned back from the foul air above the grate and took a deep breath. Knowing all of that and proving it, however, were two very different things. Putting his head close to the drain again, he said, "Listen, O'Shay, Hawley must have killed Merrivale because I sure as hell didn't do it."

"Aye, that's what I was thinking, too."

"Then for God's sake, man, tell the constable about it!" Jeff struggled to remain calm. "With your testimony to go on, maybe Tolbert will start looking into Merrivale's death again. He'll have to see that Hawley could have killed Merrivale just as easily as me and that he had more of a motive."

"Can't do that, Holt," the answer came back from the grate. "In the first place, a man like me learns to keep a tight lip where the law's concerned. And in the second, it probably wouldn't do any good. Do you think Tolbert's going to believe a man like me? Not for a second he wouldn't."

Jeff was desperate. "But then what am I going to do? After telling me all this, you're not going to turn your back on me, are you?"

"I told you, Terence O'Shay pays his debts," the big Irishman growled. His voice continued to issue from the drain grate. "Just you sit tight, boyo. I'm getting out of here tomorrow, and once I'm free again, we'll see what we can do."

"You may be free, but I won't be," Jeff snapped. "Not unless you give me a hand."

Suddenly an idea occurred to him. From the first he had not even considered the idea of breaking out of jail, but that had been when he had no concrete idea who had murdered Merrivale. Now that he was certain Hawley was the killer, things were different. He felt confident that if he was free, he would be able to find the evidence he needed to clear his name and prove that Dermot Hawley was the real killer.

Besides, Hawley had amply demonstrated how ruthless and dangerous he was, and the last thing Jeff wanted was for Melissa to start sniffing around the trail of a man like that. The best way to forestall that was to trap Hawley himself.

A moment of silence passed, then O'Shay asked, "Are you talking about me breaking you out of here, Holt?"

"That's right. Somebody's got to go after Hawley and bring him to justice."

"You sound mighty sure he's the one who done the killing."

"I'm convinced of it," Jeff said bluntly.

"Well, then, maybe I could give you a hand. I've had a few run-ins myself with Master Hawley, and that's one reason I ain't working for him anymore. You and me made a pretty good team this afternoon in that fight; maybe we could do the same thing on the outside of these walls."

"You can think about it," Jeff told him. "It's up to you whether you help me or not."

"Yes, I suppose it is at that." O'Shay was silent again, this time for several minutes, but then he finally said, "You just sit tight, Holt. But be ready to jump when the time comes."

Jeff smiled. For the first time in days, he felt hopeful. "I will be."

If it meant clearing his name and giving Dermot Hawley his due at the same time, he was going to be more than ready for that.

CHAPTER EIGHTEEN

Clay Holt and Shining Moon strode along the riverbank from the Hunkpapa Sioux village toward the church, barely speaking. It had been that way since Clay's return a few days earlier: silences where before there had been talk. That first day he had told her about what had happened in Canada, and Shining Moon had listened intently. She had as much reason to hate Fletcher McKendrick as anyone, and Clay thought he saw a gleam of satisfaction in her eyes when he had told her of how McKendrick had been struck down and left inside the burning fort.

He had said nothing about his suspicions concerning the prairie fire and the avalanche that had injured Aaron so severely. He was convinced that McKendrick could not have survived the long trip from Canada, even if he *had* lived through the explosion at Fort Dunadeen.

No, Clay told himself, McKendrick's threat was over, and there was no point in worrying Shining Moon over nothing.

Since that first evening, there had been little conversation between them. Clay had tried again to convince Shining Moon that Josie was lying, that he had never been married to anyone except her, that Matthew was not his son. Shining Moon had been there at Manuel Lisa's fort when Zach Garwood had appeared for a final showdown with Clay, and she had witnessed the battle between the two men following the revelation that Zach had raped his own sister.

But just because Zach had admitted to violating Josie did not mean that Clay had not lain with her, too. Clay knew that doubt still lurked in Shining Moon's mind. And she no longer even wanted to listen to his explanations, turning away from him when he began talking about the situation.

Clay had grown increasingly more frustrated over the past few days. He had never wrestled with a problem like this before, and his usual course of direct action would not solve it. Not unless he got hold of Josie's neck and wrung the truth out of her lying mouth—and that was a solution he was giving more thought to lately.

At that moment he and Shining Moon were on their way to the church to see Aaron. The young man was still alive, and according to Father Thomas Brennan, his condition had even improved slightly, but he was still in danger.

The priest met them at the doorway of the church. He looked grave but hopeful as he said, "I think Aaron's fever has lessened somewhat. He was awake for a little while earlier, but he dozed off again."

"Was he making sense when he was conscious?" Clay asked. He had not given up the hope that Aaron might be able to explain the truth about Josie and Matthew to Shining Moon. She might not fully believe *him*, either, but Aaron's word would at least strengthen Clay's story.

The priest shook his head. "Not really. He was

still delirious. He was talking about that man McKendrick and the girl Raven Arrow."

Clay kept his face impassive, hiding his disappointment.

Father Brennan led them into the small back room of the church, where Aaron had been moved onto a cot that Malachi Fisher had constructed. Now the priest could keep an eye on his patient almost around the clock.

Aaron's bushy beard had been shaved off, and as Clay looked down at his sleeping friend, he saw that the lack of a beard made it more obvious how gaunt and haggard Aaron had become. His normally ruddy complexion had faded to a pasty pallor, and he looked several years older than Clay, instead of the other way around. Aaron was sleeping fitfully and muttering softly, but Clay could not understand any of the words.

He glanced over at Shining Moon, whose face was filled with sympathy as she looked down at Aaron. He had been a good friend to both of them.

After a few minutes Clay took her arm and led her back out of the room. Father Brennan followed them, shaking his head. "I just don't know," he said quietly. "Soaring Owl and I have done all we can. We keep fresh poultices on his wounds, and Soaring Owl brings him some of that tea he brews up several times a day. The wounds look better, but I'm afraid the poison from them has spread all through Aaron's body."

"What about his legs?" Clay asked. "Are the bones knitting?"

"I think the left leg will be all right, if a little stiff. As for the right leg"—the priest shrugged—"I doubt if Aaron will ever be able to walk on it again, assuming that he gets over this sickness that has befallen him."

Clay started to curse, then caught himself, in light of the surroundings and the company. He settled for saying, "I patched him up as best I could out on the trail."

"I'm sure you did. We've all done our best. It's in the hands of the Lord now."

Clay hated feeling so powerless. Taking Shining Moon's arm, he led her out of the church, with Father Brennan following.

"I must go back to the village," Shining Moon said. "The men will need many arrows for the great hunt."

Clay nodded. Soon many of the men from the band would be traveling to a rendezvous on the prairie, where they would meet warriors from other bands and take part in the huge buffalo hunt that was the highlight of each summer's activities among the Sioux. Clay would have enjoyed being part of it, since he had made it back in time, but he doubted if he would go, not with all the turmoil he had returned home to.

He told Shining Moon, "I'll be along directly."

She walked off, back straight, chin lifted, still carrying herself with some of the haughtiness that had been a part of her as long as he had known her. Clay sighed and shook his head.

"Is there trouble between you and Shining Moon?"

Clay looked sharply at the priest. "I don't know as that's any of your business, Father."

"I'd like to help if I can."

I'll just bet you would, Clay thought. But he said, "Tell me which cabin is Josie Garwood's. That'd be a help."

Father Brennan frowned. "What are you planning to do, Clay?"

"Have a talk with her, maybe convince her to straighten this mess out. It's time she stopped lying."

"The truth is important, certainly." The priest still appeared rather reluctant as he pointed to one of the log cabins several hundred yards away. "That's Josie's place over there."

"Thanks," Clay said curtly. He stalked toward the cabin without another word.

He was not sure what he would say to Josie. Appealing to reason had not done a whole lot of good. She had no real motive for sticking to her story about being married to him except sheer spitefulness, as far as Clay could see. Maybe the time had come to let her know that he was not going to stand for it any longer.

The door of the cabin was closed, but smoke wafted out of the stone chimney. Clay rapped on the door, then stood back to wait. After a moment the latchstring was lifted, and the door swung open. Josie stood there, needle and thread in one hand, a boy's shirt in the other. She smiled when she saw Clay.

"How nice. You've come to visit your loving wife."

"Stop that, Josie!" he barked. "I need to talk to you."

"Well, of course. Come in, come in." She moved back out of the doorway. "It's not much, but it's home. Leastways, it would be with a husband to live here."

Clay stepped into the tiny two-room cabin and closed the door behind him with his heel. He glared at her and said, "Have you been telling that lie for so long that you've started to believe it yourself?"

"What lie is that?" she asked, still smiling.

"You know damned well. The lie that we're married and that I'm the father of your boy."

"That's what people say," Josie replied airily.

Clay's hands clenched into fists. He straightened his fingers with effort. "Only because that's the story you've spread. I want you to stop it, and I want you to tell Shining Moon the truth about us."

"Shining Moon's my friend. Of course I've told her the truth."

Maybe she *did* believe the lie, Clay thought as he stared at her. Maybe she had forgotten the truth.

"Damn it, quit playing games," he growled as he took a sudden step toward her. "Don't you care how many lives you're ruining?"

Her smile disappeared. "You stop talking mean to me, Clay Holt! You've hurt me enough already. It's time you started living up to your responsibilities."

His hands shot out and caught her upper arms, and she gasped in pain and fear as he jerked her toward him. "It's all a batch of filthy lies! And you're going to tell the truth, goddamn it!"

"Let me go! Get away from me! You can't just come in here and—"

"I'll do as I please," Clay said, shaking her, his resolve to stay calm completely vanished now in the face of his rage. "You've been telling folks I'm your husband, so I guess I have a right to *beat* the truth out of you!"

A clear, high voice said, "Stop it!"

Clay's head jerked around, and he saw Matthew Garwood standing in the narrow doorway that led to the cabin's other room. The boy had a cocked flintlock pistol in his hands, and the barrel was steady as he pointed it at Clay. He had a finger ready on the trigger.

Clay froze. Matthew might be only six years old, and he might have to use both hands to hold that gun, but that did not make the pistol any less deadly. If anything, it was more dangerous in the hands of someone like Matthew, who might not realize its power.

Swallowing hard, Clay kept his voice level as he said, "You'd better put that gun down, boy. It might go off."

"It will unless you let go of my ma and get out of here," Matthew said, his voice as cold as a mountain stream.

"Matthew, honey, be careful," Josie said, sounding even more worried than Clay. "Mr. Holt's not hurting me. You don't have to shoot him."

"Tell him to let you go," Matthew ordered.

Josie's tongue licked her dry lips. "You—you'd better do as he says, Clay."

"Sure," Clay said, nodding. He released Josie's arms and stepped back slowly and carefully so that he would not spook Matthew. He was not sure what to do next. If an adult male had pointed a gun at him, the choices would have been simple: Clay would have taken the gun away if he could or tried to shoot the other man before he got shot himself. But he could not trade shots with a six-year-old. The very idea was ridiculous.

Matthew motioned with the barrel of the pistol. "Git."

"I'm leaving," Clay told him. "Sorry I upset you and your ma, boy. You better put that gun away."

"When you're gone."

"Oh, please, Clay, just go!" Josie burst out.

He glanced at her again. "You remember what I said." Then he backed carefully to the door, reached behind him to open it, and stepped out, never taking his eyes off Matthew. He did not relax until the door was shut again, and even then he kept looking over his shoulder as he walked away from the cabin.

By the time Clay reached the Hunkpapa village, the thudding of his heart had slowed down. He had faced plenty of dangerous folk in the past, but what he had seen in Matthew's eyes as the boy pointed the gun at him was something new: a cold emotionlessness that reminded Clay of the eyes of a mountain rattler as it was about to strike. A shiver went through him as he remembered the look.

He was on his way to his tipi when Father Brennan stepped out from behind one of the other lodges. Something about the priest's determined stance told Clay that he had been waiting for him. He stopped. It was either that or run right into the man.

"Did you see Josie?"

"I talked to her. Couldn't convince her to tell the truth, though." He thought it would be best not to say anything about Matthew's threatening him with the pistol.

"Are you sure there's nothing you'd like to tell me, Clay? I'm concerned about what I see happening between you and Shining Moon, and as I told you, I'd like to help."

Clay stared at him for a moment, then snapped, "You believe that lying bitch, too, don't you?"

"Look, there's no need to—"

"Or maybe you just *want* to believe her," Clay went on, his anger rising again. "You'd like to think that I'm really married to Josie because that'd leave Shining Moon free for *you*!"

The priest's mouth tightened at the accusation. "I'm a man of peace," he said, his voice trembling slightly with swallowed wrath, "or else I'd knock those blasphemous words down your throat, Clay Holt."

"You're welcome to try anytime, mister." Clay put out a hand and gave the priest a hard shove. "Now get out of my way, and stay the hell out of my life and Shining Moon's!" He stalked past the startled man.

Then he came to a dead stop as he looked up and saw Shining Moon standing just outside their tipi, looking horrified at what he had just done.

"Shining Moon . . ." Clay said as he held out a hand to her. She turned away sharply and ducked back into the tipi, but not before he saw the flash of anger in her eyes.

Clay looked around at Father Brennan, but the priest just shook his head and walked away. The other Hunkpapa in the village were making a pointed effort to ignore what had just gone on, and Clay suddenly felt very alone, even here in the midst of his adopted people.

He let out a long, slow sigh. He had thought that once he dealt with the threat of Fletcher McKendrick, he could get on with what he hoped would be a peaceful life as a fur trapper. Instead, he had returned home to even more trouble.

It was ironic, Clay thought, but things had been a hell of a lot simpler when he was fighting for his life against McKendrick and his men.

Even in the summer, the air was cold that high in the mountains, but Proud Wolf did not feel the chill. Neither did he see the puffs of vapor from his breath that enveloped his head. He had climbed some two thousand feet above the level of the plains below, passing the timberline and entering a region of bare rock and frigid snowdrifts tucked into pockets on the sides of the mountains, and now he sat cross-legged on a barren, windswept rock seat that had been carved out from the peak. His mind was focused inward. His thoughts were on Raven Arrow, the way she had lived and the way she had died.

For several days now, Proud Wolf had been fasting, taking in only handfuls of snow that he scooped up from shaded patches of ground where the sun never shone. The feeling of light-headedness that came from lack of food was a familiar one to him. Some years earlier, like other young Sioux braves, he had gone on a vision quest, venturing alone into these same mountains to discover who he was to be in life. He had fasted then, too, and during that fast the vision had come to him of a gigantic wolf striding easily over plains and mountains, proudly surveying the land of the Sioux as his own private domain. Proud Wolf had taken his name from that vision, casting aside the name he had been given as a child and never again speaking it or even thinking of it. After the vision, he had broken his fast by killing a deer with the bow and arrow he had with him and eating heartily of the venison. When he had come down from the mountains, he was a new person as far as he was concerned.

Some of his feelings now were the same. But instead of the anticipation of change he had felt during his vision quest, now he had sorrow in his heart for the death of Raven Arrow. When he had broken the news to her parents, her mother had wept and cut her hair and clawed at her legs until blood ran down to her ankles from the scratches she had inflicted. Raven Arrow's father had only nodded grimly, but he also cut his hair, and Proud Wolf had seen tears glistening in his eyes, although he was too much of a warrior to shed them.

Proud Wolf had not cried, either, but grief had gripped his heart. It still held him tightly as he sat on the rocky ground, weak from fasting, and chanted songs of prayer—prayer for the departed spirit of Raven Arrow . . . and for himself.

He had denied her vision, scoffed at her, laughed at her. He had steadfastly refused to see that something undeniable bonded them, even when she had saved his life, until she had died helping him and Clay and Aaron escape from Fort Dunadeen. For years she had reached out to him, and he had never done anything except push her away. Now she was gone, and never again would he see the enthusiasm on her face that could brighten a day no matter how many clouds were in the sky. Never again would he hear her voice, so strong and confident in the power of her visions. Never again . . .

A tear rolled down Proud Wolf's cheek.

Suddenly, a sound caught his attention, and he ceased his chanting. He heard the sound again, close by. It was a low, menacing growl, and as Proud Wolf turned his head, he saw a massive grizzly bear lumbering toward him across the ledge. It stopped and reared up on its hind legs, its forepaws with their wicked claws extended.

Proud Wolf blinked in surprise. He had not heard

Old Ephraim approaching; that was the name the white trappers had given every grizzly, and Proud Wolf had always thought it appropriate. With their brown hair streaked with silver and their hostile bearing, grizzlies were indeed reminiscent of crotchety old men, although far more dangerous. They moved with remarkable speed, considering their size, and they had enough power to slash open a bull moose with one swipe of a paw.

This bear was the largest Proud Wolf had ever seen. He would not be much more than a mouthful to a beast like this. Putting a hand on the rock to balance himself, Proud Wolf stood up. As he was weak from fasting, his movements were awkward and slow, especially compared to the grizzly. The bear let out another angry growl. But instead of dashing across the fifty feet or so that still separated it from the young man, the beast came to an abrupt stop and gave its loudest, most thunderous cry yet, tipping its shaggy muzzle back as it did so. It was almost, Proud Wolf thought, as if the bear were challenging him.

He wrapped his fingers around the shaft of the knife sheathed at his waist. It was his only weapon, and the steel blade would be no match for the grizzly's claws and teeth. The battle would be short and one-sided, and it would end with his death. But he would not die without inflicting some pain on the bear.

The thought of trying to run and hide never even occurred to Proud Wolf, even if there had been some place in that barren landscape where he *could* hide. He would die as he had lived—fighting.

Giving a growl of his own, he lifted the knife and took a step forward.

Suddenly something pale and extremely fast flashed past him from behind. He stopped in his tracks, shocked into immobility. A white mountain lion was making a great leap that carried it through the air straight at the head of the grizzly.

"Spirit cat!" Proud Wolf gasped.

Such albino cats were extremely rare; Proud Wolf had heard tales about them, but he had never even met anyone who had seen one, much less seen one himself. He watched in awe as the mountain lion slammed into the grizzly, raking it with claws and fangs as it struck.

The grizzly howled in fury and slammed a blow into the side of the great cat, knocking it sprawling on the ground. Proud Wolf expected to see huge, bloody gashes opened up in the hide of the mountain lion, but as the cat rolled over and sprang back to its feet, it seemed to be unmarked. It pounced again, this time dashing past the bear and tearing at one of its hind legs, trying to hamstring it. The bear was forced to drop back to all fours. It swung around and lashed out at the great cat.

The spirit cat darted away, its speed outstripping even that of the grizzly. Proud Wolf had never seen an animal move so fast. With a snarl, the cat struck again, catching the bear in the face with its claws. The bear howled in pain and lunged forward.

Again the cat avoided the attack, moving nimbly to the side. It vaulted onto the bear's back, catching hold with the claws of all four feet, sinking them deeply into the flesh of the larger beast.

Proud Wolf had heard of battles between bears and mountain lions, and the bears had always won. This time was different. The spirit cat leaned forward on the back of the bear and it bit the bear on the neck.

The bear leapt and twisted, doing everything in its power to dislodge the spirit cat, which hung on stubbornly. The grip of its claws slipped so that the bear's thrashing flung it this way and that, but the teeth that were sunk deep into the bear's neck stayed as immovable as the jaws of a trap. The bear roared again and suddenly threw itself to the ground, rolling over and over on the stony surface.

That move forced the cat to release its hold.

Tossed to the side by the bear's writhing, it landed hard and rolled over a couple of times before righting itself. As it came to its feet again, so did the grizzly, rearing up on its hind legs once more. Proud Wolf could see blood pouring out of a horrible wound on the bear's neck. The beast was doomed, but it kept going. Rage and pain drove it on. It charged at the snow-white lion.

The great cat met the charge head-on with a leap of its own, crashing into the chest of the bear. The grizzly wrapped its forelegs around the mountain lion, even as the cat's teeth tore once again into its throat. For a moment that seemed endless to Proud Wolf, the lion and the bear remained locked together like that, the bear tottering on its hind legs as it tried to squeeze the life out of the cat. Finally, the grizzly crashed over to the side like a huge tree falling and took the spirit cat with it.

Proud Wolf did not expect either animal to get up again.

Then there was a feeble stirring, and with movements that rapidly grew stronger and surer, the mountain lion slid out of the embrace of the dead bear and came to its feet, shaking all over and ridding itself of the grizzly's blood. Then the cat lifted its crimson-stained muzzle and stared directly at Proud Wolf.

The young man felt as though his blood had frozen in his veins, and a wave of dizziness washed over him. He waited, rooted to the spot, for the spirit cat to bound forward and claim him as its next victim. But the creature just stood there staring at him. Unable to tear his own gaze away, he peered into its eyes.

Instead of a lion's usual golden color or the red hue that would have been expected in an albino animal, the eyes were black. A deep, shining black, the color of obsidian—

Or a raven's feather.

A voice spoke in Proud Wolf's head, but he could

not understand the words, for they were in a language beyond his power to comprehend. Still, he understood the feeling they conveyed. The voice touched his mind and his soul like a healing caress, and a great peace spread through the young warrior. The remorse he had felt over Raven Arrow's death and the way he had treated her in life was gone, soothed away.

He had no idea how long he and the spirit cat stood there gazing at each other, but suddenly the great beast spun around and bounded off toward the mountain. It began climbing, leaping from ledge to ledge, and soon it was lost from sight in the mist that clung around the peaks.

A great shudder ran through Proud Wolf, and then he turned and looked at the corpse of the bear.

If not for the massive body lying there and the steaming blood that had pooled around it, he might have thought the entire experience another vision, a product of his fasting and the sorrow that had gnawed on his mind. But the dead bear was here. Taking a deep breath, he walked over to it and reached down to brush a hand along the coarse fur on its flank. In a curious way, he sensed that he owed a great debt to the bear.

He had thought the grizzly was going to take his life, but instead, life had been given back to him by the spirit cat. He looked up once more at the spot where the cat had vanished, and he whispered a prayer of thanks.

Then he turned and began walking down the mountain. It was time to go home.

CHAPTER NINETEEN

India St. Clair was dressed in a black silk shirt and black trousers. With her black cape, high black boots, and a black hat on her close-cropped dark hair, she could blend easily into the shadows, which was exactly her intention in donning the outfit.

Ned Holt thought she looked lovely, but then, Ned thought she looked lovely no matter what she was wearing. In fact, Ned thought with a grin, India would no doubt be even more beautiful if she was wearing nothing at all.

"What are you leering about? As if I had to inquire." Her voice was quiet as she asked the question.

"Oh, nothing in particular," Ned replied jauntily, knowing from experience that it was better to keep such thoughts to himself. India had warmed up to him over the past months, and he could steal a kiss from her every now and then without her drawing a dagger and threatening to gut him from stem to stern, but other than that she still steadfastly resisted his charm. A virtual first for the roguish Ned.

"Well, you'd best keep your mind on our mission," she suggested tartly. "These are vicious lads we're going after, and they'd as soon slit your throat as look at you. Don't forget what happened to Charles Merrivale."

"That's not likely," Ned said, his tone becoming serious. "Not likely at all."

They were walking down one of the harborside streets in Wilmington, North Carolina, bound for a tavern called Red Mike's. As they drew near it Ned reflected on the place's name. It seemed to be a universal one as far as seaports were concerned. Nearly every harbor town he had visited had a grog shop called Red Mike's—in fact, he had first laid eyes on India outside a place so named up in New York City. Ned had no idea what the significance of that was. And neither was it important.

What *was* important was finding something that would clear Jeff Holt of Merrivale's murder and point the finger of guilt toward the real killer. Anything unsavory that went on around the docks would be the subject of gossip in a place like Red Mike's. For the past week Ned and India had been frequenting dockside taverns, hoping to overhear something that might involve Merrivale's murder. So far they had been unsuccessful, and that night they were paying their second visit to Red Mike's, unwilling to give up the effort.

The grog shop was a small, dingy building in a row of small, dingy buildings bordered on either side by blocks of warehouses. A crudely lettered sign bearing the name of the place hung over the oak door, which was probably the stoutest part of the building. It had to be to withstand the occasional visits by the constabulary, who tended to try to kick it down. Usually they failed and were finally, grudgingly, admitted by the owner, but not before the tavern's patrons had time to bolt out the rear exit. Gambling went on in Red Mike's, and there were cribs out back where the serving girls could take paying customers. Smoke from half a hundred pipes hung thick in the air, not all of it from tobacco. Some of the seafaring men who frequented Red Mike's sailed often to the Far East and brought back opium from China and hashish from India.

All in all, a typical sailors' tavern, Ned thought as he and India were granted entry after slipping a coin to the man at the door as a bribe.

Ned's eyes narrowed against the stinging smoke as he and India made their way across the dimly lit room to an empty booth against the rear wall. They slid in on opposite sides of the heavily scarred table, which had been scratched and marred by countless sailors' knives over the years. Red Mike's was crowded, with men standing two deep at the bar and most of the tables and booths occupied, but an alert serving girl must have seen them come in, for she appeared beside the table less than a minute after they sat down.

"What'll it be?" she asked, leaning forward so that both of them would have a good look down the valley between her large, pale breasts. The loose, low-cut blouse she wore left little to the imagination.

"Bottle of rum and a couple of glasses," Ned ordered, taking full advantage of the view. If India chided him later about the way he had peered at the wench's bosom, he thought, he could always say that he was just trying to be inconspicuous. After all, what sailor would *not* look?

"Anything else?" the girl asked suggestively, letting her hand rest for a moment on Ned's thigh beneath the table.

"Not just now, darlin'," he said, giving her a promising leer. "Maybe later."

She squeezed his leg and winked. "I'll hold you

to that." Then she turned to India. "What about you, mate? My, you're a little'un, ain't you? 'Course, that don't mean little all over. . . ."

Ned could tell from the way India suddenly stiffened that the serving girl was caressing her under the table, just as she had done to him. He looked down at the table and bit his bottom lip to keep from bursting out with a laugh. If that wench was not careful, she was going to discover more than she had bargained for.

In the husky voice that she adopted when she posed as a man, India said curtly, "Later."

"Sure," the girl agreed. She straightened and moved off, saying over her shoulder, "I'll be back with your rum."

India glared at Ned across the table. "I can see why you like places like this," she said acidly.

"You were sailing the seven seas and venturing into grog shops such as this one when I was still an innocent lad back in Pittsburgh," Ned reminded her with a grin.

"Innocent? I find that difficult to believe."

"Pure as the driven snow."

India just rolled her eyes.

The serving girl reappeared a moment later with the bottle of rum and two glasses. Before the girl could leave, Ned put a hand on her wrist and played a hunch.

"Listen, darlin', has Hawley been in tonight?"

The girl frowned. "Hawley? Don't think I know who you're talking about, mister."

"He's a friend of mine who tells me he comes in here all the time. Says Red Mike's is the best place on the waterfront."

"Well, he ain't lying about *that*. And I'm the best girl here," she purred. "Why, if you give me a chance, I can show you some things—"

"What about a man named Dermot?" India put in, following Ned's lead. They had not discussed their approach before they came in, but he had taken this tack knowing that she was quick enough to understand what he was doing.

"Don't know him, either," the girl said. Her eyes narrowed in suspicion. "Say, you two ain't some sort of John Laws, are you?"

Ned gave a raucous laugh. "Not hardly. But we *are* looking for work, and we thought we might find some in here."

She shook her head. "Can't help you with that. All I do is serve drinks and show gents a good time. And since neither of you seems interested in anything but the drinks, you go right ahead with them."

With that she flounced off, and India said dryly, "I don't believe you made a conquest after all, Ned."

He shrugged. "That's all right. There're plenty of fish in the ocean."

"Or so they say."

"Anyway, she seemed just as taken with *you* as she did me."

India flushed slightly. "Watch where you tread. We're here to work, remember?"

Ned tipped the bottle of rum and poured drinks for both of them. He could drink quite a bit without it muddling his brain, and India had a surprisingly high capacity herself, which came in handy at times like these when they had to remain inconspicuous. Nothing would have drawn unwanted attention faster in a place like Red Mike's than not drinking.

For the next two hours, they kept up their facade as hard-drinking, hard-living sailors, moving around the room so as to overhear most of the conversations going on. Ned played a few hands of poker and lost steadily, hoping that his gain would be listening to the talk around the table. Several times—at the bar, at the gaming table, sitting at a table with men for whom he had just bought a drink—he brought up Dermot Hawley's name, only to be told in every instance that no one knew the man. Ned found that difficult to believe, since Hawley was something of a prominent businessman in the area, but such reticence was not unexpected. Men who sometimes operated on the shady side of the law tended to be rather close-mouthed.

Finally when his head began to be a bit fuzzy, he caught India's eye and gestured toward the door. They would give up for that night and try somewhere else the next. India gave a brief nod and started toward the doorway.

The buxom serving girl who had brought them the bottle of rum caught Ned's arm before he could reach the entrance. With a pout she said, "Not leavin' already, are you, before I've shown you a trick or two?"

"Much as I'd like that, darlin', we'd better be shoving along," Ned told her, trying to sound reluctant—and not having to work very hard at it.

She leaned closer to him. "I was hoping we'd have a chance to—" She put her mouth against his ear and began describing in erotic detail what she wanted to do with him.

Ned blinked and tried not to gape at the seemingly boundless imagination the girl had. He knew India was waiting for him, and he could almost feel her narrowed gaze on his back, but the wench seemed to be just getting started.

That was when he felt the slight pluck on the strings of the purse tucked away in the pocket of his trousers.

Instantly his hand shot down, and his fingers closed around her wrist. The girl gasped in surprise, and Ned grinned humorlessly at her as he said, "So that's your game, is it? Fill a fellow's head full of visions of passion so that he doesn't feel you sneaking his purse out of his pocket. Better practice some more on somebody else, sweetheart. You're not good enough at it yet."

"Let me go, you great oaf!" she hissed. "I don't know what you're talkin' about!"

"The hell you don't." Ned realized that men at some of the closer tables were watching them now, but he was just drunk enough not to care. He went on, "How many other dupes in here have you robbed tonight?"

The girl tipped back her head, opened her mouth, and screamed.

The bartender made a swift motion with his hand, and two burly men who had been lounging at a corner table hurriedly put down their tankards of ale and lunged to their feet. They ran across the room toward Ned and the girl.

"Come on, Ned!" India urged.

But now instead of Ned's holding on to the serving wench, she had latched on to him with both hands and was dragging him back, holding him in place until the two ruffians could reach them. Ned realized that picking pockets was probably part of the girl's job, and she no doubt split her take with the bartender and the two toughs. Anyone who caught her at her trade and raised a ruckus, as he had just done, would be dealt with severely and probably left in an alley with a busted head.

He finally managed to jerk away from the girl, and he gave her a shove that sent her sprawling into the path of the two men charging toward him. One of them went down with a curse as the girl screamed again, but the second one vaulted over the tangled mass of arms and legs and swung a short, wicked-looking bludgeon at Ned's head.

This was not the first brawl Ned Holt had ever found himself in, however. He ducked, letting the club pass over his head, and stepped closer to smash a fist into the man's midsection. The man doubled over in pain, and Ned backhanded him into one of the tables. The collision overturned the table, spilled a flagon of rum, and brought a couple of customers to their feet with angry shouts.

That might have been a mistake, Ned realized. Now the whole tavern was on the verge of jumping into the brawl.

Someone grabbed his collar, and he whirled with his fist cocked to strike another blow, stopping at the last instant when he saw that it was India who had hold of him.

"Let's get the hell out of here!" she cried, and he had to agree that was a good idea. Out of the corner of his eye, he spotted a chair flying toward his head. He ducked under it, just as he had the bludgeon, and dived toward the front door.

Someone snatched at him, and he drove an elbow to the side to knock the man away. At last the door was directly in front of him—guarded by the hulking brute who had admitted them. India got there first, and the big man reached for her.

She grabbed his arm, pivoted smoothly, and, remarkably, the man went flying through the air to crash down on another table, snapping its legs off and reducing it to kindling. India pulled the heavy door open and darted out into the night, followed closely by Ned. A few men ran out of the tavern and scooped up loose stones from the street to throw after them as they ran into the darkness, but the stones thudded harmlessly to the ground behind them.

Ned was laughing as he ran. It had been a long time since he had been mixed up in a tavern fight, and although the battle had been a short one, it had invigorated him.

"Well, we may not have done any good," he said as he and India slowed to a walk several blocks away from Red Mike's, "but at least we got some exercise."

"I wish we'd found out whether Hawley has any connection with any of those men in there," India complained. "We're running out of time."

"Time for what?" asked a voice from the mouth

of an alley. The curt question was accompanied by an ominous sound that Ned recognized: a pistol being cocked.

He and India both froze. "Who's there?" Ned asked sharply.

"Just somebody who saw you back there in Red Mike's asking questions about Dermot Hawley," replied the man, hidden by the shadows of the alley. "I've been waiting for the two of you to leave. Looks like you had to make it a hurried departure."

"I took offense to a doxy trying to pick my pocket," Ned replied. "And what business is it of yours who we ask after in a grog shop?"

"I'm making it my business, mate. And you haven't answered my question. Running out of time for what?"

"To get a job," India said, slipping into her husky voice. The answer took Ned by surprise. "We're running out of money, and we'd heard that this man Hawley could use a couple of fellows."

"To do what?" the shadowy figure asked.

India shrugged. "Whatever needs to be done. We ain't picky, are we, Ned?"

"Nope, we can't afford to be too particular."

Ned knew India was playing a hunch, just as he had earlier. If this stranger had overheard their questions about Hawley and had been intrigued enough to wait for them outside the tavern and waylay them like this, surely he had some connection to the man. And although there was no proof of it, both Ned and India were convinced that Hawley had had something to do with Charles Merrivale's death.

After a moment the man with the gun asked, "How many men jumped you back there?"

It was Ned's turn to shrug. "Five or six before it was over. We were a bit busy to get a good count."

"And you fought your way out?"

"It wasn't too difficult," Ned said casually.

"Not many men get out of a brawl at Red Mike's

so easily," the stranger mused. He stepped forward into the dim light cast by a lamppost up the block. Ned and India saw that he was a squat, powerful-looking man in a beaver hat and a long coat. He held a flintlock pistol ready for use in a steady grip. "So you say you're looking for work?"

"That's right," India said.

"What if I told you that I know Dermot Hawley and could get you a job?"

"We'd say thanks," Ned replied dryly.

"I'm serious."

"So am I. Anything you can do to help us will be appreciated, mister, although I'm not sure why you'd want to."

After a moment's pause, the stranger said, "It just so happens I'm an associate of Hawley's. We're in the business of disposing of merchandise for which the bills of sale have been . . . mislaid, so to speak."

Ned knew what he meant; the man was a dealer in stolen goods, which came as no surprise. And Melissa suspected that Hawley had been providing some of the merchandise her father had sold through his store and also freighted to the inland settlements. Which meant that Merrivale had been involved, either knowingly or unknowingly, with a band of thieves and smugglers.

"We can always use good men to give us a hand," the stranger went on. "But we have to know that you can be trusted."

"Give a test," India challenged, "any sort of test you like. We need the work, mister."

"I'm sure you do." He paused for a moment, then said, "All right. We'll be moving some goods out of a warehouse tomorrow night." He told them where to find the building, adding, "You come down there about ten o'clock, and we'll see what you can do."

Ned snorted. "Hell, that's the kind of work any dockworker with a strong back can do. I figured you'd want us for something better."

"You've got to prove yourself first, mate. You'll do as I say, or forget the job."

"We'll be there," India said quickly. "Don't worry about us."

The man chuckled. "I'm not worried, lad. You cause any problems, and you'll wind up in the harbor with a new mouth carved in your neck. That's how we handle troublemakers."

Ned felt a chill go through him. The man had just described how Charles Merrivale had been killed. Had Merrivale been one of those troublemakers he had mentioned?

It seemed likely, just as it seemed that he and India had finally stumbled onto some of the answers they had been seeking.

"Thanks," Ned said as the man began to back away into the darkness of the alley mouth again. The man just grunted in acknowledgment and then disappeared into the shadows. Ned heaved a sigh.

He and India walked away quickly, taking a roundabout route through the city in case anyone else was following them, before finally returning to the Merrivale house. As they approached it, Ned said in a soft voice, "Melissa's not going to like hearing that her father was mixed up with a bunch like that."

"She knew he was involved with Hawley, and she already suspected that Hawley was a criminal. Whether she wants to admit it to herself or not, surely she's already considered the possibility that her father was breaking the law, too."

"You think Hawley killed him?"

"I've no doubt of it," India answered without hesitation. "Either Hawley did it himself, or he ordered it done. He probably had a falling out of some sort with Merrivale, and then when Jeff threatened the old man in front of witnesses, Hawley saw the perfect opportunity to rid himself of two problems at once."

Ned scowled. "He must be a cold-blooded bastard."

"And a smart one. That's what makes him dangerous."

Entering the house, they found that Melissa had not gone to bed, even though it was late. She was sitting in her father's study, some of his record books spread out on the desk in front of her. The door to the room was open, but Ned knocked softly on it anyway before he and India stepped in.

Melissa looked up sharply. "Did you find anything?" she asked.

"Perhaps," India said. She and Ned explained what had happened at Red Mike's and afterward, and India concluded by saying, "The connection with your father is tenuous at best, but at least it's a start."

Melissa leaned back in the big leather chair and regarded both of them at length. Finally she said, "Do you mean to tell me that you believe my father was a criminal?"

Ned said, "I know that's not what you want to hear, Melissa, but you have to admit that it's a possibility. On the other hand, perhaps Hawley fooled him just as he fooled everybody else. Perhaps your father found out that Hawley had mixed him up in some illegal dealings, and he tried to put a stop to it. Could be that's why Hawley—"

"Murdered him," Melissa finished. Her hands clenched, and her face paled. Taking a deep breath, she said, "You could be right. What are you going to do now?"

"We'll be at that warehouse tomorrow night, as we told Hawley's man," India said. "All we can do is keep digging."

"You know that warehouse is one of my father's, don't you?"

Ned and India exchanged a surprised glance. "No, we didn't," Ned said as he looked at Melissa again. "That ties it all up even neater, doesn't it?"

"But there's no proof of anything," Melissa pointed out. She gave them a curt nod. "Go to the warehouse—but be careful. I've lost my father and perhaps my husband. I don't want to lose two such good friends."

A grin spread over Ned's face. "Don't you worry about us. We've gotten out of tighter spots than this one will be, haven't we, India?"

"When?" India asked.

"Well, surely there've been one or two," Ned said sheepishly.

"I don't think so." India's voice was crisp. "But Ned's right about one thing, Melissa. We'll be all right. And perhaps we'll soon have the evidence we need to prove that Jeff is innocent of any wrongdoing."

"No one is completely innocent," Melissa said softly. "That's one thing I've learned. If I hadn't let my father influence me so much against my better judgment, and if Jeff hadn't been so hot-headed, perhaps none of this would have happened." She looked up at them. "We're all partially to blame—Jeff and I, my parents, Hawley . . ."

Ned leaned forward over the desk, his face and tone serious for a change as he said, "But if Hawley's the one who used the knife, he's going to pay for it."

"Oh, yes," Melissa said tightly. "He'll pay."

Melissa's heart pounded wildly in her chest as she paused at the doorway. This meeting was going to take every ounce of her self-control, but she knew it had to be done. Perhaps she should have told Ned and India what she was planning to do, but she knew that if she had, they would have tried to talk her out of it—and possibly succeeded.

The time for caution had passed, Melissa told herself. It would take daring to win the day and see justice done, and if that took more courage than she would have ever dreamed she possessed, then so be it.

She grasped the doorknob and turned it, then stepped into the room to confront Dermot Hawley.

He looked up in surprise from where he stood beside an ornately carved sideboard, pouring brandy from a crystal decanter into a cup of steaming coffee. It was early in the day, but apparently Hawley needed a bracer. He quickly recovered from the shock of seeing her, set the decanter down on the sideboard, and took a quick sip of the mixture in the exquisite bone china cup.

"This is quite a surprise, my dear. I never expected you to come strolling into my rooms this way, although I had hopes of such a thing at one time."

"Good morning, Dermot," she said crisply. "I hope you don't mind, but I asked your manservant not to announce me."

"You haven't come to shoot me or anything dreadful like that, have you?"

Melissa made her mouth form what she hoped was a natural-looking smile. "Not at all. In fact, I'm here on business."

Raising an eyebrow, Hawley took another sip of the brandy and coffee. "Business? The last time we met, you said that you had no desire to do business with me. As I recall, you threw me out of your father's office rather rudely."

"I was quite upset, as you can well imagine. After all, that was the day of my father's funeral."

Hawley acknowledged her point, then said, "And I'm truly sorry about that, Melissa, but you weren't in much of a mood to accept my sympathy that day, let alone my offer of help."

"A woman can change her mind, can't she?"

Melissa felt his eyes caressing her, taking in the details of her figure in the conservative but attractive gown she wore. She repressed a shudder.

Hawley said smoothly, "A lovely woman can do

just about anything that she pleases. And you are a lovely woman indeed, my dear."

Melissa took a deep breath. He made her very nervous. "I'll be honest with you, Dermot. I've tried to take over the operation of my father's business, and it's been very difficult so far. I know that the two of you were partners at one time, and I'd like for you to consider forming such an arrangement again."

Again his eyebrow lifted. "Really? I have to admit that I'm surprised to hear such a suggestion from you, Melissa. Delighted, mind you, but still surprised. I've always thought that you and I would make an excellent team—in all sorts of ways."

"We can . . . talk about that, once we see how the business arrangement is working out."

"Fair enough," Hawley said, placing his cup on the sideboard and stepping closer to her. He smiled suggestively. "I would never suggest this with most of my associates, but perhaps we could seal the bargain with a kiss?"

She tilted her head back and closed her eyes slightly. "All right."

He took her in his arms and brought his mouth down on hers. Melissa pressed against him, fighting off the urge to tear herself away. The kiss was a wanton one, and Hawley's eyes glittered brightly when at last he took his mouth away and looked down at her.

"I'm glad you finally came to your senses," he murmured. "I do believe this will be quite a satisfactory arrangement, especially once that husband of yours is out of the way."

Melissa shook her head. "Jeff is no longer a consideration. Anyone who could do what he did—" She broke off abruptly as if she could not bring herself to say anything more about the murder.

"Don't worry," Hawley assured her, "justice will be done."

"I know. It's just been dreadfully hard. . . ." She lifted her chin and then continued, "There's one more thing, Dermot. If we're going to be working together, I don't want to be kept in the dark—about anything."

He frowned slightly. "I'm afraid I don't know what you mean."

"I'm a woman, Dermot, a woman on her own with not only a child but a mother to provide for. I have none of the reservations that my father might have had about, shall we say, certain types of business dealings."

Hawley released her and took a small step back, although still hovering close. "And what sort of business dealings are those?"

"Ones that perhaps would not be fully sanctioned by the law."

"You sound as if you believe some of those scurrilous rumors that have been circulating concerning me." He chuckled, but there was no humor in his eyes.

"I'm saying I don't care if those rumors are true," Melissa declared. "My only concern is making sure that all the Merrivale enterprises remain profitable, no matter what is required to do that. Do we understand each other?"

"I think we do," Hawley said slowly.

"Good. Then you'll have no objection if I'm at the warehouse tonight when those stolen goods are moved out."

Hawley was very good at covering up his true feelings, but not even he could completely conceal his surprise at those bold words. The reaction was the one that Melissa wanted to see, but he covered it up quickly.

"I'm afraid I don't know what you're talking about."

"Of course you do, Dermot. I'm no fool. I've been digging around in my father's affairs for over a week now, and I know all about how you and your friends stored those goods in one of his warehouses without his knowledge. I daresay that quite a few of Father's employees are still on *your* payroll, too."

This was the risky part of her plan, Melissa thought, not only for her, but for Ned and India as well. If Hawley knew about the encounter between the two of them and his associate the night before, he might figure out that the two "sailors" who had gone to Red Mike's looking for work could be connected with her, in which case Ned and India might wind up walking into a trap at the warehouse. Melissa knew she was taking a chance with their lives, but she intended for her own life to be on the line as well—just as Jeff's was.

After a moment, Hawley laughed and said, "You have been busy, haven't you? What if I said you were right about the warehouse?"

"Exactly what I've already said," Melissa replied coolly. "I want to be there so that I'll be sure the profits are divided equitably. That's only fair. After all, the warehouse belongs to my mother and myself now, and I have to think about what's best for us and my son."

"Indeed you do, and I can see that it would be a mistake to underestimate you, my dear." Hawley looked thoughtful for a moment, then nodded. "I'll meet you outside the warehouse around ten o'clock. Will that be all right?"

"Of course."

"Would you like a cup of coffee to toast our bargain?"

She smiled. "No. But I'll have some of that brandy."

Hawley chuckled. "You are a never-ending source of surprise this morning, Melissa." He took another china cup from the sideboard and poured some brandy into it. He handed it to her and picked up his own cup. There was a delicate clink of china against china as they toasted. "To success," Hawley said.

"In business," Melissa added.

"And in love."

She merely smiled enigmatically and sipped the brandy. It was strong, but she needed its bracing effect. It had taken all of her bravery, all of her daring, all of her hitherto-unknown acting skills to convince Hawley of her sincerity.

And that night in the warehouse she would finally learn the truth. At gunpoint, if necessary.

CHAPTER TWENTY

Father Thomas Brennan leaned over the cot and tucked the covers around Aaron Garwood's shivering body. Aaron was feverish again, sometimes burning up, sometimes racked with chills. The priest frowned at he looked down at the unconscious man. As much as he dreaded the prospect and the risks involved, amputating Aaron's right leg might be necessary; otherwise, the sickness that had already drained him of so much life might continue eating away at him.

"Lord, help me know what to do," he murmured as he turned and left the small room at the back of the church. He doubted his own ability to perform such a procedure. His medical training had been limited largely to being taught how to administer the cowpox vaccine. After all, his calling in life had been to heal the spirit, not the body, by carrying with him the Word of God.

But he was the closest thing to a physician within a thousand miles or more, and he could not stand by and watch Aaron waste away and finally die. That end was inevitable unless someone did something to alter the course.

And it looked as if, once again, Father Thomas Brennan had been called on to be that someone.

He walked to the door of the church and stepped outside, breathing deeply of the early evening air. The sun had dropped behind the mountains to the west, but a bright red glow remained in the sky to mark its passing for another day. In the distance Father Brennan could see smoke from the cookfires of the Hunkpapa Sioux threading into the air. Closer at hand, the settlers of New Hope were also preparing their suppers, and he could smell roasting venison and elk and antelope, along with the savory aroma of wild onions and greens cooking.

That reminded the priest that he had not eaten. He turned to go into the church to prepare his own meal when movement along the riverbank caught his eye. A man was walking unsteadily along the stream. Thomas squinted at the figure, but since the light was dim and fading fast, it was impossible to discern the man's identity, and he appeared little more than a shambling shape. But from the gait that was more of a stagger than a walk, it was apparent to Father Brennan that the stranger was in trouble.

The priest hurried along the river without pausing to wonder where the man had come from or what he was doing here. As he drew nearer, he saw that the stranger was middle-aged, with a reddish gray beard. His clothes were in tatters, and he was bent over so that it was difficult to tell how tall he was or how he was built. He was looking down, his gaze fixed on the ground in front of him, and he seemed not to see the priest coming until he loomed up right in front of him and spoke.

"Here, let me help you."

The man let out a startled yelp and drew back quickly, throwing up an arm as if to defend himself from a blow.

"It's all right, I won't hurt you," Father Brennan said, holding his hands out in front of him, palms extended, in an effort to show the stranger that he meant no harm. The priest got his first good look at the man's face and had to clench his teeth to keep from gasping in shock. A long, red scar ran across the stranger's forehead underneath the tangled thatch of hair, and the lower half of his face was also dreadfully scarred in places, giving his beard a patchwork appearance where the hair would not grow in. He could tell now that the man had what had once been a powerful frame, although hardship had wasted it away.

"Let me alone!" the stranger rasped, still backing away from the priest. "Didn't hurt anybody."

"Please, let me help you." Father Brennan kept his voice calm and soothing. "I was about to eat something. Will you join me?"

The man scrutinized him, blinking rapidly. "Eat?" he repeated. "Food?"

"Yes, indeed. Jerked venison and some panbread. There's plenty, and I'd be happy to share it with you."

The stranger hesitated, then nodded. He even let the priest take hold of his arm and lead him toward the church. The man must be very hungry, Father Brennan thought, to have overcome his fear.

When they reached the church the stranger flinched again before going through the doorway, as if terrified of entering the log building. But Father Brennan was gently insistent, and the man stepped inside and stood alongside the priest. On the crude altar two candles were burning in candlesticks that Father Brennan had brought with him from Boston. The candles cast a pale glow over the room.

The priest was about to take the man into the back room where Aaron was staying when he decided not to expose the stranger to the sight of the injured man. The scarecrow-like wanderer was already in a fragile state of mind. If he saw Aaron lying on the cot, gaunt and haggard, he might become even more frightened and perhaps believe the priest was somehow to blame for Aaron's injuries. Father Brennan did not want him dashing out of the church thinking he was in danger. The stranger was far too greatly in need of assistance.

"Sit down here," the priest said, indicating the bench directly in front of the altar. "I'll get the food."

He hurried into the back room to fetch the venison and panbread, hoping that the stranger would not take the opportunity to flee. While he was there, he checked on Aaron and saw to his satisfaction that the young man seemed to be resting a little easier. In a way, he was relieved by the arrival of the woebegone stranger; ministering to the man's needs would take his mind off the decision whether or not to amputate Aaron's leg.

Father Brennan brought the food back into the church and was glad to see that the stranger had not left. He sat down on the same bench, keeping a cautious distance so as not to unnerve the man, and extended a plate of venison strips and a hunk of bread. The scarred stranger grabbed the plate and began eating ravenously, as if he had not had any nourishment in days.

The food seemed to strengthen the man, and after a few minutes, his mouth filled with bread, he asked, "Got anything to drink?"

"I've a jug of river water."

The stranger shook his head. "Need something stronger."

"Well . . . there's some wine."

The man nodded eagerly.

Father Brennan stood up and went to get the wine. Under the circumstances, some wine was probably a good idea. It would fortify the stranger.

He brought the earthen jug to the bench, and the

man promptly grabbed it, upended it, and took a long swallow, his prominent Adam's apple working in his neck as he guzzled. Father Brennan was debating if he should take the jug away from him when the man lowered it, rubbed the back of his hand across his mouth, and sighed.

"Makes a man feel almost human again, it does."

"I'm glad you're feeling better. Tell me, how did you come to be wandering along the river?"

The man's eyes narrowed in suspicion. "What river do ye mean?"

"Why, the Big Horn. It's right outside."

"The Big Horn . . . 'Tis Sioux country, then?"

"Yes, there's a village of Sioux close by. The Hunkpapa band of a chief named Bear Tooth lives there." Father Brennan tried to steer the conversation back. "Are you afoot out here?"

"Had a horse," the man mumbled. "Good horse. Rode him a long way. Damn thing stepped in a prairie dog hole and broke his leg—what?—four, five days ago. Couldn't ride him; had to leave him there to die. Figured I'd die, too. Found a few berries and roots to keep me going, then I found this place. Or I should say ye found me."

"The Lord must have led you here, my friend." The priest smiled and reached over to pat the man's knee. "But you'll be safe now. We'll take good care of you until you're back on your feet."

"What—what'd be the name of this place?"

"The settlement is called New Hope."

"Better than *no* hope."

"I think so." Father Brennan chuckled.

The scarred stranger ate the rest of his venison and bread and drank what was left in the jug of wine. The priest did not try to stop him. The man had obviously endured a terrible ordeal, not only in the past few days since the loss of his horse, but at some time in the recent past, when he had received the puckered scars. They looked like scars left by severe burns; the priest had seen the results of more than one such blaze, including the one that had taken the lives of his own family.

Finally the stranger belched, wiped his mouth again, and asked, "Do ye know a man called Clay Holt?"

The question took the priest by surprise. He answered without thinking, "Yes, as a matter of fact, I do. He lives in the Hunkpapa village with his wife, Shining Moon."

"Wife?" the stranger said.

Father Brennan nodded, feeling slightly uneasy. "Yes, his Indian wife, at any rate. Another woman lives in this settlement who claims to have been married to Clay back in Ohio, where they both come from." He frowned. "Do you know Clay Holt?"

"Indeed I do. Old acquaintances, we are. Though he never said anything about a wife in Ohio."

Father Thomas relaxed; in truth, he was glad for the company, even though the man's hideous appearance was a trifle unsettling. "Yes, the woman's name is Josie Garwood. Her brother lives here in the settlement, too. His name is Aaron Garwood." He did not add that Aaron was in the back room at that very moment, recuperating.

"Don't know that one. Haven't seen Clay in a long time. As I said, I never knew he had a wife in Ohio."

"And a child," Father Thomas added. In the interest of fairness, he was about to explain that Clay denied being married to Josie and fathering Matthew, but he stopped himself. He was gossiping like an old woman, he realized, and a feeling of shame came over him.

The stranger shook his head. "I didn't know any of that. Thank ye for telling me, Father. I'm looking forward to seeing Clay again."

"Perhaps you should rest awhile first," Thomas suggested. "You've been through a great deal, it seems, and I'm sure you're tired. Later, or perhaps in the morning, I'll take you over to the Hunkpapa village and direct you to Clay." He stood up and gestured at the bench. "Why don't you stretch out? I'll see if I can find something you can use as a pillow." He started toward the back room again.

"No need for that, Father. Ye see, I won't be staying."

Frowning, Thomas turned back toward the man. "Won't be staying? But why—"

The stranger leapt off the bench with more speed than the priest would have thought possible, considering the seemingly half-dead state he had been in only a short while earlier. The man plucked up one of the heavy brass candlesticks on the altar and swung it with great power. Father Brennan flung up an arm in an attempt to block the blow, but he was too late. The candlestick slammed into the side of his head.

There was not even time for him to cry out as he slumped to the floor. Slipping from consciousness, he vaguely saw the stranger looming over him, the candlestick upraised for another blow.

"Why?" the priest mumbled.

The stranger paused. "Ye never asked me my name, Father." His leering smile made his scarred countenance even more grotesque. " 'Tis Fletcher McKendrick."

Then the candlestick fell, rose once more, fell yet again—and Father Thomas Brennan knew no more.

Josie was humming happily as she sat down to supper with Matthew. After years of struggling—ever since Clay had deserted her back in Ohio—it looked as if her life was finally about to improve. She had seen Shining Moon often enough to be aware of the continuing tension between the Indian woman and Clay Holt. Although Shining Moon had told Clay she believed his story about not being married to Josie, there was still a core of doubt in her; Josie was sure of it. And soon Clay, tired of all the changes that had come over Shining Moon, would realize that his so-called marriage was over.

When that happened, he would turn to Josie.

Her only regret was that Aaron would have to remain in his current condition, or worse, in order for the deception to continue working its destruction on the relationship between Clay and Shining Moon. Josie visited Aaron nearly every day, but so far he had not recognized her. Any improvement in his condition was fleeting, and overall he was getting worse. The priest seemed to be at a loss as to what to do for him, and the old medicine man from the Hunkpapa village had already done everything he could with his herbs and mystical mumbo-jumbo.

If Aaron died, Josie would mourn, of course. But she would have Clay to comfort her.

Josie put a portion of fried squirrel on Matthew's plate, along with some rough-ground cornbread, wild mustard greens, and hominy. Budd Spenser, the blacksmith, had brought a couple of squirrels to her cabin earlier in the day, a present to her from the morning's hunting. Spenser was sweet on her, Josie knew, even though he was well aware of the trade she had plied until Clay's return from Canada. Since Clay got back, she had steadfastly turned away every man who showed up at her door looking for a little loving. Otherwise, Clay Holt would be far less likely to turn to her.

So she had been leading as upstanding a life as she could manage these past few weeks, knowing that Clay would probably hear plenty of gossip about her but wanting to show him that she had changed. If he would just come to her, she could be a good wife to him, she was certain. And it did not matter that they had never stood in front of a preacher and said vows; when he had "married" Shining Moon, there had not been a preacher within five hundred miles, Josie would have wagered. And despite the fact that Father

Brennan liked Shining Moon, his church would not recognize a union between a white man and a savage, Josie thought. It just was not right.

She looked across the table and watched Matthew push his food around on the wooden plate. "You'd better eat," she told him. "It's not every day we have something as good as squirrel."

"How long are we going to stay out here?" Matthew asked in a sulky voice.

"Why, from now on, of course. This is our home."

"I wish we could go back to Ohio. I don't like it out here."

Josie frowned. Matthew had never said anything about what had happened back in St. Louis, and she wondered if he even remembered killing Gort Chambers. He certainly did not act like it. And if he had blocked the incident out of his mind, she did not want to remind him of it again by explaining why they could not return to Ohio. Going through St. Louis would be too much of a risk.

"We're here in New Hope," she said firmly, "and this is where we're going to stay. When you get old enough, you can leave if you want, I suppose. But I hope you'll stay."

He did not look up at her.

Josie's frown deepened, but she fell silent. Arguing with the boy was pointless. When he got that way, silent and sullen, there was no way to bring him out of it. All she could do was wait for the mood to pass. Lately, he had been like that more often than not, and Josie worried about him.

A sudden knock on the door broke into her thoughts, and she lifted her head sharply. *Clay!* she thought. Maybe Clay had come to see her. Maybe this was the start of what she had been waiting for.

She pushed back her chair, stood up, and went to the door. "Who is it?" she called out, a faint smile of anticipation on her face.

"Is this the cabin of Josie Garwood?"

Her smile disappeared. She did not recognize the man's voice, but he was not Clay Holt. Probably some newcomer to the settlement who had been told that she was the one to see for some easy loving. She hoped he would not be angry when she sent him on his way with his lust unfulfilled. And on the slight chance that he might be looking for her for some other reason, she opened the door and said, "Yes, I'm Josie Garwood. Josie Garwood Holt," she corrected. She was going to have to start remembering things like that. "What do you want?"

Then the light from the lantern inside the cabin fell on the face of the man standing just outside her door, and she let out a startled gasp. He was a ragged, ugly figure with torn clothes and hideous scars on his face. He tried to smile at her, but that just made him look more frightening.

"Ye do not know me, madam," the stranger said, "but I'm a friend of Clay Holt's. He sent me to fetch ye. Aye, and the boy," he added.

"What?" Josie asked, confused. "Fetch us where?"

"He wants to speak to ye, madam. Please hurry. It's important."

Josie shook her head. She had never seen this man before, either around the Hunkpapa village or in the settlement. Night had fallen, and she was not going to leave her cabin in the company of someone she did not even know.

"Tell Clay that if he wants to see me, he knows where he can find me," she said firmly, taking a step back so that she could shut the door.

The scarred man quickly put a hand on the door to keep it from closing. "No, he can't. Clay's been hurt, and he's asking for ye."

For an instant Josie believed him, fear for Clay's safety and pleasure at his asking for her winning out momentarily over her caution. But then the instincts that had helped her survive as long as she had took over, and she realized that the man's claim had been too quick, too glib. Clay was not really hurt; she was sure of it. But then why—?

Why was unimportant, she quickly told herself. She said, "I'm sorry, but I can't go out tonight. Tell Clay I'll see him in the morning." *If Clay even sent you,* she thought, *which I doubt.*

The stranger's face hardened, making it even more fearsome. "You're sure of that, are ye?"

"I'm sure—"

The man rushed forward, and had Josie not moved back, he would have bulled into her. He kicked the door shut behind him.

"That's the boy, eh?" he said, nodding toward where Matthew sat at the table.

Josie glanced over her shoulder at her son. Matthew had finally looked up from his plate and was watching the unexpected confrontation with hooded eyes, eyes that seemed much older than his years. Josie knew that cold look all too well.

"You'd better get out of here and leave us alone," she told the intruder, trying to make her voice sound firm and brave. "You can't just burst in here—"

"I can do whatever I damn well please," the man said. He was gaunt and haggard, almost emaciated, but some inner strength seemed to be animating him, and as he stepped toward her again, Josie recoiled in fear, as if he were some sort of wild beast rather than just a man.

Judging from the insane glint in his eyes, maybe he *was* more beast than man at this moment, she thought. But she could still handle him. She had handled plenty of trouble before. All she had to do was keep her wits about her.

"You're going to be in plenty of trouble if you don't leave," she warned. "Not only will Clay come after you, but so will every other upstanding man in this settlement. I have friends, you know."

"I'm not worried about your friends, only Holt. And he bloody well *better* come after ye, if he ever wants to see ye alive again."

"You're crazy!" Josie gasped. "You plan on taking me as some sort of hostage to get to Clay?"

"Aye, now ye understand." He lifted a hand and beckoned with gnarled fingers. "Come with me, ye and the lad both."

Josie was still slowly backing away from him, and she bumped up against the edge of the table. She put a hand down to steady herself, and her fingers touched something smooth. She recognized it as the handle of the knife she had used to cut up the squirrel after she had roasted it. The stranger probably could not see the knife; her skirt would be concealing it. Wrapping her fingers around the handle of the weapon, she picked it up and held it behind her.

"We're not going anywhere with you," she countered, "but if you'll just leave, I won't say anything about this to anybody."

The man shook his head. "You're what I need to get to Clay Holt, and I'll not be leaving without ye." He lifted a hand and came toward her.

Josie's self-control broke. She let out an angry shout and threw herself at the man, the knife thrust out in front of her.

He moved with unholy speed, slapping the knife aside. Josie cried out in pain as his fingers closed around her wrist and twisted. Her fingers opened involuntarily, and the knife slid out of her grip.

The man's gnarled face distorted even more with rage. He caught the knife as it fell and brought it back up, growling, "Trying to gut me, are ye?"

Lantern light flickered on the blade, giving it a hellish red glow. Josie tried to jerk aside, but he still was holding her wrist. He squeezed hard, and she felt the bones grind together and then snap. She screamed in pain.

"Shut up!" the stranger bellowed. "Shut up, damn ye!"

Then something burning hot slashed into her chest, and her scream was cut off.

Josie sagged against the intruder, her mouth working without sounds. There was a numb spot in the center of her chest, but from it radiated waves of pain that seemed to fill her entire being. She turned her head toward the table and saw Matthew sitting there looking stunned and terrified. Then the man let go of her crushed wrist, and she fell to the floor, her legs folding up underneath her as if all the bones and muscles in them had turned to dust.

"Come here, boy," the stranger growled.

Matthew flinched, but the man was too fast. He grabbed hold of the child's upper arm and jerked him out of the chair. Then he gave Matthew a vicious backhanded blow across his cheek, knocking his head to the side. The boy slumped, unconscious, the cruel grip on his arm the only thing keeping him from falling.

Josie watched the attack on her son in dazed silence. All her strength had deserted her, and she could not even get up, let alone go to Matthew's aid. Somehow she managed to move her uninjured hand to her chest and felt the handle of the knife protruding from her body, but she was unable to pull it free or even grasp it firmly. Her fingers fell away from it.

The stranger loomed over her. He was holding the unconscious boy as well as the rifle and pistol that Malachi Fisher had given her for protection, along with a powder horn and shot pouch. Josie hoped her son was only unconscious. She wanted to reach out to him, to touch his cheek, but she could not.

"I should not have killed ye," the scarred man said to her with regret. "I lost my temper when ye came at me with that knife. But I have the boy, and he'll do to bring Clay Holt to me. Holt will not turn his back on his own son, and if he wants to see the little bastard alive again, he'll have to walk right into my trap."

Josie's lips moved, and a single hoarse word choked out. "Who—?"

"McKendrick," the man said, and then he was gone, striding out of the cabin and carrying Matthew with him.

Josie lay there, not moving. The pain had eased, but the numb spot in her chest was growing, and she knew she was dying. She had to do something, had to do it now before the darkness claimed her, or Matthew would be left in the hands of that madman—for it was clear that he was truly mad.

She willed her muscles to work again, and her hands pressed against the floor. Slowly, she lifted herself.

Clay! Clay could save Matthew, if only she could get to him in time. With a strength born of desperation, Josie pushed herself to her feet. She felt a fresh trickle of blood from the wound but ignored it. She had to reach Clay before it was too late.

Clay would save Matthew. Her son . . . *their* son. The thought drove Josie out of the cabin and into the night.

Clay took the pipe from Proud Wolf, drew in a mouthful of smoke, and blew it out, a puff to each of the four winds. They sat cross-legged beside the fire in the center of the tipi. Shining Moon was sitting to one side on one of the buffalo robes, mending a buckskin shirt. She wore the blue dress Clay had brought her. She took it off only to wash it, and Clay figured she intended to wear it until it was completely tattered. He was not sure what significance it held for her, but whatever it was, it seemed to be important. That was enough for Clay.

He passed the pipe back to Proud Wolf. The Hunkpapa warrior had returned from the mountains several days before; so far he had said nothing about what had happened to him up there while he was mourning for Raven Arrow. Something had happened, however, Clay was sure of that. He could see the change in Proud Wolf's eyes, a maturity that had not been there before and an expression that sometimes made Proud Wolf seem many miles away.

"I went to see Aaron today," Proud Wolf said. "He did not know me."

"He doesn't recognize me when I go to see him, either," Clay replied. "I'm not sure if he ever will again."

"The white shaman thinks there is no hope. He will not say this, but I can see it in his eyes."

"Father Brennan is a priest, not a shaman," Shining Moon said without looking up from her work.

Proud Wolf shrugged, the distinction clearly lost on him. He went on, "I have been thinking about that avalanche. I do not believe it was a natural thing."

Clay stiffened slightly. He had come to the same conclusion quite a while earlier, but he had avoided saying anything. It was just possible that Fletcher McKendrick had survived the head injury and escaped from the burning fort in time to save his life. It was also possible that he had followed them, especially if he had been lucky enough to come across one of the horses that Clay had never found. The Scotsman could have started the rockslide, and the prairie fire, too, for that matter. But could he have followed them all the way back from Canada? That would have required an almost superhuman effort, and Clay did not think a man so severely injured would be capable of such a thing. Surely McKendrick had died somewhere along the way.

Clay hoped so, for Shining Moon's sake; things were already strained enough between them.

"Doesn't matter how the avalanche happened," he said curtly. "Aaron was hurt. But I won't give up on him."

"I am not giving up on him," Proud Wolf said. "But it is true that he is no longer himself."

Clay sighed. No point in arguing against something so obviously true. Over the past year they had all changed, painfully and dramatically. And it was doubtful that life would ever again be the same for any of them.

A couple of dogs set up a howling and barking outside. Clay thought it came from the edge of the village. He became more attentive as the barking grew louder. Something really had the critters spooked, he thought, and he got to his feet. Perhaps a grizzly had wandered too close to the camp. He gripped his flintlock rifle tightly as he stepped toward the entrance of the tipi.

Before he could reach it, the hide flap was pushed aside, and Josie Garwood staggered in. Clay's eyes widened in horror at the sight of a bone knife handle protruding between her breasts, the fabric around it sodden with blood. There was a deathly pallor to her face and it was a wonder she was able to stand. Her eyes were wide and unfocused at first, but she managed to settle her gaze on Clay, and she whispered his name before she sagged forward toward him.

He dropped his rifle and caught her under the arms as she fell.

Curious faces peered in through the entrance as Clay gently lowered Josie to the ground next to the firepit. Shining Moon and Proud Wolf came quickly to his side.

Eyeing the knife, Proud Wolf said, "I will find Soaring Owl."

As he ducked out of the tipi Shining Moon knelt beside Josie and asked anxiously, "Who did this to you, Josie?"

She seemed not to hear. Blinking rapidly, she looked up at the top of the tipi and then found Clay's face again after a moment. "So far away . . ." she murmured.

Clay's jaw was tight with anger. There had been times when he was so furious at Josie that he felt as if he could have killed her himself, but he never would have. Never would he have done something as awful as this.

He reached out and touched her cheek. It was cold, so cold that he would have thought she was already dead had it not been for the fiercely intent gaze fastened on him and the harsh, irregular rasp of her breathing.

"What happened, Josie?" he asked.

"Mmmm . . . McKendrick," she managed to say, though it cost her an obvious effort.

A chill far colder than the winter winds slid through Clay's veins. His heart pounding, he leaned closer to her and said in a half-whisper, "McKendrick? Here? He did this?"

Josie's head moved slightly in a nod, and she caught Clay's hand. "He . . . he has Matthew. Said you would have to . . . come after him. . . . Save him, Clay. . . . Save . . . our boy. . . ."

He swallowed hard. The lie had taken hold in Josie's mind, all right, such a strong hold that even now, on the verge of death, she would not let go of it. But that was insignificant compared to McKendrick's presence here at the Hunkpapa village—and the pain and suffering he was still bringing to Clay Holt and those around him.

There was no question about what he had to do now. He squeezed Josie's hand and said, "I'll get him, Josie. I'll get Matthew away from him. McKendrick won't hurt anybody else, I promise you."

"You'll . . . take care of him? Raise him . . . to be a good man . . . like you?"

Clay hesitated only for a moment, but in that moment a flood of thoughts went through his mind. He had never liked Matthew Garwood; there had always seemed to be something *wrong* about the boy. Considering who his father was—Zach Garwood—that was not surprising. Matthew was also the living embodiment of the blood feud that had taken the lives of Clay's parents, Bartholomew and Norah, as well as the lives of Pete and Luther Garwood, brothers to Zach and Aaron. He remembered the hellish night when the Holt barn had gone up in flames, ruining the wedding of Jeff and Melissa. He remembered finding the bodies of his mother and father in their burned-out cabin. He remembered saying good-bye to Edward, Susan, and Jonathan, his brothers and sister who had gone to live with relatives in Pittsburgh while he and Jeff went west in an effort to put an end to the senseless feud, only to have Zach Garwood follow them. So much had happened, and most of it could be blamed directly on the lie Josie had started about Clay being Matthew's father.

And now she was asking him to take the boy and raise him as if Matthew were his own son.

He saw the light fading in her eyes, and he glanced up, meeting Shining Moon's intense gaze. She nodded, and that was enough.

"I'll take care of him," Clay told Josie. "I swear it."

The faintest smile touched Josie's mouth. That was all she had left within her. Her face relaxed, and Clay thought he saw peace in her eyes at last, just before the glaze of death swept over them.

"Was too late," a voice said behind Clay. "Knew when I got here I could not help."

Clay looked up at old Soaring Owl, the medicine man. "I know," he said. "She'd lost too much blood. No one could have helped her. I don't see how she made it all the way here."

"She wanted you to help her son," Shining Moon said. "Her fear, and her love for the boy, gave her strength."

Clay sighed. "I suppose so." He reached out for the rifle he had dropped earlier. As he stood up he said ominously, "McKendrick's lived too damn long."

Shining Moon stood as well and shooed the on-lookers out of the tipi, leaving it empty except for her, Clay, Proud Wolf, and the body of Josie Garwood. "I will prepare her for burial. She was my friend."

"That would be best, since she has no family left except the boy and Aaron." Clay looked at his wife and went on, "Shining Moon, do you really think we ought to take Matthew in when I get him back from McKendrick, or were you just telling me to say that to ease Josie's passing?"

"We must," she said simply.

"Dammit, I don't care what Josie said there at the end, that boy is *not* my son—"

"I know."

Clay blinked in surprise. For the first time Shining Moon sounded completely convinced. "You do?"

She smiled sadly at him and said, "I know you, Clay Holt. You are outraged that this man McKendrick killed Josie and stole her child, and I know you will risk your own life to rescue Matthew. But if he were your own flesh and blood, you would be as enraged as a grizzly. And the pain in your eyes would be far stronger."

"I've still got to go after him."

"Yes, you must."

"And I will go with you," Proud Wolf added. "I thought I had struck McKendrick down when he killed Raven Arrow, but somehow he survived. This time we will make sure he is dead."

"Damn right," Clay said. "We'll start tracking him at first light. It shouldn't be too hard. I have a hunch he *wants* us to find him. He wants a resolution as badly as we do, but he wants it on his own terms. That's why he took the boy."

The dogs started barking again outside, and Clay heard a man's voice call his name. He stepped out of the tipi, followed by Proud Wolf, and saw several of the inhabitants of New Hope coming toward him, led by Malachi Fisher and Budd Spenser.

"Got bad news, Holt," Fisher said without preamble. "Looks like some madman went on a spree over at the settlement. We heard yellin' from Josie Garwood's cabin, but when we got there, we couldn't find Josie or the boy, just a lot of blood on the floor."

"Josie's here," Clay told the group. "She died a few minutes ago, but she lived long enough to tell me that an old enemy of mine attacked her and kidnapped Matthew. I'm going after the boy in the morning."

"Damn!" Spenser exclaimed. "Poor Josie. She oure didn't have that comin'."

"There's more," Fisher said. "We found Father Brennan in the church. Somebody clubbed him with a candlestick, and I'm bettin' it was the same person."

Clay winced. He and Father Brennan had never gotten along that well, but he respected the priest for the good he had tried to do. "Is he still alive?"

"He's alive," Fisher replied grimly. "His head's stove in a mite, but he woke up long enough to tell us he's got a hard Irish skull. He's got at least a fightin' chance. Said the fella who hit him was named McKendrick. That the same man who went after Josie?"

"The same man," Clay confirmed angrily. "But he won't live to hurt anybody else." Even as he spoke the words they sounded slightly hollow to him. He had made the same vow once before, and lives had been lost in what he had thought was the fulfilling of the pledge.

He had been wrong, and now the evil that wore the name Fletcher McKendrick had struck again, bringing more death with him.

"We'll go with you," Spenser said, breaking into Clay's bleak thoughts. "We'll help you track down the bastard."

"No. Proud Wolf and I can travel faster alone,

and we can deal with him. We'll bring Matthew back safe and sound."

And this time McKendrick would definitely die, Clay thought. Even if he had to carve the man's still-beating heart right out of his chest.

CHAPTER TWENTY-ONE

The wait seemed interminable for Jeff Holt the day Terence O'Shay was released. He had been freed during the morning, and as a couple of jailers led him past Jeff's cell on the way out of the cellblock, the big Irishman did not even glance in Jeff's direction.

Maybe O'Shay had forgotten all about his promise to help, Jeff thought. Maybe the man had been just talking through his hat the night before and had not meant a word of what he said.

Jeff tortured himself with that possibility as the hours crawled past.

No one came to see him, and he was thankful for that since he was in no mood to be good company for Melissa or India or even Ned. He hoped things were going well for them and that Ned and India had been able to give Melissa a hand running the company.

If his name was ever cleared, he thought, maybe

he could do the same thing. He was sure that together, he and Melissa could continue to make a success of the enterprise Charles Merrivale had founded —if that was what they wanted to do. But so often now, possibly as a result of his confinement, Jeff found his thoughts straying to the West, to the great mountains where he and Clay had shared so many adventures.

One of these days they were going to get together again, Jeff promised himself. One of these days . . .

The light in the cell faded as the sun settled below the horizon. Two of the jailers brought Jeff his supper, one of them standing outside with a cocked pistol, as usual, while the other one took the bowl into the cell. Jeff ate without really tasting the food and did not even look up when the men came back later to get the plate and spoon. He just sat on his bunk, staring down at the stone floor and brooding.

Sometime after full dark had fallen—Jeff was not sure how long—he heard a noise in the alley outside the small window. He cocked his head. It had sounded like the creaking of wagon wheels, but he was not sure a wagon could even come down that alley, it was so narrow.

"Hsst! Holt!"

The whisper jolted him, and he came up off the bunk as if he had been poked with a stick. Grabbing the bars in the window, Jeff pulled himself up and peered out into the darkness.

"O'Shay?" he whispered. "Is that you?"

"Aye, so 'tis," came the reply. "Are you ready to get out of that hole?"

"But how—"

"Just grab these chains and put them around the bars. Then stand back, and be ready to wiggle out in a hurry."

By the faint light from the moon and stars, Jeff saw that there was indeed a wagon in the alley, drawn by a team of four sturdy oxen. O'Shay threw a set of chains up to the window, trying to keep the clinking down to a minimum. Jeff caught them, wound them around the bars, then let the chains hang down outside the window. O'Shay grabbed them and fastened them tightly. Jeff craned his neck to look down the alley and saw that the chains were attached to the massive doubletree of the wagon.

He dropped to the floor of the cell, shaking his head in disbelief. O'Shay apparently believed that the oxen would be able to pull the small window out of the wall—and counted on enough of the surrounding masonry wall going with it to allow Jeff to escape through the opening. And it might actually be possible. Jeff thought: those oxen were big and no doubt as strong as—well, as strong as oxen. But there would be a lot of noise, and Constable Tolbert and his men would come running with pistols ready.

However, he did not mind dodging a few bullets. If it meant a chance to bring Dermot Hawley to justice, he would willingly run that risk.

Quickly he pulled his boots on and shrugged into his jacket. The chains clinked again as the oxen started plodding forward, taking up the slack. Jeff lifted himself up to the window and risked one more quick look. The chains were taut now, and he could feel the iron bars trembling under his hands as the tension hit them. He dropped back to the floor.

The seconds passed with agonizing slowness as the oxen strained against their burden. Suddenly, with popping sounds that reminded Jeff of gunfire, a few of the bars jerked free of the mortar affixing them. The other bars held, but the window itself gave way, tearing out of the wall with a rumbling, rasping noise. The window went flying and clattered to the ground as the chains went slack.

"Come on!" O'Shay urged from outside.

There had been less noise than Jeff had expected, but it was enough to alert the authorities that something was amiss. Jeff heard faint shouts coming from the front of the building as he grasped the rough edge of the opening and pulled himself up, then thrust his head and shoulders through.

The shouts were getting louder now. Jeff wriggled and squirmed, trying to fit his body through the hole. It was a good thing he was rather lean to begin with, he thought, and that he had lost a bit of weight during his incarceration. As it was, his hips caught on the sides of the opening.

"Let's go, let's go!" O'Shay exhorted.

"I'm trying," Jeff replied between gritted teeth as he struggled to extricate himself. He heard the cell-block door slam open, heard rapid footsteps coming down the corridor toward his cell. He shoved again, harder.

Jeff let out a yelp of pain as he came free and sprawled into the alley. He had left a piece of his trousers behind as well as a little skin and blood, but he was free—at least for the moment.

He scrambled to his feet, and O'Shay caught hold of Jeff's arm. "Over here," he said, pointing. "I've got horses for us."

Beyond the wagon, where they had been obscured by the bulky oxen, were two tethered horses. "What about the wagon?" Jeff asked as he ran over to the horses with O'Shay.

"We'll leave it and the oxen right where they are," the big Irishman said, his grin lit by the moonlight. "They ain't mine, anyway."

O'Shay sounded rather nonchalant about the whole thing, Jeff thought. Maybe it was not that unusual for him to steal a wagon and a team of oxen to break a friend out of jail. Jeff had the feeling he had never before met anyone quite like Terence O'Shay.

The horses were saddled and ready, and as Jeff swung up onto one of them, a man's head and shoulders poked through the gaping hole in the wall of the jail. "Hey!" he yelled. "There they go!"

The next instant a pistol boomed, lighting up the

alley for a split second with the blast from its muzzle. Jeff heard the ball thud into the wall behind him, but the shot was a clean miss, and that was all that counted, no matter how close it was.

More shouts sounded from the mouth of the alley beside the jail's entrance. A shot thundered down the alley's narrow confines, but again it missed. Jeff and O'Shay whirled their horses and headed for the far end of the alleyway. The wagon and the oxen almost completely blocked the way behind them, an obstacle that would considerably slow down any pursuit from that direction. With hooves pounding, the horses raced out of the alley and into the small street beyond the jail.

More shots were fired, but as far as Jeff could tell, none of them came anywhere close. The night wind blew in his face as he and O'Shay galloped away from the jail, and it had never smelled so wonderful to him, harbor stench and all.

"Come on," O'Shay called as he swung his horse into another street. "We've got to get to the waterfront!"

"Why?"

"I did some nosing around today. Hawley's got some sort of big deal happening tonight, and I know where. What say we pay him a visit?"

Jeff's heart began to thud heavily, sounding louder to him than even the hoofbeats of the horses. He had been waiting for just such an opportunity, and now the time had come. No longer did he have anything to lose. He was an accused murderer, a fugitive who had just broken out of jail, one whom the constable and his men would probably shoot on sight. The only chance he had left was a confrontation with Dermot Hawley. If he could force the truth out of Hawley, he might still clear his name and be reunited with his family.

Tonight the truth would finally come out—or he would likely die. It was that simple.

*   *   *

"Where are you going at this hour, dear?" Hermione Merrivale asked as her daughter put on her bonnet.

"I need to go to the office for a while, Mother," Melissa Holt replied, hoping that her nervousness was not audible in her voice. She hated lying to her mother—but it was not *too* big a lie, she reasoned. She would be passing the office on her way to the meeting at the warehouse with Dermot Hawley.

Hermione frowned in disapproval. "You're going down there this late? I'm not sure that's a good idea, Melissa."

"I'll be fine, Mother," Melissa assured her. "And I won't be gone long."

She hoped that was true. She hoped that Hawley would readily admit his part in the murder of her father. When he was facing the small pistol that was weighing down her purse, he would talk, she thought.

Besides, Ned and India would be there in their guises as new recruits for Hawley's criminal gang, and if there was trouble, they could give her a hand.

"What about Michael?" Hermione asked.

"He's had his dinner, and he's asleep. He'll never know I've been gone." *And when he wakes up in the morning, perhaps his father will be back here with us again.*

"What if he wakes up and calls for you?"

"Just tell him I'll be back soon," Melissa said, her impatience growing. She knew her mother had only her best interests at heart, but—

"All right. Just be careful," Hermione said with a resigned sigh. "And come home as soon as you can."

"Of course, Mother." Melissa leaned over and brushed a kiss across her mother's cheek. Then she hurried out the front door. She had asked one of the servants to bring the carriage around, and it was waiting for her in the street.

She climbed into the vehicle and took up the

reins, flapping them to get the pair of horses moving. The carriage rolled through the nearly empty streets of Wilmington. At that hour, just before ten o'clock, few people were out and about in the residential area, but as she neared the waterfront, more wagons, carriages, and equestrians were in the street, as well as more pedestrians. Most of them were men, and the few women were gaudily painted and garbed prostitutes. Melissa felt more than one curious gaze follow her as she drove past, but she tried to ignore them. She was not going to allow anything to deter her from her mission.

Ned Holt scratched his head under the knitted cap he wore and tried not to let his nervousness show. If the men surrounding him and India ever found out why the two of them were really here, they would be in trouble—bad trouble.

But, Ned thought, why worry about something before it happened? After all, back in Pittsburgh he had not wasted a lot of time worrying about a few stray husbands showing up while he was visiting their wives; he had had more important things to focus on. Of course, that had meant diving out of more than one bedroom window to avoid an angry charge of buckshot when he had been found out, but everything in life had its risks.

Those happy-go-lucky days were far behind him now. He had found a way of life that was infinitely more rewarding. But from time to time he felt it was important to remember the luck that had carried him through so many scrapes. It was not going to desert him now—or at least so he hoped.

"I wish they'd get on with this," India said in a whisper that only Ned could hear. He nodded slightly.

They were standing just inside a large, dim, echoing warehouse near the harbor, along with a half dozen other men. The burly individual in the beaver

hat who had accosted them the previous night after
the brawl at Red Mike's was in charge. Ned had heard
one of the other men call him Bullock, which seemed
an appropriate name.

Several mule-drawn wagons had been pulled inside the warehouse, and then the heavy doors were
closed behind them. Only a couple of lanterns were
lighted, and their illumination did not reach to the
corners of the big building. Despite the gloom, Ned
could see stacks of wooden crates that filled up about
three-quarters of the warehouse—crates containing
stolen goods that would be loaded onto the wagons
and taken away to be disposed of somewhere else.
Ned was not sure what they were waiting for, but so
far there was no sign of Dermot Hawley. Maybe
Hawley's absence was what was causing the delay.

Ned and India were not the only ones growing
impatient. One of the other men complained, "Are we
goin' to be gettin' on with this any time soon, Bullock? I got a little gal waitin' for me."

"She'll just have to wait, and so will you," Bullock retorted. "We don't move this stuff until the time
is right."

A few of the men muttered among themselves,
but no one else complained to Bullock. The time
stretched, and Ned calculated that it was now around
ten o'clock.

Suddenly hoofbeats sounded close by the warehouse, then drew to a halt. After a moment there was
a soft knocking at the entrance in a pattern that Bullock evidently recognized, for he nodded in satisfaction and went to open one of the big doors. The door
swung back, and a man and a woman came into the
warehouse, the man's arm linked with the woman's.

Ned and India both stiffened in surprise. Judging
from the way Melissa had described him, the man
was Dermot Hawley, whose presence was not unexpected. But the woman was Melissa Merrivale Holt.

"What the hell?" India said under her breath. "She didn't say anything about being here tonight!"

"No, she didn't," Ned said. "I guess she has plans of her own. Let's just keep our eyes and ears open and wait and see."

That was all they could do—that and pray Melissa knew what she was doing.

"You sure about this?" Jeff asked.

"I got you out of jail, didn't I?" Terence O'Shay replied.

That was true, Jeff had to admit. But looking up the rickety stack of boxes O'Shay had piled into a makeshift ladder leading to a boarded-up window high on the rear wall of the warehouse, his confidence was about as shaky as the boxes.

"This is where Hawley's supposed to be," O'Shay went on, "and the only way in where they won't notice us is through that window. Sorry I couldn't come up with a real ladder to get us up there."

"Guess we'll just have to take the chance," Jeff said with a shrug. He had come much too far to turn back now. But if those boxes came crashing down while he and O'Shay climbed them, the fall would probably injure both of them as well as alert the men inside.

O'Shay stepped up to the boxes. "I'll go first," he volunteered.

"No, hold on. You weigh more, so I'd better go first."

"You sure you want to?"

"Wanting to's got nothing to do with it," Jeff said dryly. He stepped onto the lowest box, reached up for a handhold on another one, and began climbing.

The stack of boxes was steadier than he had expected it would be. The ascent to the window was not like climbing stairs, but it went quickly and smoothly enough. When Jeff reached the window, a hurried examination told him that some of the boards across the opening had already been loosened. O'Shay had been a busy man since being released from jail earlier in the day, he realized.

Grabbing one of the boards, he wrenched it free with only a slight squeaking sound as the nails gave way. He could hear voices inside the cavernous warehouse and hoped that the conversation would cover up the small noises he would have to make to get the window open.

He dropped the board to O'Shay, who caught it deftly, then repeated the process with two more. Now he could reach inside and shove up the window sash, which was not fastened. The boards nailed over the window had apparently been considered enough of a deterrent to keep out thieves.

But Jeff was not here to steal anything. He wanted to reclaim what had been stolen from *him*: his good name and his freedom.

He leaned through the window and peered around. A couple of lanterns at the front of the building cast large shadows on the walls. The tall stacks of crates concealed the people themselves, but he could see their shadows moving around and hear them talking.

Jeff pulled back from the window and motioned down to O'Shay to begin climbing. Then he ducked his head and again looked through the window. Crates were piled below the window, so he wouldn't be able to drop to the ground. He would have to land on the crates—quietly. He clambered through the window and twisted around as noiselessly as he could. Getting a firm grip on the windowsill, he hung from it and waited until there was a sudden burst of conversation from the occupants of the warehouse; then he let go.

Luck was with him. He landed solidly on a crate and balanced himself so that he would not overturn the stack. Carefully, as soon as he was certain that nothing was going to collapse beneath him, he crawled to the edge of the large crate and slid off, landing on the floor in a narrow walkway that had been left between the piles of boxes. It was very dark, but he was able to follow the winding path through the labyrinth of crates until the light from the lanterns grew brighter. Then he crouched even lower and edged forward until he could peer around a corner into the large open area at the front of the warehouse.

His heart seemed to stop beating.

Dermot Hawley stood not far inside the big double doors of the warehouse—and standing next to him was Melissa!

Melissa had found Hawley waiting for her outside the warehouse, and he had smiled and taken her arm as she stepped down from the carriage. It was if he were escorting her to a party rather than leading her into a warehouse full of stolen goods.

"How are you this evening, my dear?" he had asked.

"Looking forward to doing business with you," Melissa had replied, hoping she sounded convincing.

Hawley had knocked on the door of the big building, and a moment later they were admitted by a powerful-looking man in a beaver hat.

Melissa had shot a glance at Ned and India as she and Hawley walked in, confident that they would be able to conceal their surprise at seeing her. They would have no choice now but to follow her lead.

She let her gaze sweep over them, carefully not paying any more attention to them than she did to any of the other members of the gang.

"Now that you're here, boss, we can get on with this," the man in the beaver hat told Hawley. He was staring curiously at Melissa, as were the other men, but he did not ask Hawley who she was. She took that as an indication of how much respect, or fear, the man had for Hawley.

"Go right ahead, Bullock," Hawley told his lieutenant. He added, "You have a couple of new men here tonight, don't you?"

Bullock grinned. "Yeah, they handled themselves damn well in a little row at Red Mike's last night. I thought they'd be good to have around."

"Well, you know I trust your judgment. Let's get on with it."

Melissa looked up at Hawley as the men began loading crates onto the wagons. "What will you do with these goods, Dermot?"

"Several merchants down the coast who do business with me need supplies to sell in their stores, and they're not too particular where those supplies come from. These boxes will go overland in the wagons and reach their destination in a day or two, resulting in a pretty profit for me."

"And what about for me?" Melissa asked quickly. "Need I remind you that you've stored them in *my* warehouse?"

Hawley chuckled. "It's a shame your late father can't see this, my dear. I'm sure he would have been proud of you. You're a daughter after his own heart."

Melissa kept her feelings tightly reined in. "You're saying that he knew about all of this?"

Hawley hesitated. "When Charles and I were partners, he must have suspected something of the sort, but I can't be certain of that. However, he was a man who dearly loved to make money, so I don't think he really cared what I did, as long as it was lucrative for both of us."

"And you would have continued doing business with him behind my back if he hadn't been killed, wouldn't you?"

"Actually, the last day I saw him, he was telling me that he thought he might try making that arrangement with your husband succeed—but then, of course, Holt came bursting in and attacked him, so that changed everything."

Melissa stared at him, hardly able to believe what she had just heard. "My father told you that he was going to try to get along with Jeff?"

"Yes, he did. He was polite enough about it, but he was letting me know that the arrangement between us, informal though it was, was about to come to an end."

Melissa's pulse had begun to race. They had all misjudged her father, she saw now; he really had intended to work with Jeff. But what Hawley had just told her was the final bit of proof she needed. Not proof that would hold up in court, perhaps, but she was still convinced of his guilt.

Hawley's attention had drifted back to the men loading the wagons, so Melissa took advantage of the opportunity to slip her hand into her purse. Her fingers closed around the butt of the small pistol. Taking a deep breath, she pulled out the gun, stepped back, and leveled it at Hawley.

"So that's why you killed him," she said, "because he was not going to be part of your crooked schemes anymore."

One of Hawley's eyebrows quirked upward, but he did not seem particularly surprised that Melissa was pointing a pistol at him. A couple of the men let out startled curses and abruptly stopped their work at the sight of their boss being held at gunpoint by the lovely young woman who had accompanied him.

"Melissa, what the hell . . . !" The exclamation burst from Ned Holt, who immediately looked chagrined that he had given away his connection with her.

"It's all right, Ned," Melissa told him without taking her eyes off Hawley. The barrel of the pistol was surprisingly steady. "You and India can come over here. It's all over now. Mr. Hawley and I are going to the authorities, and he will tell Constable Tolbert everything he has told me."

Hawley smiled. "I've admitted nothing."

"Only that you had just as compelling a reason as my husband to want my father dead," Melissa said, and for the first time a slight tremor in her voice revealed the strain she was under. "I think you'll tell the truth once you've sat in a cell for a while."

Ned and India came over to flank her. Bullock glared at them, his anger at being deceived evident. Both of them took pistols from under their belts and held them ready, in case trouble broke out.

Hawley still seemed unshaken. "You've really underestimated me, my dear," he told Melissa. "I *thought* you were a bit too quick to accept your father's involvement in shady dealings and want to be part of them yourself. That's why I told you that story about your father wanting to end our arrangement. I figured it would draw you out and make you reveal your true motives."

"Story?" Melissa repeated. "You mean it wasn't true?"

Hawley shrugged. "Your father may have *suspected* that something was wrong, but he had made no move to change things. He was a fool and quite easy to dupe, made all the more so because of his greed."

"No!" Melissa cried. "Shut up, Dermot, unless you're finally willing to admit that you killed him."

"Of course I did," Hawley snapped. "You don't think I'd pass up an opportunity like that, do you? Surely you realized that I got rid of him and that wretched husband of yours at the same time, and all it took was one stroke of a knife blade."

"You—you—" Melissa was unable to find the words she needed.

Ned had no such trouble. "Come on, you goddamn bastard. We're going to see the constable." He gestured with the barrel of his pistol.

Hawley shook his head. "I don't think so. You see, I knew Melissa was up to something, so I took some precautions."

Almost lazily, he gestured with his left hand, and

a pained cry sounded from the thick shadows on the far side of the warehouse. Two men emerged from the darkness, one of them roughly pulling a small, resisting figure in a long nightshirt.

"*Michael!*" Melissa screamed.

Ned and India tensed, but neither of them dared to do anything, with Michael in the hands of Hawley's men. The gun in Melissa's hand sagged toward the floor, forgotten in the face of such a terrifying development.

"Your two friends will have to be killed, of course, since they now know the truth," Hawley said smoothly, nodding at Ned and India. "But you'll be spared, Melissa. After all, a wife cannot be forced to testify against her husband—and you *will* agree to marry me if you want your son to survive this night."

Jeff had nearly lost control during Melissa's conversation with Hawley. When she pulled the pistol from her purse, he almost stepped into the open, but he had forced himself to wait and see what Hawley had to say. Hawley's confession came as no surprise; Jeff had already concluded that Hawley murdered Charles Merrivale.

When Hawley's men roughly dragged Michael out of hiding, every muscle in Jeff's body tensed. It was time to make his move, but where was O'Shay?

The big Irishman's hand came down on Jeff's shoulder, and Jeff's nerves were drawn so tightly that it was all he could do not to let out a startled yell.

"Had a bit of unexpected delay," O'Shay whispered. "Couple of gents coming in the back door nearly tripped over me before I got hid. That's them out there, with the boy. Who is he?"

"My son. Come on."

Everyone's attention was focused on the drama unfolding in the center of the warehouse, which was exactly what Jeff was counting on as he slipped out of the jungle of crates and catfooted toward one of the wagons a few yards away.

"Put those guns down," Hawley was saying. "There's nothing else either you or your friends can do, Melissa. I'm afraid you've gotten in far over your pretty little head."

"You son of a bitch—" Ned began hotly.

India cut in, "Give them the guns. Otherwise, they'll harm Michael."

"That's quite right." Hawley stared at her for a moment. "Good Lord, you're not a man at all, are you? It would seem I'm not the only one who enjoys a bit of deception."

"I'm not a deceiving worm like you," India snapped as she handed over her pistol to one of the gang members who stepped forward. Ned did likewise, turning over his gun to Bullock.

Hawley himself plucked the small pistol from Melissa's unresisting hand, then made a small gesture. Watching from his hidden vantage point, Jeff felt infinite relief when the man holding Michael released him and the boy ran across the floor to his mother, throwing himself into her arms as she bent to embrace him.

"Mama! The men scared me, Mama."

"It's all right now, Michael," Melissa assured him. Her voice was filled with outrage as she said, "No one else will hurt you." She looked up at Hawley. "What did your brutes do to my mother?"

Hawley looked at the men, and one of them answered, "The old lady's fine, just shook up a mite. We didn't hurt her when we grabbed the brat."

"Very good," Hawley said. "You see, Melissa, I'm not the monster you seem to think I am."

"You're worse," Melissa replied bitterly. "But you've the upper hand, so there's nothing I can do."

"Nothing but marry me," Hawley said with a smile.

A few feet away, Bullock was still glaring at Ned

and India. "I don't like being made a fool of," he snarled. Without warning he brought around the hand holding the pistol he had taken from Ned. The weapon caught Ned on the side of the head, opening up a nasty gash just below his temple. As Ned staggered from the blow, Bullock told him, "I'm going to enjoy killing you, mister."

Jeff knew he had no time to lose. He and O'Shay had circled around and reached the wagon, and now he reached out and grabbed the handle of a bullwhip that was coiled around the brake lever of the wagon. He pulled it free without making any noise, but one of the mules in the team suddenly snorted and shifted its feet. The closest of Hawley's crewmen glanced around and opened his mouth to yell a warning when he spotted Jeff.

But the long whip was already uncoiling onto the floor with a sound like the hissing of a snake, and before the man had the chance to shout, Jeff's arm shot back and then forward. The whip's deadly, sinuous length cracked forward, the weighted tip catching the man on the cheek just below the left eye with a sound like a gunshot, and he screamed.

"Give 'em the lashing they deserve, Holt!" O'Shay boomed as he lunged forward toward Hawley's men.

"Jeff!" Melissa screamed as she turned and saw him.

At that instant Bullock cocked the pistol he had just used to hit Ned and started bringing it to bear, but before he could do so, Ned slammed a fist into his face, knocking him backward into a couple of other men. With a roar of rage, Ned leapt after Bullock, his arms sweeping out to grab more than one man.

"Kill the boy!" Dermot Hawley cried as he turned and ran for the door.

Jeff lashed out again with the whip as one of Hawley's men jerked out a pistol and pointed it at the back of Michael's head. This time the tip of the whip caught the eyeball itself, and the man screeched in agony as he stumbled forward, dropping the unfired pistol, and clapped both hands over the ruined eye.

The massive O'Shay grabbed a couple of men by their necks and slammed their heads together. At the same time, Ned was swinging brutal blows right and left, toppling several of the men. Bullock threw one more futile swipe at him before Ned clubbed his hands viciously into Bullock's jaw. Bullock dropped limply, his jaw crushed.

Grinning, Ned shook his left hand, which had taken the brunt of the blow. A couple of knuckles were probably broken, he thought, but he was enjoying the fight too much to care.

Melissa had dropped to her knees and gathered Michael into her arms, trying to shield him from the melee. One of Hawley's men swung a club that would have crushed the skulls of both Melissa and the boy, had it had connected. But before the blow could land, India St. Clair drove the heel of her right boot into the back of the man's knee, causing his leg to crumple beneath him. India pulled a small knife from her trouser pocket. The blade briefly flickered in the lantern light as she stabbed the man in the back, then quickly withdrew it. As that foe collapsed, she spun to meet the attack of another, ducking underneath a wild punch and then slashing the man's face with the knife. He screamed as the blade opened his cheek all the way to the bone.

Jeff whirled around. Seeing that Hawley had almost reached the doors, Jeff cracked the whip again and wrapped one of Hawley's ankles with it. Jeff tugged hard on the whip, upending Hawley, then dropped it to finish off the man with his bare hands.

Hawley landed hard but rolled over and came to his feet just as Jeff reached him. He blocked Jeff's first punch and threw one of his own that caught Jeff in the chest and rocked him backward. The man's desperation seemed to give him added strength, and Jeff had his hands full warding off blows.

But a missed swing by Hawley finally gave Jeff the opening he needed, and he hammered a series of punches into his foe's midsection. Hawley doubled over, and Jeff helped his momentum along by shoving a knee into his jaw. Hawley went down.

Jeff threw himself on top of him, first driving his knees into Hawley's chest, then smashing his fists into Hawley's face. Jeff was panting, sucking air through his teeth, as he struck again and again. This man had tried to steal his wife, had murdered Charles Merrivale, had framed him for the murder, had kidnapped his son and threatened Michael's life. . . . Jeff let his anger and outrage at everything Hawley had done take control of him, and he slammed blow after blow into Hawley's face until the man's features only vaguely resembled anything human.

Strong arms caught Jeff around the middle and hauled him up and back. "Stop it, Jeff!" Ned shouted at him. "You're killing him."

"Let me go!" Jeff ranted. "He deserves to die for all he's done."

O'Shay appeared on Jeff's other side to give Ned a hand. "Aye, maybe he does," O'Shay said firmly, "but if you kill him, he can't confess to the constable that he's the one who killed Merrivale, now, can he?"

That logic got through to Jeff, and he slumped in their grip. "I'm all right now," he muttered. "Just let me go."

"Sure," Ned said, releasing him. "I think somebody's waiting for you."

Jeff turned and saw Melissa and Michael being led away from the scene by India. He took a step toward them, then broke into a run and swept both of them into his arms. A sob of relief shook him.

"I don't know how you got here, Jeff," Melissa whispered into his ear, "but thank God you did! I love you. Oh, God, I love you!"

"I love you, too, both of you. And I'll never leave you again. I swear it."

A few feet away Ned and India were exchanging looks with Terence O'Shay. After several moments Ned said, "I don't know who you are, mister, but you were on the right side in this fight. You a friend of Jeff's?"

"Aye. Haven't known him for long, but I'm proud to call him friend. We met in jail, before I busted him out of there tonight. Name's Terence O'Shay."

Ned extended a hand. "I'm Ned Holt, Jeff's cousin. And this is a friend of ours, India St. Clair."

O'Shay shook Ned's hand and grinned at India. "You're a mighty pretty colleen to be dressed up as a man, if you don't mind my saying so, ma'am."

"Actually, I do, but under the circumstances . . ." India smiled. "I'm pleased to meet you, Mr. O'Shay. I—"

She stopped short as the doors of the warehouse crashed open and Constable Tolbert, followed by a contingent of his men and a handful of hastily sworn-in volunteers, burst into the building. As they all leveled pistols and muskets at the people still on their feet, Tolbert exclaimed, "What the devil—? We heard the yelling and fighting in here four blocks away, but I didn't expect to find a damned battlefield inside a warehouse! You there, Holt! Stand still!"

Jeff ignored the order and strode over to Hawley, the muzzles of the guns following him all the way. He reached down, grasped Hawley's collar, and hauled the man to his feet.

"Here's the man who really murdered Charles Merrivale, Constable. Everyone in this room heard him confess to the killing, and if you don't believe my friends and me, some of Hawley's own men will probably confirm our story, once they realize just how much trouble they're in."

Tolbert frowned, his confusion evident. "Well, it's

a good thing we were out looking for you after you escaped, Holt. You're going to have to answer for that, you know." He looked over at the big Irishman. "And you, O'Shay! I should've known you had something to do with this, you blackguard!"

Jeff let go of Hawley, who would have collapsed to the floor had Tolbert not motioned to a couple of his men to catch him. As Jeff started back toward Melissa and Michael he said over his shoulder, "We'll sort all this out later, Constable. Right now, my family needs me."

For a second Tolbert looked as if he would explode with anger, but then he put away his pistol. "We'll sort it out, all right," he muttered, "but I got a feeling we've got the right man this time." He jerked a thumb at his men. "Take Mr. Hawley and these other gents back to the jail. No need to be any too gentle with them, either."

Jeff reached down and picked up Michael, who snuggled against him. With his other arm, Jeff embraced Melissa.

"Is it really over?" she asked.

"It's over."

Then, followed by Ned and India, O'Shay, and the constable, Jeff led his family out of the warehouse, into the soft summer night.

They were going home.

CHAPTER
TWENTY-TWO

Setting out after Fletcher McKendrick the morning after Josie Garwood's death and Matthew's kidnapping, Clay Holt and Proud Wolf discovered a clear trail that was probably the Scotsman's leading toward the mountains. They took off on horseback at first light, when the glow in the sky was barely enough to allow Clay to see the tracks in the buffalo grass. Although most of the grass had sprung back into its natural position, some of the blades were broken, and to Clay that might as well have been an arrow drawn on a map.

Malachi Fisher, Budd Spenser, and other men of New Hope had wanted to accompany them, but Clay refused the offer. His hatred for McKendrick was far too personal, as was Proud Wolf's. Clay knew they had to keep their wits about them, however. McKendrick was capable of killing the boy on a whim or in hopes of so angering his pursuers that Clay and Proud Wolf would become careless.

By midday they reached the edge of the mountains, an area of steep, wooded foothills and rocky outcroppings. The trail became more difficult to follow here, but Clay always managed to find a broken branch, an overturned rock, something to tell him that McKendrick had passed that way. The conspicuousness of the signs told Clay that McKendrick was blazing a trail for him, just as he had suspected.

He and Proud Wolf would have to be more alert than ever. McKendrick was bound to try an ambush. The only questions were where and when.

The trail led them through a narrow, winding canyon. Clay and Proud Wolf rode along, their eyes scanning the pine- and spruce-covered slopes.

"Ought to be catching up to him soon," Clay commented in a quiet voice. "He's on foot, and the boy will be slowing him down."

"Unless he has already killed Matthew and hidden the body," Proud Wolf suggested.

Clay winced. The same thought had occurred to him, but he had not wanted to voice it.

"He won't let go of the boy unless he has to," he said, trying to convince himself as much as Proud Wolf. "Matthew is what gives him his advantage."

Proud Wolf agreed but still looked somewhat dubious.

Clay could not figure out why he was so worried about Matthew. He had never even liked the boy; Matthew was a strange child and always had been. He supposed that he would be just as concerned about any innocent victim of a madman's scheme— and McKendrick qualified as a madman, without a doubt. Clay simply had to rescue Matthew and make sure McKendrick never hurt anyone again.

By late afternoon they still had not spotted their quarry. It seemed impossible that the Scotsman could have outdistanced them for so long, but Clay reminded himself that McKendrick was driven by the power of madness. They had no way of knowing just how much the man might be capable of, and underestimating McKendrick would likely prove to be a fatal mistake.

Suddenly, as they neared another bend in the canyon, Proud Wolf put out a hand to stop Clay and said urgently, "There! Did you see it?"

Clay followed the Hunkpapa's gaze, which was directed at the thickly wooded slope up ahead and to their left. "See what?" Clay asked as his gaze swept over the hill without noticing anything unusual. "Did you spot McKendrick?"

"No. It was . . . something else." Proud Wolf hesitated. "A mountain lion."

Clay felt a surge of impatience. "Plenty of big cats up here," he said.

"Not like this one," Proud Wolf rejoined, his voice hushed. "I have seen it before."

Clay shot a glance at his brother-in-law. Proud Wolf was still looking at the slope, and his eyes shone with a peculiar light.

"What do you think it was?" Clay asked.

Without hesitation Proud Wolf answered, "A warning."

Clay rubbed his bearded jaw and frowned in thought. "That's a mighty sharp bend up there. Could be a good place to set up an ambush. I've been up this canyon before, and it seems that I recall a ledge around here. It would give a man a good field of view of the whole trail."

Proud Wolf slipped down from his horse. "I will go over the hill on foot and get above that ledge."

"And I'll ride around the bend and draw his fire if he's up there," Clay finished. If they were wrong about the possibility of an ambush, no harm would be done by their caution. But if they were right, they might manage to turn the surprise around on McKendrick.

Clay reached out and took the pinto's reins, leading it down the trail as Proud Wolf, carrying his flintlock rifle, trotted into the trees on the steep-sided hill. If McKendrick was waiting around that bend, he would be able to hear the hooves of both horses hitting the rocks of the trail and would think that both pursuers were still coming on.

Clay could feel his nerves drawing taut as he neared the curve. He wondered what was so special about that mountain lion Proud Wolf claimed to have seen. He certainly had not spotted any such big cat when he looked up the slope. Somehow he thought it was connected to the retreat Proud Wolf had gone on after they had returned from Canada. When this was all over, he would try to get Proud Wolf to tell him what had happened then. If the young warrior did not want to talk about it, though, Clay would not pressure him. Some things were personal and had to stay that way.

He had gotten to within a few yards of where the trail turned sharply to the left. Steeling himself, he pressed the heels of his moccasins against the flanks of the dun, urging it on. As he rode around the bend he lifted his eyes to the outcropping of rock looming above and just ahead of him.

The late afternoon sun suddenly glinted on something up there.

Clay was dropping from the back of the dun even as the boom of a rifle sounded. The ball whipped past his head and took off a chunk of rock alongside the trail. Landing lightly on his feet, Clay yelled and swatted the dun's rump, sending it and the pinto galloping down the trail, out of harm's way. Then he flung himself toward a cluster of boulders at the base of the slope.

"Holt!" a voice howled. "Is that ye, Holt?"

Clay crouched behind a good-sized rock and did

not say anything. Let McKendrick wonder, he thought. He edged the barrel of his rifle over the top of the boulder and looked for a target.

McKendrick had had time to reload, and he got off another shot. The ball splintered off the rock Clay was using as cover, kicking up grit and small chips of rock at his face as he ducked down again. The Scotsman had a good eye; Clay would give him that. But he had seen the flash from McKendrick's rifle and now had him pinpointed at the edge of that sheer, rocky bluff. He squeezed off a shot of his own at a faint flicker of movement.

"Ye missed me, Holt! Ye just don't seem to be able to get me, ye sorry sod," McKendrick taunted as Clay began to reload.

"Holler all you want to, McKendrick," Clay muttered under his breath as he seated the ball and patch atop the charge of powder he had poured down the barrel of his rifle. "All you're doing is leading Proud Wolf right to you."

When the flintlock was loaded and primed again, Clay ventured another look. From where he was, he could not see the top of the hill very well, where Proud Wolf would sneak up on McKendrick from behind. Clay had to assume that by now the young warrior was almost in position.

"I don't want to play games with ye, Holt," McKendrick called down. "'Tis time for ye to die, laddie, for all the trouble you've caused me these past two years. So step out and take what ye have coming, or I'll kill this boy!"

Clay scowled. Just as he had feared, McKendrick was going to use Matthew to draw him out into the open. There was no doubt in his mind that McKendrick would kill the youngster without a moment's hesitation.

"Hold on, McKendrick!" he shouted. "Don't hurt the boy. I'll do what you want."

"Step out from those rocks so I can see ye!"

Taking a deep breath, Clay stood and walked out of the clump of rocks. He held his rifle ready to lift to his shoulder and snap off a shot—if McKendrick gave him a chance to do so.

Clay tilted back his head and looked up at the top of the bluff. Suddenly two figures appeared there, one large and one much smaller. He recognized Matthew Garwood, but McKendrick was a gaunt, scarred shell of the man he had been. Still dangerous, though, Clay reminded himself. What had happened to Josie and Father Brennan was ample proof of that.

McKendrick had a hand clamped around the back of Matthew's neck and was holding him tightly. He shoved him perilously close to the edge of the outcropping. In McKendrick's other hand was a pistol, and the barrel was pressed up under Matthew's chin.

"Very good, Holt," McKendrick said with a hideous grin when he saw that Clay had done as ordered. "Now put your rifle down and back away from it, or I'll blow the lad's head off."

For an instant Clay debated the idea of trying a shot. But even if he hit McKendrick, the Scotsman would probably be able to trigger the pistol before dying. And if *that* did not happen, the chance remained that both McKendrick and Matthew would topple over the edge since they were so close to it. Clay could not risk either of those possibilities. Carefully he placed the rifle on the ground by his feet, then backed away from it.

McKendrick took the pistol from Matthew's throat and aimed it at Clay. The distance was a little far for a pistol shot, but not so much out of range that Clay could count on McKendrick to miss.

"I'm going to kill ye now, Holt," McKendrick called, "but perhaps you'd like to see this lad of yours die first. Let's see how high he'll bounce when he lands at the bottom of this cliff!"

McKendrick shoved at the back of Matthew's

neck. The boy twisted and writhed in the madman's grip, his feet scrabbling for purchase at the very brink. Clay was about to dive for his rifle and try a desperation shot when a buckskin-clad form suddenly flashed across the ledge and slammed into McKendrick. At the same instant as he collided with the Scotsman, Proud Wolf snagged Matthew's collar with one hand and dragged him away from the edge. All three figures collapsed out of Clay's sight, falling back on the broad ledge.

Clay snatched up his rifle and sprinted toward the hillside. A path led up to the top of the bluff, and he bounded up it, taking chances as rocks slid under his feet. He heard McKendrick shouting above him.

Clay darted along the path, putting his free hand down to steady himself as he kept his gaze fastened on the top of the outcropping. He could hear the sounds of fighting up there but had no way of knowing who was winning. After several minutes that seemed much longer, he finally reached the summit and vaulted onto the ledge.

Some twenty feet away McKendrick and Proud Wolf, on their knees, were locked in struggle. In his right hand Proud Wolf held his knife, but McKendrick gripped the young man's wrist, thwarting the thrust of the blade. McKendrick still held the pistol in his other hand, but its deployment was equally thwarted by Proud Wolf, who kept a tight hold on the Scotsman's arm. Meanwhile, Matthew Garwood was cowering against the rocky wall at the back of the ledge, watching the standoff with wide eyes. The boy was dirty and scratched up, Clay saw with a quick look, but he did not seem to be badly hurt by his ordeal, at least not physically.

Clay clutched his rifle tightly. He did not want to risk a shot while Proud Wolf and McKendrick were locked so close together; all he could do was wait for an opening.

Suddenly McKendrick's grip slipped, and Proud

Wolf stabbed with the knife. McKendrick was able to deflect the blow, however, so the blade merely sliced across the top of his left shoulder. At the same time the effort threw Proud Wolf off balance, and McKendrick jerked his gun hand loose. He slashed at Proud Wolf with the barrel, knocking him back, then leaned away from the young warrior and fired. The ball slammed into Proud Wolf's body and sent him sprawling.

"No!" Clay screamed. He brought the Harper's Ferry rifle to his shoulder and fired, letting instinct do the aiming for him. He had wanted a clear shot at McKendrick, but not this way.

McKendrick flung himself to the side as Clay's rifle blossomed fire and smoke, and through the haze Clay saw the Scotsman's left arm jerk. The ball had merely clipped him, Clay realized. McKendrick landed hard and rolled over, and as he came up again he flung the empty pistol away. With a howl that sounded more animal than human, the Scotsman plucked a knife from his belt and charged straight at Clay.

Clay dropped his rifle. He pulled out the brace of pistols tucked beneath his belt, his thumbs looping around the cocks. McKendrick never wavered in his charge, even when Clay lifted the pistols and pointed them. McKendrick just shrieked out his insane rage and kept coming.

Clay pressed both triggers, and the pistols discharged with a thunderous roar that echoed far down the mountain canyons. McKendrick was slammed back as if he had run into a stone wall, his knife slipping from his fingers, but somehow he managed to stay on his feet. Blood welled from the twin holes the pistol balls had torn in his chest.

Behind him Proud Wolf staggered to his feet. He still held the knife, and with a Sioux war cry he half fell, half lunged at McKendrick, plunging the blade into the Scotsman's chest between the two pistol wounds. Proud Wolf sprawled on the ground as Mc-Kendrick stumbled backward, his hands pawing feebly for the handle of the knife.

"Damn ye, Holt!" he managed to rasp, and then his feet slid off the edge of the bluff. The scream that came out of his throat lasted only a second before it was cut off by an awful thump.

Clay was suddenly aware that he had been holding his breath.

Hurrying to Proud Wolf's side, he knelt and rolled over the young man. Blood stained Proud Wolf's buckskin shirt, but it was low on the left side, which meant there was a chance the wound was not as serious as it looked.

Proud Wolf opened his eyes, and Clay asked, "How're you doing?"

"I will be . . . all right," Proud Wolf replied between teeth clenched against the pain. "What about . . . the boy?"

Clay looked up. "You all right, Matthew?"

Matthew nodded shakily. The icy reserve that he usually exhibited was missing. He looked exhausted and terrified, just as any normal six-year-old would under the circumstances.

"I think he'll be all right," Clay told Proud Wolf, "and you will be, too. I'll patch up that wound, and then we'll get you home."

"McKendrick?"

"Dead."

Proud Wolf tried pulling himself into a sitting position. "Help me up," he said. "I—I must see for myself."

After everything that had happened, Clay could understand Proud Wolf's need. He slipped an arm around the young warrior, trying to avoid the wound, and helped him to his feet. Together they walked over to the edge of the bluff to look down at the body sprawled on the trail below. As if it were not enough that McKendrick had been shot twice and had a knife in his chest, his head was twisted at a grotesque angle, indicating that the fall had broken his neck. Clay did not have to climb back down the path to know that this time Fletcher McKendrick was truly dead.

However, they still needed to get off the bluff. Keeping one arm around Proud Wolf, Clay looked at Matthew and held out his other hand.

"Get my rifle, boy, and then come on. It's time to go home."

Shining Moon was waiting for them when they rode back into the Hunkpapa village the next day. In fact, the entire village had turned out to welcome them, as well as quite a few of the settlers from New Hope—but Clay saw only Shining Moon. He saw the smile that spread across her face when she looked at him, saw the smile widen when her gaze took in Proud Wolf on the pinto with Matthew riding perched in front of him. Proud Wolf's midsection was bound tightly with bandages torn from Clay's shirt, but a night's rest had restored some of the strength he had lost along with the blood from the wound. Clay was confident that he would be all right.

As for himself, he felt as if a burden had been lifted from his soul with McKendrick's death. And maybe now he could finally get back to the normal life he craved.

He swung down from the dun and took Shining Moon in his arms, cradling her gently against him and stroking her hair. "It's over," he told her. "For good this time."

"You are all right?"

He looked down into her eyes and smiled. "I'm just fine," he said, and he meant every word of it.

Shining Moon's happy expression turned grave as she said, "We must go to the church. Father Brennan is amp-amputating Aaron's leg."

Clay frowned. "What the hell is he doing that for?"

"The sickness is getting worse. Father Brennan says that is the only way to save Aaron's life."

"Hell, that priest was clubbed senseless by McKendrick just the night before last. He's got no business trying such a thing!" Clay fumed.

"Father Brennan says he is all right. He was lucky that McKendrick did not kill him."

"What about Josie?"

"She is buried behind the church. Father Brennan held the service yesterday."

Clay gave a brief nod. It was a shame Matthew could not have been at his mother's funeral. But the boy had come close to dying himself, and life had to go on; that was one thing the mountains had taught Clay.

"Okay, let's go see how Aaron's doing." He turned to Proud Wolf. "And you need to have Soaring Owl take a look at you while we're gone."

However, Proud Wolf would not be talked out of accompanying Clay and Shining Moon. Aaron was his friend, after all, and he wanted to see him before he had the shaman tend his own wound.

Together with Matthew, the three of them walked quickly to the church beside the river. Father Brennan was standing just outside the door, wiping his bloody hands on a piece of cloth. He looked tired and haggard, but a smile lit his bruised and battered face.

"Aaron came through the operation just fine, and he's going to be all right," he said before Clay had a chance to open his mouth. "That leg had gone bad on him, and it would have killed him if it didn't come off."

"You're sure about that?" Clay asked suspiciously.

"I'm sure." The priest looked at Matthew. "Thank God you found the boy. What about McKendrick?"

"He's dead. No doubt the wolves and buzzards have taken good care of him by now."

The priest frowned. "Every man deserves a Christian burial, no matter what he's done."

"I won't argue religion with you, Father," Clay said, "but we didn't have an extra horse, and Proud Wolf's pinto was already carrying double. I sure as hell wasn't going to tote him back with me."

Father Brennan touched one of the swollen lumps on his skull from McKendrick's attack. "Under the circumstances, I suppose there was nothing else you could do. But I'll say a prayer for his soul anyway."

"You do that," Clay said coldly. He had figured out that the priest had inadvertently sent McKendrick to Josie's cabin with his remarks about her claim of being Clay's wife, and although he was sure the priest had meant no harm, he still could not bring himself to feel overly charitable toward him. He turned to his companions. "Let's get back to the village. Come along, Matthew."

Instead of following, the boy stood his ground. He looked up at Clay, his face set in a stony mask once again, and asked, "My ma's dead, isn't she?"

Clay had tried to avoid discussing Josie's death, since Matthew had not asked any questions until now, but he could no longer get around it. Sighing, he said, "That's right."

"What's going to happen to me?"

Father Brennan began, "You can stay here at the church—"

"No." Shining Moon spoke softly but firmly. She went to Matthew's side and held out her hand to him. "You will come with us. We will take care of you. We promised your mother."

Clay started to object. No one would hold them to the promise he had made to Josie; after everything that had happened, folks would understand if he did not want Matthew around.

But none of it had been the boy's fault, Clay realized, and he kept his mouth shut as Matthew reached out tentatively and slipped his hand into Shining Moon's. If she was willing to put the past behind her, Clay thought, maybe it was time he did the same.

He stepped over to Matthew, took the boy's other hand, and squeezed hard. "Let's go, son."

"What are you doing?" Shining Moon asked a week later as she came into the tipi and found Clay hunched over a piece of paper, laboriously printing on it with a quill pen that he dipped from time to time in a small pot of ink.

"Something I don't think I ever did before," Clay replied. "I'm writing a letter. Malachi says there's a boatload of supplies for his trading post coming upriver, and when it goes down again, I'm going to send off this letter to Jeff. Been a long time since I've seen him, and I want him to know we're still all right."

Shining Moon sat down beside Clay with a rustle of skirts. She still wore the blue dress, and she was clutching the Bible she had taken to carrying after Father Brennan gave it to her. She was able to read it after a fashion, and she was spending a lot of time doing just that. She went to the church every day to pray and take religious instruction with some of the other Hunkpapa women who had decided to take up Christianity. Clay had never been much of a churchgoer himself, and since coming to the mountains, it had seemed to him that it did not really matter whether somebody chanted to the Great Spirit or sang psalms. It was all the same thing when you got right down to it, he believed. But if it made Shining Moon feel better to call herself a Christian, that was all right with him, although it struck him as a bit strange sometimes when he looked at her in her store-bought dress, studying the Bible, and remembered the haughty beauty in buckskins he had first met.

But things changed.

Aaron was doing well, or as well as could be expected after losing a leg. The sickness had gotten better just a few days after the amputation, and although he was still terribly weak, he had regained consciousness and was coherent again. Clay had told him about everything that happened since the avalanche, and Aaron had verified to Shining Moon that Josie and Clay had never been married. Without revealing the facts of Matthew's parentage, Aaron had stated unequivocally that Clay was not Matthew's father. Shining Moon had already been convinced of that, but hearing it from Aaron was a welcome confirmation.

Proud Wolf was healing quickly from his wound and was almost back to normal, except that he spent a lot of time gazing off at the mountains. When Clay had asked him about the mountain lion, he muttered something about a spirit cat and then refused to say anything else. But that was enough for Clay. He had heard the legend of how a person's spirit could come back in the form of a great white cat.

Something had warned Proud Wolf about that ambush, and Clay was not in the habit of questioning good fortune. When Proud Wolf gazed at the mountains, Clay figured he was seeing that spirit cat—and Raven Arrow.

He sighed and tried to force his wandering thoughts back to his letter. An idea had occurred to him, and although he was not sure how Shining Moon would feel about it, he thought he would suggest it to Jeff. Assuming the letter ever found its way to Jeff; Clay had no idea what his younger brother had been up to during the past couple of years. He missed Jeff, and he missed Edward, Susan, and Jonathan, as well. The Rockies were home now, and Shining Moon, Proud Wolf, Aaron, and, yes, even Matthew, were his family. But Clay had not forgotten his sister and brothers, and he never would.

It would be mighty nice to see them all again, he mused.

"I am worried about Matthew," Shining Moon said, breaking into his reverie.

"So am I," Clay said.

For a day or two he had held out some hope that the boy would start to warm up to them, but Matthew was as withdrawn as ever. He was polite enough, but it was as if there were a wall between him and them, a wall too high ever to see over. Matthew had been raised to hate the Holt family, and suddenly he found himself one of them. Whether or not taking him in and raising him had been the Christian thing to do, as Shining Moon claimed, Clay worried about how the arrangement would turn out.

But nobody could predict the future, Clay told himself. And maybe, just maybe, a trip back East would make Matthew feel more like one of the family. It was worth a try.

A faint smile on his face, Clay Holt dipped the pen in the ink once more and began to write again.

CHAPTER
TWENTY-THREE

"What's that?" Melissa Holt asked her husband, looking at the sheets of paper he was reading as he sat in the rocking chair in the Merrivale parlor. Michael was sitting on the floor at Jeff's feet, playing with a toy wagon that Ned had carved for him.

Without looking up, Jeff replied, "It's a letter from Clay."

"Really?" Melissa said as she sat down on the divan opposite him. "How in the world did you get it?"

"Clay sent it to the post office at Steakley's Trading Post, back in Marietta, and Castor and Pollux picked it up."

He explained to her how Castor and Pollux Gilworth, the two brothers who were sharecropping on the Holt farm in Ohio and tending the property in the absence of any family members, had forwarded the letter from Clay along with a message of their own.

"What does he have to say?" Melissa asked.

Jeff smiled. "Quite a bit, actually. Sounds as though he's been just about as busy as I have these past two years. Had more than his share of trouble, too."

"We all have," Melissa murmured. "Tell me what he wrote."

While Melissa listened, Jeff told her about the adventures and tragedies Clay, Shining Moon, Proud Wolf, and Aaron Garwood had shared, culminating in the final showdown with Fletcher McKendrick. From time to time Jeff quoted passages directly from the letter.

"This McKendrick fellow was the authority behind that renegade Duquesne whom Clay and I tangled with," he concluded. "I'm glad to hear he finally got what was due him."

A tiny shudder ran through Melissa, and she glanced down at Michael. "I'm glad a certain someone wasn't paying any attention to all of that," she said quietly.

Jeff grinned as he looked down at his son. True, Michael seemed to be engrossed in playing with the wagon and appeared not to have heard any of the story, but Jeff would not have bet money on that. Michael had a way of listening and absorbing things even when it seemed his attention was elsewhere. That was part of the frontier heritage in him, Jeff thought. A man had to have that quality if he hoped to survive in the wilderness.

Of course, it was unclear if Michael would ever

see the frontier. Melissa wanted to stay in North Carolina and make something of the business she had inherited from her father. During the time she had been running the operation, she had discovered that she thrived on the business world. Ned and India were still in Wilmington, too, lending a hand, and Jeff had to admit that after the turmoil they had all been through, a stretch of peacefulness was welcome, indeed.

And things had been quiet lately. The murder charge against him had been dropped, of course, after Dermot Hawley's confession, and the local magistrate had talked Constable Tolbert into not pressing any charges related to the jailbreak. Jeff's partnership with the late Charles Merrivale had proven him to be a respectable, successful businessman, the magistrate had reasoned, and Wilmington needed more fine citizens like him.

Yes, he was sure enough settled down, Jeff thought with a faint smile. For now, anyway . . .

"Does Clay have anything else to say in his letter?" Melissa asked.

"As a matter of fact, he does. And it ties in with a problem Castor and Pollux have. It seems the farmhouse needs extensive work, and they want to expand the place, too, since the crops have been so good. They want to know what the family would like for them to do." Jeff looked up at his wife. "I really ought to go out there and see about it."

"Just for a visit, you mean?"

"That's right." Jeff held up the letter from his brother. "And Clay suggests sort of the same thing. He wants us all to get together again at the farm. A family reunion, I guess you'd call it. He says he'll bring Shining Moon, Matthew, and Proud Wolf— Aaron, too, if he's up to the trip—and you and I could go up to Pittsburgh and get Edward and Susan and Jonathan and bring them out."

Melissa smiled. "He doesn't even know about Michael, does he?"

"Nope. But I'd say it's time all of them got to know their nephew."

"You want to go, don't you?" Melissa's voice was soft as she asked the question.

Jeff nodded.

Melissa leaned forward. "Michael, come here." The toddler stood up and went over to her, and Melissa pulled him into her lap. She asked him, "Would you like to go out to the frontier and see the farm where your daddy used to live?"

"Yes!" Michael said eagerly.

Jeff stood up, folded the letter, and put it away. He stepped over to the divan and sat down beside Melissa. "You can meet your uncle Clay," he told Michael, "and your uncle Edward and aunt Susan and uncle Jonathan."

"Can we, Pa?" Michael asked breathlessly. "Can we go?"

Jeff looked at Melissa, saw the love shining in her eyes, and nodded. "We can go," he told his son.

Michael slid down to the floor, his happiness and exuberance too much to contain. "I'm going to the frontier!" he cried, hopping up and down. "I'm going to the frontier!"

Jeff put his arm around Melissa's shoulders and drew her close against him as he watched their son capering around the room.

With each new generation, he realized, the frontier was moving ever onward.

And so were the Holts.

BENEATH THE SKY
by
Paul Block

In 1837, eighteen-year-old Queen Victoria ascends the British throne, ushering in a tumultous age of expansion. The tiny island nation vies for supremacy of the seas, seeking new trade routes to the East—setting England against the ancient Celestial Empire of China.

As the first shots of the conflict are fired, the tempestuous destinies of two family lines are played out. Ross Ballinger, son of a prosperous tradesman, sets sail for China, where the raging Opium War plunges him into a storm tide of dangerous adventure and ill-fated love. Back in England, his cousin, aristocratic Zoë Ballinger, finds herself caught between her family and a young, hot-blooded man named Connor Maginnis, who has vowed vengeance against the all-powerful Ballinger.

Their lives are inexorably woven together in an age of bold adventurism, blazing pageantry, and unconquerable desires. From the teeming ports of Colonial Britain to the exotic shores of the Far East, the two clans fight to carve their place in history—one born to great wealth and nobility, the other thrust by an act of betrayal into a world of devastating hardship. In this time of empire and expansion, two families—and two nations—wage a bitter war as they seek their destiny . . . beneath the sky.

Keep reading for a preview of BENEATH THE SKY, on sale August 1993 wherever Bantam paperbacks are sold.

"Clo'! Clo'!" an old man barked, his voice muffled by the pile of clothing draped over his head and shoulders. "Good clothes to buy or sell!"

"Out o' my way, you old codger!" another voice shouted as the throng of people pushed forward down the street, nearly knocking the clothes man off his feet.

The old man staggered under the weight of his load, took another jarring blow from one of the passersby in the crowd hurrying en masse down Petticoat Lane, and came to rest against the stone wall of an adjacent building. "C-Clo'!" he shouted in a weak, gravelly voice, then started to lower his bundle.

"Here, let me help you," a friendly voice offered, and a pair of strong hands reached up and relieved the man of his burden, lowering the heavy pile of clothing to the ground, still wet from the morning rain. "You really shouldn't be trying to walk about on a morning such as this," the stranger said, extending his hand. "My name's Connor Maginnis."

The clothes man was rubbing his shoulders, and he paused now and looked the stranger up and down, paying particular attention to his outfit. The young man named Connor was dressed in a neat but fairly modest brown suit that complemented his striking brown eyes and thick, dark hair. The old man reached forward with his gnarled hand and fingered the jacket lapel, then gave a low murmur of approval. Though not the outfit of a gentleman, this was by no means one of the secondhand suits bought by most commoners at the Old Clothes Exchange. The trousers were fashionably snug, though not so tight-fitting as to show the shape of the legs, like those favored by the dandies. And the outfit was nicely set off by a white waistcoat and modest cravat that held the upright points of the collar suitably close to the cheek.

Seeing that Connor was still offering his hand, the old man seized it with a surprisingly strong grip. "You lookin' for some new clothes?" he asked.

"No. Not today."

The old man harrumphed. " 'Not today,' he says. Just like all the rest." He stooped to count the items in his bundle, as if checking to make sure no one had stolen any off his back.

Connor chuckled. "Well, you can't expect to do very much business on Coronation Day. Perhaps if you were selling ginger beer or fish cakes or the like." He motioned down the lane toward the vendors who lined the buildings, selling everything from oysters to "cokernuts" to trays heaped high with tiny sponge cakes. "But clothes? On a day such as this?"

"And why not?" the man demanded with a challenging frown. "Folks need clothes, Coronation Day or no."

"I'd say that folks are more concerned with the queen's clothing than their own this morning."

The clothes man grunted. "All a bunch o' foolishness, I say. 'Tis for young folks like yourself. It means nothin' to the likes o' me."

Connor raised his forefinger to his brow as if in salute. "Well then, a good day to you, sir. And good luck with your clothes."

The man grunted again, but there was the trace of a smile as he went back to counting and sorting his clothes. Connor continued down the lane and heard the man take up his call: "Clo'! Clo'! Good clothes to buy or sell!"

Despite the persistent threat of rain, the street vendors—at least those who sold food and drink—were doing brisk business, with passersby snatching up the assorted cakes and fried fish that were the staples in this most popular of the street markets. Most vendors merely stood beside their stands, heads bobbing cheerfully as they exchanged food for coin. Some of the more enterprising went among the crowd, enticing people toward their stands with cries of "Lemonade! Raspberryade! Ha'penny a glass! Ha'penny a glass! Sparkling lemonade!"

The sellers of items such as penny scissors, steel pens, stockings, stationery, sponges, and "chewl-ry" were not faring nearly so well. In fact, most of them appeared to be asleep at their stands or sagely meditating on the smoke curling up from their pipes. But should anyone indicate, even by a glance, that he might be interested in the proffered goods, the vendor would be on his feet at once, diligent and attentive and promising "the best goods and price in all London—indeed, in all Her Majesty's empire!"

Connor was nearing the corner that marked the end of the Petticoat Lane business district when he saw that much of the crowd had come to a halt around something in the street. As he neared the area, he caught glimpses of what seemed to be a fight in the middle of a ring formed by curious onlookers. Some jostled for a better view, while the less interested surged around the sides and continued down the street.

Connor moved through the crowd toward the source of the commotion. All around him, women in tattered dresses and men in threadbare suits raised their fists and cheered as they egged on the combatants, who could not be discerned through the press of people. At a small pub nearby, the somewhat better-dressed patrons set aside their whiskey and beer and poured outside to see what was going on.

"Black his eye!" one particularly disheveled old Londoner yelled, foamy yellow spittle glazing his bristly chin. He smacked fist against palm, then leaned over and spat a gob of tobacco juice onto the hard-packed ground.

Connor stepped to the side to avoid the mess, then continued forward, drawn by the high-pitched squeal of whoever it was who was taking the beating—one of the local street women or perhaps a child.

"Damn Jew boy!" shouted another voice in the crowd. "Kill the damn Jew!"

Connor knew at once that the object of derision was one of the many young Jewish street sellers who frequented the district, hawking their wares from small pushcarts or, in the case of the poorest of the lot, from canvas sacks slung over their shoulders.

As Connor pressed forward, he saw several of the onlookers clutching oranges, while other pieces of the fruit lay squashed on the ground. The boy being assaulted was obviously a costermonger of fruit, and the crowd had seized the opportunity to divest him of his wares.

"Get out o' the damn way!" a burly, relatively well-dressed man exclaimed as Connor pushed past him to the front of the crowd.

Connor glowered at the man, whose broad, flat face was a mass of veins bursting from mottled red skin. When the man grabbed Connor's sleeve to haul him aside, Connor jerked his arm free and stepped into the clearing formed by the crowd surrounding the combatants. The boy who was the object of the attack was in his early teens. He had curly brown hair that was badly tousled just now, and he wore an old but well-kept corduroy suit of the square-cut style favored by his class. His three attackers were barefoot and far more poorly dressed; Connor took them for young Irish toughs. They had the Jewish boy squatting on the muddy ground and were kicking him relentlessly, all the while shouting, "Jew bastard!" "Clipped Dick!" and "Wooden Shoe!" This last epithet had nothing to do with Jewish attire but was a popular rhyming slang for "Jew"—an indication of the widespread prejudice against anything considered foreign.

Though Connor was American by birth, his ancestry was Scots-Irish, and he had lived in England long enough to be considered a native. Still, he often felt like an outsider, which made him naturally sympathetic to the Jewish lad, who probably had been born right here in London but would always be a foreigner, an outcast in his own land. And Connor could never abide someone's being ganged up against, no matter the cause—even if it were overcharging or passing off rotten fruit as good. More than likely the Irish toughs were simply moving in on the Jewish boy's territory, and today they were driving home the point that they wanted the

"Wooden Shoe" costermonger to clear out for good. It was a sight becoming all too familiar on the streets of London, with the more recent arrivals, the poorer Irish, seeking to supplant the Jews, who formerly had a monopoly on such trade in many of the districts.

"Get up and fight!" one of the toughs bleated as he kicked the squatting boy in the back, almost knocking him over. The other two toughs grabbed hold of the sack and tried to yank it off the boy's shoulder. Several more oranges and a lemon spilled out, and as the boy reached to grab them, the sack slipped from his shoulder and was wrenched away. A moment later it was tossed into the crowd and immediately torn open, the contents snatched up by eager, clutching hands.

"Enough of that!" Connor Maginnis shouted, moving into the center of the clearing.

The young toughs glanced up, then returned to their business, one of them taking hold of the boy's curly hair and twisting it, forcing him onto his back.

"You heard me! Enough!" Connor dashed forward and clasped a powerful hand around the tough's forearm until he released his grip on the hair.

"Wha' the hell?" a voice in the crowd shouted. "Leave 'em to their sport!"

Connor felt someone grab the back of his brown jacket, and he spun around to see the burly man who had argued with him before.

" 'Tis none o' yer damn business!" the man blared, staring up at Connor, who was a good bit taller and, at twenty-one, perhaps half his age.

Connor jerked his jacket free, and when the man again grabbed at him, he pushed the fellow back, not roughly but enough to warn him off. But the man would not be dissuaded; he took one step back and swung wildly at Connor's head. The younger man easily ducked the blow and, straightening up, drove his right fist into the man's ample belly, doubling him over.

An excited cry came from the crowd, and Connor knew that if he did not make quick work of the fellow, a brawl would break out. He waited until the man stopped sputtering and gasping for air. Then, when the man straightened up and moved in for the attack with both fists raised, Connor planted his feet firmly, drew back his right arm, and feinting to the left, delivered a crushing blow to the man's temple. The punch staggered him, and he went down on his knees, swaying left and right before finally crumpling to the ground.

A great cheer went up; apparently the crowd did not much care who was fighting or why, so long as there was some action to see. Connor noticed that his own fight had drawn the attention of the young toughs, who for the moment seemed to have forgotten their prey. Using their lapse to his advantage, Connor stepped toward them and shouted, "Be gone with you! Leave the fellow alone now!"

The three did not react other than to stare at one another, as if wondering what they should do. Connor took hold of the nearest one's collar and pushed him toward the crowd. "Get going! The lot of you!"

The other two hesitated. Then one of them glanced down at the boy curled up on the ground. Turning to his companions, he muttered, "Come on. We're done here." He gave Connor a smirk, then stalked off with his mates into the crowd, with many of the onlookers slapping them on their backs as they passed.

The crowd stirred, tiring of the spectacle. Connor spied the Jewish boy's canvas sack lying in a tattered heap near the edge of the crowd, and he snatched it up and took it back to where the boy was lying. Kneeling beside him, he clasped the lad's arm. "It's over. You can get up now." Realizing the boy was sobbing into his sleeve, Connor handed him the sack and said, "Wipe your face on this."

The boy did as he was told, then with Connor's assistance struggled to his feet. People paid him little attention now as they continued their march down Petticoat Lane toward the coronation route. The incident seemed all but forgotten; even the man lying on the sidewalk where Connor had downed him drew little reaction from the passersby.

The boy was choking back his tears, trying his best not to look childish. He allowed Connor to smooth his hair and even smiled faintly when his benefactor commented, "It's nothing to be ashamed of. I cried myself the last time a trio of Irishmen beat me up."

"Th-Thank you," the boy stammered.

He waved off the thanks. "Forget it. Are you injured?"

"I'm all right. They . . . didn't really hurt me."

"That's good. I'm sorry I couldn't save your goods. Did you lose much?"

Frowning bitterly, the boy looked down at the empty sack, which hung limply from his hands. "My whole stock. Near twenty shillings."

Connor straightened the lad's jacket and brushed off some of the mud, then adjusted his own cravat and collar. He noted the boy was wearing a coarse, collarless shirt that was several sizes too large; probably purchased at one of the stalls along the lane or perhaps at the nearby Old Clothes Exchange.

Just then the man lying on the ground nearby began to rouse, and Connor said, "Come on. Let's be off before that brute tries to finish what he started." He led the boy back into the business district of Petticoat Lane. After they had gone several blocks, he asked, "You've a family?"

"Just my grandfather, and he's mostly laid up in bed. He helps with the sellin' when he can."

"Has he got enough stock money put aside for a new sack of goods?"

The boy halted, looked curiously at Connor, and asked, "You know a lot about mongerin'. But you don't look like one."

Connor glanced down at himself. "The suit, eh? Well, don't let such things fool you. I've done my share of mongering. Still do when I have to."

"You ain't a Jew, though?" the boy asked, more a statement than a question. When Connor shook his head, the boy's eyes narrowed suspiciously. "Irish, then?"

"No. American," Connor said simply.

"I never seen me an American street monger. Nor an American, I suppose. What're you doin' here?"

Connor placed his hand on the boy's shoulder. "This is my home. My father was from Edinburgh, my mother from New York. I was born there, but we moved to London soon after. Then they . . . they died. I've made my living on the streets ever since."

They started to walk again. Seeing how the boy kept glancing over at his well-tailored brown suit, Connor said, "Like I told you, don't let these clothes fool you. In my line of work, a fellow needs a good outfit."

"What do you sell?" the boy asked cautiously.

Connor's eyes brightened. "Let's just say I've learned there are things to be sold that don't need much of a stake, other than a fancy suit and a smile."

"You mean, you're a fancy man?" The boy's voice was filled with wonder. "It's all right; I'm old enough to know about those things."

Halting, Connor turned to look at him. "Exactly how old *are* you?"

The boy drew himself up tall. "Sixteen in November."

"And your name?"

"Mose. . . . Mose Levison."

"Well, Mose, I'm Connor Maginnis, and I suppose when I was your age I knew as much. But I wouldn't have called someone a fancy man—at least not to his face."

Mose's face blanched. "I'm sorry. I didn't mean—"

Connor laughed and clapped him on the back. "Think nothing of it."

"But it ain't my business how you earn—"

"I said forget about it. Let's just say I'm a monger of a different sort."

As they began to walk again, Connor asked, "About that stock of yours—has your grandfather got enough money put aside to stake you to another sack?"

Mose looked down. "We spent the last we had on that fruit. We won't have any more till the end of the week. He put all our savings in commemoratives."

"Commemoratives?"

"You know . . . of the queen. We stand to make a good profit when we sell 'em."

Connor looked at him curiously. "So what were you doing with those oranges? I'd think Coronation Day, with such crowds all over London, would be the best time to be selling commemoratives."

"We ain't got 'em yet. We bought 'em on speculation. They're booklets tellin' all the news of today's events. They'll be printed up tomorrow, and I'll sell 'em to the Saturday crowds at the park."

"I see."

"Is that what you're doin'?" Mose asked, cocking his head and examining Connor's outfit more closely. "Are you attendin' the coronation?"

Connor couldn't help but laugh. "Me? At Westminster Abbey? I should think not. I was hoping one of the queen's Ladies of the Bedchamber would send me a personal invitation, but . . ." He gave a sly wink. "No, a coronation's no place for a fancy man like me."

"She'll be passin' by in the state coach on the way to the abbey," Mose said, his expression growing more animated. "And after the coronation's finished, she'll be ridin' back through the streets wearin' her crown and carryin' the scepter and orb."

Connor snapped his fingers. "I'll tell you what. Why don't we head over to Hyde Park Corner; the procession is going right past there. Then, if you come along with me for a while, I think I know a way to get you a fresh stake."

"You do?"

"I'd loan you the money myself, but a few pennies for boolers is all I've got. But I know someone who's got a lot more than a few pennies . . . a whole lot more."

"Are you sure?" The boy looked up expectantly at his benefactor.

"Just stick with me, Mose. We'll get that sack filled, and then some. Just do exactly what I tell you." He gripped the boy's sleeve and motioned him down the street. "Now come along. The first rule of a fancy man is never keep a woman waiting. Especially the Queen of England."

Mose Levison stood among the bushes at the side of the big brick house on St. James Square, drawing circles in the dirt with the toe of his shoe. Every now and then he glanced up at a second-floor window. It seemed as though hours had passed since the fancy man named Connor Maginnis had signaled him from that very window to remain where he was. Mose was tired and bored, and from the sounds of cannons and cheering in the distance, he was certain that Queen Victoria was already riding from Westminster Abbey to Buckingham Palace.

It was true that he had caught a glimpse of the young queen on her way to the abbey earlier that day, but now she would be wearing her crown and purple robes of state. He found himself wondering if it was worth waiting any longer for the few pennies Connor probably would squeeze out of the lady of the house— the woman he had been entertaining all afternoon up in that second-floor room.

Mose jumped with a start at the sound of a carriage clattering around the corner of the square. Drawing back into the bushes, he peered out at the cobbled street and saw a smart-looking black hansom cab halt in front of the same house in which Connor was "plowing his trade," as he had called it.

Mose's breath caught in his chest as the carriage door opened and a man well into his sixties emerged, looking dapper in a black cutaway coat and silk top hat and wearing the stockings and knee breeches still favored by many of his generation. Mose strained without success to hear what the man was saying to the liveried driver. The man handed the driver a coin, and the hansom cab pulled away and drove right past Mose and on around the square toward central London.

There was no doubt in Mose's mind that the well-dressed passenger was the master of the house—and of the mistress who was doing God-only-knew-what in the upstairs bedroom with Connor Maginnis.

The gentleman turned toward the house and walked briskly up the drive, his silver-knobbed cane tapping jauntily on the ground. Mose risked leaning out of the bushes far enough to see the man inserting a key in the lock of the front door. His suspicions confirmed, he ducked around the side of the house and searched frantically for some means of warning his friend. Spying the gravel surrounding a nearby flowerbed, he picked up a small stone and hurled it at the window, missing by inches. He tried a second time, but his aim was even worse. Snatching a whole handful of pebbles, he let them fly, and enough struck their mark to set the pane rattling.

Mose had just let loose a second handful when the drapes were thrust aside, revealing a scowling, bare-chested man. Mose waved his arms, signaling that some-one had come home and was on his way inside and perhaps upstairs. It took a moment for Connor to realize what was going on; then a sudden shock of awareness came over him—either he understood Mose's message or had heard something in the house.

Connor let the drapes drop in place and disap-peared into the room. A moment later he yanked the drapes open wide and, clutching his clothing against his chest with one hand, reached up with the other to re-lease the window latch. With some difficulty he got it unlocked and pushed the window outward on its rusty hinges. Behind Connor, Mose glimpsed the woman's corpulent, naked body as she pulled a flimsy dressing robe over her shoulders. Connor and the woman ex-changed words, as if debating what to do, and then she pushed him toward the open window. Connor looked around wildly and with an expression of fearful resigna-tion stepped over the sill and onto the narrow ledge just below the window.

Mose couldn't believe what he was seeing. Connor was stark naked, his modesty protected only by the clothing clutched against his abdomen. He cautiously moved to the right, away from the window, as the woman started to pull it shut. Abruptly she halted, dashed off for a moment, then reappeared carrying something, which she heaved outside. It was a pair of boots, which went spinning through the air and landed with a thud on the ground, one of them right-side up at Mose's feet, the other upside down a few yards away.

Mose retrieved Connor's boots, then looked up to see him on the ledge, struggling into his pants. His lady friend was still at the window, attempting to close it, when a shadowed figure surprised her from behind. Mose could almost hear her gasp. She spun around to the man behind her, blocking the window with her body while she spoke to him. Just when it appeared as if he was about to move past her to the window, she raised her arms and threw herself at him in the most passionate embrace Mose had ever seen—or imagined. The man did not seem averse to her attentions, and in a moment Mose saw the dressing robe slip off her shoulders to the floor. The man's hands sank into her copious flesh, and then the pawing figures moved back from the window.

Only a couple of feet away, Connor stood on the ledge, one leg in his pants, his gaze transfixed on the open window. Apparently he had been able to see or hear enough to know what was going on, for now, disregarding his state of semidress, he inched back to the window and leaned toward it far enough to catch a glimpse inside the room.

Abruptly he spun away from the window, as if something or someone had surprised him. Losing his balance, he teetered on his perch, his naked leg struggling to maintain its footing, the clothed leg hovering over the abyss, like a tightrope walker fighting to stay on the wire. Grabbing at the wall, he had to release the pants—along with the rest of his clothes—and as his shirt, jacket, waistcoat, and undergarments went flapping to the ground, the pants slid down his leg and hung off his foot.

Connor shook his leg to free it from the dangling pair of pants. The movement only served to unbalance him more, and with a gasp and a last desperate lunge toward the window ledge, he lost his footing and went flailing through the air.

Mose gasped as his benefactor landed unceremoniously on his rear end in the middle of a well-trimmed bush below the window. Racing to his side, the boy reached into the tangle of arms, legs, and branches, then held back as Connor opened his eyes. He looked upward and his focus returned, his eyes widening, and Mose followed his gaze to see the woman of the house framed in the partially open window. Her body was screened by one of the drapes, which she held in front of her as she grabbed hold of the window. Staring down at her lover and the youth beside him, she raised a finger to her lips and frowned, then pulled the window shut and disappeared from view.

"Help me up," Connor grunted, holding out a hand to the boy, who started to reach for it. "First get my pants."

After gathering the items, Mose carried the bundle to Connor, who was still sprawled in the middle of the bush, his skin a maze of scratches.

"Give it here," Connor directed him. "And stop all that staring."

"I—I'm sorry," Mose stammered, dropping the bundle onto Connor's midsection.

"You've seen a grown man before, haven't you?" Lifting himself up slightly, Connor shook out the pants and slipped his feet into the pant legs. Seeing what a struggle it was for the boy not to stare where he shouldn't, Connor shrugged and asked, "Well, what is it? Is something wrong?"

"Why, no," Mose insisted, flushed with embarrassment. "It's just that . . . well . . . you really *ain't* Jewish."

Looking down at himself, Connor grinned. "That's what I said, isn't it? Now help me out of here."

Mose clasped Connor's wrists and hauled him out of the bush. Connor's pants were still around his knees, and he reached down and pulled them up. Then he scooped up the rest of his clothes and quickly donned them, stuffing the undergarments into the pockets of his jacket and hastily arranging the cravat and collar.

"Let's get going." Connor prodded his young companion toward the street.

Hesitating, Mose muttered, "I guess you didn't get a chance to ask her about puttin' up my stake."

"Is that what's got you frowning?" He reached into the pocket of his waistcoat and produced a gold coin, which he presented to his young friend, whose expression lit with excitement as he took it and turned it round and round, examining both sides. "In my trade, you learn early to get your money up front—before the husband comes home."

"But I don't want to take your—"

"That coin's for you," Connor insisted, pushing the

boy's hand away. "A present from the good Lady Henrietta Wellesley. I've got my own right here." He patted his waistcoat pocket.

"But how did you convince her? What'd you say?"

"I told her that my nephew just arrived in London, orphaned and penniless. She said she's more than happy to—how did she put it?—'to help a strapping young country lad get started on the right track in life.' If I'm not mistaken, Lady Wellesley would love to tell you that herself after you've got yourself 'properly situated.'" Connor's eyes twinkled with mischief, and he cuffed the lad's chin.

"Are you suggestin' . . . ?" Mose's voice trailed off with uncertainty.

"Like I told you, there's lots of ways to earn money that don't need a stake or a sack of fruit—just the right education from a fancy sort of fellow like me." His eyes sparked with merriment. "Something tells me a good-looking Jewish lad like you would be quite a novelty for the womenfolk." He jabbed the boy dangerously close to the groin and started to chuckle.

At first Mose looked quite uncomfortable, but then he found himself laughing, as well. He followed Connor away from the building but halted abruptly, tugging at Connor's sleeve. "Just promise me one thing." He motioned toward where Connor had landed when he fell from the ledge, and his lips quirked impishly. "If I let you show me the ways of a fancy man, you'll teach me a better way'n that to end up in the bush."

"Mose, my friend, I'll show you a thousand ways." Connor led him onto the street. "And here's your first lesson—the first rule of a fancy man: 'A bird in the bush is worth two in the hand.'"

Mose looked at him curiously. "But this mornin' you said the first rule is to never keep a woman waitin'."

"That all depends, my good man, on whether she's going . . . or coming."

Mose shook his head in confusion.

"Give it no mind. There're plenty of rules for a fancy man, and plenty of time to learn them . . . and to break them."

It all began with
WAGONS WEST
America's best-loved series by Dana Fuller Ross

❑ *Independence!* (26822-8 $4.95/$5.95 in Canada) A saga of high adventure and passionate romance on the first wagon train to Oregon territory.

❑ *Nebraska!* (26162-2 $4.95/$5.95 in Canada) Indian raids and sabotage threaten the settlers as "Whip" Holt leads the wagon train across the Great Plains.

❑ *Wyoming!* (26242-4 $4.95/$5.95 in Canada) Facing starvation, a mysterious disease, and a romantic triangle, the expedition pushes on.

❑ *Oregon!* (26072-3 $4.50/$4.95 in Canada) Three mighty nations clash on the fertile shore of the Pacific as the weary pioneers arrive.

❑ *Texas!* (26070-7 $4.99/$5.99 in Canada) Branded as invaders by the fiery Mexican army, a band of Oregon volunteers rallies to the cause of liberty.

❑ *California!* (26377-3 $4.99/$5.99 in Canada) The new settlers' lives are threatened by unruly fortune seekers who have answered the siren song of gold.

❑ *Colorado!* (26546-6 $4.95/$5.95 in Canada) The rugged Rockies hold the promise of instant wealth for the multitudes in search of a new start.

❑ *Nevada!* (26069-3 $4.99/$5.99 in Canada) The nation's treasury awaits a shipment of silver just as the country is on the brink of Civil War.

❑ *Washington!* (26163-0 $4.50/$4.95 in Canada) Ruthless profiteers await wounded Civil War hero Toby Holt's return to challenge his landholdings.

❑ *Montana!* (26073-1 $4.95/$5.95 in Canada) The lawless, untamed territory is terrorized by a sinister gang led by a tough and heartless woman.

❑ *Dakota!* (26184-3 $4.50/$4.95 in Canada) Against the backdrop of the Badlands, fearless Indian tribes form an alliance to drive out the white man forever.

❑ *Utah!* (26521-0 $4.99/$5.99 in Canada) Chinese and Irish laborers strive to finish the transcontinental railroad before corrupt landowners sabotage it.

❑ *Idaho!* (26071-5 $4.99/$5.99 in Canada) The perilous task of making a safe homeland from an untamed wilderness is hampered by blackmail and revenge.

❑ *Missouri!* (26367-6 $4.99/$4.99 in Canada) An incredible adventure on a paddle-wheel steamboat stirs romantic passions and gambling fever.

❑ *Mississippi!* (27141-5 $4.95/$5.95 in Canada) New Orleans is home to an underworld of crime, spawned by easy money and ruthless ambitions.

❑ *Louisiana!* (25247-X $4.99/$5.99 in Canada) Smuggled shipments of opium and shanghaied Chinese workers continue to invade the country.

❑ *Tennessee!* (25622-X $4.99/$5.99 in Canada) Unscrupulous politicians lead an army of outlaws and misfits to threaten America's cherished democracy.

❑ *Illinois!* (26022-7 $4.95/$5.95 in Canada) One of the nation's most awesome catastrophes tests the courage of the tough, new immigrants to the Midwest.

❑ *Wisconsin!* (26533-4 $4.95/$5.95 in Canada) Wealthy lumber barons seek to destroy those new enterprises that dare to defy their power.

❑ *Arizona!* (27065-6 $4.99/$5.99 in Canada) The comancheros who rule this sun-scorched frontier with brutal terror are sought by the U.S. Cavalry.

❑ *New Mexico!* (27458-9 $4.95/$5.95 in Canada) Law-abiding citizens infiltrate a cutthroat renegade gang to bring law and order to the Southwest.

❏ *Oklahoma!* (27703-0 $4.95/$5.95 in Canada) Homesteaders and ranchers head toward an all-out range war that will end their dreams of a peaceful existence.

❏ *Celebration!* (28180-1 $4.50/$5.50 in Canada) As Americans prepare to honor their nation on its centennial, the enemies of democracy stand ready to move in.

And then came
THE HOLTS: AN AMERICAN DYNASTY
The future generation by Dana Fuller Ross

❏ *Oregon Legacy* (28248-4 $4.50/$5.50 in Canada) An epic adventure of a legendary family's indomitable fighting spirit and unconquerable dreams.

❏ *Oklahoma Pride* (28446-0 $4.99/$5.99 in Canada) Buckboards and wagons get ready to roll as the "Sooners" await the start of the biggest land grab in history.

❏ *Carolina Courage* (28756-7 $4.95/$5.95 in Canada) As a dread disease runs rampant, hatred and blame fall on the last great Indian tribe of America's East.

❏ *California Glory* (28970-5 $4.99/$5.99 in Canada) Riots and strikes rock America's cities as workers demand freedom, fairness, and justice for all.

❏ *Hawaii Heritage* (29414-8 $4.99/$5.99 in Canada) Seeds of revolution turn the island paradise into a land of brutal turmoil and seething unrest.

❏ *Sierra Triumph* (29750-3 $4.99/$5.99 in Canada) A battle that goes beyond that of the sexes challenges the ideals of a nation and one remarkable family.

❏ *Yukon Justice* (29763-5 $5.50/$6.50 in Canada) As gold fever sweeps the nation, a great migration north begins to the Yukon Territory of Canada

And now
WAGONS WEST: THE FRONTIER TRILOGY
From Dana Fuller Ross

❏ *Westward!* (29402-4 $5.50/$6.50 in Canada) The clock is turned back with this early story of the Holts, men and women who lived through the most rugged era of American exploration.

❏ *Expedition!* (29403-2 $5.50/$6.50 in Canada) In the heart of a majestic land, Clay Holt leads a perilous expedition up the Yellowstone River.

Available at your local bookstore or use this page to order.

Send to: **Bantam Books, Dept. LE 13**
             2451 S. Wolf Road
             Des Plaines, IL 60018

Please send me the items I have checked above. I am enclosing $_____ (please add $2.50 to cover postage and handling). Send check or money order, no cash or C.O.D.'s, please.

Mr./Ms._____

Address_____

City/State_____Zip_____

Please allow four to six weeks for delivery.
Prices and availability subject to change without notice.   LE 13B 2/9

They were the valiant men and women who fought and died to bring independence to a struggling young nation...

PATRIOTS

by Adam Rutledge

❏ **VOLUME I: SONS OF LIBERTY** 29199-8

Boston, 1773. A secret band of patriots plans defiant actions to protest the Crown's injustices. It is a heady time for young Daniel Reed, pursuing his education in Boston. While he cloaks his insurrectionist sympathies with caution, his teenage brother rushes headlong into freedom's fight. $4.99/$5.99 in Canada

❏ **VOLUME II: REBEL GUNS** 29200-5

Mustering soldiers to capture British munitions, Daniel Reed must vanquish a madman in order to carry out his mission. At the same time Quincy Reed, joining with the fearless Green Mountain Boys, is swept into a perilous raid on Fort Ticonderoga. In the tumultuous days of war, the lives of these courageous men and women may be the price of victory. $4.99/$5.99 in Canada

❏ **VOLUME III: THE TURNCOAT** 29201-3

War becomes a reality as redcoats and rebels alike swarm toward the bustling seaport of Boston, while a growing band of patriots gathers across the Charles River in Cambridge. Daniel Reed, his brother Quincy, and fiery patriot Roxanne Darragh risk their lives for the dream of a free country. $4.99/$5.99 in Canada

❏ **VOLUME IV: LIFE AND LIBERTY** 29202-1

It is a treacherous time for freedom fighter Daniel Reed, who has thrown in his lot with General Washington's Continental Army. Risking exposure and death threats, undercover patriot and daring double agent Elliot Markham will fight a deadly battle against a lawless legion of ruthless criminals who could extinguish the flame of independence forever. $4.99/$5.99 in Canada

Available at your local bookstore or use this page to order.

Send to: Bantam Books, Dept. DO 35
            2451 S. Wolf Road
            Des Plaines, IL 60018

Please send me the items I have checked above. I am enclosing $_____ (please add $2.50 to cover postage and handling). Send check or money order, no cash or C.O.D.'s, please.

Mr./Ms._____

Address_____

City/State_____Zip_____

Please allow four to six weeks for delivery.
Prices and availability subject to change without notice.   DO 35 7/9